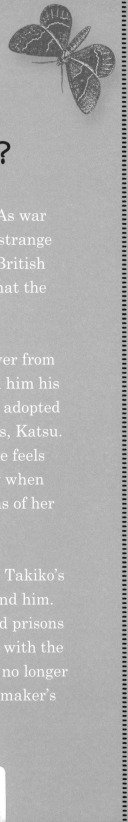

Has time run out for the Watchmaker?

Strange things are happening in Tokyo. As war with Russia looms, the city is plagued by strange electricity storms, while the staff at the British Legation have gone on strike, claiming that the building is haunted.

Civil servant Thaniel Steepleton is sent over from London to act as interpreter, bringing with him his partner, Keita Mori the watchmaker, their adopted daughter, Six, and Mori's clockwork octopus, Katsu. Thaniel is dazzled by life in Tokyo, but he feels increasingly out of his depth – especially when he meets Takiko Pepperharrow, and learns of her connection to Mori.

But then Mori disappears, and Thaniel and Takiko's paths diverge as they desperately try to find him. As their searches lead them to snow-steeped prisons and mountainside shrines, Thaniel is faced with the terrifying revelation that Mori's powers are no longer enough to save them – and that the watchmaker's time may have run out.

THE LOST FUTURE OF PEPPERHARROW

ALSO BY NATASHA PULLEY

The Watchmaker of Filigree Street

The Bedlam Stacks

THE LOST FUTURE OF PEPPERHARROW

NATASHA PULLEY

BLOOMSBURY PUBLISHING
LONDON • OXFORD • NEW YORK • NEW DELHI • SYDNEY

BLOOMSBURY PUBLISHING
Bloomsbury Publishing Plc
50 Bedford Square, London WC1B 3DP, UK

First published in Great Britain 2020

A catalogue record for this book is available from the British Library

Library of Congress Cataloguing-in-Publication data has been applied for.

ISBN: HB: 978-1-4088-8516-1; TPB: 978-1-4088-8518-5 EBOOK: 978-1-4088-8519-2

2 4 6 8 10 9 7 5 3 1

Typeset by Integra Software Services Pvt. Ltd.
Printed and bound in Great Britain by CPI Group (UK) Ltd, Croydon CR0 4YY

To find out more about our authors and books visit www.bloomsbury.com
and sign up for our newsletters.

For Jacob

Prison at Abashiri

HOKKAIDO

JAPAN

SEA OF JAPAN

Tokyo

Mt. Fuji
Aokigahara
Forest

Nagasaki

Aokigahara Forest

Mt. Fuji

S

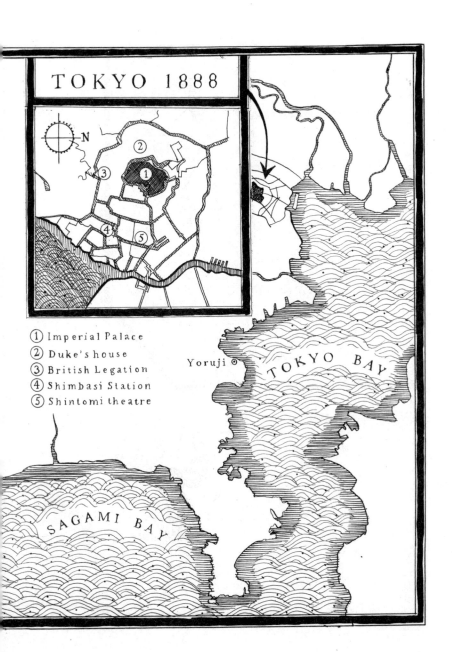

TOKYO 1888

① Imperial Palace
② Duke's house
③ British Legation
④ Shimbasi Station
⑤ Shintomi theatre

Yoruji ⦿

TOKYO BAY

SAGAMI BAY

PROLOGUE

It's easy to think that nobody could really arrange the world like clockwork. All sorts of things would get stuck in the mechanisms; history is full of queens and generals who've given it a damn good go but failed because of nothing more complicated than the weather. But clairvoyants have a knack for arranging time, and it was not without a sense of irony that Keita Mori was a watchmaker.

In his workshop, it was difficult to see what he was making until it was done. A sort of organised chaos characterised the way he worked, so much so that he could be constructing something for months or years and it would only look like a tangle of something generically worrying – right up until it got up, walked off, and turned out to be an octopus.

It was even harder to tell what he was making when he was using time and not steel. But if you knew him quite well, it was possible to discern when he was arranging something, and sometimes even sketch the shape of its tentacles. One tentacle began to take a clear shape – to anyone watching closely enough – on the last day of October, in eighteen eighty-eight, in St Petersburg.

Pyotr Kuznetsov was surprised when, after not having seen each other for five years, Mori sent him an invitation for coffee at the Hotel Angleterre.

'Hotel bloody Angleterre,' Pyotr snarled at nobody as he crossed the road, which startled a boy who'd been shovelling snow.

On the great official map, Japan hated everyone. It was one of those deliciously rich but under-developed little countries that everyone wanted to invade – Britain, Russia, America – but Russia was closest and so if there had to be a ranking, it was number one on Tokyo's to-be-stabbed list. Pyotr and Mori shouldn't have been friends. Officers in enemy countries' secret police were expected not to be. But they'd always been exact counterparts throughout their service careers. They both existed with one foot in often unpleasant, boring business, the other at black-tie events at embassies. They both disliked flag-waving and Americans. Mori could drink properly and Pyotr knew all the rules of sumo. They had a lot more in common with each other than with the flag-waving ministers they worked for.

One small spanner in the otherwise smooth works was that Mori was, and there was absolutely no getting round this, rich. He did horrible things like invite Pyotr to fancy hotels – as though any normal human would even get through the door at the Angleterre. Tolstoy was staying there now. Pyotr had never lost an instinctive anxiety about places with gilded frescoes and resident novelists.

Mori had retired from the Japanese service a few years ago, or so he said. He had been living in a suite at the Angleterre for six months, making clockwork for the Tsarina. It was the most stupendous cover story Pyotr had ever seen, because Mori actually *was* making clockwork for the Tsarina. She had given the Home Minister a watch a few months ago and he'd been showing it to everyone, including Pyotr. It was gorgeous.

Pyotr was willing to be called Katerina for a year if Mori really was here for clockwork.

Pyotr paused outside the hotel. It was still only ten to eleven; he'd left himself extra time in case the doormen wouldn't let him in. Decently, he'd wait, but it was so cold he couldn't stand still. The snow had flurried on and off for four days now; along the edges of the pavements it had been shovelled up seven feet high. Like icing sugar, it was fine and dry, and the passing of every cab and carriage blew wisps of it glittering into the air. Just along from the hotel, some men were repairing a telegraph line that must have snapped in the cold. And still only October; it was going to be a wolf of a winter.

In fact, the doormen did let Pyotr in. He didn't even have to show his Okhrana badge.

The cafe was busy, a singing clatter of cakes being delivered on three-tiered plates and women talking – you knew you were somewhere well-heeled when the men spoke more softly than the women – but he saw Mori straightaway by the window, because the spray of mechanical parts on the table caught the light. He was making a toy octopus. He was adjusting something in its insides. The octopus was trying to steal the silver spoon from the sugar bowl.

'Is that alive?' Pyotr asked, mainly to avoid exclaiming that Mori didn't look one single bollocking day older than the last time they'd met up. Pyotr had gone grey.

'No,' said Mori in his courtly Russian. He had the most unexpected voice of anyone Pyotr knew. He was a nymph of a man, but he sounded like petroleum fumes would if they'd had anything to say. 'Just pretending.'

The octopus was nearly perfectly round, a shiny blob with silver and glass panels. Pyotr gave it the spoon. The little thing made a joyful mechanical noise that sounded a lot like *wob wob wob wob* and dived under the table, where it hugged his ankle. He leaned down to stroke it, trying hard not to make embarrassing cooing noises at it. It only had seven legs. The eighth was a tiny bronze wheel.

Opposite him, Mori was turning his sleeves down. Pyotr caught a snatch of a tattoo, Japanese writing, just at the top of his forearm. It must have been done today or yesterday, because it still looked sore. Belligerently, he decided not to ask.

'So,' said Pyotr. 'What are you really doing here? Should I expect a clockwork bomb in the Tsar's bedroom?'

Mori smiled. Life had been treating him so well that he had a glow. He could have illuminated a broom cupboard at least. Pyotr had a fantasy about shoving him in one. 'You know I'm not working. I've lived in London for years; Tokyo wouldn't be able to talk to me. Have you met the Royal Mail?'

'London could talk to you. Did you defect?' It came out sounding a lot more hurt than Pyotr had meant. He'd always hoped Mori would come across to Russia.

'Of course I didn't defect, I opened a watchmaking shop. I wouldn't defect without defecting to you, would I? How are you?' He did look honestly pleased to meet up again.

Pyotr melted. Nobody ever looked pleased to see him. 'Ticking along,' he said, and Mori was chivalrous enough to laugh. 'All right for coffee?' he asked.

'Yes, thanks,' said Mori, and bang on cue, a waitress arrived with two new cups.

'How do you do that?' Pyotr demanded. 'I'm ten minutes early.'

If there was an answer, he didn't catch it. There were three owls sitting on the ledge of the window behind Mori, all lined up and huddled together. They were looking inside as if they were at the theatre. Pyotr found himself cocking his head to see if any of them would copy him.

'Listen, I heard something from Tokyo you might like,' Mori said, and then kicked him as Pyotr took out his wallet to ask if he ought to pay.

'What sort of something?' Pyotr said, settling finally.

'A friend of mine's about to become Prime Minister.' Mori was lifting the sugar bowl and the coffee pot away from the edge of the table, neat and delicate. 'Kiyotaka Kuroda. You know—'

'The crazy one who keeps invading Korea?' Pyotr exploded, and banged down his already-empty cup. The table juddered. At least four different waiters frowned. 'They let him into the Palace? Aren't there rules? Don't give me that bloody Pyotr's-so-naive look, I was waterboarding a trade unionist fifteen minutes ago.'

Mori gave him the pistachio macaron that had come with the coffee. 'Kuroda's first order of business will be to establish himself. He'll take the Kuril Islands and Vladivostok off you if he can.'

Pyotr snorted. 'Vladivostok? Don't be stupid—'

'He's about to finalise an order for forty ironclads from Liverpool,' Mori said over him, without raising his voice. 'The British will sail them to Nagasaki in February. Each ship will take two hundred sailors.'

There was a long silence. This was not the kind of information they had ever, ever given each other before. They'd mentioned it if their respective mad nationalists were planning anything especially explosive, but that was small stuff. Never on this scale.

'Mori,' Pyotr said at last, 'why are you telling me?'

'Because Kuroda needs managing. If he starts invading new places and spouting rubbish about the Glorious Empire of the Sun, he'll take Korea first and then China, and before you know it we'll be at war with America.' Mori stared into his coffee for a strange second. Now that Pyotr was looking at him properly, he didn't seem like himself. His collarbones were taut, even under his shirt and waistcoat. The tendons in the backs of his hands showed when he shifted his grip on the cup, as close to the surface as a ballerina's, and Pyotr felt protective. 'I'd prefer not to be at war with America,' Mori said eventually. He tilted his eyes up again. 'They'll win, and then you'll have no buffer zone between Russia and the United States.'

'I'll look into it,' Pyotr promised faintly. He hesitated. 'But you know what the Minister will say, don't you? That if Kuroda's ordering new ships, then the old ones are clapped out. He's going to say that this would be the moment to take Nagasaki.'

Mori tipped his head. He was too well bred to shrug. 'If Kuroda is fighting for Nagasaki, he is not building an empire.'

'Christ,' said Pyotr. He couldn't help glancing around. The Japanese must have been livid that Mori was even here. No secret service, surely, let a retired operative set up in an enemy state and invite his old opposite number to tea without at least having him followed. 'Mori, do you understand how stupid this is? If they even suspect this is coming from you, you're in the Winter Canal tied to a brick.' It was stating the obvious, but Mori couldn't possibly have thought it through. Rich people never thought about consequences.

'I trust you,' Mori said quietly.

Pyotr struggled. The shape of it felt wrong. 'You say he needs managing, but this can't just be from your great moral sense of the good of nations. What are you really doing?'

Mori set his cup down too precisely. It didn't make a sound on the saucer. He was losing his colour.

Pyotr frowned. 'Are you all right?'

Mori nodded, but it looked strained. 'Something is about to happen to me and it's going to look bad, but I am all right, so you don't need to call a doctor or anything. But … if you could perhaps see me into the cab?'

'What?' Pyotr said blankly. Behind Mori, beyond the window, a cab glided up to the edge of the pavement. For the first time, he noticed that Mori had a travelling bag with him. He always packed lightly, and Pyotr knew, without a doubt, that it would be everything. He was leaving St Petersburg. 'What do you mean, bad?'

'I'm about to lose all my Russian.' He was pushing his fingernails into the tablecloth. Behind him, the owls had straightened up.

'You're about to what? What are you talking about?'

'It's going, I'm sorry,' Mori said, and Pyotr stared at him, because he was right; he was losing his Russian. He had an accent now, and he was having to talk slowly, like he was remembering the words from a textbook. It was nothing like the natural way he'd spoken thirty seconds before. 'Can you … tell the driver that I need the railway station?'

'Mori,' Pyotr tried, shocked. He went around to him and caught his elbows, and felt a slow wave of horror when he saw that Mori's eyelashes were full of tears. Poison, it had to be; some kind of toxin that affected the mind. They'd come for him after all. 'We need to get you to a hospital …'

'Ah, cab for Baron Mori?' a beautifully uniformed door-man interrupted.

'I don't need a hospital,' Mori said to Pyotr, in English now. Pyotr could follow it, just about. 'I just need to get back to London. This is just − a condition I've always had. No need to worry.'

'Well − are you sure?'

'I'm sure. Thank you.'

'Just to Tsarskoselsky station, please,' Pyotr said helplessly to the doorman, and handed over Mori's bag. The clockwork octopus, which had been stealing all the spoons from the free tables, hurried back and swarmed up Mori's arm.

'Send me a telegram,' Pyotr called after Mori. It was so cold today that someone had changed the breakfast menus by hand, because on the short walk between the market and the kitchen, the eggs had frozen in their shells. This was not the weather to travel in even if you were fighting fit. 'Tell me when you get safe to Paris, all right?'

Mori nodded and let the doorman chaperone him away.

Pyotr went to the window to see the cab go. At exactly the same moment the horse clopped out into the white road, the owls glided away too. Pyotr watched for a long time, trying to work out what in God's name had just happened.

———

Two days later, the Russian fleet began what they called practice manoeuvres just off the southern coast of Korea. To anybody watching for the shape of arranged things, what was really remarkable was that the exercises began just in time for Kiyotaka Kuroda, the new Prime Minister of Japan, to see them himself.

He hadn't been Prime Minister for long. His bones still thought they belonged to a naval officer, someone solid and normal, and definitely not someone with an entire staff who thought he should be wearing a carnation in his lapel. It was good to be back on the deck of a ship, inspecting harbour defences: he knew how to do that, at least. Spread out across the shore, the Nagasaki docks were magnificent: an industrial maze of cranes and dry docks, steelworks, and vast piers for the navy destroyers. Galaxies of blowtorches winked and flared, and men swarmed over one of the ships in for repair.

But it was only magnificent if you'd never seen Liverpool. Kuroda had.

His least favourite person in the world pointed out that it all looked splendid. Arinori was the Minister for Education. He wore a pink carnation. That, as far as Kuroda was concerned, should have disqualified him from government.

'I don't know why you're wittering on about a new fleet. If it ain't broke, don't fix it.' English.

Kuroda stared at him. Arinori was one of those people with absolutely no sense of irony. He wanted – and he had said so publicly, and often – to make English the national language or, failing that, to convert Japanese into Roman letters, to make it easier for children and foreigners to learn. Kuroda still kept the article from the *Japan Times* in the top drawer of his desk. It has been there since eighteen seventy-one, but he was still going to make Arinori eat it one day. 'In England,' Kuroda said, concentrating hard on not shoving him over the side, 'they hang people like you.'

Arinori only laughed.

Kuroda went straight to the admiral's cabin to tell him they would order forty new destroyers from Liverpool today, and bugger what the cabinet had to say about it. If he dithered any longer, the British would only sell the bloody things to the Americans, or worse, the Tsar.

He and the admiral were still finishing off a bottle of wine when a lieutenant hurried in to report that there was enemy movement ahead.

'Enemy movement?' the admiral scoffed. 'What d'you mean, enemy movement? We're only twenty miles offshore.'

The lieutenant looked anxious. 'Perhaps you'd better see, sir.'

Kuroda went with them to the bridge. The admiral leaned down to see into the long scope, and stayed bent for a long time. When he straightened up, he wasn't smiling anymore. Kuroda looked into the eye-piece too, puzzled.

Right on the horizon, about thirty miles away, there were ships. A lot of them. They weren't passing through. They were all facing in different directions, and even as he watched, an arc of smoke shot out from the heavy guns of the largest destroyer. They were running combat drills.

'What are we looking at, sir?' the lieutenant whispered.

'We are looking,' the admiral snapped, 'at the entire Russian Pacific fleet wanking at us off the coast of Busan.'

Kuroda sent the order to Liverpool from the Admiralty office at Nagasaki. He was just checking the wording with his secretary when another secretary, sounding worried, announced his favourite aide and general fixer-upper,

Mr Tanaka. Everyone needed a Tanaka. Although the rest of the government wore smart black morning suits and those ridiculous lapel carnations, Tanaka swanked around in a bright red coat with mismatching buttons. One, which always glittered in strong light, was a miniature Fabergé egg. Kuroda had a feeling that Tanaka had decided the corridors of power needed a splash of completely tasteless colour – Tanaka often decided things – and he liked him a lot for it.

'Tanaka,' Kuroda said. 'Get the scientists up to Aokigahara. They're on.'

Tanaka lifted his eyebrows, but he didn't ask questions. He only bowed and vanished.

———

Tokyo University was the best in the country. Dr Grace Carrow would have liked to think that her lecture room was full because some of the brightest students in the world wanted to know what she had to say, but she was nearly certain that it was because the rain was torrential outside, and the physics department was right above the boiler room. The novelty of a woman tutor had worn off weeks ago.

The course was a ten-week general introduction to various branches of physics for second-year undergraduates, but this fortnight block covered her field: ether theory. She always looked forward to it.

Even though, for a few days beforehand, she always felt uneasy. Ether theory was the only viable scientific explanation for clairvoyance; inevitably, it made her think of the one genuine clairvoyant she knew. She didn't know Keita Mori well, just well enough to know she didn't ever want to see him again. He was a quiet man, but she knew what it was like to be extremely clever in a very small space. You got bored.

She was just starting her lecture when a man wearing a red coat came in. The coat had mismatched buttons. One of them was a Fabergé egg.

'Sorry, all,' he said easily. 'Lecture's cancelled, order of the Home Ministry. Off you all sod.'

Grace didn't argue. You didn't, with men from the Ministry. The students looked worried, but they trooped out. She waited by the blackboard, trying to scrape up enough of her abysmal Japanese to ask what was going on. Lectures were always in English, which was just as well, because she had the linguistic capability of a sea cucumber. As far as she could tell, the word for 'husband' and the word for 'prisoner' were identical. Half the faculty were still worried that she'd got Baron Matsumoto locked away in her attic.

'It's all right, Dr Matsumoto,' the man said in English, looking amused. 'You've not done anything wrong. My name's Tanaka.'

That was the Japanese version of Smith. It must have been a false name; people who were actually called Smith introduced themselves by their first names. Unease stiffened her back. One of the reasons she liked Tokyo was that, even if you were a little woman of five foot three, you were titanic in comparison to most people. Grace went walking at midnight here and never worried. She hadn't realised before what an invisible weight it was in London, being – not afraid or even nervous – but aware all the time of people on the street. She'd nearly forgotten what it was like.

'And mine's Carrow,' she said slowly. 'I didn't take my hus-band's name. How may I help you, Mr Tanaka?'

Tanaka smiled. The jewels on his Fabergé egg button were winking bright shadows onto her lecture notes. 'You can hear me out. The government are running a defence project and it's about to get going. We need ether scientists. I can't tell you the exact specifications until we get there, but you'd be perfect. It's very new, very secret. We'd have to go right now. You can't tell anyone where you're going. I'll inform the university, your husband, all that.'

'Well, that sounds insane,' Grace said. Two men in smart suits had appeared by the door.

Tanaka nodded. 'It does. But, the most insane measures are always the ones that are surrounded by silly amounts of money.' He tipped his head. 'You get next to no funding here. The department hired you because your husband's rich. You don't have a lab. You barely have an office. You should be in research, not wasting your time with a bunch of snotty undergrads. But what I'm talking about – it's serious. The department mentioned your name to me because they want to be shot of you, but I've read your work, Dr Carrow, and you are exactly who we want.'

She hesitated. He wasn't wrong. 'Where will it be based?'

'Can't tell you til we get there.'

'If … look, you needn't tell me yes or no, but I'm going to tell you what I think you're doing. If this is military, you're not interested in theories, and there's only one obvious practical application of ether theory. I think you're starting a project that will determine whether or not clairvoyance is reprodu-cible in laboratory conditions.'

Tanaka winked. 'As you say, I can't tell you.'

'It's impossible without a clairvoyant to test,' she said, slowly, because that wink had made her want very much to annoy him. 'Unless you have one handy, it will be pointless.'

'You'll get whatever you need,' he said easily.

The men in dark suits were checking their pocket watches. Grace glanced at Tanaka.

'You're not really asking me, are you?' she said quietly. She wondered about making a run for the window.

'No, love,' he said, and ushered her out.

PART ONE

ONE

London, 2nd December 1888

Fog rolled down Filigree Street early that morning. It was a great brown mass, darkening the lights from one window and then the next, engulfing the gilded shop signs until there was nothing left but a crooked trail of bright dots that might have been the street lamps. At the narrow end of the road – it became narrower and narrower the further you went – laundry on the lines between the gables turned sooty. Lamps went on in upstairs windows as people hurried to take it in, too late.

At number twenty-seven, Thaniel eased the door open just wide enough to slip through, so he wouldn't let too much of the fog or its chemical smell into the hall, and wound his scarf on high over his nose. It should have been daylight by now, but the fog made it look like midnight, and he had to walk close to the shop fronts to keep himself in a straight line. He shoved his hands into his coat sleeves.

Normally, even though it hurt everyone's eyes and lungs and probably everything else as well, he liked fog; it was a novelty, like snow, and it was hard not to feel a thrill when he saw how different the world looked under the weird brown pall. But all he could think today was that the post wouldn't come. It never did in fog. No post; no telegram from Russia. Like he did every morning, he looked back at number twenty-seven, and the dark workshop window, then pinched himself. Mori wasn't just going to magically reappear overnight.

———

South Kensington station was eerie with so few people there, every step clocking loud on the wooden platform in a way he never noticed in a crowd. The big new posters for Milkmaid condensed milk were optimistically bright, plastered over the older soot-stained ones. They always seemed to appear around the same time the fog did; the milk carts stopped running, of course, because nobody wanted to try and take care of five hundred glass bottles when the streets were full of fog-skittish horses. When the train came, the carriage wasn't even half as crowded as it would usually have been.

When Thaniel came up from the Underground at Westminster, the streets were deserted. There were no cabs, no carriages, not even doormen outside the Liberal Club or Horse Guards. The white buildings loomed spectral and huge, the roofs lost in fog, and he could see what it would look like in a thousand years' time, when it would probably all be in ruins. It was a relief to get into the heat and light of the Foreign Office.

It was a glorious building, with a huge entrance hall and a main stairway built to impress visiting sultans and diplomats. The great chandeliers were unlit today, the vaults of the ceiling lost in a brown gloom, and the clerks at the desk were handing out candles. Thaniel took one and caught himself grinning, because the novelty gave everything a holiday feeling, like going to church on Christmas Eve. One hand cupped over the little flame, he set off away from that first grand, frescoed hall, into the tangle of little corridors that weren't meant for visitors. There were some lamps going, the gas popping and stuttering, but they gave off much less light than they did their odd chemical smell. The gas line had never been brilliant.

The Far Asia department was much brighter. He couldn't tell how official it was – not very, knowing his manager – but this floor of the building was lit electrically, as a kind of pilot experiment with one of the electric companies who wanted to light the whole of Whitehall. Instead of that popping of gas lamps, there was the friendly sizzle of Swann lightbulbs. It was much quieter, and Thaniel liked it, but sometimes, if the power supply waned too much, they fizzed with a noise that, to him, sounded green. The whole corridor had a green tinge to it now.

The department was mostly empty. A few people were playing a delicate game of skittles in the long corridor that led to the Minister's office. Given that the balls sometimes missed and thumped the door, the Minister probably wasn't in either. Thaniel looked up and down the corridor, then dropped onto the stool of the grand piano nobody else ever played and went over the opening of Sullivan's new show. The piano had appeared, mysteriously, about a month after he'd started working here. His manager, Fanshaw, was a huge Gilbert and Sullivan fan, easily avid enough to acquire a piano if it meant he got snatches of the new shows before anyone else. He usually frowned on clerks doing other things at weekends – the Foreign Office was a vocation, thank you, not a job – but he never looked happier than when he was taking Thaniel off weekend shifts in favour of rehearsals at the Savoy. Thaniel kept up a decent supply of free tickets to say thank you.

He kept his weight on the quiet pedal, so that the sound wouldn't hum through the whole building. He was pleased about the new show. It was different to the music Sullivan had written before, richer, less funny, and there was a fantastic moment in the overture when, if everyone hit the big crescendo like they were meant to, the sound was coronation anthem, cathedral-filling grand, and the theatre lit up gold.

Thaniel looked round when the lights buzzed. The green was worse than ever. He shut his eyes hard and pushed one hand to his temple. He did like seeing the colours of sound. He liked seeing the colour of Mori's voice, and the lights that hovered like an aurora above an orchestra, but he was starting to think that electricity might not be his favourite thing.

'The hell is that music coming from?' a courtly voice demanded. Thaniel froze.

He got up gradually and looked around the door of the office. Lord Carrow was inside, talking to Thaniel's manager and looking uncomfortable even to find himself in an office space, as though working for a living might be catching. He was gripping his cane hard, horizontally, in both hands.

'Oh, it's you,' Carrow said blackly. 'I forgot you worked here.' He glared at him and turned back to Francis Fanshaw. 'As I say, if you could drop her a line and encourage her to remember she has a father who would occasionally enjoy confirmation that she hasn't been abducted by savages.'

He didn't wait for anyone to say yes or no and strode out, banging Thaniel's shoulder hard on the way by. Thaniel watched him go.

The last time they had seen each other was in a bland little registry office in Kensington four years ago, when Thaniel and Grace Carrow had been signing divorce papers. They'd all been brittly polite to each other, and then Lord Carrow had punched him in the eye in the foyer.

'You haven't heard from Grace, have you?' Fanshaw said once Carrow was well out of earshot.

'We don't talk to each other. Um ... why was he asking you?'

'She lives in Tokyo now, didn't you know? She married that Japanese fellow – you know, the anti-you. Dandy, annoying; I forget his name. Apparently she hasn't written for a while.'

'Well,' said Thaniel, 'I wouldn't write if Carrow were my father.'

'My feeling too.' Fanshaw paused. He had never asked exactly what had happened between Thaniel and Grace, and Thaniel was glad, because he couldn't think of a good lie even now. 'Say,' he said, 'how's that watchmaker of yours?'

It might only have been that Fanshaw had gone from thinking of one Japanese man to another, but Thaniel had a horrible zing of fear that hurt his whole spine. He hated it when people asked him about Mori. Fanshaw had every right to, he'd met him, but the very first thing Thaniel always thought whenever anyone asked was, *do they know?*

It was prison if you were lucky, an asylum if you weren't. Hard labour or electroshock therapy; and beyond that, he had no idea, because the newspapers couldn't print those kinds of stories, and asylum doctors didn't publish their treatments. They didn't hang people anymore, but that was only because the doctors had managed to classify it all as a kind of madness – moral insanity.

He'd rather hang. That was clean. A scaffold didn't have the rancid horror of an asylum.

'Yeah, fine, probably. Dunno, he's been away.'

'Listen to me very carefully.'

Thaniel frowned. He was too hot now; all his internal engines were revving, ready to run, even though there was nowhere to run to.

'It's "yes" and "I don't know", Steepleton. Promotions come to he who enunciates.'

'Piss off,' said Thaniel, so relieved he had to lean back against the wall.

Fanshaw laughed. 'Anyway. Something for the fog?' He held out a silver hip flask.

A few years ago, Thaniel would have refused, but lately he'd realised that refusing was only polite if you were talking to a poor person. If you refused a rich person, you looked like you were worried you'd catch something. He took a sip and the brandy seared nicely down the back of his throat. 'Thanks.'

'Actually there's something else I need to talk to you about,' Fanshaw said, and stood aside so that Thaniel could see his own desk. The telegraph had been overactive across the weekend. It was covered with ribbons of transcript paper.

'It's all from our legation in Tokyo,' said Fanshaw.

'Have the Russians declared war?' Thaniel said, trying to find the end of the tangle. When he did, he pinned it to the China desk with a Kelly lamp.

'No,' Fanshaw said. 'It seems that the Japanese staff of the legation believe that the building is haunted. They're all leaving. And now the British staff are getting the raging collywobbles as well. There's a danger the whole place will shut down.'

Thaniel straightened, still holding a ribbon of transcript. The later messages towards the end of the ribbon had gone into shouty capital letters. *APPARENTLY THE KITCHEN IS HAUNTED BY SOMEBODY'S DEAD WIFE STOP PLS ADVISE GOD'S ACTUAL SAKE STOP.* 'Did someone enrol us in the Psychical Society without telling us?' he asked, nearly laughing.

Fanshaw shook his head. He was smoothing transcripts as Thaniel cut them up, and he didn't look like he thought it was very funny at all. 'I seriously doubt they mean figure-in-a-sheet ghosts.' He sank his head and surveyed an invisible dictionary about three feet off the floor. It took him a while to find the right words. 'I'm worried it's something the servants feel is unspeakable, and so they're telling stories about ghosts so they won't have to say what's really going on. They know we're all stupid. They know that if they make up something supernatural then we'll write it off as native flightiness and ask no more questions. I've seen this sort of behaviour before, in farther-flung countries. It's usually caused by diplomats ... abusing their immunity, and so forth.'

Thaniel nodded. He could believe it.

Fanshaw looked uncomfortable. 'And if that is the case, it means a local interpreter is no good. They could be inter-preting to the person who's actually the problem. I have to send in someone from outside.'

'Will you go over there and sort it out, then?'

Fanshaw looked up. 'No. You will. You're far more fluent than I am, it's idiotic that you aren't already on a Tokyo posting.'

Thaniel was quiet while he let it sink in. 'How long for?'

'As long as it takes. I'll put it down as a full rotation translation posting, though, so you don't arrive to a building full of people who know you're investigating them. Year, year and a half, on paper.' Fanshaw frowned. 'Are you all right? You don't look happy.'

It caught Thaniel off guard and he didn't know what to say.

Mori was still in Russia. Whatever he was doing there, he had been doing it for six months, and before that, he'd been in Berlin for three. Thaniel had no idea why. Almost certainly the only reason they had managed to rub along together for four years was that he never asked too many questions, but he felt hollowed out with missing him. When the time came to expect a letter – every week or so – the walk home was tight with a sort of nervous buoyancy that veered between dread and hope. There hadn't been any-thing for three weeks. He had a grey feeling now that there wouldn't be, since the entire Russian infrastructure was buried under sixteen feet of snow.

He cleared his throat. 'It's just the fog,' he said, and then almost exactly on cue, had to turn his head away and cough into his hands. 'My lungs aren't too good. I used to work in an engine factory.' He tried to thread some sensible thoughts together. They kept rolling off under the furniture. 'How long do I have to think about it? I've got a little girl.'

Six was going to hate the whole idea. She hated it if he took her on a detour on the way to school, never mind to Tokyo.

'Not long, I'm afraid,' Fanshaw said. He twisted his nose regretfully. 'Think it over tonight, but I need an answer tomorrow. The Russians are still parked in the Sea of Japan. They're not moving at the moment, but if they do move, they're going to go straight for Nagasaki and then all the passenger ships will be put on hold. Everything goes through Nagasaki.' He looked as though everybody had arranged it that way specifically to annoy the Foreign Office. 'So you need to be there sooner rather later.'

Thaniel hesitated, because he didn't much like the idea of taking Six into a war zone. 'But they won't, will they? The Russians. They can't invade.'

Fanshaw shrugged. 'They could. They wouldn't be there if they didn't know something, and I suspect what they know is that the Japanese fleet is on its last legs. I think they're going to inch nearer and nearer til someone from the Japanese navy loses his nerve and fires. Then it'll be the Opium War all over again. The Russians will have the right to do whatever the hell they like once a Russian ship takes a hit.'

'If it's just about not firing on them, then why would anyone do that?'

Fanshaw waved his hands at the whole department. 'Because! Have you seen the heights of gibbering indignation the upper echelons of the Japanese armed forces can achieve? They're still samurai. They grew up being unofficially allowed to test out new swords on unwanted foreigners. They're still getting to grips with the idea that there are forces in the world they can't bully. I almost guarantee someone will fire.'

Thaniel tried to match that idea to Mori, who had never bullied anyone.

Fanshaw let himself slouch. 'Anyway, as I say, have a think tonight. But you do need to go, if you're going to go much further with the Foreign Office. If you get stuck in England, you'll be a clerk forever.'

Thaniel nodded again. Japan; he'd never been further than two hundred miles from home. The idea of it was so big that it was warping everything around it, even sitting here in the same old chair with a folded up Chinese passport stuck under the back leg to keep it level. Ten minutes ago, the office had just been the office, familiar, and cosy in the fog. Now, it didn't feel safe. Instead of the fog, Japan was pawing at the windows, vast and nebulous, and for all he spoke the language and lived with a man who had grown up there, it was dark to him.

Fanshaw clapped him on the shoulder. 'There are things poor people don't teach their sons, and one of those things is that there's a link to home you must sever, if you're to do anything real at all.'

TWO

Tokyo, the same day

Kuroda had met Mori for the first time on a battlefield. The fighting was over by then. The field was beautiful, with mist hanging softly over the broken parts of men, horses, and artillery chassis, the grass black with blood and gunpowder burns. The only people standing upright were the relatives of the soldiers, looking for survivors, or at least relics to take home. Nearly all of them, including Kuroda, moved in a half-grim, half-panicky way, sometimes jolting forward to turn over a body and check who it was, sometimes having to pause at the edge of the field when they saw something too bad.

There was one figure who moved in clear, straight lines between corpses. He didn't hesitate, he didn't look at them, and he walked serenely through the slaughter like it was a rice field. Before long, Kuroda found himself staring, because he was overcome with the certainty that he wasn't seeing a man at all, but a death god, collecting souls.

He didn't believe in death gods, so he went and introduced himself. The young man laughed and promised he wasn't a death god, just a very junior samurai from House Mori come to collect the armour of his fallen brothers. They'd got on well ever since. But Kuroda had never completely shrugged off the suspicion that Mori might actually have been lying about not being something other than entirely human. He hadn't been in the least surprised to find that what had looked, to begin with, like a knack for luck, was actually an ability far more precise.

And then suddenly, after ten years in government service, Mori had moved to London. Almost certainly to defect. No doubt the British had given him a better offer. The Prime Minister at the time would have liked him killed, but Kuroda had quietly made sure nobody tried. It would have been stupid. Ironclads were all well and good, but when the Russians finally did come – he'd always known they would – it would be a hell of a lot better to have a death god. Or whatever you wanted to call him.

———

This morning, walking through the building site that was the Imperial Palace, Kuroda couldn't help feeling put out that Mori hadn't turned up yet. The Russians had been inching closer for two weeks, all but mooning the southern ports, and there was still no sign of him. Not even a telegram. Defector or not, Mori was still a samurai, not to mention a proper friend. Kuroda had honestly thought he would come home to help, if he were ever really needed.

He ducked as some men went by with bamboo scaffolding.

Everywhere, new glass panels winked. The Palace had burned down not long ago, and now builders were replacing all those very flammable old paper walls with brightly coloured glass. Walking through the new corridors was beautifully like navigating a kaleidoscope. Some things the Royal household got right.

Not very many, mind.

Ideally, Kuroda would have convened this Privy Council meeting at the local pub. It was impossible to discuss anything with the full pedantic weight of the Imperial Household leaning over your shoulder. You weren't allowed to take the Emperor to a pub, though, and he was not feeling very optimistic. They needed to get to the point, not priss endlessly. While everyone was agonising over the place settings and the correct forms of address, the Russians were drifting nearer, and nearer.

All they had to do was make someone fire. If someone shot at a Russian ship, it would be war. Everyone might as well learn Russian now.

If no one fired, there were two possibilities. One, everything would be fine; the Russian fleet would end up nearly anchored in Nagasaki, where, given the spirit of Nagasaki, all the boardwalk traders would make a shedload of money rowing out and selling excellent Chinese food to the Russian sailors, and in general everyone except the Home Ministry would consider the whole thing quite funny. It was just about possible that at that point the Americans or the British would get jealous enough of their trading rights to chase off the ships.

Two, the Russians would anchor at Nagasaki, invade, and then look sorry later at the international war tribunals, before utterly failing to hand back the land they'd taken. The British had built an empire out of doing that and Kuroda saw no reason at all why the Tsar wouldn't think it was a splendid idea.

It was two in three, then, for an industrial war the like of which had never been fought before. Part of Kuroda itched to just sink their flagship and get on with it.

The meeting that morning was in a grand room at the Palace with an echo that could be heard even from the corridor outside. The household steward, butler, imperial whatever – Kuroda hadn't bothered to learn his title – bowed at him meticulously at the door.

'Prime Minister! Despite your scheduling difficulties it is hoped that this chamber will prove appropriate,' he said, with an air of triumph that put Kuroda strongly in mind of a dog that had brought back all the old shoes you'd tried to throw away earlier. Kuroda had come up with the scheduling difficulties on purpose. He had suggested moving rooms four times, trying to outrun the uniformed men with rulers and name cards.

'Superb,' he growled, wondering if anyone would really bother to prosecute him if he smacked the man with his own ceremonially embossed ledger.

Government ministers sat in a great horseshoe of chairs upholstered in deep purple velvet, behind a table draped in green damask. They were all in perfect morning suits or, in the case of the military ministers, black uniforms, the thin gold brocade across their chests glinting in the light that flooded in through the huge windows and the chandeliers. Kuroda thumped into a chair.

Beside him, the Emperor's table was draped in red in case, Kuroda supposed, any newcomers or wandering foreigners perhaps hadn't noticed that the youngish fellow kicking around court with too many servants was the Emperor. Like he often did, Mutsuhito came in quickly, to keep ahead of the comet tail of staff behind him, and waved in some men with tea and coffee as everyone jerked to their feet.

'Sit down, sit down, I haven't got my crown on yet,' he murmured.

They sat, stiffly, and only gradually unstiffened as the bright teapots and cafetières went around. Mutsuhito wore a beard and a perpetual frown to seem older, although he had a bleak manner that made both unnecessary.

'The thing is,' he said suddenly to Kuroda as if they were still at the tail end of their conversation of yesterday, 'what if they *do* end up nearly anchored in Nagasaki? It's Nagasaki. People will have sold them fourteen different kinds of chicken and then stolen their lifeboats before they can even say *priviet.*'

'Yes, and then every single country in the world will be giggling at us, sir,' Kuroda said tiredly. It was treason, but he would have given anything for the Empress to attend these things instead of the Emperor. She told people things, and then the things happened. It was how command was meant to work. Mutsuhito was totally unsuited to being in charge of anything more complicated than a dinner party.

'So?' said Mutsuhito in his unbearably neutral way. 'We shan't be in violation of any treaties. They shan't be legally allowed to invade.'

Kuroda stared into his coffee. He hated coffee. 'Quite right, sir, but there will come a point when they don't especially care what they're legally allowed to do, and nor will anyone else. The British and the Americans will shrug and say it's our own silly fault for failing to defend our own borders. And even if they don't invade this time, someone else will, because we didn't fight.'

'Even though it would … be illegal for us to fire on the Russians. But aren't they in violation of our waters?'

'Yes, sir.'

'That's a conundrum.'

Kuroda wondered if he was in Purgatory.

Mutsuhito was looking at the next few pages of affairs to be gone through, altogether serene. He let the corners trail through his gloved fingers. 'I think this young man is hoping to talk to you,' he added.

Kuroda twisted round in his chair. Tanaka had been waiting just by the door, ignoring the steward, who was trying to insist that a red coat with patched elbows and a Fabergé egg was not appropriate attire. Kuroda went out to him as quickly as he decently could.

'I could kiss you,' he said.

'Prefer it if you didn't,' Tanaka said, and seemed to notice the steward for the first time. 'Yeah, mate, no offence, but will you fuck off?'

The steward, amazingly, did as he was told.

'Any news?' Kuroda said quietly. He just about kept himself from saying, is Mori coming.

Tanaka nodded once and handed him a file. 'Yes, sir. These are the findings so far from Aokigahara. The scientists are settled in, they seem pretty happy. We're getting a few reports of ghosts from the greater Tokyo area now, mind you, but so far it's mainly people in coal warehouses and flour mills. None of the papers have picked it up yet. But, one big request from the head physicist.'

'What is it?'

'What they've been saying all along. There's only so much they can do without a real clairvoyant to run tests on.'

'I know,' Kuroda said. He sighed. Mori wasn't coming of his own accord. Fine. He was surprised, though, because Mori must have known what Kuroda would do if he didn't turn up. 'Send a telegram to our ambassador in London, tell him we want to make an accusation against a British civil servant. Nathaniel Steepleton. Indecent assault against the son of a major samurai house.'

'Hey?' said Tanaka.

'It's England,' Kuroda prompted him. 'They're religious fanatics. Their favourite hobby is policing people's bedrooms.'

'Oh yeah.' Tanaka thought about it. 'Culty weirdos. Dunno why anyone would put up with it, myself. Are they brain-washed, sort of thing?'

'Visit and you'll see,' said Kuroda. He would have paid a lot for a phonograph recording of Tanaka's reaction to a Baptist church sermon. 'Anyway, Mori should turn up pretty sharpish if he doesn't want his boy in prison by next week.'

Tanaka nodded slowly. 'Surely he already knows you could make that threat though?'

'I'm sure he does,' Kuroda said. It was vaguely troubling that Mori had waited for him to make it. 'But let's hurry him along.'

'And we're definitely sure he isn't going to kill us all?'

Kuroda snorted. 'Tanaka, he's a knight. Promise him a decent fight and he'll come. It's called fun.'

Tanaka looked like he could come up with a few other words for it than fun, and he had begun to turn away when a very young aide appeared with an envelope.

'Um, sir?' the young man squeaked.

'What?'

'Telegram – for you? From a Baron Mori?'

Kuroda waved it at Tanaka, then tore the envelope open.

This doesn't bode well for not firing at the Russians, does it? My nine-year-old is better at playing chicken than you. See you on Dec 18th.

19

Like a banner, the old familiar joy of the fight unrolled in Kuroda's heart, dusty for having been packed away for so long, but no less bright. He'd been starving for it ever since he left the Navy, only he hadn't understood how badly until now. A proper tournament, with a proper knight, for the first time in years. All at once he wanted Mori to be here right now, to see what happened next, with the wonderful fitful kind of excitement he'd had on his wedding day.

Tanaka lifted his eyebrows when he saw the telegram. 'You're all insane,' he said.

'The only way you get any good at war,' Kuroda said, still so full of elation he could probably have floated quite a respectable hot-air balloon with it, 'is if you love it. That's what a real samurai is.'

'Great, great, and how are we going to make a clairvoyant stay in a room long enough for a bunch of scientists to ask him things? You know, if he doesn't gracefully submit the second he arrives? He doesn't sound like he means to.'

'The scientists have some ideas,' Kuroda promised.

———

When Kuroda got home, his steward was in a tizz. There was, apparently, a woman in his study and she wouldn't go away. Puzzled, he went through. He did keep a geisha, but she was the real thing: an exquisite professional who had an ethereal way of not always turning up even when you were hoping she would. When he opened the door, though, the woman in his study wasn't a geisha. She was little and plain and looking into his aquarium, where his octopus was prodding at her fingertip with one tentacle in what was definitely a handshake. He felt betrayed. He'd started keeping a pet octopus ever since he'd met Mori's clockwork one. They were a lot more endearing than cats and, usually, a lot more loyal.

'Mrs Pepperharrow,' he said, honestly shocked. Like a fool, he found himself searching around for a reason to get away from her, and then felt angry with himself, and with her for making him feel that way. 'I'm busy, what do you want?' he said roughly.

'The owls have come back,' she said. She didn't sound offended, or worried, or vengeful. 'Mori is coming home.'

'I – yes, I just got a telegram,' Kuroda heard himself confessing.

'Good stuff. Want some help?'

'What? But – you hate me.'

She nodded. Her strange eyes were ticking over him, up and down. Rather than step towards him when he came in, she had stepped backward, well out of reach. 'Yes. But we both know he's far more dangerous than you.'

THREE

London, the same day

Thaniel and Fanshaw were still talking about ghosts when the electric lights hummed worse than ever, everything went green for a good five seconds, and then the power supply failed completely and plunged the office into a candlelit murk.

'I vote,' Fanshaw said firmly in the dark, 'that we take the day off. You live near Kensington still, don't you? Shall we share a cab?'

'Ah, I've got an Underground ticket,' said Thaniel, who could cope with brandy but not unexpected cab journeys. It wasn't that he couldn't afford it now. Foreign Office salaries were good. It was just that poverty was as much a state of mind as a fiscal reality, and sometimes he couldn't smother the angry squawk of his father's voice demanding to know why the buggery he was wasting his money.

Fanshaw smiled. 'Is that your oblique northern way of asking me for a raise?'

'No, it's my oblique northern way of saying you're too fancy for your own good with your unnecessary cabs,' Thaniel said, but he was relieved to let his smile fade once Fanshaw turned away to find his coat. He still didn't know how he was going to convince an angry little girl that they were going to move to Tokyo next week. And Mori; he couldn't help thinking that if Mori had had anything particular to say about it all, he would have turned up by now.

By the tall front doors, the desk clerks were squashing candles into pools of melted wax so that people could navigate a way out without falling over the hat stands. Thaniel pulled his scarf up over his face and slipped outside into the gritty dark.

He could just make out that the street lamps were lit, but they didn't illuminate anything. They were just disembodied glows. The people on the street were invisible until they passed a few feet in front of him. But he could hear them. People were whistling as they came to the corner to warn anyone coming the other way. The whistles made bright wisps in the pall.

He was almost at Westminster Underground station when he heard someone ringing a bell and shouting that the line was shut. He stopped and looked around, not sure what to do.

A flare went by, a real one, and then another hissed alight right in front of him with a sharp gunpowder tang.

'Light the way for a shilling?' the little boy behind it said.

'Ah,' said Thaniel, undecided. There might have been cabs in the road – he could hear horses – but the chances of flagging one down without being run over seemed small. An omnibus crawled past, top heavy with passengers, the big advert for Lipton's tea on the side only just visible in ghost letters. The driver was leading the horses, a lantern hanging on his wrist.

'Hit you with my cosh,' the boy said experimentally.

Thaniel pulled the cigarette out of the boy's mouth and dropped it into the flare, which sputtered. 'Don't smoke while you threaten people. But all right. What about two shillings if you take me across to Knightsbridge?'

'Knightsbridge!' the little boy said. It had startled him enough to drop the cockney bravado. 'That's far.' He rallied. 'Did you say two shillings and six?'

Thaniel laughed. 'I did.'

They set off towards St James's Park. All he saw of other people were other flares, mostly at waist height because they belonged to the link lighters. The brambles of telegraph wires overhead were just low enough to make twisting shadows.

By the time they came to the park gates, he had a tight headache and his lungs hurt. The little boy was coughing, though he had a neckerchief over his face. It sounded too bad to have come on today. It was cold, too; the sandy path was sparkling with frost under the boy's flare, and so was the grass. It was just possible to make out the string of lamps that marked the lake. When they reached them, Thaniel touched the little boy's shoulder. He didn't think he could be older than eight, and it was another mile to the Knightsbridge gate.

'I'll go by myself from here. Two shillings and six, all right?' The boy smelled of cigarette smoke and gin, and the sulphurous damp of the fog.

'Right,' the boy said seriously, and then coughed again. 'Bye, mister.'

'Bye.' Thaniel stood and watched til he was out of sight, which was barely ten yards.

———

Thaniel rearranged his scarf and sank his hands into his pockets.

His left closed around some folded sheets of manuscript paper. He took a couple of pieces everywhere so he could write on the train. He had the bones of a symphony, but lately he couldn't pull them into the right shape. It had begun strong last year, when he had taken over one end of the long bench in the workshop and worked while Mori did. Mori had never said anything, too gentlemanly to make anyone feel like they were being scrutinised, but if Thaniel turned shy over a difficult section and tried to write in the parlour instead, Mori started making tea, which might as well have been a summons, because something in Thaniel's knees was wired to get up the second he heard a kettle sing.

But lately there was a dampness in the part of his mind that fired when he was really writing, not just tinkering. Whenever he tried to dig down into himself for more verve, all he found was a maddening mental IOU note that said he would think about it after the post arrived. And of course, after the post arrived, there was always tomorrow's post.

And now – now, he was going to Tokyo by himself. Possibly Mori would appear if the weather was all right, but Thaniel couldn't picture it. There was every chance he wouldn't see him for a year. A year of waiting for the post.

'Oh, shut up,' he told himself aloud. 'You sulky bloody mess.'

Away over the other side of the lake, a cluster of flares hung suspended, will-o'-the-wispy. The light upset a heron, somewhere among the reeds. It made a prehistoric noise and clattered away.

He walked for what felt like the right amount of time and then slowed again, worried that he had gone past the gate. In a tree that must have been very close, an owl hooted.

'Thaniel,' Mori's amber voice said from a little way off. 'It's this way.'

Thaniel swung around and didn't believe what he'd heard until he saw him. Mori was waiting between a pair of trees in a thinner patch of fog. He didn't look how Thaniel remembered. He never did; he had a changeling's ability to alter nearly everything about himself depending on where and when he was. His coat had a fur collar, there was silver stitching on his gloves, and he had cut the last of the light dye out of his hair. It was back to its own glassy black.

For a long time, it had struck Thaniel as unlikely that a clairvoyant samurai would ever bother with a gamekeeper's son who'd left school at fourteen with all the natural refinement of a shovel. But Mori was one of those men who liked anybody willing to be tenacious with him.

His clairvoyance was the reason for that. Not many people wanted to live with someone who knew nearly everything, or so he said.

Mori remembered possible futures. It was just like ordinary memory, but it worked forwards as well as backwards. If something was about to happen, he knew it clearly – in just the same way anyone else knew what had just happened a minute ago. If something was only a distant, hazy possibility, he remembered it like it had happened twenty years ago, buried under all the more recent, more likely things. The second a thing was no longer possible, he forgot it. It was why he maintained that a book was nothing but a dead story, thank you, and he preferred them while they were still alive, fluttering about in someone's mind, with lots of possible endings and interesting side bits, before the editor pulled them off and pinned it down on paper and he forgot all the good parts. Mori was still annoyed with Arthur Conan Doyle for reasons he couldn't remember anymore.

So it was a funny sort of acquaintance. Anyone sensible would have thought they could never have anything in common, or a solitary thing to say to each other. They didn't even have mutual friends. But Thaniel was good at making up better endings for Sherlock Holmes stories, and Mori seemed to think that was more than enough to be getting on with.

'Kei.' For a long second Thaniel was paralysed with relief and joy, and awkwardness. 'You came back,' he managed.

'Of course I came back,' Mori said, laughing. 'How are you?'

'Good.' Thaniel tried to think of something sensible. It occurred him that the polite thing would be to ask if everything was finished in Russia.

'It is more or less,' Mori said before he could ask. 'I'm sorry I haven't written for a bit, I was ill and I got stuck in Paris.'

Thaniel saw Mori notice that he'd replied to something that hadn't happened aloud yet, and the flicker of anxiety and irritation that always came with it. He didn't like doing it, even with people who knew he could.

'Ill?' said Thaniel. Mori was either upright and going about his day, or unconscious. By ill, he didn't mean he'd had a cold. 'Are you all right now, what—'

Mori looked lost and exhausted for a moment, before he shook his head and cast the look off like a scarf. 'Yes – I just hate Paris. I'm surprised more people don't have some sort of allergic reaction.'

Thaniel decided to let it lie, whatever it was. 'Only you could hate Paris.'

'Thaniel, I grew up bowing to immediate family. Every random Frenchman thinks that the only proper way to say hello is indecent assault. I thoroughly hate Paris.'

Thaniel laughed. Mori tipped his shoulder to suggest they go. They skirted a coughing family coming the other way, then set out across the grass, which crackled as the frost shards broke. If Thaniel had been king of everything, this would have been the test he gave to anyone who claimed they were clairvoyant – to walk unguided through London in fog. Mori went as fast at night and in fog as he did on bright mornings.

He took Thaniel's hand. They would have lost each other even a foot apart. The tea-stain haze was thicker outside the park, where Knightsbridge had funnelled it into a dense column. Thaniel squeezed his fingers. It felt safe and private. Mori pressed his knuckles and pulled him to the right, onto Filigree Street.

Not for away, the electric lights at Harrods were bright enough to give the shop doors a halo, but Filigree Street was medieval. The houses leaned further and further towards each other in a way that always put Thaniel in mind of a row of companionable drunks, so close at the far end that even on a sunny day the road was always in shadow, and far too narrow to ride through. In the confined space, the fog closed in and concentrated itself all the more, until it furled in almost solid patterns, tentacles brushing at the tiny-paned windows. The lower floors were mainly occupied by small, exquisite shops and they were still open, each one with ten or twelve candles outlining the path to the doors. The lights were so dim they were hardly more than phantoms.

A caped policeman coalesced from the murk just ahead of them, and touched his hat.

Thaniel let go of Mori's hand. He couldn't help it. He felt like his skull had turned to glass and any casual observer would see all his thoughts finning around.

Number twenty-seven was all alight. When Mori pushed the workshop door open, the clear air inside tasted sweet. In the window, the clockwork birds were all sleepy, though usually they fluttered about between each other's perches in little silver and bronze flashes. The mechanical fireflies had come out instead. They pootled gold lines around the ceiling and down among the birds, which sometimes stirred in the light. Thaniel had caught one once, but he still couldn't work out what it was that glowed inside the glass case. It was a powder of some kind which flared brighter the more it was disturbed. A sort of pollen, Mori said, from Peru, although privately Thaniel suspected he'd made that up because he was embarrassed about having invented something completely anachronistic.

A barn owl settled on the window sill. Thaniel smiled. He'd got so used to owls haunting Filigree Street that he'd stopped noticing them, but a while ago they'd stopped coming. It was good to see one again. He had a silly feeling that it knew Mori had come back.

Mori took off his coat. Thaniel watched him in the reflection. His image in the glass looked much more solid than Thaniel's did, because his colours were clearer and deeper.

Thaniel was the rough mock-up someone's apprentice had folded together out of paper scraps, and Mori was the real thing, enamelled, and finished in gold.

———

Six leaned out of the kitchen doorway, then came across speculatively. She was nine, or so they thought, but she was miniature for her age, and when she was worried, she tended to look like a solemn toddler. Because she hated anyone touching her any more than absolutely necessary, they kept her hair short so that no one else would have to brush it or plait it, and that made her look even younger. She had a spanner behind her ear today.

'Hello,' said Mori, very soft, because appearing unexpectedly after six months had a fifty percent chance of eliciting no reaction from her whatsoever, but an equal chance of helpless lifelong rage. Thaniel doubted that even Mori could tell accurately which it would be. Six was built differently to the rest of the world.

'Good evening.' She said it in stiff Japanese. She was studying Mori, and clearly struggling to take in how he looked. 'Your clothes are different,' she said, unhappy. He was in a beautiful blue waistcoat full of silver threads that made him look like he had just that second been caught in the rain. Thaniel had never been able to tell exactly why she hated it when one of them wore anything unusual, but he had a theory that she took an evening suit or a new coat as an external sign of some dangerous internal change.

Behind her, Osei winced on the threshold and put her hand up a conciliatory fraction to say that usually she looked after a better-trained child. Osei wasn't a professional nanny – in fact she ran the local tea house – but she was much kinder than anyone Thaniel had interviewed from proper agencies. 'Miss Charlotte. You should say welcome home.'

'I'm Six,' said Six. 'Not Charlotte.'

'No, you're nine,' Osei said. She swiped away the spanner. 'You have to have a proper name.'

'I'm wearing this because I didn't have anything else warm enough,' Mori said gently, just over them both. 'Come here, I've got something for you.'

Six looked unwilling but did as she was told. Quietly, Thaniel was on Osei's side. Charlotte was Six's real name, the one her mother had given her in the workhouse register. But the workhouse staff had numbered the children rather than bother with names. Thaniel had tried to tell her that that was awful. Six had only said blankly that if he wanted to call her Charlotte, then she would be calling him Henry.

Mori took a box from his coat pocket and gave it to her.

Thaniel came nearer. It was a lightbulb. Inside, the filament had been arranged into something that suggested shapes, but he couldn't tell what they would make once they were alight.

Six didn't make a sound, but she rose onto the balls of her feet and put her arms up. Mori lifted her up. She didn't want affection, just the empty lightbulb socket above him. He held her while she screwed the bulb in. When it came to life, the filament buzzed, and then flared into an octopus. It writhed and moved, swimming inside the glass. Six laughed. It was an abrupt monotonal bark. Thaniel had thought it was fake for a long time before he realised that there hadn't been enough laughing at the workhouse for her to have a good grasp of the way it was usually done.

'What do you say?' Osei prompted her.

'Arigatou gozaimashita.'

'You're welcome.' Mori set Six down and didn't make any more fuss of her. He had never treated her like a child, only a small adult, with the same dignity as one. Thaniel had forgotten that, but watching her now, he could see her sinking into it with a relief that gave him a pang. She took Mori's sleeve and leaned against him. It was just at an angle that hid her from both Thaniel and Osei. Mori put his arm around her and she put her face against his waistcoat pocket. She seemed to have forgiven him for the change of colour. She was just old enough to enjoy how glamorous Mori was. Her friends at school had god-fathers who were bankers or tweedy, moth-ballish landowners in Nottinghamshire.

Osei looked anxious and bowed to him. Mori bowed back and thanked her for helping so much. Six let go of him, but stayed close. She had stolen his watch, but she hadn't unclipped it, which left a small slack of gold chain between them. He moved slowly so that she could keep up.

She had used to make the very smallest clockwork parts for him. A lot of fine clockwork came from workhouses, where the children were tiny enough to make chain that might as well have been golden hairs, or dust-specks of cogs. Mori claimed not to like children, but near Christmas in the first year Thaniel had lived here, he had brought Six home and then refused to take her back again, and that was that.

Thaniel found a lamp for Osei, then felt guilty when he looked at the fog again. She was only the size of a link lighter. She always refused to stay for dinner.

'I'm just going to walk back with Osei,' Thaniel said over the murmur of Japanese from Six.

33

Mori straightened up. He looked like he might have meant to say something, but as Osei passed him, with a polite nod, he frowned and leaned back like he'd caught brimstone on her. Thaniel widened his eyes at him to ask what the matter was. Osei didn't smell of brimstone. Her clothes just drifted jasmine through the air. Mori shook his head.

When Thaniel looked back at the window, Mori was taking Six through to the kitchen. They walked still linked by his watch chain. Despite the grit in the air, Thaniel felt like he could breathe properly again, but he could tell it was temporary. When he got back, he was going to have to talk about Tokyo – about who would take Six, about whether any of them would see each other, everything – and this delicate, filigree peace would break.

It only took twenty minutes to see Osei home, and when he came back, Mori had already cooked. The heat from the range curled up to meet him at the dented steps down into the kitchen from the workshop. Sitting on the stove and soaking up the heat was Mori's octopus, mechanical, like everything else. With bright steel casing over his clockwork, Katsu looked like a mercury spill, except for the copper wheel that had replaced one of his tentacles. He had disappeared for a while once, but a fortnight or so later he had trundled back, minus a leg, and Mori had given him a temporary wheel while he made a new leg. When the time had come to fit it, Katsu had hidden on top of a cupboard, and whenever anyone brought up repairs, he disappeared until the subject moved on. Mori thought that something had been skewed in

34

his clockwork. Thaniel was nearly sure that Katsu liked the wheel. It improved his cornering.

Thaniel touched one of his tentacles to be sure he wasn't too hot, then picked him up and gave him to Six, who had just sat down after setting the table. She put her nose against Katsu's and did a silent fish impression. After such a long time away, it struck Thaniel as freshly odd to have a pet octopus, but it did make sense really. Real pets were out, because Mori didn't like things that couldn't look after themselves. You couldn't have fluffy clockwork, and a clever snake would have been sinister.

There was food already on the table. It was chicken and proper rice, proper vegetables, proper soup, and a box of beautiful French cakes it would be a shame to eat. One had a marzipan octopus on it.

As he sat down, Thaniel had to twist away and cough into his hands. Six studied him.

'Are you dying?' she asked. 'People who cough like that always die.'

He managed to smile. He was trying and failing to think of a way to mention Tokyo that wouldn't land on the table like an anvil. 'No, petal. I don't mean to.'

'Nobody does. Mori,' she said, untangling Katsu. 'If Dad dies, must I go back to the workhouse?'

Thaniel choked. It was the sort of question she asked at least twice a year and although it upset him more each time, he had never been able to find a way to convince her that in some things, people didn't change their minds. 'Six, that's ridiculous, of course you're not going back; you're never going back.'

'No it isn't ridiculous. Mori might not want me,' she said reasonably.

'Six—' he began. He had explained to her before – several times – that she belonged to them both, and the only reason she was legally his was that the registry office would sooner arrest Mori than let him become the legal guardian of a white child. She always ignored him. Even though it was Mori who had taken her from the workhouse and Mori she went to for justice and reassurance, she never seemed able to let go of the nagging worry that any link she had with him was unofficial. Thaniel didn't blame her.

'Whether I want you or not is irrelevant,' said Mori. Thaniel looked up slowly. 'You can't take children back to a workhouse without a receipt. I haven't got one for you anymore.'

Six frowned. 'But some of the boys used to come in and out nearly every day. For school.'

'With receipts.' He gave her some rice. 'The octopus fed yours to the koi.'

'Oh,' she said, and seemed satisfied.

Thaniel felt wry. It had never been a secret that Mori had the comprehensive Six instruction manual, although it was annoying not to have deduced more than a quarter of it without him.

She interrogated Mori about France and, having decided it was a generally unworthwhile place, she said in her upright Japanese that dinner had been a real feast, and looked solemnly approving when Mori gave her the octopus cake. She turned to go without saying anything else. Thaniel poked her.

'Hey. Show me an uppercut, soldier.'

She did, and smiled when he pretended that catching it in his palm had hurt.

'That's good.'

'I know,' she said, 'but I can't play with you now, it's cake time.'

'Fair enough.'

Thaniel watched her go, trying to tell if she was all right or not. She wouldn't sulk if she was unhappy or angry. She would behave normally, but then she would change all the door handles.

'I'll get it in the neck later,' Mori said. 'But she's got a perfect right to that.'

'No, she hasn't. She can't keep you in the house forever,' said Thaniel.

Mori studied him for a while, heedful and unhurried. 'And how are you?'

He still didn't know how to say it, so fast and all in one go seemed best. 'Francis Fanshaw wants me to go to Japan. There's some trouble at the legation in Tokyo. I'm supposed to sort it out. I don't know what your plans are, but ...' His throat had gone dry again. 'I suppose we need to decide where Six goes, here or there.'

'No, we'll all go. Friend of mine's just got himself elected Prime Minister over there. He wants me to come home.'

Thaniel stared at him. 'Sorry?'

'There's a liner going out on Thursday. It only takes twelve days now, so we'll be there for Christmas.' Mori smiled a little. 'That's why I'm here. If you'd – like to go together, that is.'

'I'd like to,' Thaniel said, and couldn't summon up anything else at first. He had to clench his hands under the table, ludicrously close to crying with relief. 'You never said?'

'I know, I'm sorry. I wasn't sure any of this was happening until a few weeks ago, and then I got stuck in Paris. Flu or something. I'm sorry.'

'You might have given me a bit of warning, before it was a certain thing? Steepleton, look sharp, you might be moving to Japan?'

Mori looked uncomfortable. 'I'm sorry. I didn't … want to think about it too much. I know that's stupid, but it's always odd. Going home.' His black eyes came up again, full of awkward apology. By odd, he meant deeply unnerving.

'How do you mean?' Thaniel said, annoyed with himself.

Mori inclined his head unwillingly. 'Well; my house is haunted in bad weather.'

Thaniel hadn't known that Mori believed in ghosts, but he was never surprised anymore when they hit little pockets of difference like that. It would have been much stranger if they'd grown up six thousand miles apart and agreed about everything. Besides, at this precise moment, Mori could have announced he often had high tea with a talking fox and Thaniel would have gone along with it. 'No wonder it's not your favourite place.'

Mori smiled and shook his head once. 'It's nice, though. An estate in Yokohama. That's the posh residential bit on the edge of Tokyo. Good air, by the sea.' He twisted back to take something from the drawer of post he never bothered to open. It was a postcard. 'This is it.'

When Mori had said house, Thaniel had imagined one of those tall neat places in Belgravia, but maybe with rickshaws going to and fro outside instead of hansom cabs. On the postcard, though, was a photograph of a sprawling ramble of beautiful traditional buildings among lush gardens and pools that steamed, and cherry trees that snowed their petals onto the curved rooftops. The name was printed in Japanese in the corner on the other side of the card. Yoruji: it meant The

Evening Temple. And then, in small sepia print, *Yokohama residence of House Mori.*

'Christ,' said Thaniel, who had gone straight from impressed to uneasy. That kind of money was like a bright light. It showed every single rough edge in horrible detail. Even just sitting and holding an image of the place, he was acutely aware of being made of rough edges. 'Sure they'll let me in? I'm not – really your sort.'

Mori's shoulders flickered with something like incredulity. When he spoke, his voice was full of smoke. 'What? You're exactly my sort.'

Thaniel had to laugh. Whatever nerves he might have about high society, it was hardly a bad problem to have. Going together was better than anything he'd thought of, or even hoped. 'So – Japan, then.'

Mori smiled, shy like he always was if anyone was too pleased about something he'd said. 'I think that deserves a toast.'

There was a hum from upstairs as Six turned on her generator to power her lightbulb collection, and then a squeaking that must have been the new addition going into a socket. Thaniel fetched down the brandy and a pair of glasses. As he set them down, he caught the smell of lemon soap from Mori's clothes. It was on his skin too, hotter. Mori looked back as Thaniel leaned forward to kiss his cheek. He touched their heads together, just cradling the base of Thaniel's skull for a careful moment before he kissed him back. Thaniel felt a flood of white hot relief.

He had never known what the agreement was. It was an unbearable thing to ask him. If Thaniel tapped on Mori's door at night, he always let him in, but he never touched

Thaniel first, and never spoke about it; no endearments, no promises, and no discussion. Thaniel liked it that way, but he was always afraid. Mori was from a generation and a country where carrying on with a friend was unremarkable, something you could do idly for a summer or two, or, worse, submit politely to even if you didn't much want it, like a boring work dinner, for the sake of a bit of company. Thaniel had decided a long time ago he could live without knowing.

FIVE

Eight o'clock had just begun to chime when Six fetched Thaniel to read. The attic ran the length of the house. There was a trapdoor above the landing and a brass-fitted ladder that unfolded itself when the hatch opened. She hurried up ahead of him. Thaniel went more slowly. The insides of his elbows ached and he felt feverish.

Six's lightbulb collection had turned the rafters starry. The bulbs were all different sizes and shades, wired up at different heights, because where they were depended on what she had found to climb up on. There weren't dolls or normal toys. She had yelled and hidden from the doll Thaniel's sister had once tried to give her. Instead, winking like sequins all across her desk were rows and rows of minuscule cogs she'd filed down herself. She loved going with Mori to the factory where you could buy them rough in bulk. She was making a naval chronometer.

Mori was there ahead of them, building a pyramid of kindling in the fireplace. He never let her go without a fire even if there was only a little chill in the air, and Thaniel loved him a lot for that. Growing up, his own father had had an unbreakable rule that there would only be a fire in the tiny gamekeeper's cabin on days when you had to crack the ice on the water pitcher. It had been fair enough, but Thaniel had never hated anything like he'd hated winter then, except maybe his father, who hadn't done it because of the cost – the cabin was right next to the woods and firewood was free as part of the job – but on principle. Really it had been a healthy experience, because now he knew that if anyone said 'it's the principle of the thing' then the correct response was to punch that person in the throat, but he was glad that Six wasn't having to learn that way.

She gave Thaniel the generator instruction manual and bumped Mori hard on her way by him, which made Thaniel pay attention even before she did anything else. She rolled a die along her desk, looked at the number and folded her arms. She was holding something else. Thaniel couldn't see what it was. Mori jumped as if a huge noise had gone off in his face, even though there was nothing but the skitter of the die. He didn't say anything.

She rolled the die again. Mori flinched hard, then eased when it landed on four.

'Six,' Thaniel said, slowly, because he had just understood what she was doing.

A die had exactly even sides. Mori had no way of knowing on which side it would fall, since nothing was more likely than anything else. Exactly even chances, one in six. Random was random whether you were a clairvoyant or not. Coins, dice, and lightning: that was the random trinity. Mori could watch a thunderstorm or a game of roulette for hours, just for the novelty of having no idea what was going to happen next.

The die landed on a six.

She slung down what looked like a teabag, but when it hit the floor, it went off with a bang much too loud for the attic.

'Christ,' Thaniel said, taken right off guard. She had always done peculiar things, but fireworks indoors weren't something he'd ever expected. He had a feeling that she would be a lot older before she understood the ordinary rules most people took for granted. No stealing, no staring too hard, no fire-crackers in the face. 'What are you doing? You can't have those in here.'

'But they're mainly only potential firecrackers,' Six reasoned evenly.

Mori clenched his hands hard on his knees. 'I think three times is enough, don't you?' he said quietly through the chemical smoke. The die had landed right on the edge of the desk and now it fell into his lap. He jerked back from it like most people would have from a spider. Thaniel heard his breath catch.

'No more dice,' Thaniel decided. He picked it up and slung it in the fire. It made her squeak. He knelt down to her so he wasn't looming over her. 'Come on, Six, if you're angry, you have to tell people, you can't throw dice and firecrackers. That's not very …' He stopped, because he had been going to say 'ladylike', but ladylikeness was the reason Mori thought women shouldn't be allowed to vote. 'Honourable.'

She hid under the bed before he was even halfway through speaking. Mori was staring at the fire as if he were worried the die wouldn't burn but crawl back out of its own accord. When Thaniel touched his shoulder, his bones were so tight they thrummed. He seemed not to feel it.

'Kei,' Thaniel said.

'No, I'm fine,' Mori said. 'It's just – it's …' He let his breath out. He was much more bothered than he should have been by a firecracker.

Thaniel pulled him gently to make him move away from the fire. Mori let him, but only by a couple of inches.

'I didn't mean it to be that bad!' Six said anxiously. She sounded near to crying. Thaniel's heart squeezed. She had no middle ground; she was either content, or so deeply ashamed it scared him.

'I know that, roku-chan. Come out,' Mori said. He wound up one of her clockwork mice and scooted it under the bed to her. 'The decent thing is to stand up straight and look someone in the eye.'

She sniffed.

Mori leaned down. He kept his hands clasped, holding himself just on the strength of his spine, though he had to go low enough for his hair to brush the floor. 'I can't do that if you don't come out.'

She hesitated, then edged out. There was real fear in her. She expected a cane or worse, even now, though Mori had never so much as raised his voice at her. Mori pushed gently on her chest to make her uncurl, because she tipped forward over her knees when somebody had told her she was in the wrong. She would do it even when she was standing up. Usually she would find a corner first, and then creep down the wall. It was appalling and animal. Thaniel hoped she didn't remember why she did it anymore.

Mori bowed where he was kneeling. 'I'm sorry I left you for so long.'

She stared, then nodded and bowed back. 'I'm sorry I let off fireworks inside.'

'Square?'

'Square,' she agreed, broadcasting relief.

Not all of Mori's colour had come back. Thaniel propped Six into his lap and opened the generator manual. 'Are you sure you don't want to try Princess Kaguya tonight?' he tried.

Six shook her head. 'I already know how princesses work.'

———

When they went downstairs, Mori opened the kitchen door just as the Haverly boys kicked a rugby ball right over the fence. He caught it, but rather than give it back, he threw a firecracker back at them and then pulled the door shut. There was a bang and a lot of yelling. Thaniel poured them both some more brandy. Mori gave the ball to Katsu, who whirred delightedly and hurried off with it.

'Are you all right?' Thaniel asked.

Mori was unsettled enough to have been thrown out with his timing. He answered the next question – has something happened? – rather than the present one. 'Nothing—'

'What will happen, then?' Thaniel said. He frowned. 'Is someone going to blow something up again?'

'No, no, it wasn't the firecracker. It was the die.'

Thaniel felt like he was drifting even further out to sea. 'Traumatic backgammon game?' he hazarded.

'No, but anything random – it's a bit … you know, like someone jumping at you from behind the bins.'

'When did that start?' Thaniel said carefully. They had played with dice before and Mori had been fine.

'I don't know,' Mori hedged. 'Lately I suppose.'

'The last time you were scared of anything, it was heights, and it turned out you were going to fall off a building.'

'I'm not going to fall off any buildings.'

'I think we both agree that that was such a specific truth it was really a lie, can't we?'

Mori laughed, though it was more like patience than humour. It just cracked the lines around his eyes. 'I'm fine, I've just been a bit fragile the last few weeks. As I say, I – came down with something in Paris.'

Thaniel thought about pushing, but Mori shied away when he overheard that future. 'Listen, let's ask Mrs Haverly to look in on Six. I'm taking you out.'

Mori's mind must have been elsewhere, because the idea seemed to clip him from the side. 'Out, out where?'

'To a show.' Thaniel gave him his coat. 'With humans and laughing, like normal people do. *Jekyll and Hyde*'s on at the Lyceum.'

SIX

London, 3rd December 1888

The room was still dark when Thaniel woke up. Fog pressed against the diamond-paned window, but the fire was still glowing from last night, and his skin carried the warm, sherry and candied-almond smell of the theatre. At next door's hearth – the two houses shared a chimney flue – Mrs Haverly was singing to her baby.

It wasn't until he shifted that he realised Mori wasn't there. As he sat up, all the muscles between his ribs hurt. He must have been coughing in the night. He'd only just had time to worry he might have driven Mori out when Mori came in with two cups of tea.

'God, thank you.' Thaniel took it carefully, enjoying how it felt to hold it. His normal morning trajectory for the last nine months had been sink-clothes-Osei's, with Six in tow. He hadn't been bothering with tea until he reached the office, not because he didn't want it, but because he'd developed a private hatred of making it just for himself.

'Did I keep you awake?' he said, embarrassed. Even when he didn't have a cold, he was always acutely aware of just how much space he took up in this room, Mori's room. Mori was a person who made society girls look doughy and huge, never mind someone who had a permanent locker at a boxing gym.

'What? No.' Mori leaned down over him and kissed his throat, and the awkwardness dropped away. 'I've only been up five minutes.' He folded down on the quilt and crossed his legs, facing the headboard. He could never get back into bed once he was up; he thought it was decadent. He was wearing a heavy Aran jumper with sleeves that came to his knuckles, and a green scarf Thaniel's sister had sent at Christmas. The wool made him look soft, and it had caught the smell of woodsmoke. 'They're sending people home from the Foreign Office today. You could stay,' he said. He tipped his eyes away as though despite everything, he wasn't sure Thaniel would want to stay at home. 'See Dr Haverly about that cough, maybe.'

So Thaniel had coughed all night. 'I will,' Thaniel promised, and then hugged him, trying to communicate that he was sorry about what must have been quite a lot of lost sleep without having to mention it.

Six creaked down the loft ladder then. Thaniel sat back fast and pulled yesterday's shirt back on. The bolt of shame-fear woke him up much better than tea could.

'There's no school,' Six reported from the doorway. She had her hands clamped around fistfuls of her dressing gown. As she spoke, she glanced wretchedly back along the corridor. 'They said no school if there's fog and – there's fog.'

Mori held up a piece of paper folded into a star.

If Six moved at anything quicker than a walk, she looked off-balance, and so it was with a kind of tripping lurch that she hurried across. She took the paper star and opened it up. It was a schedule for the day, divided into half-hour slots. Her whole posture loosened and she touched her palm to

Mori's, which was the nearest she could manage to a hug when she'd been worried. Thaniel trapped his hands under his knees so he couldn't scoop her up. Hers was always such a frail happiness that whenever he thought about sending her out into the world, his tongue turned to paper.

The Haverlys lived next door at number twenty-nine, and they had six children, who were all terrible, and so getting a doctor's opinion was really only a matter of leaning over the fence in the back garden and tapping on their kitchen window. Given the children, Dr Haverly didn't charge.

When Thaniel stepped into the garden, where the silver birches were mainly invisible under the chemical haze, Katsu hurried out ahead of him with a piece of toast. It was for the birds, although less out of octopussy good feeling for his fellow fauna than to catch one. He hadn't managed to pin one down yet, but Thaniel doubted that he would do anything with it when he had. It was more a prestige thing for Katsu to hold over the Haverly cat.

Thaniel blinked slowly as he reached over the fence to tap next door's kitchen window. Now that he was up and moving about, he felt sluggish. Dr Haverly came out, sneaking, with a lit cigar.

'Pretend to be more ill than you are so I can smoke this,' he said hopefully.

'I might have malaria,' said Thaniel.

'Good man, good man.'

'But as well as the malaria, I've got a cough, which is — not an emergency, but you haven't got anything for it, have you?'

'Oh, I expect so,' Haverly said, glancing back into his own house, gloomily. It was cacophonous. The children were fighting about something.

'No rush. Don't put that out,' Thaniel added when Haverly moved to stub out the cigar on the fence post. Thaniel had never smoked, but he could recognise a good cigar; the Foreign Minister smoked so much he was volcanic. He had to turn away and cough. His hands had begun to shake.

Haverly was frowning. 'Hold on. Come here, I want to listen to that. Just to the fence. Pardon me.' He leaned down and set his ear to Thaniel's chest. 'Breathe in. And again.' When he stood back, he had swept his expression neutral. 'How long have you been coughing like that?'

'Oh. A few weeks I suppose. Same every year though.'

'I think you arrived in London, didn't you, with some damage to your lungs? Cotton factory, was it?'

'Engine factory.'

'And your father had similar problems, didn't he, despite always working outdoors in the countryside?'

Thaniel nodded. 'He was always bad in winter.'

'Yes. I'm afraid you're on the sticky end of both the environmental and inherited sticks,' Dr Haverly said carefully. 'Unavoidable in London. In your case, I suspect that actually it would have been unavoidable unless we'd put you in a specially oxygenated box on the Isle of Skye. I'm surprised it hasn't happened before. Better get yourself off to the seaside. Brighton's a favourite, for this sort of thing. I should give it five or six months at least.'

'What?' Thaniel said, after a second in which he was too confused to speak. He had thought Haverly would say a week, or just to stay out of the fog. He glanced back at his own kitchen window. Mori was there but facing away, the small of his back against the edge of the range. He was talking to Six, his arms folded. 'Are you sure? I feel all right, couldn't it just ...'

'Certain, I'm afraid. Your lungs are struggling much more than they should. I think when you say you feel all right, you mean you feel normal, but normal for you is getting dangerous. You've always taken colds harshly, but this fog – well. Strong people can recover with the right air.' Haverly's eyes slipped away before he dragged them back. 'But it's very easy to contract something like phthisis once you're already in this condition.'

'What's – no. I see,' said Thaniel, but too late.

'Tuberculosis.'

'Right.' He closed his teeth. 'You mean it's going to kill me, don't you?'

Haverly sighed. 'Impossible to say. If you keep very well, you could stave it off for twenty years. I mean, you're terribly fit; you walk everywhere, and you box, don't you? But London will kill you by summer. You're breathing poison here.'

'Right. Thank you.'

'I am sorry,' Haverly said.

'Um ... no. Actually we're going to Tokyo on Thursday,' Thaniel said gradually. 'It's by the sea. Probably a lot nicer than Brighton. Big parks, that kind of thing.'

Haverly cheered up. 'Oh, well, in that case! What good timing, hey?'

'Extremely,' said Thaniel, looking back through the window of number twenty-seven again. He tipped sideways to catch Mori's eye. Mori saluted, looking awkward to have been found out.

SEVEN

Yokohama, 10th December 1888

The scientists at Aokigahara sent a list of specifications. Kuroda took it to Yoruji on a lowering grey morning with so much static electricity in the air that it dragged at his teeth. Tanaka and his men came too, to scout the place. Kuroda did not envy them the task of learning the corridors in the week it would be before Mori arrived.

Yoruji, the ancestral northern home of House Mori, was an ancient, rambling place that stood on the highest point of the Yokohama cliffs, facing out to the roiling sea. That morning, the patchwork stormlight fighting through the clouds made sections of the house bright and warm, and some dark. Pieces of it had been rebuilt and rejigged, walls moved, and new buildings added for about five hundred years, and none of the builders had been especially concerned about its making sense. There was even a rumour that the monks who had once lived here had gone out of their way to make it difficult and strange, to better protect the shrine at the heart of the old temple. Kuroda was inclined to think there was some truth to that. Yoruji was such a dim, confusing, odd house that it was hard to think anyone could have made it by accident.

Mrs Pepperharrow met them at the strangely positioned front door with maps of the house drawn out neatly and labelled for the soldiers.

'Thank you very much, ma'am,' the captain said, careful and wary.

On the way over, at least three of the men, including Tanaka, had asked Kuroda exactly who Mrs Pepperharrow was, and why she ran Yoruji in Mori's absence. He'd decided not to tell them. If a tiny woman was going to have twenty armed soldiers in her house for a fortnight, it was a good idea for them to be puzzled by her. So he'd only told them she ran an important kabuki theatre. Ever since his wife had died, he'd felt overprotective about women.

Mrs Pepperharrow was an unprepossessing lady, and her main feature was that she was never one thing or another; neither young nor old; not wholly Japanese, which was obvious immediately because she had grey eyes, but not especially English either; not feminine but not manly. At home, she was usually outside, in boots, helping with the upkeep of the grounds. She led the way inside now to a big room with a glass wall that looked out over the gorgeously tailored cascade of the cliffside gardens.

'So,' she said, as the steward appeared with enough tea and little biscuits to feed an army. The soldiers gave her an adoring look. 'You've got some ideas, you said.'

Kuroda explained the report.

The scientists had used words like simple. All one needed to catch a clairvoyant was an electrograph, a decent signalling system, and twenty well-trained soldiers. They had made it sound like the volcano baking soda experiment.

'We suggest using the main temple bell in your tower here as a signal,' the captain said, a little full of himself.

'No,' she said straightaway. 'The Russians are forty miles off Nagasaki, the newspapers say; is that still right?'

She had the streety Tokyo accent that you usually over-heard quietly saying 'fuck' after it had spilt its drink at one of those pubs where you sat on orange crates rather than chairs.

'Thirty-five, actually.' Defence pedantry.

She seemed not to mind. 'If we start ringing huge bells on the sea shore, people are going to think we're being invaded. They're going to come and ask what the hell is going on. We need to keep it much smaller.'

The soldiers glanced at each other. 'But — it has to be something we can hear throughout the house and grounds, or none of this will work.'

'Can't you use these radio telegraphs you mention here?' She held up the report.

'Their range is very short, ma'am, it won't carry the whole length of the house. We have to talk in chains, if you see what I mean. One person every fifty feet or so.'

'All right. We can use the servants' bells. We'll have to put up more, but that'll be a lot better than ringing the temple bells.'

Everyone nodded.

'I'll order them in,' she said. She scanned down the document, then looked at Kuroda. 'Have you got any theories as to why he'd walk into all this, if it's so foolproof?'

'Honestly I think he's just doing it to make us work hard,' Kuroda said. He was still feeling bubbly about the whole thing. 'He's always done things like this in the past.'

She frowned. 'What, so he's arranged for the Russian fleet to come here just to make you a better Prime Minister? I doubt it. If he were to ride into a joust, it wouldn't just be to teach some other knight an especially vivid lesson. It would be because breaking that particular lance on that particular man would catch the eye of someone you've not noticed in the crowd, who might then have an idea and become the next Newton or the next Lady Murasaki. I wouldn't mind knowing who that is.'

Tanaka looked amused.

'Why, have you changed your mind about helping us?' Kuroda said with a small edge, wishing she would see her way to not making him look like such a prick in front of everyone.

'No. Even if he means to gain something by walking into a trap, a trap is exactly where he should be. All right, lads, get on with your business then,' she added to the soldiers, who nodded and hurried away as if she'd always been with the unit. 'Don't be embarrassed about getting lost, everyone does. Just yell and the servants will sort you out.'

There was a chorus of yes-misses.

'Oi,' she said, quite gently. 'Are you going to take those biscuits with you or what?'

Kuroda smiled. Abrupt or not, he liked anyone who was kind to soldiers.

'You don't fancy getting a divorce and marrying me?' Kuroda said once they were gone.

She studied him. 'No. We're only here because of what happened to the last Countess Kuroda.'

It needled him more than it should have. 'Bloody hell, woman, do you have to bring it up every time—'

'Calm,' she said over him, full of patience, 'the fuck down, and have your bloody tea like a normal person.'

He settled. It was always nice to have a little tiff to make sure everyone knew where they should stand. He poured himself some tea, or started to, but then paused. Behind her, all along the huge glass windows, owls had lined up. There were twenty at least, different species and sizes, and they were all looking out to sea, as though they expected some-body.

PART TWO

EIGHT

Yokohama, 18th December 1888

Thaniel jerked out of a nightmare with the absolute certainty that there was someone in the corner of the cabin, watching him. It didn't go away even once he had been looking around for a while. Unsettled, he went out to the balcony for some air. They were sailing close to the land, much closer than he'd thought. It was misty, but above the mist, unreal because it was so vast, was Mount Fuji. There was a click above him. Some ladies on the next deck up were taking photographs – or rather, *the* photograph, the one everyone wanted for a postcard.

Fuji wasn't like other mountains. The slopes were shallow, the tip truncated. It looked like it should have been small, but it was a titan. From less than a third of the way up, it was white. There were other mountains ghosting around it, but in comparison they were miniature. Right around the skirts of the whole range sprawled Aokigahara Forest, bluish in the mist bands.

Near the shore was a great murmuration of birds. Thaniel couldn't tell what they were, but something had upset them. The swing of their flight wasn't the peaceful twisting of a playing flock; they were shooting away from something, and the shapes they made were strobing.

Thunder growled from inland. The sky was pewter, and there was a migraine pressure in the air. Up on the mountainside, something flashed blue. He yanked his sleeve over his hand when the rail gave him a shock. Whatever was wrong with his lungs, he'd started to feel the cold badly and he'd slept in a jumper since leaving London. The wool stuck against itself now, staticky.

Above the land, the birds were crying, and there was a salt-coloured haze over everything. But the sky was clear. The mist, most of it, was the noise of the birds. The world looked clearer when he covered his ears.

He wondered about tapping on the connecting door to see if Mori was awake yet. He folded his arms to stop himself. Mori had been cheerful all through the journey, and kept the door between the two cabins open always. A few days ago, when they reached the southernmost tip of Korea, he had brought Six through so they could watch from the balcony as they passed the Russian fleet. Thaniel had never seen real warships before. He'd thought the liner was big, but the Russian ironclads were juggernauts. Friendly juggernauts, though; the men in the rigging waved and the liner passengers waved back, and Six pealed into delighted laughter when the flagship let off its guns in a huge, fantastic salute.

The music in the first-class lounge that night had been Tchaikovsky. Mori taught him to waltz. Thaniel couldn't always remember where or when to turn, but it didn't matter; the bones in Mori's hands were close to the surface, and they flickered before a change in direction, as clear as weathervanes.

Then Nagasaki had materialised on the horizon. It was a strange place, full of ramshackle shipyards and markets that everyone had poured off the liner to explore for a few hours while the crew refuelled. Everyone except Mori, who wouldn't even go near the gangway. There was something wrong with Nagasaki, he said; it gave him nightmares.

That had been early yesterday, and Mori hadn't got back his cheer. The connecting door was shut now. It seemed the decent thing to give him some time to himself, to get used to home and everything it meant, instead of following him around like an asthmatic puppy.

There was a green clack as the connecting door unlocked. Mori came through.

'Speak of the devil,' Thaniel said, surprised.

'I know, I'm sorry.' He must have got up in a hurry. His cuffs were undone and his shirt was open to his collarbones, and it wasn't clear what he was apologising for. 'Could you come inside a minute?' he said. 'Away from the balcony.'

Thaniel did as he was told. Mori shut the balcony door and stepped back from it, just before the murmuration reached them and birds smacked into the windows, dozens of them. Thaniel jumped. Yells came from the cabin above, and more from the one on the right. The bang of each small body burst black stars across Thaniel's vision, followed by the tin scritch of cracking glass. The birds were blue and grey, the size of tennis balls. One smashed through a weakened patch of glass and Mori caught it, very softly, between both hands.

It stopped as quickly as it had started. All that was left were floating feathers. Dead birds covered the balcony floor. The living one in Mori's hands cheeped feebly. When he let it go, it wheeled away, still panicking.

'She's on the bridge, she's all right,' Mori said, just as Thaniel took a breath to ask about Six.

Some of the birds on the balcony weren't quite dead yet but jerking brokenly. He opened the door and knelt down to snap the neck of one that was getting frightened and frantic. White-breasted with dark speckles, it was a lovely little thing, something like a finch. He set it down gently. 'Why did they do that?'

'Something on the mountain.' Mori watched Fuji go by.

A few of the other birds twitched, but none of them was alive enough to save.

Six had made friends with Second Lieutenant Hopkins, who was mechanically minded and happy to show her things. At first, Thaniel hadn't been too pleased with the idea of letting her go off with strange men; not because he thought Mori would let anything bad happen, but because it seemed dangerous to teach her to trust everyone. Mori, though, had pointed out that it was just as dangerous to teach a little girl that one foot wrong would mean a lunatic and a dungeon. It made it sound inevitable, whereas if you were brought up safe in the knowledge that people were supposed to be good, you approached the bad ones with a healthy fury that might just see you out of the dungeon.

None of the windows had broken on the bridge, but some of the officers were peering down through the cracked glass.

'Mr Hopkins says it's electrical,' Six reported when she saw Thaniel and Mori. She was studying the wing of a dead bird, which Hopkins had spread out to show her. 'The compasses have gone strange. Look.' She pointed to the navigation panel just beside her.

The needles skittered and stuck in odd places.

'Hopkins,' the captain said distractedly. 'Put that child back where you found it.' He was leaning close to a telegraph, listening.

Thaniel took her hand and nodded to Hopkins. He started to turn away, meaning to take her downstairs again to find some food, but Mori stayed where he was. He was watching the captain.

'You're about to get a shock from the key,' he said.

'Since when did we allow passengers on the bridge?' the captain said. He had one hand over his ear in an effort to listen to the telegraph. 'If you wouldn't mind terribly ...' He faded off. 'Hopkins. The tower on shore is broadcasting. They're saying to stay five miles off the coast until Yokohama. Turn us away. Engine order full steam— Jesus Christ!'

The telegraph hadn't only shocked him; the wiring had caught fire. Mori had been waiting by him with a bucket of sand, so it didn't get far. The captain gave him an unnerved look.

'How did you know?'

'If it's electrical, then it will affect the telegraphs. I wouldn't use that,' Mori added to Hopkins.

Hopkins stopped with his hand almost on the Chadburn telegraph, on the point of cranking its bronze lever around to 'full steam ahead'. As Hopkins stepped away from it, it juddered by itself and the needle skittered. A man covered in coal dust pushed through the door.

'The engine-room bells are going off all over the place, sir – what's the order?'

'Full ahead, please,' the captain said. 'Something funny going on ashore.' He glanced at Mori.

Mori shook his head. He looked more troubled than any of them.

'Ah,' said Hopkins. He had been studying Thaniel, who he'd not acutally met, looking increasingly anxious. 'Miss Steepleton? Is – one of – these two unlikely gentlemen your father?'

Six looked up at him, solemn. 'No. They stole me from a workhouse and now I live in the attic.'

Hopkins opened his mouth, shocked. Thaniel folded his arms and inclined his head down, not sure what to do. Saying that it was a lovely attic wouldn't help.

'Chocolate?' Mori said to her.

'Yes!' she squeaked, full of joy. He didn't usually let her have anything sweet. There was a reason, he said, that white people were all fat and short-lived. 'And then please may I go down to the engine room and look at the engines, say yes onegai shimaaaas—'

'Yes,' Mori said, and Hopkins looked puzzled but let them go.

———

Not long later, the ship steered back towards the land. Instead of unbroken coast or the odd scattering of wooden houses they'd passed before, there were warehouses and piers. Thaniel went outside. His lungs wheezed and he had to stand still at the rail while he saw stars. Signs for tea cargoes appeared through the haze, painted in white on wooden boards at the ends of the nearer wharves where the clippers from China anchored, and men in work clothes and bandanas loaded crates onto carts pulled by oxen with ribbons tied to their horns. Above the narrow road that looped round the harbour, a dyer had hung kimono sashes. They were thirty feet long and they writhed in the wind.

There were two other liners already at the big main wharf, which was full of gentlemen in Western suits and women in plain day kimono, although some of them, looking much more well-to-do, had bright silk belts and flowers in their hair. Either for colour or an occasion, strings of blue and red bunting fluttered between the wharf lamps. Along from the wharf, the houses were neat and wooden, close-set, jumbled with advertising signs running lengthwise from the roofs, and dotted with little warm lights where people had set up cooking stalls. At short intervals there were telegraph poles, just like in London, but they were a different shape; they had fewer arms, so they looked more like tall keys than trees. It stuck in his mind later because it was the first really unfamiliar thing he saw.

Mori had come out too, much more slowly, to give him time to catch his breath without waiting ahead of him.

'We're going up there,' Mori said, pointing to their right.

Thaniel couldn't see anything there but a lighthouse. It was a red wooden tower with a lamp and an anemometer, to measure the wind. Neither moved. The lighthouse itself leaned forward, as if there was something interesting in the sea.

A steward called that they were all very welcome to Yokohama, and that they would be free to disembark in a few minutes. Trains into central Tokyo ran from the station, which was a short walk or rickshaw ride away, and would arrive at Shimbashi terminus shortly before three. Passengers staying in Yokohama would find rickshaws on the dockside. Mori was still watching the lighthouse where, as if the keeper had noticed that he was being observed, the lamp came on.

NINE

Mori said that it wasn't far to Yoruji. Luggage had disappeared into the meticulous accounting of the ship's staff; it would appear at some point, though all the stewards seemed to think it was vulgar to ask.

The rickshaws at the harbour were one of the strangest inventions Thaniel had ever seen. They were like one-horse hansom cabs, except instead of a horse between the bars, there was a man. Dozens of them waited at the harbour, just after the line of customs officers, and when people climbed up into the little chariot-type carriages, even with luggage, the rickshawmen took off at a jog. Sometimes the wheels were rubber-tyred and beautifully sprung, and sometimes they had no more suspension than a hay cart. He wondered if people had something against horses.

Six looked thoughtful when someone offered her a steamed bun. She sniffed.

'No. Vile,' she said.

Mori pushed the side of her head, very gently. She meowed at him.

Thaniel ought probably to have said something about manners, but he was too distracted by the mist. It was real mist, not the London soup. It was white, cold, and pristine. It even tasted clean. Slowly over the years, he'd begun to think of white mist as existing only in memory. He hadn't seen it since he'd left Lincolnshire. But here it was, hanging luminous in the air above the stony unpaved road and the frost that glittered in the verges. It looked like home, and he had a sudden and completely absurd surge of belonging. Six tugged his sleeve to ask what it was.

'What fog's meant to look like, petal.'

'Oh, dear,' she said.

Mori was careful about the way he smiled. He didn't laugh at them.

In the open paper window of a tall house, a woman in full geisha paint was talking into a telephone. She tipped the receiver absently away from her face and rubbed the chalk powder off it with her sleeve. Thaniel felt embarrassed about staring when Mori touched his arm, but it wasn't a rebuke; he was pointing out a girl walking away down an alley, towards the same house, in the full paraphernalia. Usually Thaniel didn't hold with taking photographs – it was better to remember the thing, not remember carting around an omnipresent camera – but he wished he had one just then.

The docks fell away quickly. Soon they were walking on a path above an open beach with black sand. The little streams by the path were gurgling not because they ran over so many rocks, but because they were boiling. Six bent down to see, Katsu on her shoulder. They really did smell like something rotten. The rocks in the streams were sometimes covered in pale, yellow brine: sulphur. Thaniel had known Japan was volcanic, but it was a bit startling to see the obvious evidence of it right there on a beach. He had a sudden sense of standing not on solid ground at all, but a sort of gangway over the heavings of the lower earth. As if it heard him, the ground shook softly.

'What was ...'

'Earthquake,' Mori explained.

Thaniel smiled. The novelty of it was completely disproportionate to the tiny little shudder, but it had made Six giggle too. She stole Mori's watch so that the chain made a fragile gold link between them.

Mori pointed out the house up ahead. It was just visible. It stood alone, a collection of curving roofs and gantries that spilled down the cliffside. At first Thaniel thought they must have been walking away from Tokyo, not towards it, but just after the next curve in the cliffs was the glitter of the city's dockyards and the huge machines that lifted in freight. He felt stupid for having expected everything to be cherry trees and temples. Even from here, he could see that there were ironclads in dry dock. Furnaces in the shipyards glimmered like fireflies. A wilderness of masts reached up for the sky there, and great bramble-clusters of waterwheels.

They came level with a fence. It wasn't high, and beyond it was a roll of land that led down to a park, full of black trees. There were men there, raking the leaves. It looked like an enormous job; the place had a wildness to it. He nearly said it was nice to live near a park when he realised it wasn't a park at all, but the grounds of the house.

The path tipped them down onto the beach. Even through shoes, despite the cold weather, the sand felt warm. Six looked down at it.

'Fancy a walk in the sea?' Thaniel said. 'I can take your shoes.'

'No,' she said. 'I find it all very suspicious.' She wound Mori's watch chain once more round her hand, which reeled him in nearer.

'It's just civilised,' Mori said. 'Free underfloor heating.'

'Will we explode?'

'No.'

'I suppose that's all right then.'

Thaniel was starting to feel light-headed. He put it down, firmly, to the sulphur, and ignored the voice at the back of his mind that had begun to sound like Dr Haverly, that said of course it wasn't the sulphur. He had to slow down. All he wanted to do was sleep, though it was only two o'clock in the afternoon. Mori slowed to a dawdle and paused to pick up a shell, then another, and wondered aloud whether it would be twee to make a miniature astrolabe to sit in a clam like a pearl. There was nothing more certain in the world than Mori's perfect disinterest in shells.

The shale of the shore swung upwards, and onto a gravel road. Gingkos were raining yellow leaves down across it with a continuous scratching sound. And then there was a high red gate, just two posts and an up-curving cross bar. Mori stopped just before it and looked up. He didn't look happy to be home. He looked like he had come to the very edge of a battlefield.

'If you catch a leaf, it's lucky,' Thaniel said, rather than ask what the matter was. The yellow leaves were eddying around them in a tiny sea wind.

Mori looked up. 'Why?'

'Just is.'

Mori held both hands out to either side. Two leaves settled in his palms one after the other. He gave Thaniel the nearest. 'One each,' he said quietly.

Thaniel took it. 'Kei ... what's going on?'

If he heard, Mori didn't show it. He was already looking up among the trees, quietly, as if he'd heard cannon shot coming and had no particular hope of getting out the way.

A woman whistled at them from a balcony half hidden in the trees.

'Joy Featherworth, as I live and breathe!'

She'd said it in English. It was Mori's name, translated; Thaniel had always known it without ever really thinking about it. It was jarring to hear in a stranger's voice. He felt obscurely like she'd stolen something from him.

Mori laughed. There was something hopeless about it. It was happiness and despair together. 'Pepper – are you coming down?'

The woman was in a plain white under-kimono, but her hair was swept up high and studded with jewelled pins that winked rainbows in the sun. She was having to hold some leaves aside to talk down to them on the path. An older lady batted at her, plainly wanting her not to, but she only batted her back with a tea-towel.

'I'm being held hostage by the tailor, but I thought I'd shout at you from a tree and then you'd feel loved and wanted.'

Mori was still smiling. 'I do.'

'Miss? I don't suppose there's any sort of electrical supply,' Six called up.

'There is actually. Are you Miss Steepleton?'

Thaniel wondered how she knew. She wasn't a servant. Servants didn't yell from balconies. They certainly didn't call noblemen by their first names.

'Yes. Six Steepleton. I don't like alliterating,' Six said, casting a narrow look at Thaniel as if his last name were his own personal fault, 'but not doing so would have caused terrible legal difficulties.'

The woman was nodding. 'Tell me about it. The whole Mori house went mad when Keita and I were married. They refused to let me take his name, so I'm still Pepperharrow.'

TEN

Shintomi Theatre, Tokyo, 1878
(ten years ago)

Until she was nearly thirty, Takiko Pepperharrow had been convinced that good things come to unobjectionable people. Saying yes and simpering all the time was silly – her mother did that and even noticeably anxious ducklings walked all over her mother – but she had always maintained that just marching in and annihilating everyone was a bad idea too, in the long run.

It was a kiln-hot afternoon in July, on the day her theatre master Ayame handed her the role of a lifetime, when Takiko decided it was time to give annihilating everyone a chance.

Princess Yaegaki was one of the greatest roles in all kabuki theatre. The play was incredible. There was a scene where the princess floated through the air among foxfire. Countess Kuroda had requested that the company perform the play on her birthday. And because she was terribly modern and fashionable, she wanted, said Ayame, to see a real woman in the role.

For about forty seconds, Takiko couldn't believe it. After ten years making costumes and working the oily mechanisms under the stage that moved the scenery and the curtains, limping along in tiny roles with fewer lines than an eviction notice, it was everything she'd been waiting for.

'We don't have the licence to perform the play of course,' Ayame added, glittering. Even if he was just talking about lunch, he sounded like he was confiding a secret, so when there was a real secret, it was impossible not to feel pulled in. 'But it'll be a private performance. Just the Countess, the Count, and their friends. No need to spend all that money on a licence when it's just an informal thing that isn't even for the general public.'

Takiko took a breath, because that was definitely wrong. The Guild would torch alive anyone who so much as breathed a copyrighted word without the proper licence.

But then she understood what was going on. Ayame had given her the role so he could report her. The others must have finally demanded he stop training her. That would be it. Career over. She might even end up in prison.

Balls to that.

When the day came, Takiko thought she would be nervous, but it was too hot to feel anything except thirsty. The dressing rooms trapped the heat inside their paper walls, and if anyone left the back door open for some air, the hot wind powered in like someone had put a blast furnace there.

Out in the auditorium, completely audible from the dressing rooms, Count Kuroda was growling that he would have preferred to go to the sumo. A bit deliriously, Takiko thought she would have quite liked to be at the sumo instead too. It was like theatre, with all the rigid ceremonies and the stiff judges sitting at the edge of the ring, but unlike the theatre, there was a certain necessary lightheartedness. She'd always thought the theatre would take itself less seriously if there were a healthy chance that the senior management might be skittled by an enormous man being flung across the room by the back of his belt.

While she stitched the new gold threads into Ayame's best wig, she took care to look diligent, and not like she was plotting.

'Get out of the way,' someone snapped. She only glanced at him and didn't catch who it was, only the white sweep of the paint down his neck and the cloth band that hid his hair, ready for a wig. Made up, all the actors were interchangeable swans. It was so hot in the warren of dressing rooms that everyone was walking about without shirts, the white paint drawn to inverted triangles right down their spines. They moved slowly to keep from sweating through it. 'And shouldn't you be ready by now?'

'I'm leaving it til the last minute or I'll keel over,' she said. 'It's so hot.' The costume was sparkling on its mannequin, all fire colours in layers and layers, some fox-trimmed, some purple, some bronze. She was already wearing the harness that had to go underneath it for the flying scene.

He narrowed his eyes at her. 'If you were ever going to be a real actor, you wouldn't let a bit of heat bother you. Women don't have the constitution for the stage.'

'We'll see,' she said.

'Put that away,' he said, and lobbed a pot of paint at her.

The lid wasn't quite on properly, and some of the white spilled across her fingers. She rubbed it off on a cast-off scrap from one of the samurai costumes. The others had clusters of paint pots and jewellery in their places; hers, right on the end near the back door and the boiling draught that blew under it, was mainly taken up with a Singer sewing machine. She had come to like the Singer a lot. She was worried she liked it in the way that long-term prisoners felt safe behind the bars.

A small owl came in through the window and settled with a great deal of purpose on her sewing machine. Takiko tried to shoo it. It sat down. Its beak was sharp. She decided it could have the Singer if it really wanted to and stood back, puzzled. Something must have woken it up early.

'Is that an owl? How lucky!'

Ayame had just floated in with a blast of hot air that smelled of dust and stagnant drains. He was dressed like a waitress, apron and everything, his beautiful hair piled up out of the way. There was a pencil stuck in it. He did hours at the teashop next door to practise being a woman.

'Lucky?' Takiko said.

'Didn't your mother tell you? Owls are called "fukurou" because they bring "fuku".' Luck. He'd said it in English, like he would have to a tourist. 'They know things, owls. They have a way of turning up when something extraordinary is about to happen.'

'My uncle says that if you're followed by an owl it's because a shinigami has marked you out to die,' someone said in passing. 'It's not about luck, it's about fate.'

'Or that,' Ayame said cheerfully.

Takiko sighed and didn't ask how owls were supposed to know the business of passing death gods. 'Did you send the owl in here?'

'Beg pardon?' said Ayame.

She couldn't tell if he was acting. He was brilliant at looking innocent.

'How are you feeling?' Ayame added. 'You mustn't be nervous, I'm certain you'll be splendid.'

She bowed and then watched him, and wondered if she'd got it all wrong, and she was about to crucify someone who was trying to do her a favour.

'You look terrified,' he laughed, and squeezed her knuckles. His hands were cool. 'The gentlemen might be very illustrious, but nonetheless they are here to see the play. You've got your role, same as any other night. Do it well, and you'll have your new name at the next ceremony. Yoshizawa Ayame IX; we'll stitch it on your costumes together, hey?'

It was what she'd wanted ever since she'd joined the company.

It was the great evil of plays that every character had some kind of purpose. Absorb too much of them, and you could go about believing there was something wrong with you if you drifted unremarked towards your thirties, and coasted into a quiet beach of no interest to anyone. Whenever those thoughts arrived, she always heard her mother's voice pointing out, not unreasonably, that she should be grateful. There was plenty to be grateful for, and it was childish to say it was hard to have seen Christopher Pepperharrow's world, where everyone spoke three languages and travelled four times round the world in four years, and learned, and learned, and did things. A lot of people saw that and didn't pine. None of her sisters did. Fumiko had married a lawyer.

'Now paint over that ugly little badger face of yours,' Ayame said. He patted her head.

'Yes, sir,' she said. She pulled her sleeve over her forehead. She was so hot she felt like she was melting. Sweat was creeping down her back.

'Come along, owl,' Ayame said, and picked it up without any hesitation, as if it didn't have a beak or talons. He put it just outside the door, where it walked off.

As soon as he'd gone to see the other actors, she took off the harness, picked up her bag, and slipped down the back stairs, fast. All she had to do was disappear. Going out the front door, by the ticket office, would be much easier than going out the back where everyone could see her.

She was only halfway down the stairs when someone caught the back of her collar.

'Where in the world are you going?' Ayame said in his bright way. However good he was at being a girl, he was very, very strong, and now she was nastily aware that he was a head taller than her. 'Back in here.'

'I just felt a bit faint. I thought I'd get some water from the bar—'

'I'll fetch it for you.' He hadn't let go of her collar. 'You've no time. Get dressed.'

She pulled, and heard the stitching in her dress creak. 'Just to get a bit of air that isn't full of actors—'

He smacked her ear, hard. 'You're being hysterical. Don't be nervous. In you go.' He all but threw her up a couple of stairs.

She spun around and realised firstly that she was going to have to charge past him, and secondly that it wasn't going to work. She might get to the bottom of the stairs, but then he'd be after her, and he was fit. Even if she got to the foyer, nobody would think anything of seeing an actor box a set girl's ears.

She banged him aside with her shoulder. He caught her by her hair just as she reached the bar. The smell of hot wood and paper from the corridor vanished, replaced right on the threshold by caramel nuts, wood polish, and brandy vapour. It was so close to the main doors that she tried to wrench away, but it hurt too much.

'No, no, no,' Ayame said, still jolly. 'Back you come.'

'No—'

'Hello,' said a cultured voice. 'What's this?'

A gentleman was watching them. He was dressed in Western clothes, gorgeous ones, his hands sunk easily into his pockets and his shoulder against the wall. Even with Ayame's fist clamped through her hair, Takiko thought he looked familiar: she'd seen him in the newspapers. He was one of those famous wealthy bachelors the society pages loved to gossip about. Southern-bronze, good looking, still young but not very.

'Just a lazy girl, sir; don't worry,' Ayame smiled. Takiko tried to twist, but he clamped his hand tighter through her hair. She banged her elbow into his ribs and heard herself make a stupid helpless squeaking noise when he twisted her arm up too high behind her back.

Nobody except the gentleman was paying any attention. The bar was full of more men in lovely clothes, and there were two geisha with them – real, expensive, older geisha. A few people glanced over, but no one showed any more interest than that. Ayame pulled her back towards the stairs.

'Wait. Miss – it *is* you,' the gentleman said suddenly, as if they knew each other and he was delighted to see her again. 'I haven't seen you for years! You wouldn't mind letting me borrow her?' he said to Ayame. 'I'm sure you can find someone else to do whatever she does.'

Takiko thought Ayame would say no, but the gentleman was watching him hard and suddenly the air was heavier than before. Ayame knew that if he annoyed the scion of a noble house it would stop people like Kuroda coming here. Any chance of royal patronage would be snuffed out. That was very definite. But he didn't know for sure that Takiko meant to report anyone.

Ayame let go of her hair. The gentleman inclined his head to ask Ayame why he was still here. Ayame vanished back into the corridor.

Takiko couldn't believe it at first. Then her mother's voice pointed out that things which were too good to be true generally weren't. She turned slowly back to the gentleman and wondered what he expected, in return for rescue.

'Sorry,' said the gentleman. 'I've seen you in the paper; you're the actress, aren't you?'

Takiko rubbed the back of her head. Her scalp hurt. 'How do you know that? I've barely been on stage.'

'They all seem to think it's very edgy and exciting to have a woman on the stage at all.'

'Oh, right. Yes. I've seen you in the paper as well, but I don't think I … yeah. Listen, I didn't mean to have to be rescued like a little twerp; you don't have to calm me down or make friends. I'll let you get on.' She started to edge away.

'I can see that, but I only did it so you could rescue me. Kuroda's going to spend this whole thing yelling in my ear unless I find someone else to sit with.' He looked awkward. 'Would you mind?'

'I'm not a prostitute,' she half snapped.

'I know,' he said. He bowed, just as low as he would have to a lady of his own rank. It made her hesitate. It wasn't how men behaved when they expected things. 'I'm Keita Mori.'

'Takiko,' she said, and paused, because she knew he was only going to say pardon when she said Pepperharrow, and she didn't want to explain to yet another person that actually she was a bit foreign but yes she did talk properly thanks, and yes, that was probably why she was ugly. 'Pepperharrow.'

'Good to meet you, Miss Pepperharrow,' he said, and didn't even stumble over the pronunciation. He had a British accent in English. 'Would you...?'

She meant to say no, and get out, but he looked nearly as helpless as she must have a minute ago. 'All right.'

Takiko tried to stay sceptical, because there must be another shoe about to drop.

She always remembered how he'd seemed on that first afternoon, sitting in the auditorium in a sunbeam. It was a strange quality, but Mori distinctly didn't belong in a place with steam engines. If you had taken away his modern clothes and put him in courtly black, he could have come straight from the council at the old palace in Kyoto – the sort of man you might have found, once, on one of the fabulous gilded bridges with their vaulted roofs, and who the ladies watched in the mirror water while they pretended to look at a convenient heron.

'I've never seen you here before,' she said. He was even giving her a good amount of space, sitting fully an arm's length away. 'Are you a fan of kabuki?'

'I hate kabuki,' he confessed. He looked guilty about admitting it, but not confident enough in his own ability to lie to say anything else. 'The dances always look a lot like a cat trying to wrestle a sock puppet; I've never really understood.

But this is what Countess Kuroda wanted to do, so, here we are.' He paused. Two rows down from them, Count Kuroda was still talking hopefully about the sumo. 'What was all that, by the way? With that man before.'

'He's the theatre master,' she explained. 'We don't have a licence to perform this play, and he doesn't like me, so he gave me the title role. I think he wants to report me to the censor's office and have me disbarred from the Guild. That would mean a lifetime acting ban. So I thought I'd duck out, then go to the censor's office myself and get *him* disbarred.'

Mori laughed. 'Brilliant.'

'And then I thought I'd threaten to disbar all of them unless they make me a gift of a controlling share in the company.' She pressed on the sore place on the back of her head again. 'I've lost patience with sewing.'

He thought about it. 'How are you going to stop them all beating you up behind the bins?'

'If they do that, I'll shut the theatre.'

He smiled again. There wasn't even a flicker of disapproval in him. He glanced towards the stage a few seconds before the announcer arrived.

'I'm afraid, ladies and gentlemen, that there's been a last-minute change of casting—'

'Get the fuck on with it!' Kuroda called. He had a klaxon voice. Beside him, his beautiful wife winced. Takiko recognised them both from the papers. They were ten times more vivid in real life. The Countess was wearing a green dress that was probably worth about what Takiko earned in fifteen years.

'—but the performance will begin in a very few minutes!' the announcer said hysterically.

'Believe it when I see it, mate!' Kuroda shouted.

Mori had bought some candied nuts for them to share. Takiko threw a walnut at Kuroda's head. 'Hey. You. Be quiet. They're doing their best.'

Kuroda swung round and started to say something, but then he saw Mori, who was laughing, and started laughing too. 'Yes, ma'am.'

She had a stupid suffusion of belonging and tried to squash it down. If you let yourself believe you belonged with people like this, you drowned, because they were sirens and they breathed another element. Mori must have noticed she'd stopped smiling too quickly, because he was watching her. She had to look away. There was too much song in his eyes.

That evening, after she had watched the suited men from the censor's office serve up an official Guild revocation of Ayame's name, Mori bought her a bottle of champagne. Kuroda came along too, and the Countess, and all their brightly coloured friends. Kuroda shook up the bottle so that the bubbles poured everywhere. Mori touched their glasses together with a quiet low cheers. Kuroda whooped. He had, far from disapproving when Mori explained what she'd done, thought it was funny.

'To Kali the Destroyer!'

She laughed, embarrassed and happy at the same time, and lonely despite it all. That was the trouble with the floating world that artists and geisha and actors made. You sat on a raft on clear water, snatching glimpses of a life that wasn't yours. There was a sort of grace you had to learn, one that let you see it all and dive down for a few minutes, but then come back up and watch the tide go out without feeling resentful. She wasn't very good at it.

In fact Mori came back every Saturday, with all his friends. Then more wealthy people followed, and then, one day, the princesses. Partly because she loved it and partly because she was scared of getting above herself now she had money, Takiko still lived in the little room in the playhouse attic, but it wasn't a place where you could make tea for a princess. With an unhappy, dragging reluctance, she started to look for houses. She could buy one outright. She ought to have been ecstatic – she could hear her mother's voice saying so – but she didn't want to go. The attic was never quiet, voices always filtered up, and sometimes someone hurried in to ask about costumes or switching roles, and it meant there was never the awful, dead silence that would hang over a detached house with a fine garden somewhere proper. She was lonely enough as it was, among all the reassuring theatre sounds. She'd go mad without them. She said as much one evening to Mori, who didn't care where he drank his tea as long as it was warm. He was sitting in front of her tiny stove, his back propped against a broken mannequin.

'I've been trying to get someone to buy the east wing at Yoruji. I don't need all the space and it bloody echoes.'

'You can't break up that lovely house.'

'I can, I'm spiting the Duke. He wants me to marry some Shirakawa idiot *for the family*.' He cut his eyes away, annoyed. She'd never worked out how his family worked, but as far as she could tell, samurai houses were more like big companies than normal families. They had employees and board members and directors. The Duke of Choshu was the director of House Mori. She had no idea what Keita was. Something high up, but still answerable to the Duke, sometimes in vague, obscure ways to do with property deeds and taxation, sometimes in sharp, specific ones. Like marriage. 'If he doesn't back off I'll chop it into holiday apartments for American tourists.'

He didn't ask if she would take it. Instead he poured them both some more tea and wondered aloud if it was giving in to actual robbery to pay the half yen at the bar downstairs for two biscuits.

'I'll take it,' she said. She swallowed, then ordered herself not to be such a bloody coward. 'Do you want to get married as well? I can't repay you for everything you've done, but I can save you from the Shirakawa idiot.'

He lifted his eyes slowly. They were southern black mirrors. 'That's a lot, Pepper. You ... the Duke would never give you full status in the family, he'd treat you like my mistress. It wouldn't be an upward step for you, more of a side shuffle.'

'I don't want advancement, I want to help you. I wouldn't have the theatre if you hadn't come when you did; I wouldn't have anything. I owe you this. I'd be honoured to fight off the Duke for you, if you'll let me.' She smiled, because he looked a fraction better persuaded at that, like she'd thought he might. He was among the youngest of that last generation of real samurai. Someone being kind to him was puzzling; someone who wanted to have a good fight was normal.

He looked down, then smiled too. 'Thank you.'

ELEVEN

Yokohama, 18th December 1888

Beyond the red gate, the way to Yoruji zigzagged up
through gardens and gingko groves. All the way up,
the house appeared in odd disjointed sections. It had a small
tower, like a real temple, and when Thaniel said so, Mori
nodded; the place was a deconsecrated monastery. They
passed tiny pockets of perfect gardens, all arranged around
pools that shone red and yellow with the reflections of the
trees, which bent over them curiously. Thaniel just made out
a stone bridge. All the pools steamed.

And then suddenly, there was a riot of jasmine. It was
brilliant white after the autumn yellow of the gingkos, and
there was so much of it that it looked unnatural, sprawling
over the trees and eating other shrubs, and clawing right up
the front of the house. The scent of it was a bit shocking, a
wall of sweetness. Thaniel wanted to get away from it. The
bone-white flowers, blooming and falling everywhere,
looked waxy and false, like someone had drained them of all
their real colour and pumped them full of formaldehyde to
make them last.

A full staff had come out to greet them.

There were twenty at least, maids and stewards, and
several serious men with plain suits and swords. Thaniel

couldn't take any of it in properly. He felt like he was trying to swallow a piece of glass.

Married. Mori was married. But of course he bloody was. He was forty-four and he was from a major samurai house; it would have been a miracle if he'd managed not to be. And it was hardly a surprise that Mori hadn't mentioned her. She was official, legal business. Mori had about as much reason to mention a wife as he did to mention property tax or the acreage of the estate. It had nothing whatever to do with Thaniel, and it was none of his business. He still felt like she'd taken a hammer to his ribs.

He was damned if he was going to say a word about it. He came across as a whiny little prick enough of the time as it was.

An expressionless steward in a plain black kimono said a very formal good afternoon and asked them to follow him into the house, up irregular flights of steps and around steep corners. Thaniel walked feeling more and more disjointed.

Yoruji was an unsettling place.

Parts of it were very old, the wood dark with decades of varnish, and parts had plainly just been rebuilt, still bright and smelling of cedar. No corner quite led in the direction it should have, and, because the winter sky was so dim, the lamps were lit. The corridors took you suddenly outside onto gravel paths, even onto stepping stones over pools with water so deep and pristine they shone an eerie turquoise, then plunged back into the gloom again. Occasionally there was an odd mismatched section of wall where there had used to be different doorways, wainscoted around now, but the lintels were still there. The house was hardly more than a shell; the walls were almost all paper and wood, not integral to the structure, and easy to take down and switch about.

And even though the corridors were empty, he had a strong, weird feeling that they were being watched. He could feel eyes on him at every single turn, and all the time they were walking, he could have sworn that unseen people were always vanishing just around the next corner, a split second out of view. He shifted his shoulders. Stupid. It was just an unfamiliar place with an unfamiliar logic. Mori had told him, on the journey, that Japanese buildings would feel strange at first.

Everything smelled of jasmine.

The steward took them to a wing that overlooked the sea and the lighthouse on its crooked rock. There were two neat rooms there side by side, with broad sliding doors that led outside. Thaniel couldn't see much beyond them but sky, but Six shot out.

The steward managed, despite being completely proper, to emanate disapproval at the idea of having foreigners in the house. If they would kindly not cross about in the corridor too much after ten at night, he said, the ladies upstairs would be grateful to be spared the noise of the floor.

'It is creaky, isn't it,' Thaniel said, to say something that wasn't to do with Mrs Pepperharrow, or with that scritch over the back of his scalp that insisted there were people peering at them from inside the walls.

The steward gave him an antarctic look. 'Of course. It is a nightingale floor.'

'Were you afraid he might get about the house unattended?' Mori said, a laugh just under his voice.

The steward bowed minutely. 'I shall return shortly with the Baron's clothes.'

'I can just wear a jacket. Suzuki—'

'I'm certain the foreign gentleman would enjoy taking a photograph of the Baron in proper attire with the Baroness's clever new apparatus.'

The Baroness. Thaniel tried to smile. 'The foreign gentleman would enjoy that a great deal.'

'Excellent,' said Suzuki. He glided away over the squeaking boards, making no effort whatever to seem gracious in victory. He looked surprisingly young when he passed into a sunbeam, but even so, he left behind an impression of dust.

'He's something,' Thaniel said. English sounded savage after a break.

Mori looked at him hard. 'You are a traitor, and if you take a photograph of me, I will make you eat it.'

'Kimono are nice,' Thaniel protested. He wanted to say, does everyone call her the Baroness.

'Morris dancers' costumes are *nice*,' Mori said. He turned away to the other room. The dividing wall was only paper and there must have been a bright window on the far side, because Thaniel saw his shadow through the panes. It was hard to tell if it was actually Mori's own room, or if Suzuki had expressed his disapproval of extraneous foreigners by abandoning him in a guest room. 'This is why the Americans steam-roll us in treaty agreements; we all look like little dressed-up dolls. Imagine turning up to major international negotiations in ribbons and bells.'

'Fair. No photos. Photography does steal your soul, doesn't it?'

'Without seasoning. Raw silver nitrate and paper.'

Thaniel made himself laugh. He went to the balcony doors.

They led out into a garden. It was small but dense with contorted trees and tiny gravel lanes, and beginning almost right outside the door were cloudy pools that steamed. They were warm even from the doorway. A fox was sitting on the edge of the nearest, studying the glass windows above theirs and evidently waiting for more birds to knock themselves out on the panes. There was already a collection of downy bodies around its paws, and feathers on the window ledges. He heard children's voices at the far end; Six had found a little boy over that way, a gardener, unless he carried round a spade of his own accord. He looked serious and puzzled, broke into a chesty baby giggle, and then they ran off down one of the steep paths. It was a relief. Thaniel had been worried that all the new things would be too much for her and he'd have to spend the afternoon coaxing her out from under a table.

Mori came back with a kettle. When he turned to set it down on the low table, Katsu was coiled around his arm. Mori put him on the floor, where he hurried off towards the nearest pool. There was a splash as he dived in. A few seconds later he climbed out on the other side and left tentacle-and-wheel tracks on the slate before disappearing into the grass. The fox rushed away.

Everything was incredibly, unrealistically clean. The reed mats were perfect, the paper walls looked brand new, and there was no clutter. Nothing, not even curtains. Just the table, the tea things, and a tall cupboard where Suzuki had explained all the bedding was kept in the daytime. The floor was warm. There must have been hot pipes just underneath. It was wonderful. Thaniel felt like something fleabitten Mori had brought in off the sea shore.

'They're for people too,' Mori said. 'The onsen. Springs,' he translated, when Thaniel hesitated.

'I imagine there's something complicated you have to do first.'

'Suzuki's coming to show you now. I'd go in with you but I just want this tea before I have to get dressed.' He said it as if he were talking about starting on another long journey.

Suzuki glided back in with towels and a host of other things, soap and razors and combs. There was a whole ritual to it, one Thaniel didn't like at first, but the process forced his whole mind to slow down. It was too complicated to stray onto thoughts about Mrs Pepperharrow in the background, but straightforward enough not to be difficult.

'I'm sure we can make you presentable yet,' Suzuki said. He didn't look like he thought so.

At the low table, Mori had fallen still. He looked less like he was holding himself upright than resting exactly on the balance of his spine.

'Now then,' said Suzuki, 'the pool nearest to us is the coolest, but I recommend the farthest. There is an excellent view over the bay and it would perhaps be best to make use of it before the other gentlemen arrive for the hunt.'

'A hunt?'

'Oh yes,' he said. 'Do you ride?'

'No,' said Thaniel. He'd never liked horses except to talk to. They were more than clever enough to work out who they didn't like and find a strategic fence to sling him over.

Suzuki lifted his eyebrows. If Thaniel had said he didn't know about crockery and usually ate off the floor, he would have pulled the same expression. 'It is edifying to watch. Of course you'll attend.'

'I'll see,' said Thaniel, starting to enjoy meeting such a caricature of a person.

Mori was pouring himself another cup of tea, slowly, all his concentration on the iron kettle. Once he had set it down again, he sat holding the cup, very still and breathing the steam. A bloom of women's laughter came from somewhere above them. Thaniel wondered where Mrs Pepperharrow's balcony was.

Suzuki shepherded Thaniel outside. The five pools were scattered about among the rocks and under the trellises, which were set just far enough back for most of the falling leaves to miss the water. The last pool was right on the cliff edge. Steps carved into the rock led down into the water, and then to stone benches all the way around so that you could sit looking out over the bay.

The feeling that he was being watched got ten times stronger. It was ridiculous. The steam was so dense that nobody could possibly have seen much of him even from four feet away.

'I'll take that for you,' Suzuki said, and held out his hands for the towel.

'I'll keep it.'

Suzuki frowned. 'You'll do no such thing, it would be vulgar.'

'I'll be vulgar then, thank you.'

Suzuki watched him. 'Very well. But there are people of quality here. The Prime Minister is here.' He pointed away beyond the pools, to the next level along, where a man dressed in a plain dark suit was pacing on the verandah out-side another room, with the distinct bump of a gun under his jacket. A bodyguard.

'Kuroda, really,' Thaniel said, only half listening. He'd known that already. Mori had warned him there would be a welcome party. He was still scanning the steam, certain he was going to see someone.

He sighed. He'd known it would be odd, coming so far from home to somewhere so different, but he really had had higher hopes for his own nerves than total failure in the first fifteen minutes after arriving.

'Yes, really.' Suzuki pointed to a corner of the pool which had a clear view over the sea and the roofs of the monastery next door. 'That is the Baroness's favourite place. She has excellent taste.'

Thaniel waited until he'd gone before he stepped down into the pool, not where Suzuki had suggested. He sat down slowly on the stone bench underwater. The heat burned at first but then worked into his spine. It was good – much better than an ordinary bath.

The steam from the water carried an edge of sulphur with it, but it wasn't unpleasant. It only smelled of heat. Whether it was that or some rocky mineral in the water, it tasted much cleaner and fresher than normal steam. When he lifted his arms out and onto the side of the pool, his skin felt polished. Now that he was by himself, he let his neck bend while he waited to stop feeling like the whole place had punched him.

In the background somewhere was a faint, odd, crackly beeping. He frowned, because it had the rhythm of Morse, but he'd never known a house to have its own telegraph, and anyway, there were no telegraph lines. The tiny sound made little starry lights. It stopped, and after a moment he wasn't sure he'd heard it at all. He wondered if he was hallucinating telegraphy. He hoped not. If you were going to hallucinate something, Morse was very dull.

Voices came from the open doors behind him: Mori and Suzuki, arguing about clothes. Suzuki won. Through the space under the curving trees and the verandah roof,

Thaniel watched Suzuki unwrap the packets he had brought until the floor was covered in geometrically folded paper. Inside were traditional robes, layers of them. They went on thinnest first and Thaniel understood why Mori hadn't wanted to bother; dressing was a long process, and he must have been cold at first. Each layer had its own belt, tied with a ceremony that made the knots look like they meant something, and then the final layer, which would have been a coat in the West, was like nothing Thaniel had ever seen, even in a painting. It was thousands of pounds' worth of silk if it was a penny, with black on black embroidery that shone where it caught the light. He couldn't make out the patterns from so far away, but he could see that they were there. The last belt was sacerdotal red. As Mori turned around to chase the end of it from Suzuki, he was starker and neater than human. Not the Mori he knew at all.

'And the foreign gentleman—'

'Will be left well alone,' Mori said.

Suzuki seemed to see that he couldn't have a total victory. 'Very well,' he said smoothly, and set to folding up all the pieces of rice paper individually.

When Mori came out into the sun, the black silk writhed with naphtha colours. He stepped over the stones between the pools without breaking his pace, though the hem of his coat brushed the water.

'Careful,' Thaniel said. It was a banal thing to say, but he couldn't think of anything else.

'If Suzuki wants me to wear it, he'll have to put up with my actually wearing it. Anyway, it's not supposed to be clean, it's riding gear for this bloody hunt.' He knelt down on the slate edge of the pool. The brocade was a riot of bird patterns;

blackbirds, flocking from left to right. It must have been designed to be seen only by the person wearing it or someone sitting right next to him, because it had been obscure even from a few feet away. The collar of each layer was starched so well that they didn't move when he did. They left a hollow at the back of his neck. At home, Thaniel's sister had a silk scarf she never wore. It stayed wrapped in tissue in the top cupboard. It was probably an offcut of something like what Mori was wearing now. If someone had suggested she take it anywhere near a horse, she would have spat. 'You're invited. I didn't say that before, did I? Pepper's got half of Tokyo staying.'

'Suzuki told me,' Thaniel pointed out.

'You always look like someone who knows what's going on,' Mori said, looking sorry. 'I never know what I have or haven't mentioned.'

Thaniel glanced up. 'Any children you might have forgotten to bring up?' It came out sounding much more forced than he'd wanted.

'No,' Mori said, laughing.

'And Mrs Pepperharrow; she's not going to be annoyed that I'm here?'

'No? She's half-English. She doesn't mind foreigners.'

Thaniel wanted to drown. 'That's good then.'

He thought Mori would go, but he let himself drop flat onto his back on the warm slate. The red silk shone across his hips and the flocks of blackbirds shifted and shimmered. Yesterday, this morning even, Thaniel would have reached out to touch it.

He sank further back, towards the middle of the pool. The water was too hot there, but he didn't care. Actually burning was better than burning inside.

The sounds of the house filtered out. In another garden just below them somewhere, some girls were putting out laundry. He could hear the creak of the pegs against the sheets. Someone was walking over the nightingale floor, which made a constellation of white squeaks.

Out in the bay, the lighthouse flashed on, unpleasantly bright even in the daylight. Thaniel looked down at the water, hearing a kind of violin-high whine from the white blast. Mori's hands flickered. The lighthouse had made him jump.

'If the Baron is to be on time,' Suzuki began, and then stopped, because from the lower garden came the odd but very distinctive sound of several people chiming handbells. 'Oh, where's the dratted ...'

Thaniel straightened up and watched, puzzled, as Suzuki took a bell of his own from a loop on his belt, shook it three times, and then put it back. He didn't offer a word of explanation.

'If the Baron is to be on time he had best come now,' he finished.

The last silvery-blue coils of the sound faded off into the rain. 'What was that?' Thaniel asked, wondering if it was some kind of ceremony he hadn't heard of.

Suzuki sighed. 'Just a little fad of the Baroness's.'

Mori had jerked upright when the bells rang, and now he had turned too still, his hands balled to fists against his knees. Suzuki paid no attention and herded him back inside.

Thaniel was still wondering about it when the Morse crackle sounded again, this time much nearer. He twisted around. A man in a dark suit had appeared right at the far end of the pools. He was pacing there now, and he was holding a strange little box, pressing a button like a telegraph key. It wasn't wired to anything, but it was what was making the noise. Thaniel sat back a little. Real, wireless telegraphy; he'd never seen it before.

'Hey,' he said to the man. 'Is that a radio?'

The man looked round, and then seemed surprised when he saw who had spoken. 'Why?'

'I was a telegraphist for ages, I've never seen one. Can I have a look?'

'No, lad. Government property.' He looked amused. 'I can't go round showing it to random gaijin.'

Thaniel nodded and sank back in the water again, a bit disappointed but not surprised. The man was sending another message. Now he was close, Thaniel could hear it quite clearly. The man mustn't have been used to telegraphy, because he was slow and easy to follow.

He's inside still, east wing. All well.

Thaniel felt a little cheered up. It was bloody impressive. According to every dispatch he'd ever read, Kuroda was a terrible choice for Prime Minister, but it was hard to completely disapprove of someone who invested in new inventions like that. Six would love it.

TWELVE

At the back of the house, a wide courtyard was full of horses and men. Thaniel recognised the Prime Minister from photographs in the newspapers. He'd always been suspicious of the man, because Kuroda's favourite hobby seemed to be war with Korea. And 'Kuroda' meant 'Blackfield', and anybody who walked around central government sounding like a pirate couldn't have been wonderful news for anyone. Thaniel thought he was probably being unfair, especially given the wonderful radio things, and started out willing to be proven wrong, but, quite quickly, he was proven right.

Kuroda wasn't tall, but he was a bull of a man, and stable-boys were spraying away from him as he threw orders about. His voice was one of those that would carry across battlefields and he had the gruff clipped samurai way of talking that Thaniel could never understand first time round. Suzuki went ahead of them and murmured to him. He swung round. Kuroda had an open face and neat short hair, and wide, serious eyes. He was dressed just as well as Mori, in fantastically expensive-looking forest green. Beyond him were five men in dark suits, standing at the gates and doors. They were all watching.

'Mori,' he said, brisk. 'Here to help me with the Russians, are you?'

'No,' Mori said. 'I absolutely am not. You're going to have to try harder than that.'

Kuroda gave him a stern look, but then engulfed him. He lifted him right off his feet, though Mori was taller, and spun him around twice. 'You're back! You're back, you bastard, what were you *doing* out there? Watches, stupid waste of time ...' He dropped him again and thumped his shoulder. Thaniel had never seen anyone look more delighted. There was a sort of fever-excitement coming off the man in waves. His horse, which was just behind them, nudged at them both, wanting to know what all the fuss was. Kuroda looked over at Thaniel, full of frank interest, both hands still on Mori's arms. 'This your monkey?'

'Pleased to meet you,' Thaniel offered.

Kuroda blinked. 'It can talk. How does it talk?'

'The usual way, I should imagine,' Mori said.

Kuroda didn't seem convinced. 'Do you understand Japanese, then?'

'Yes, sir,' Thaniel said.

'D'you ride?'

'I can't.'

'Hm.' He looked Thaniel over again, like he was trying to decide whether or not he really wanted him so close by, but then abruptly he lost interest.

'Kuroda,' Mori said, pointed but not quite sharp yet.

'Delighted to meet you, of course,' Kuroda said smoothly to Thaniel. He was plainly only in it to needle Mori; he had the glow of someone who had just been given such a wonderful toy to play with that he barely had any idea where to begin. In a child it would have been endearing. In a man it was unnerving.

'I don't believe you,' Thaniel said.

Kuroda laughed much too suddenly. 'You're fun.' He turned away. 'Mori. Got a nice horse for you. She's a bit skittish yet, but you're not bad with horses, are you?'

A boy came out with a black mare. Thaniel couldn't tell a thing about it except that it was expensive and strong. Mori wound the reins around his hand. 'She seems all right to me.' The horse nudged him.

'Baroness!' Kuroda shouted. It was klaxon loud and Thaniel saw purple splotches. 'Where the hell is that beautiful woman of yours when I want to show off to her?' he added to Mori. 'She has a knack for vanishing.'

Mori was leaning against the horse, which seemed to like him. 'Just around you, is it?'

Kuroda snorted. 'There she is. Mrs Pepperharrow!' It was too loud again. Thaniel blinked hard. It wasn't a volume he would have thought a human could produce. If politics fell through for Kuroda, there would be a fine career in opera ready and waiting. 'We're all here! Come and hostess.'

When she came, people hurried to get out of her way, though she was tiny. Thaniel wasn't surprised it had taken her this long to get dressed; she was wearing more than he earned in a year. Her dress was all hummingbird colours that made Mori and Kuroda look austere. There were real jasmine flowers in her hair. Thaniel caught the smell of them, warm and sweet. Despite all that, she wasn't a stunningly beautiful person. In ordinary clothes she would have been boyish.

'Gentlemen, hello.' She bowed a tiny doll's bow. 'Lovely to see you properly and not hanging out of a tree. Welcome home.'

Mori bowed back to her, not half as formally as he had with Kuroda, but still full of gentility. She'd lit a candle in him somewhere, because he glowed a bit when he said thank you. 'And this is Mr Steepleton.'

She ducked her head to Thaniel, gradually, because the silver combs in her hair must have been as heavy as she was. 'The musician, yes, wonderful; I've got the phonograph recording of your Mozart concert, it's absolutely the best one there is.'

'Baroness,' he said, and felt real despair, because she wasn't being false-charming. She really sounded honest.

'No-o,' she laughed. 'Just Takiko, please.'

'Nathaniel,' he said bleakly.

'You'll watch the hunt, Baroness?' Kuroda put in, clearly of the opinion that she wasn't paying him enough attention.

'Ecstatically,' she said. She nudged Thaniel and, when he glanced down, glinted the edge of a deck of gilded playing cards at him from just under her sleeve.

Kuroda noticed, but he looked pleased. 'Baroness,' he said, 'would you come and take the edge off me for these nice people?'

She bowed wryly to Thaniel and Mori and went away with him. Kuroda slowed right down for her, clearly happy to have something so bright in tow. Mori was watching them too.

'She ...' Thaniel couldn't think of anything to say. 'She seems not to mind him. I'd have hidden in a barn when I was her age.'

Mori did smile, but not much. 'You're not her age yet.' Like it often did after several other people had been talking, his voice sounded even more unusual than normal. Everyone else's was normal unremarkable cotton, but he sounded like velvet to which someone had just held a match.

'Oh,' said Thaniel. He was already getting a growing sense that a white man was likely to fall apart before any normal person was halfway through their warranty.

'Hurry up!' Kuroda shouted. 'Get on your horse, Mori!'

'Would anyone mind if I chucked him in a well?' Thaniel said, already tired of the purple splotches and glad to change the subject.

Mori smiled properly this time. 'No, I think that's wholly to be encouraged.' He climbed up on the stirrup and settled in the saddle. The horse shifted to see what the new rider felt like. He sat straight and still, listening to his own balance. Under the hem of the black kimono, he was wearing proper riding boots. Although they were fitted for spurs, with a bronze loop round the heel, he had taken off the sharp edges.

Kuroda pulled a white stallion right up alongside and Thaniel jerked backward, an inch from being trampled. The clank of horseshoes shot silver into everything. He had just long enough to feel Mori's stirrup dig into his back and a knife edge of panic before Mori leaned over his head to smack Kuroda with his crop in time to make him pull back again. Kuroda looked down, surprised to see anybody there.

'Well? Should've got out the way,' he said. 'D'you still shoot, Mori?'

Thaniel clenched his hand and thumped his knuckles against his own leg to vent the need to swear at him.

Mori swung his horse and shoved Kuroda out of his saddle. There was a thump as their shoulders met and then another when Kuroda hit the ground. Motes of hay puffed up around him.

'Should've held on,' said Mori drily.

There was a silence in which it seemed almost certain he would be taken away and shot. Half the men in the stable yard now were the same ones who had met Mori at the front door, and hands went to sword hilts. Not far away, Kuroda's men in their dark suits eased away from their posts and more towards Kuroda. One was dressed differently – loudly, Thaniel thought – maybe to make absolutely sure people noticed him. He wore a bright red coat and one of the buttons was a tiny Fabergé egg. He was holding a revolver in the easy way of someone who used it all the time, and it was aimed at Mori's kneecap.

Kuroda slung some hay at him. 'Fuck off!'

Everyone relaxed. Thaniel stood still, waiting for his heart to stop banging. He didn't mind jokes. But if Mori hadn't hit Kuroda, the horses would have collided and he would have gone down under their hooves. After a second, he went around and helped Kuroda up. He understood. Kuroda was a frightening man who liked people who weren't frightened of him. It was still an effort to brush him down and clap his shoulder like he was harmless. Kuroda was laughing now. He climbed up onto his stirrup again and paused when a boy came to look at the buckles on the saddle. It was a relief not to be the focus of his attention.

Around them, other men were climbing into their saddles, and the women dropped back from the horses. Mori nodded at Thaniel to step back before Kuroda whistled sharp and hard and the riders spun away as fast as a cavalry regiment. The ground was scattered with pine needles, which jumped under the horses' hooves. It shook until they were well away. Someone threw a bow and a quiver between horses and someone else caught it, and then he heard the snap of a string and a bird fell from the sky. One of the dogs tore across to fetch it.

Thaniel watched them from the stable gate, digging his fingernails into the wood. He'd never thought of Mori's barony as being real in any sense but money. Mori described Japan as a tiny place in the middle of nowhere with no trains and a suspicious attitude toward telegraph lines. Somewhere along the way, Thaniel had filed it away with other middle-of-nowhere bits of the world and pinned on a matching idea of its aristocracy. Tiny African states had kings, though they were kings of less land and fewer people than a Suffolk farmer oversaw in an afternoon. It wasn't the kingship of England or Germany, the sort that turned the world rather than crops.

'Are you all right?'

He looked around, didn't find anyone, then looked down. Takiko Pepperharrow was there again, looking half concerned and half amused.

'I saw Kuroda up to his usual,' she said. 'He's jealous of Mori. He's possessive about his friends. Doesn't want you on his patch. He hasn't got very many friends.' It was perfect cut-glass English.

'Oh. No, I'm all right.'

'You're from Yorkshire,' she laughed.

It seemed pedantic to point out that actually it was the next shire down. He'd already found on the ship that he would settle happily for anything in Britain. If someone guessed that he was from near Edinburgh, he said yes, because Lincoln was very near Edinburgh if you were coming at it from Nagasaki. 'How did you know?'

'My father was an English diplomat and my governess was from Whitby.' She nodded again towards the hunt. The wind brought a breath of jasmine perfume to him. 'He tries it with me all the time, Kuroda. He wants to see if he can make you flinch. He's like a sumo wrestler; he throws his weight about but all he wants is a good fight. You just say rhinoceros and he laughs and trots off on his merry way.'

'Rhinoceros?'

'There's a rumour he killed his wife,' she said. She was watching him now, too closely, but perhaps it was only something she had taught herself to do in order to keep big men unsettled. 'And you know the *Marumaru*, the cartoon newspaper? They published a sketch of him in bed with a new girl and a rhinoceros ghost looming up out of some sake fumes. You know, rhinoceros is "sai", wife is "sai" ...'

'That's funny,' he said automatically, then pictured it properly and frowned. 'Did he? Kill her.'

'Yes. Ow,' she added. She snatched her hand off the rail and bit her knuckle. 'Static.' She left teeth marks in her finger. Thunder snarled to the south and then lightning sparked very high, not a fork but a hanging flicker that looked like the tendrils of a jellyfish.

'Sorry, what? He did?'

'Yes, he's a drunk,' she said, as if people who killed their wives were normal. She turned her sleeve back, carefully, and winced when the silk nipped at her again. 'It's the mountain,' she said. 'There's been odd weather from there lately.' She tapped the fence to tell him to step up on it and then she did the same, pointing between a gap in some trees. Fuji showed, lunar, through the grey storm haze. While they were looking, light snapped up in the sky again. There was no bang this time, no thunder, and no rain either. But the air had turned crackly. Somewhere through the woods, a horse shrieked.

'Why is he Prime Minister if—'

'Because Keita wants him to be,' she said mildly. She studied Thaniel properly, her forearms still resting on the fence. 'So how do you two know each other? You and Keita.'

It was horrible hearing her call Mori by his first name. She had introduced herself by her first name in a bid to be modern and Western maybe, but Mori wasn't modern. First names were only for children and people you wouldn't be surprised to wake up with. 'He's my landlord. I rent his spare room in London.'

'How well do you know him?' she said.

'Well enough. Why?'

She was looking at him hard now. 'I'm asking if you know what he can do.'

'Is it polite not to throw coins or dice too near him, yes, I know that.' He could hear he was being brusque, but more than anything he wanted her to go away. All the questions felt like pressure on a bruise.

Takiko must have been used to a different league of unfriendly men, though, because she didn't even seem to notice. 'Then you must also know that people near to him aren't really people in his eyes. They're tools. You're *for* something. I'm for something, Kuroda is for something, there is nothing I'm more sure of in the world – or maybe it isn't you, maybe it's your interesting little girl.'

'Sorry, what do you want to say?'

'Why are you here?' she asked softly. It was urgent, not a threat. 'You seem like a nice person. Nice people don't do well around Keita, Mr Steepleton, they end up dead. He is the king of useful deaths.'

Thaniel frowned. It was one way to describe Mori, but he couldn't help thinking it sounded dramatic. 'Why are you still married to him then? You could walk out if you wanted.'

'To warn people like you. I hope you don't mind my saying, but you're ill, aren't you? You sound ill.'

'Yes. So?'

'The king of useful deaths,' she said again, very quietly this time.

'I'm not here to die, I'm here because I can breathe here. London's a mess.'

'Right.' She sighed. 'You probably think I'm just trying to get an annoying gaijin off my territory. I'm not. Ask him what happened to Countess Kuroda.'

'I'm all right, thanks,' Thaniel said, a touch sharp. It was just one of those things, with Mori; there was a temptation to hold him personally responsible for every evil that happened nearby, given that he could have put a stop to it. But that was a nasty way to think. It didn't allow for Mori being a person, one who could be tired or ill, or distracted, or upset. Whatever had happened to Kuroda's wife, Thaniel was inclined to call it Kuroda's fault.

'All right. But in case you haven't noticed, you've walked into a war. Kuroda wants him here to help beat the Russians; he forced him to come. Keita doesn't want to help beat the Russians, but I expect he does want to remind Kuroda who not to annoy. Don't get caught between them.'

'I'll bear it in mind,' said Thaniel, who couldn't see how Kuroda would force Mori to do anything. 'They look like they're just having a laugh.'

'They are. But they're samurai. Their idea of fun is dangerous.'

He nodded. More than anything, she sounded like someone who would have preferred not to have a herd of men in her house thumping around like a bunch of walruses. If he'd been her size, he would have found Kuroda terrifying. Perhaps Mori, too; perhaps he'd have even hated him a bit, for letting Kuroda charge around so much, and particularly if being married to him meant being his legal property. He didn't know what the Japanese marriage system was like, but given the way Mori thought about women, it couldn't have been too dignified.

'You think I'm a woman being worried about woman things,' she said wryly. 'I know Kuroda and Mori must look harmless to you from up there, but that isn't what I'm talking about it all.'

'Well,' he said. He smiled a bit, annoyed with himself for having been rude before. 'Thanks for the warning, then.'

She opened her hands to say she wasn't going to push any more.

The blue light flickered again over Fuji. They both watched it for a while. The air felt stormy, but there was still no rain.

She called something to the other women. He didn't catch it. A march of bright sleeves and sashes later, and snatches of conversation about the Russian fleet, they were all past him and he was alone on the narrow road.

Somewhere close by, little bells rang. He couldn't tell where from. It must have been some kind of signal, because one of Kuroda's guards hauled himself down from where he'd been perched on the fence about fifty yards away from

Thaniel, and started to trudge towards what must have been the back gates of the grounds. He stabbed at the radio.

Still got him?

Pause. Thaniel listened, just idly.

Yes all well. Wish Suzuki had put him in something brighter though, red and black is bloody difficult to keep track of. Every second person's tack is red and black.

Thaniel frowned, because he could have sworn Kuroda had been in green. It sounded like they were talking about Mori.

THIRTEEN

Between the stables and house was a long, pretty greenhouse. The glass roof traced two curves like a temple to match the old house, each pane fitted at odd contours to make the shape. Wanting to breathe warmer air for a minute, Thaniel let himself in. It faced what must have been the temple grounds at the far end, because it looked out onto a graveyard. On the way, some overladen pear trees made an archway over the little path. There was a bench at the end. He sat down carefully to give his lungs time to soak up the humidity and the green smell of water on leaves.

It all helped. Even after half a minute, breathing was easier. He stole a pear for later. Beside the bench was a beautiful glass terrarium, full of fat and happy caterpillars. A couple of them were already spinning their cocoons. It was mesmerising. He sat bent towards the glass, wondering how a caterpillar recognised its friends once it was a moth, or if you had to start again as a moth and reintroduce yourself.

To windward, the glass panes bumped. The weather had turned blustery. Dark clouds had gathered over the sea and the light was struggling through them. There was still no rain, not even in the distance, just more fog, rolling in from the north.

A child shrieked. It was a horrified primeval sound and he jerked upright in case it was Six. He followed the vivid white after-tone of it down the hill to the graveyard.

It wasn't Six. It was the little garden boy. He had a scarf over his face, because he had been shovelling quicklime over a shallow grave. Just beside him was a crate full of dead birds. Crows, mainly.

'What happened?' Thaniel asked.

'I saw a ghost!' He sounded panicked.

Puzzled, Thaniel went to the grave to look in. There were a couple of crates' worth of birds already there, half covered by the powdery lime. 'Where ...?' He trailed off, because the boy had begun to cry. 'What's your name?' he said, more softly.

'Hotaru,' the little boy managed. 'Yoshida.'

Thaniel picked him up. He was probably older than he looked, but he was tiny and buttony, and he was so light he was easy to carry back towards the house. He suited his name; he was a little firefly of a person. 'Where's your mum, then?' Thaniel said quietly.

'At the salt, the salt works down the beach,' the boy said, still sobbing in uneven gulps. 'But Mr Suzuki won't like me to go ...'

'Mr Suzuki will live with it,' Thaniel said. 'Come on, let's find him.'

The boy was right; Suzuki didn't want to let him go home.

'For heaven's sake, you can't send staff home whenever they take some silly fancy—'

'How old are you?' Thaniel said to Hotaru.

'Seven.'

'He's seven, Suzuki, I'm taking him to his mother. Unless you think he'd be more productive in a weeping heap behind the greenhouse.'

Suzuki sighed. 'The salt burners are vulgar people, Mr Steepleton, superstition is only to be expected. The boy will grow out of it sooner if you don't pander to it.'

Thaniel took the little boy down to the beach. They passed one of Kuroda's bodyguards at the gate, looking out to sea, bored. The man didn't even bother to nod. Above them, despite the grey weather, the lighthouse sat on its leaning rock, unlit. But there was a washing line with a white shirt pegged on it, fluttering.

He could smell the salt works before they came into sight. They were burning seaweed, and smoke was pouring out into the sky. There was something odd about the way it moved. The smoke coiled sometimes like something was nudging it. There was no wind. The quiet made the shore eerie. It should have been full of seagulls and sandpipers, but there was nothing.

He thought the birds must have just flown somewhere safer. It was wishful. Before long, he saw them all in the tide-line, downy corpses washing up against the mess of seaweed and pebbles, the softer, lighter feathers masquerading as foam. When he went to look, the weed was swarming with spider crabs having the time of their lives with the carrion. Not much further along the beach, other people had noticed too. They were lifting the crabs out into buckets. Children mostly, with old pails and grey clothes. The smoke from the salt works drifted through them too much for him to see how many. Still unhappy, Hotaru stayed close to him.

The salt works were set up on what looked like a natural tumble of rocks. He climbed up carefully, his gloves catching on old limpets. At the top, a broad figure with a rake paused and watched him through the smoke and the whirling cinders.

'Afternoon,' said Thaniel. 'I'm from the big house. Are you Mr Yoshida?'

'Who's asking?' the man rumbled. He had an inhumanly hoarse voice. He must have spent his life breathing the smoke. Just beside him was a deep pit, full of burning seaweed that hissed and popped as its air pockets burst.

'Your boy's had a bit of a fright, he's upset.' He touched Hotaru's shoulders to put the little boy in front of him. 'Is his mother here?'

'Why, what's happened?'

'He says he saw a ghost.'

'What do you mean, he says?' the man said crossly. 'If our Hotaru says he saw one then he did. We all have.'

Hotaru had turned small and still, his eyes fixed on the ground.

Thaniel frowned. 'All right.'

The man grunted at him and then called back to a woman. She came by without a word, only a cringing nod that probably didn't do her husband's bullishness much good, and hurried Hotaru away. Thaniel wished he hadn't brought him, and wondered if Suzuki had been trying to tell him, in his stuffy way, that it would make a bad day worse.

'You said you'd all seen them?' Thaniel said to the salt burner.

'So?'

'Where?'

'Here. What do you care?'

'Would you show me?'

'They don't come just because some cracker wants them to.'

112

The smell of the place was something between charcoal and seaweed. Thaniel would have liked to go closer, but the rocks were uneven and he couldn't see a path through the burning pits. 'Why are there ghosts here?'

'If you don't believe me you should just say that and get on your way.'

Thaniel could imagine that if you made your living burning seaweed in these grit clouds, not many people would want to hear what you had to say about anything. 'Did something happen here?'

The salt burner was still at first. Thaniel waited. However odd he found the salt burner, he must have looked stranger himself. He was a full head and shoulders taller, and his coat was shroud grey.

'Ask the Baron at the big house,' the man said at last.

'Why?'

'Started when we knew he was coming back.' He wrung his hand once around the handle of his rake with a scraping noise of bad wood and calluses.

'What does it matter that he was coming back?'

But the salt burner had had enough. 'Look, fuck off, you're distracting my men.'

Thaniel looked around. There were men all around, paused by their own fire-pits to listen, leaning on rakes. They had scarves over their faces. He could have mistaken any one of them for a ghost.

———

'I told you they were odd people,' Suzuki said when Thaniel traipsed back. 'You're covered in ash,' he added. 'Don't walk it into the house.'

Thaniel went around the courtyard instead. There was a pine tree whose middle branches were still hung with ancient, decaying prayer cards, from when the house had been a monastery. It was broad and old, the ridges in the bark as thick as saplings themselves, its boughs starting low, about chest height, and covered in dark moss. The needles shushed in the wind.

Someone had just recently begun to use it as a holy tree again. There were six or seven new cards on bright ribbons tied to the lowest branch. A little wind clocked them together. It sounded ecclesiastical, like church bells did, or footsteps alone on a stone floor. There was nothing else he could do for Hotaru, so he took a new card from the box someone had left out and looked at the hanging ones.

So that Midori's headaches get better before the wedding
So that I stop seeing the ghosts
So that the baroness's play goes well
So that the ghosts go away
So that the ghosts go away.

All of them were in different handwriting. He took the pen tied on a string to the tree and filled in a spare card, wishing Hotaru well, and flicked a coin into the shallow pool. A good few sen coins already sparkled under the lilies.

He jumped when something shrieked at him, then laughed at himself. It was only an owl. There was a mother and two half-grown chicks, all lined up in the roots of the pine tree. One of them was pecking at a dead crow. Other birds littered the grass; there was another glass window just above. One of the chicks came to investigate his bootlaces.

'Hey! Get out!' A girl with a broom had appeared from the side door. 'Go on, go!'

The owls flapped away, the little ones leaving behind a few of their last downy baby feathers.

'They weren't doing any harm,' he protested. 'They just wanted the birds.'

She looked uneasily after them. 'Owls are bad,' she said. 'You understand? Something bad will happen if there are too many together, they steal your luck. They shouldn't come near a holy tree. We're having a hell of a time keeping them away, this whole place is infested with them. Always is when the master comes home.'

He paused. 'I didn't mean to spy, but I saw the cards. Did you write one of those about the ghosts?'

She nodded. 'There's an evil spirit in the well, a woman.'

Thaniel tried not to look openly unconvinced. Practically every Japanese castle and mansion he'd ever read about had some sort of story about a woman in a well. Medieval lords had seemed to think that that was where women generally belonged. 'Was there a real lady who died in the well, then?'

She looked blank. 'You don't know about Countess Kuroda?'

'Oh,' he said, not sure why he was surprised.

The girl pointed through to another section of the garden. 'Go and see,' she said.

The well was just beyond some gingko trees. It had been sunk deep, but there must have been some seismic change since the building of it. If the water had ever been clean, it wasn't now. It had left a thick, vivid yellow sulphur-salt around the well walls. The water at the bottom was boiling, pouring more steam upward. It was impossible to see through, and even if you could have, it would have boiled all the flesh off a corpse before anyone could get down to take it out. It must have been forty feet down, but he could hear the hiss and roar of the water. The heat was uncomfortable, even leaning against the well lip.

'I didn't know Countess Kuroda died here,' he said at last.

The girl had come too. 'Well, no one was surprised,' she said. 'You know how to write down Yoruji?'

'Sorry?' asked Thaniel, confused. 'Er – yes. Evening Temple, doesn't it mean?'

'They write it like that now to posh it up. It never used to be. *Yoru* is tomb.'

Disconcerted, he went back to the graveyard to bury the rest of the birds, so that Hotaru wouldn't be in trouble. Ghosts; like at the legation. Maybe this was just a haunted country. The quicklime puffed into odd shapes as he worked. When he finished, he stuck the spade in the disturbed soil and straightened, feeling better for having done something useful, though he was much, much more tired from it than he ought to have been. Brushing off his hands, which were stiff right in the bones and crackly when he flexed them, he drifted through the nearest graves to see if there was anyone famous here.

There was a tall, stone shrine gate to mark the boundary. It was old; there was moss around the base, and a wind-eroded fox carving. He couldn't tell what it meant. Beyond it, the graves were set far closer together than they would have been in the West. Some of them were Christian. Others were simple columns with vertical text, scattered with the curving skeletons of old incense sticks. The moss clung to everything, and so did delicate spiders. With the constant earthquakes, some of the older stones had listed or fallen, and in turn the moss anchored them to the loamy grass.

He stopped by one, because worked into the headstone was a sort of periscope pipe, and at the top of the pipe, a bell. People were so afraid of being buried alive that they had a bell pull put round their fingertip in the coffin. It must have been quite a fashion, because a lot of the graves had bells. On a couple of them, the bells had plainly been added a long time after the grave had been laid. Some of the little bell towers were wooden, brand new, even on graves from last century. They smelled fresh. It must have been some legal thing they had to do. He had no idea if people here believed in resurrection. Mori talked about past lives sometimes, but only in the way Thaniel talked about Hell – not with any real feeling.

One of the graves had a kind of scope with a shutter at the top, so you could see down into the coffin. He opened the shutter. Bounced back by two mirrors, gone cloudy now, was the image of someone's small, inoffensive skull, chin tucked down. It was oddly pleasing.

From away at the far end of the graveyard, there came the soft, prism-coloured jingling of a single bell. He looked around to find it and frowned. She had changed her clothes, and without all the finery she was nearly unrecognisable in plain things, but the woman kneeling by the oldest graves was Takiko Pepperharrow. She was tying up a new bell. On her left, she had a whole basket of them still to go. They sang merrily when she picked them up and moved them to the next grave.

Gripped by the need to not talk to her again, he turned away.

FOURTEEN

By the time dinner was served, Thaniel was so tired he felt delirious, but Mori promised the food would be worth it. It was a real effort at first, but as he, Mori, and Six walked through the peculiar house, hearing other people coming down from other obscure staircases, the men still fizzy from the hunt and the women talking about the weather on the mountain, he woke up more.

The dining room was a long, lush space with a huge view out to sea through a pair of double doors that almost opened the entire back wall. The tables were long and low with hollows underneath so you could sit on the floor, and, despite the open doors, they trapped the heat. At intervals along them were gorgeous arrangements of hothouse flowers in glass vivariums, set around pebbles and moss and half-flowering twigs. In some were tiny hummingbirds which, on close inspection, were clockwork, the silver oxidised to gleam blue. People called compliments for the hostess from all along the tables.

Thaniel overheard a lady telling her husband that the hummingbirds had been part of Mori's wedding present to Takiko, and that *some people* might do well to borrow a leaf from his book on their next anniversary.

Thaniel closed one hand hard over his watch. Mori had made that too.

If you were just entering into a friendly business arrangement, you did not spend hundreds of hours making ten clockwork hummingbirds for her. You bought her a nice set of china and that was that.

The food arrived in small but beautiful portions — sushi parcels wrapped perfectly and decorated with fish eggs that looked like tiny jewels, fried rice, ordinary rice but flecked with purple grains, a kind of tofu cake that came with a pot of honey to pour across, beans still in their pods and steaming through salt crystals and spices. The servants moved fast; the kitchen was right next door and it hissed and steamed brilliantly. Rather than signalling meekly when they wanted something, the women yelled and someone came speeding along. It was nothing like he'd expected and ten times more alive than the same house would have been in England.

'Explain why I'm wearing this, to eat pub food? Which I hear you insisted on?' Mori said to Kuroda, who was sitting on his other side. Suzuki had chased him into another kimono, even more beautiful than the last, and plainly the equivalent of white tie. Everyone had them, each one made of layers and layers. Thaniel had resisted Suzuki's best efforts – it seemed excruciatingly and indefinably disrespectful – and now he felt drab.

'Not a damn thing wrong with pub food,' Kuroda said happily. 'And you're wearing that so I can have a flower on each hand.' He put one hand out to Mori and one to Takiko Pepperharrow, who was on his right. Mori looked at his hand sceptically and Kuroda laughed.

Thaniel made a quiet fuss of Six, who was between him and Mori. Someone had put her in a kimono too. It suited her, and there were pockets in the sleeves into which a determined person could fit quite a lot of nuts.

Mori gave him a glass of amber wine. It tasted of plums, cut with tea, and it was by far and away the nicest kind of alcohol he'd ever had. Its fumes blended well with the pipe smoke floating in the air. It wasn't making him cough; with the open doors, the smoke was drifting outside, and the sharp nip of the oncoming sunset seeped in. The servants started to light little candles in paper lamps that hung from the rafters. Before long Thaniel had lost the thread of the conversation completely.

Every so often a bout of flame went up along the table, because the chefs were cooking trout with blowtorches in front of people as a party trick, and new gusts of laughter and snatches of punchlines followed. Lured by the candles, fireflies drifted in. They looked like constellations that had decided to go wandering. They looped here and there through the smoky air and trundled about when they found the lights, puzzled. Some of the women caught them in their sleeves, and before long there were jars full of confused fireflies up and down the table.

The woman on Thaniel's other side, who turned out to be Lady Shimazu, called across a footman and made Thaniel request new dishes for at least five people in a list. When he managed it, she whooped and refilled his glass. He could see he was half being mocked, but it was funny all the same. Lady Shimazu asked him about the journey and they all chipped in when he mentioned the birds. The birds had been doing bizarre things for weeks now. Lord Shimazu's groundsman had piles of them in the woodshed. The peasants were getting superstitious about it.

'Maybe the mountain will blow,' someone said, and they all hmmed and said 'hope not', not in the least as if they were talking about being incinerated by a volcano.

They were directly opposite the lighthouse, so when it came on, the electric light strobed right across the room. It was the colour of a foghorn. He had to thump his hand against his ear to convince himself he wasn't really hearing it.

All the servants stopped what they were doing, straightened up, and each rang one small silver bell. The chimes sang their metallic blue through the smoke. There was a girl right behind them and to get to her bell, she dropped a cup. It fell straight into Mori's lap and tipped steaming hot tea across his knee. He didn't gasp. He only froze.

People were looking round expectantly, to see who was about to speak. The lighthouse lamp went off again. Thaniel had to tip his head one way and then the other to try and chase away the after-tone.

'Time for the proper wine!' Kuroda called, to general cheers.

Everyone seemed to accept that as the reason for the bells. Six went back to her dinner. Around the room, Kuroda's bodyguards rotated; some switched with each other, and a couple of them left.

Mori was staring at the cup in his lap, white and unmoving, though he must have been burned. Thaniel had never seen anyone lose colour so completely and so quickly. He looked as if a body had just fallen out of a cupboard and cracked at his feet.

'Mori,' Thaniel said quietly. He reached past Six to move the cup and give Mori his wine glass, which was empty except for a good shard of ice.

Mori looked at it without understanding. Then, 'Sorry. Yes. Thank you.' He put his sleeve over his hand and tipped the ice into it for a makeshift poultice.

'What the hell is going on? What are the bells for?'

'It's just the signal for Kuroda's men to change their posts. They rotate to stay awake.'

'Oh,' said Thaniel. He frowned. While they were speaking, some new men had come in to take over from the ones who had left. 'Made you jump, though.'

'I'm just foggy from the journey,' Mori said.

One of the men passed just behind them. He was keying at his radio. He was better than the others Thaniel had heard, faster.

Still in the dining room. The cup worked. He didn't catch it.

Thaniel snapped round, then looked back at Mori. 'That was on purpose. She dropped the cup on purpose. They're talking to each other about you.'

'I know,' Mori said patiently. 'They have to protect the Prime Minister. A clairvoyant who possibly defected to the enemy is every security officer's worst nightmare, I expect.'

'But how—'

'Leave them be,' Mori said. 'They're just doing their jobs.'

Thaniel swallowed down the urge to say that spilling boiling water on someone was a bit beyond the purview of most people's jobs.

'Mori,' Thaniel said on the way back to the rooms. He was carrying Six, who was asleep. The house was creaking and counter-intuitive. Whenever his sense of direction wanted to turn left, they went right. Sometimes the shadows of other people flickered on the other side of the paper walls. He kept his voice right down. The whole house would hear a whisper. 'About Kuroda. I heard he killed his wife.'

He had expected a hot denial, but Mori only put his shoulders back while he thought about it. 'He had a hand in it.'

Thaniel lifted his eyebrows at the floor. 'And he's shot past slightly odd, through possible lunatic and right up to the top prize of the Napoleonometer! This is really quite extraordinary, ladies and gentlemen, Mr Mori, you have won a coconut.'

'Why?'

'Why? If Kuroda's in the habit of murdering people – Mori. This stuff with his bodyguards; if he decides you're – I don't know, if he decides to have a proper go at you—'

Mori wasn't looking at Thaniel. He was studying a patch of air just ahead of them, for all the world as if somebody were there, his eyes full of quiet reproof. Just for a second, Thaniel saw something like the outline of a person in the dust where it winked in the soft light.

'He didn't kill her. I did.'

Thaniel slowed down. It was hard to believe what he'd just heard and instead his mind skipped around to find other things to think about. They had come out into a big room partitioned into sections, empty but lit with oil lamps. The nearest screen was a hell triptych that showed a woman burning in a falling carriage. The style looked ancient, but the colours were still bright. Demons swam in the smoke. It was a horrible thing, and hallucinatory, because he still couldn't place where they were in the house. Not the kind of thing Mori would choose, either. Of course he hadn't; it would have been her. 'Was there a good reason?'

'Depends what you mean by good.'

'I've never known you do a bad thing,' Thaniel said honestly.

'You haven't known me long,' Mori pointed out.

Thaniel didn't think he was under special illusions about it. He'd heard plenty of shady stories. A dead cousin, a host of unlikely accidents, including the odd death of the Matron from Six's workhouse. But at the end of it all, Mori was a quiet man who had been at war with the Haverlys' cat for four years and made lightbulbs for his little girl. Thaniel said so.

'The irritating thing about evil people is that they have a way of doing good things too,' Mori said.

'You've gone dramatic,' Thaniel said.

Mori didn't look convinced, but he did smile. 'Why don't you care? You should.'

Thaniel put his cheek against Six's hair while he tried to think of something to say that wasn't the truth. The truth was that he loved Mori so hopelessly he could have found a way to excuse cemeteries of dead wives. 'None of my business,' he said at last.

FIFTEEN

Yokohama, 19th December 1888

Thaniel had the same dream he'd had on the ship: that someone was in the room, watching him. It snapped him awake. His watch said half-past four in the morning.

He sat up and raked his hair back from his face. The bedding was all traditional, just a thin mattress and sheets set up on the floor, which was good, because you could surround it with books and cups. He sipped some water and gazed around. Even though he could see that the room was empty, he couldn't shake the feeling that someone was there. The feeling was so strong that he got up with a candle to scrutinise the paper walls for eye-holes hidden among the paintings of cranes and trees. He didn't find any. But even while he was looking, he kept catching maddening flickers right at the corners of his eyes. Even Mori, who had such a mathematical mind that he barely understood the point of art galleries, had said this place was haunted. And all those prayer cards in the garden; and Hotaru. Something was wrong about the place, whether it was ghosts or not.

He went to look at Six. She breathed silently, and he had to kneel with his hand on her shoulder to know that she was. She had set up her mattress by the balcony door, which was open. The air was freezing and she'd already given herself a cold this year, but she was claustrophobic at night. He tucked her in better, wishing she'd consent to having a dolly or a bear he could put in with her. She looked neglected without. He propped the generator manual up against the edge of the door where she would see it if she woke up.

Bright light shone through the whole room.

It was coming from next door, like the echo of a foghorn. Just on the other side of the paper wall, Mori's silhouette was very clear. Thaniel could see his eyelashes. Katsu was curled up flat on his chest, tentacles shifting sometimes. The light was too much for candles or the soft oil lamps. It was the lighthouse.

Mori shifted uneasily. Katsu clung tighter to his arm to keep from falling.

From somewhere in the house, faint but clear in what was otherwise absolute silence, someone rang a small bell, and then there was another and another, until just for a second, the whole house was full of the sound. Mori jerked upright like someone had kicked him. It made Thaniel jump.

The lighthouse beam went out again. Mori sat frozen. He was holding his breath.

Thaniel touched the paper, which scratched against the telegraph-roughened tip of his forefinger.

Mori jolted back from the screen. If he had heard a dead thing rattle and hiss, and seen it scratch decaying fingertips against the translucent paper, he couldn't have gone faster.

'It's me,' Thaniel said quickly. He went outside and round to Mori's open door. 'Wake up.'

'I'm awake,' Mori whispered.

'Nightmare?'

'No, I'm fine.' Mori was breathing again, but not much. He was holding himself still and terse. Thaniel knelt down next to him, meaning to take his hands, but Mori brushed him away. 'Don't – don't,' Mori whispered. He glanced at the door and Thaniel looked back with the sudden certainty that Six was there, but the threshold was empty except for the soft furling of the steam from the hot pools. 'Go back to bed.'

Thaniel did as he was told, his heart squeezing, shut the door, and stood still on the verandah while he waited to stop feeling like he wanted to vanish into the ground.

The second the door was closed, he heard moving fabric and the inner door of Mori's room open and shut. Nothing on the nightingale floor, but then a tap on another door, and, very quietly, so quietly he wouldn't have heard if he hadn't been listening for it, Mori's amber voice said 'Pepper' and another door opened and shut.

Thaniel walked out to the hot pools, which steamed in the cold night. Where the moonlight striped across them, there were curling patterns in the vapour.

He must have been caught in the flinders of the nightmare still, because for a split second he saw someone outlined in the steam before it blew apart again. His ribs hitched. He sighed at himself and knelt down on the edge of a pool to scoop a handful of hot water across his face.

None of his damn business if Mori wanted to talk to his own wife in the night.

He stayed by the pool, breathing the steam. Inch by inch, the sky lightened. It turned violet and then pink, and then almost blue. He got dressed properly. He'd meant to spend the whole day asleep and not talking to anyone except the piano, but though it had sounded like heaven yesterday, the whole idea was purgatorial now. He found Suzuki, who gave him a train timetable, and set out for the railway station.

The British legation wasn't far away. From Yokohama to the big Tokyo terminus station at Shimbashi it was an hour on a brand new train. Shimbashi was the size of King's Cross and heaving with people at nine o'clock in the morning. The name meant Newbridge, and there was indeed a great new bridge across the river, churning with carriages and rickshaws and overfilled oxen carts, everyone going in whichever direction they felt like. As Thaniel came out from under the high brick arches of the station, a herd of students came the other way. One of them was wearing a fez.

It wasn't until he was in that ordinary, chattering, anonymous crowd that Thaniel realised just how much of a relief it was not to feel like he was being watched. A weird pressure on the back of his neck had lifted since he'd left Yoruji. He rubbed at the bones there. No wonder people thought the house was haunted.

From Shimbashi to the legation was a short ride in a cab. It was in a borough to the west, Kojimachi. It was all big open spaces, parks, and brick buildings. But quite close, sometimes in clear view down the broad and clock-towered streets, there was another Tokyo altogether – a leaning, rambling, tangled clutter that looked much older and much less polished.

'This is the nice part of town,' the cabbie said, wrinkling his nose at the crowd of curving roofs away down the hill while Thaniel paid. He had stopped at the top of the grand sweep of the legation's gravel drive, outside the front doors. 'No need to look that way, hey?' He sounded a lot like a Whitehall chauffeur might have if a foreign envoy had found Anglo-Saxons still camped in Clerkenwell.

Thaniel didn't say that the cluttered places looked much more fun. He thanked the man and turned towards the legation. He was almost at the steps when someone said, a bit half-heartedly,

'Foreigners go home!'

There were two men holding a banner that drooped in the middle. They were dressed in the traditional way he'd expected Kuroda to, purposefully rough and scruffy, kimono sleeves tied up despite the cold. They must have been freezing.

'Morning,' he said, interested. 'What are you protesting?'

'Foreigners,' one snapped. 'You shouldn't be here.' He even came up and gave Thaniel a push.

It was like being shoved by a quail. He had to bat the man's small fist aside with his knuckles. 'Steady on. Foreigners generally?' he added, halfway up the steps.

'Foreign oppression!'

'All right. I'll see you both later.'

'See you,' the man's less angry friend said, gloomily.

'Fukuoka!'

'Sorry.'

Inside were chandeliers and deep silk rugs. At a glance it might have been somewhere in London. A pair of palms leaned over the main doors and the walls were full of oil paintings, the gilt frames shined up and glittering. The nearest door led to what looked like an office, full of men too young to be diplomats but who almost certainly were. He tapped his knuckle on it.

'I'm looking for the Secretary,' he said. 'Is he in?'

'And who might you be?' someone said in a pompous voice.

'I'm the new translator from London.'

The young man straightened, flustered, then got up. 'Yes, of course – we didn't expect you until after New Year – very

129

keen, aren't you? Good train, I suppose? You've come from Yokohama, did your wire say? Nice down there.'

Thaniel inclined his head. 'Steepleton,' he said, to give the boy a chance to get onto a normal conversational track.

'Pringle, Pringle,' he said, holding out his hand from much too far away. 'Hajimemashite and so forth.'

Thaniel smiled and waited until he was near enough to take it comfortably. 'Yeah, yoroshiku onegai. The Secretary?'

'Yes, sir, of course, I'll show you. He's just through here,' he said, walking Thaniel to the door even though it was in obvious view. Then he retreated back to the office. The second he was inside, just out of sight, he let all his breath out in a rush. 'God, I thought he was someone's servant!'

'You absolute snotweasel, he can hear you,' someone else laughed.

Thaniel pretended not to have heard and tapped on the Secretary's door, then opened it when another cultured voice told him to come in.

The man behind the desk didn't stand up. He was Thaniel's age, but blond and handsome.

'You're Steepleton, are you? Didn't I just see you get in a fistfight by the front door?'

'Well,' said Thaniel. 'A quarter of one.'

'What a good start.'

Thaniel waited. Things seemed to be going this way increasingly in the last couple of years when he met someone new at work. At first he'd thought it was his accent and that he didn't sound educated enough, but eventually he'd realised it was just because, while he hadn't really been paying attention, and through some alchemy to do with eating properly and Fanshaw chasing him down to the boxing club, he'd become a big man. Nobody wanted to feel loomed over by an immediate subordinate. It was annoying, he could see that, but he wasn't going to apologise for having not been punched in the face by a nationalist.

'I'm Tom Vaulker,' the Secretary said at last. 'Well, have a seat. I must say, it does seem hysterical for Francis Fanshaw to send someone just to sort out a ghost problem.'

Thaniel sat. He knew from dispatches that Vaulker was very paper-presentable, except that he hated Japan. He was doing his obligatory nine months before a nicer posting in Berlin. If someone was bullying the staff, he was a good candidate.

'It's more that we were worried that it isn't a ghost problem,' Thaniel said.

Vaulker ignored him. 'Immaculate timing though. We've just had another man give his notice. Apparently saw the ghost of his late wife, again. In the kitchen, as usual. Very distressed. Apparently she went missing a while ago in ... somewhere called ...' He checked a form. Thaniel wondered if he knew he'd said *apparently* twice. 'Ow-kee-ga ...?

'Aokigahara,' Thaniel offered. The sun was pouring in and he could see through the paper.

'I won't try,' Vaulker decided. 'Anyway, it's near Mount Fuji. Now, he's not wholly making sense, but I think we can excuse him that, given his wife is missing.' He had bright blue eyes and they ticked unevenly over Thaniel to make sure he wasn't going to make fun of the idea of shock. 'But he seems to think her spirit is unquiet. They never found the body, apparently—'

Thaniel decided to kick the table leg every time another *apparently* came along.

'—so she's unburied – if she didn't just do a bunk – and I think he's angling for us to make the police investigate properly.' He looked up again. 'I wonder if you can wangle that? I can't find a damn soul among the police who speaks English.'

'I don't think the police will investigate a disappearance in Aokigahara, sir,' Thaniel said carefully.

'Why not?'

'It's the suicide forest. People go there to hang themselves.'

Vaulker dropped his hands onto the edge of the desk, which made his cufflinks clink. 'What a charming country this is.'

Thaniel smiled. He had never known, before he worked for the Foreign Office, that there was a hierarchy of countries according to Whitehall. If you did the standard diplomatic circuit, it usually began somewhere like Khartoum, and up a rung would be Peking, somewhere that was more war-nibbled than war-ravaged, but still wasn't good enough to have a proper embassy instead of a legation. It was Germany and America everyone wanted, or Paris, where you could have glamorous tiffs with the other side about secret military plans. It looked, on the surface, like it was about acceptable weather and significant international clout, but Japan had English weather and fabulous amounts of money, and it was still lower down the whole thing than Khartoum.

His theory was that it was about how much translation you had to do before you could talk about anything interesting. The Sudan was horrible but people there spoke English.

'I don't know, it seems sensible to me,' Thaniel said. 'Polite really, not to do it on a railway.'

'Polite ...' Vaulker touched his own temple and seemed to give up. 'Look, he's only spoken to Pringle, who's probably poked himself in the eye with the wrong end of the stick. See what you make of it. Fellow's name is Nakano, I think he's still in the kitchens. His mother's the head cook. You can catch him if you go now. Ridiculous as it all is and past the point of caring as I am.'

Thaniel nodded once.

Vaulker seemed to notice the absence of any sympathy. He shifted uncomfortably. 'While you're here – how do you say the forest name again?'

'Aokigahara. "Aoi" means blue, "ki" is tree, "hara" is plain.'

'Blue?' Vaulker sounded almost interested. 'Is it?'

'No. There wasn't a separate word for green until after they'd named everything,' Thaniel said, feeling sorry for him.

Vaulker slouched again. 'Have you brought all your things? Are you staying with us from now on? I wasn't expecting you until after New Year; your contract doesn't start until the third of January.'

'No, I'm staying in Yokohama. I just thought I'd come in and introduce myself.'

'Yes, very thorough. Talk to Nakano, would you. Apparently he's leaving in half an hour – what was that? What just banged the table?'

'I didn't see, sir,' Thaniel said, and then went to find his own way to the kitchen.

Perhaps because there had been one going spare, and certainly not because it especially fitted the place, the legation had a bell tower. The kitchen was directly below, tucked up and then down two tiny, unnecessary sets of steps. Thaniel only found it because he followed the smell of coffee through the dining room. The dining room couldn't have been more grand. It had huge floor-to-ceiling windows, beautiful draped curtains, and long tables; designed, he suspected, to look like the Oxford and Cambridge colleges the diplomats were coming straight from. The kitchen was low-ceilinged and the windows were long slits high in the walls. They weren't open, so the room was full of steam.

There were four people inside and none of them were working. An old lady was trying to calm down a weeping man, and two girls were staying quiet and awkward, pouring more tea for everyone. They all looked round when Thaniel tapped on the door.

'Are you lost?' the old lady said. She had a gravel voice and a cigarette in her hand.

'No, ma'am, I'm the new translator. My name's Steepleton. I heard that Mr Nakano was upset and I wanted to see what was going on.'

She tipped back speculatively. 'Well, aren't you unusually good-mannered.'

'I think I'm normally mannered, but Mr Vaulker seems like a ...' You couldn't really say 'unreserved cock' in Japanese. It didn't translate. 'Difficult person. May I sit down?'

'Suppose you do,' she said, and nodded to one of the several spare seats. They were all high stools. The table was covered in flour.

'So what's going on?' Thaniel asked Nakano, who had dragged his sleeve over his eyes.

'I saw my wife over there.'

'She went to Aokigahara?'

'Yeah.' He was staring at the edge of the table. 'I don't know why.'

'Well, you did hit her a lot,' the old lady said, unmoved.

'Mum,' one of the girls whispered.

'Eh,' she said, and breathed out a lungful of smoke. 'He should feel lucky she didn't hang *him* from a tree. Classy woman.'

'Mum!' the girl said hopelessly.

More smoke. Thaniel had to make a tectonic effort not to laugh. Nakano had shrunk with shame.

'And it's not the first time you've seen things in here?'

'Where d'you think everyone is?' the old lady said, motioning at all the empty stools with her cigarette, which looped a nearly perfect smoke ring. 'Started November. We've lost one a fortnight since. You can't expect people to put up with that kind of thing.'

'What did they see?'

'Ghosts!' Nakano snapped.

'Mm,' said Thaniel, careful not to show that he had already sided with the old lady and the dead wife. 'Whose ghosts?'

'Just – I don't know, do I?'

'Drink your tea,' the old lady said at Nakano. She dipped her cigarette towards Thaniel. 'I'm Marie Nakano. Ginger snap's mother.' She nodded at her son, who went an angry red. 'We don't know whose ghosts they are. Ririka was the first one we recognised. She was standing right where you're sitting, staring at nothing like she'd got all the world on her shoulders. The others, no idea. People, ordinary people. None of them did anything frightening, but the young people, well.' She blew smoke again.

'What were you doing when you saw her?'

She shrugged. 'Making bread.'

The two girls exchanged a glance.

'What was that for?' Thaniel asked them.

The old lady sighed. 'They think the spirits disapprove of this place. Foreigners on their ancestral ground and so forth. That is, naturally, a load of shit,' she added, more at them than him, and blackly. 'We've had foreigners in and out since I was your age and only ghosts since November.'

'Can we call an exorcist?' he asked.

They all looked surprised.

'Expensive,' said the old lady.

'If you know someone who can do it, I'll put it under cleaning. The legation can cover it.'

There was a long quiet.

'Unless there's ... something else?'

More quiet. The girls looked uncomfortable.

Vaulker banged on the door. 'Really, this is unacceptable. It's half-past nine and not even the first sign of breakfast. There are fourteen hungry people here. Mrs Nakano, even toast would be greatly appreciated, if you wouldn't mind?'

'I never know what he's saying,' the old lady said, devastatingly unworried. 'But I suppose we'd better get going. Can you tell him it would be easier to cook rice? He always wants bread.'

Thaniel relayed it.

Vaulker only looked annoyed. 'No. Pardon me if I don't want to go entirely native. Do you have flour? Water? Yes? Marvellous.'

The girls must have understood, because they got up at once and picked up flour packets. Both of them hesitated before they sprayed a handful each over the worktop.

'Sorry about your wife,' Thaniel said to Nakano, and then bowed to the old lady. Vaulker, he noticed, rolled his eyes. 'Thank you, ma'am.'

'Yes, yes, you can come back,' she said, mostly into her cigarette. 'Good manners make up wonderfully for being ugly, don't they, girls?'

'Mum!'

Thaniel laughed.

Vaulker tapped his fingertips on the door to make him hurry up.

Thaniel pulled the door to behind him and backed Vaulker down the little stairs more forcefully than he needed to.

'They need a raise,' he said.

'A raise, why?'

'Because you're not the easiest person to get on with, and I think they're talking about ghosts as a polite excuse to get out of here and work at one of the other legations. I think someone saw something once and the rest latched onto it. I'm bringing in an exorcist, so they won't be able to use that particular excuse anymore, but they'll probably find another one if you don't give them a reason to stay.'

'How dare you!'

'See? You're prickly,' said Thaniel.

'You're insubordinate!'

'I'm doing my job,' Thaniel said.

Vaulker sighed. 'How much is an exorcist going to cost?'

'I don't know, but if it solves the problem for a bit then it's worth it.'

'Or I could sack them all,' Vaulker said flatly.

'It's New Year. You wouldn't be able to hire anyone else.'

'A raise and an exorcist, that's your official recommendation, is it?'

'Yes, that's what I'm wiring to Whitehall now. Have you got a telegraph I can use?'

137

'Of course, but no telegraphist, because he left after he said he saw a samurai ghost ride through the front lawn. You'll have to go to the post office.' He might as well have said, 'check'.

'No, it's all right, I was a telegraphist for years,' Thaniel said, having fun now.

Vaulker must nearly have been too, because he snorted rather than lose his temper. 'Of course you were.'

SIXTEEN

Thaniel got back to Yokohama towards three, and by then the idea of collapsing in his room and talking to no one but the piano had regained its shine. Although it hadn't been far, he was exhausted. The ordinary effort of getting to the right platform and the right train was four times magnified when it was all in another language on a shaky tannoy. The stations were laid out differently too. If you went along one local platform for long enough, you ended up at another one that was on its way to Shinjuku, a couple of miles away, and on the same platform five minutes later – to the second – there was a sleeper train going in the opposite direction. In the end he'd had to guess and hope he wasn't going to Osaka.

———

At Yoruji, he sat at the piano and worked properly for the first time in months. He drew the music where he couldn't be bothered to write out each note and it came out in chiaroscuro, like one of those old candlelight paintings. Lately he'd started to really notice that the more a piece of music looked like a painting or sculpture, the better it was. Symphonies had contours and angles, and where something sounded wrong, it was always because a movement or a phrase was sticking out in a funny way and you had to poke it back into shape. It was very refreshing to be able to see the shape. He hadn't, not for months.

The weather had turned freezing, though, so he had to stop before long to hide under the kotatsu.

Kotatsu were the best thing anyone had invented on either side of the Pacific. Under the table was a pit in the floor, lined with velvet, and in its base was a grille. Below the grille was a fire in a tiny stove. The heat built up under the table, trapped by its thick cloth. You could sit with your heels resting on the grille without being burned, which meant that it was more than possible to keep warm even with the sliding doors wide open. The only downside was that if you sat completely under the tablecloth, like a cat or a child might, you would die of carbon monoxide poisoning, but when Thaniel had asked about that, Mori's stance was that if children never faced any household hazards, they would only grow up useless and frightened of scissors.

Mori came around the sliding door. He was looking for something, and after a moment it was clear he hadn't noticed there was anyone else in the room. Thaniel smiled. He was naturally unobtrusive, but he'd never been invisible. He waited to see how long it would last. He wasn't hidden behind anything.

Mori climbed the ladder against the high bookcase. He leaned to make it roll and caught the edge of the next shelf along, and took down a book that looked like it might be ghost stories – the cover was black and the figure on the cover was chalky and strange – which Six liked when she wasn't reading the generator manual. Once he had it, he stayed on the ladder without holding on, the book propped against a rung while he leafed through.

'Tea?' said Thaniel, because it had passed fun and become spying.

Mori dropped the book. His hands and shoulders flickered upward as if they'd been at one of those technology fairs and Thaniel had applied an electrode to the top of his spine.

'Christ, you look like you've seen a ghost,' Thaniel said.

Mori smiled. He looked shaken. 'You know when you think you've left a cup of tea on the desk, you can walk straight past it even if it's doing a jig on the kitchen table?'

'Where did you think you'd left me?'

Mori's expression opened helplessly. Thaniel saw his mechanisms move as he tried to think of a reasonable lie.

'I was in Tokyo until just now,' Thaniel put in, puzzled. 'At the legation.'

'Right,' Mori said gratefully. 'How was it?'

'Haunted. I think the staff are just being polite about finding an excuse to work at the Chinese legation because the British Secretary's an idiot, but we've called an exorcist. People are – really superstitious here, aren't they? I've heard three ghost stories already and two were from this house.'

'Mm,' said Mori, looking like he was trying to work up the will to say something else. He was watching Thaniel hard, studying him inch by inch. 'It's a strange house.'

'Am I growing new bits I shouldn't be?' Thaniel asked.

'What? No – no.' Mori was chronologically out, because he added, 'Yes please,' before Thaniel could ask again if he wanted some tea.

Thaniel hesitated, not sure what was going on. 'I'd go down for tea with everyone else but I'm not going anywhere else today. If I stand up again in the next hour I'll die on Suzuki's nightingale floor and you'll not hear the end of it.'

'Wouldn't bother him. He'll have it cleaned pretty recently.' Mori knelt down across from him. He sounded all right, but he didn't make mistakes like that unless his mind was elsewhere. Recent and soon looked the same to him, and Thaniel suspected he had to concentrate to get the right one. 'How is it?' he asked, motioning to Thaniel's lungs with his eyelashes.

'Much better here,' Thaniel said honestly. 'Maybe it's the sea.'

Mori put his head a tiny fraction forward, just one inclination of one vertebra in his neck. 'I'm sorry about last night, by the way. It was – like just now; you were unexpected.'

'Unexpected? You looked like I'd crawled out of the grave-yard still in a shroud,' Thaniel began, and then stopped, because Mori had fallen so still that he might have been turning to glass.

He understood what was happening in stages. The confusion cracked, the realisation oozed out, and then egg-yolked down his spine.

'You mean you can remember me being dead, don't you?' He couldn't believe he hadn't understood before. 'It's a pretty heavy possibility at the moment, so … you've got it in mind that I'll not be here soon – *recently*. Seeing me walking about is like seeing a ghost, isn't it?'

'Of course it's not,' Mori said, more like himself again. 'I'm sorry. I'm full of fog, it's the time difference.'

It wasn't enough to smooth down the memory of the haunted look he'd had before.

'You should go and talk to the others,' Thaniel said. He'd said it smiling, but even as he did, it felt heavy. Though he'd had a fortnight to get used to the idea, it was the first time he'd had to be graceful about perhaps dying. He'd been determined that if the worst happened, he *would* be graceful and there wouldn't be any hysterics or dramatic regrets aired endlessly to the profound boredom of everyone else. But he hadn't realised that grace was not a thing you performed, but a weight you carried. 'Anyone who's going to live more than fifteen minutes and who won't seem like the waking dead in the middle of the night.'

'No. I was half asleep, I'm not—'

'Shut up,' Thaniel said. He was glad his voice was still coming out steady. 'You've got a ghost following you about, don't pretend you haven't. I'll try and find a cheerful hat or something; there's no reason I can't be a jaunty ghost.' He hesitated. 'Listen. Dr Haverly said I'd probably be all right here. Is that not true?'

'You're going to be fine. I promise. Like I say, I'm just a bit scattered.'

Thaniel tried to let it go, but then lost the battle. 'Can you stop lying for a minute? I don't speak samurai. I can't tell if you're hating every second of my being here because it's driving you mad with horrible nightmares but you're just being polite, or if you really don't mind. Can you tell me straight? If you'd rather I go and stay at the legation, I'll go. That's fine. It's a nice place.'

Mori looked up with shatter lines around his eyes. 'Thaniel. I'm so at the mercy of this stupid thing my brain does. It's a kind of sickness more than anything else. Now this minute, yes, you're right, I can remember – I can remember your dying. It is odd to turn around and find you here after all, it is … like seeing a ghost.'

Thaniel had worked it out before like a crossword puzzle and it hadn't sunk it truly, but hearing Mori confirm it aloud felt like some terrible unseen physician had closed a steel clamp around his lungs.

Mori must have seen his expression change, because he was shaking his head. 'I'm only remembering the worst now because the things that will help you haven't happened yet. But they will happen. I'll be back to normal when they do.'

'Right.'

Mori sighed. 'I know it's terrible to have to put up with that from me. If you can bear it, though, I'd rather you were here. I understand if you can't. Not everyone wants to – to see himself reflected a ghost in someone else's eyes.' He looked away outside as he finished, as if he'd become suddenly aware that the daylight really was making good mirrors of his eyes.

Thaniel poured them both some more tea for something to do with his hands. He wanted urgently to lean across the table and take Mori's. 'I can cope. And you bloody knew I'd say that, so why all the palaver?'

'Pride,' Mori said ruefully. 'I think there was a very small unlikely future where I pretended well enough for you not to notice.'

'No there wasn't. There might have been one where I pretended not to notice you pretending.'

Mori laughed. 'Right. Yes.'

His eyes slipped over Thaniel's shoulder then, and then lifted to the height of a standing person. It was so marked that Thaniel twisted round, expecting to see Suzuki lurking, but there was nobody. When he glanced back at Mori

144

again, puzzled, Mori only shook his head and shrugged a fraction.

'Anyway,' said Thaniel, and cast around for a reason to get himself out of the house for a little while, and give Mori a break from his haunting, 'I should send a wire to the legation. Let them know where to reach me.' It was a lie. Vaulker didn't care where he was. 'Is there a post office?'

Mori closed both fists against his knees, but his collarbones dropped as he let some of the pretence go, relieved even in defeat. 'Just down the road, opposite the man with the cat on the lead. I've got a parcel, if you'd post it?'

'No trouble,' Thaniel said, glad for a real reason to go. He set the teapot down again, carefully, because as though gravity had shrugged, the effort it took to lift was wrong. When he opened his hand, his fingers felt nerveless. He clenched it in his lap under the table, but it still shook. 'Where's it going?'

'Aokigahara.' Mori went to fetch it. It was marked 'delicate' in insistent letters. 'They're cocoons. Moths.'

'Moths? The ones from the greenhouse?' Thaniel asked.

'You saw? There's a ranger up there who collects them.'

'Why is it you, providing moths?'

'We've been breeding them here. They're rare, they come out in February.' He let his fingertips rest on the edge of the box even after he had let go. He closed up like a fan when he saw that Thaniel had noticed. After a long, strange pause with vaults that echoed with the things Mori wasn't saying, he finally took a breath.

'Don't let anyone stop you sending that off. Kuroda's men are a bit twitchy about his security.'

'I won't.'

'Sorry,' Mori said obscurely.

'Mori, even if one of them rugby tackles me, there are fairy princesses who would think this lot were a bit delicate-looking.'

He'd hoped Mori would laugh, but he only got an absent nod. 'No, you're right.'

Thaniel went to the post office, feeling like a poltergeist.

SEVENTEEN

Shintomi Theatre, Tokyo, 1878
(ten years ago)

Takiko was ready for the Duke of Choshu when he came. Mori had sent her a warning telegram an hour before.

It gave her time to change. She put on a Western dress cut from vivid kimono silk, all brocaded with blossom patterns. Kimono were too easy to bow in. It was very British, forbidding yourself over-servility and enforcing that resolution with whalebone, and she had a feeling that it would be a good idea to remind the Duke that she was at least half foreign, with one foot outside the circle of his influence.

The actors went into an interested flutter when she said he was coming. They were rehearsing a kabuki version of *Swan Lake*, so the stage was a beautiful chaos of white feathers and the constant genteel fight between their own dancing master and the Russian ballerina they'd brought in to give the performance a Western flair. It all looked satisfyingly modern, and not like the sort of place to be perturbed by a fuming patriarch.

The Duke turned out not to be a fuming patriarch at all.

The man who sat down opposite her at her table in the empty bar was papery. He looked like a book that had been left in the sun for too long. He was excellently dressed in a Western morning suit, and he wore spectacles whose lenses carried a slight gold tint. They must have been for some kind of vision problem, but they made him look like his constitution was so refined that he couldn't bear to see the world without a golden veneer.

'Miss Pepperharrow,' he said, without introducing himself. He didn't seem surprised that she'd obviously known he was coming. 'I believe you are soon to marry into my house.'

'I am,' she agreed. 'Tea?'

His eyes ticked over her. She got ready to shake his hand English-style if he started out in too offensive a way. He looked like he might combust if a stranger touched him.

'This theatre is yours, I believe?'

She poured the tea. 'It is.'

He looked troubled. 'You don't seem like a stupid person. Do you understand what Keita is? I don't mean who, not family, I mean what.'

Takiko sat back, because it was so far from the attack she'd expected that it took her a minute to put down the shield and relax. 'Yes,' she said slowly. 'I've noticed. He always knows when I should bring an umbrella to go out, if that's what you mean. He knew when you were coming today.'

The Duke took off his spectacles and put them back on again, and slowly, with a lot less glee than she'd have thought, she realised that he was flustered. 'Miss Pepperharrow, the girl I wanted him to marry is extremely stupid, and incapable of anything but looking nice at parties. Did you not imagine, when you swooped in, that I was trying to prevent him from getting to anyone else?'

'Sorry?'

He looked down at the tea and poured himself three drops more, though his cup was already full. 'I knew his mother.

Keitsune Mori.' His eyes came up again. 'He gets it from her, you see. Heaven knows how much of modern history she shaped while she was pretending to be occupied at that loom of hers. It was a joke, you see. The loom. Weaving fates.' He snorted at himself, but only as if he thought he ought to find it funny, not as if he really did. 'But her great trick was that she would let you see just what she was, and you would want to do as she asked all the same.'

Takiko hesitated. 'I see,' she said, untruthfully.

The Duke put both hands on the edge of the table, just his fingertips, but he was such a restrained person that it made her lean back. 'Do you imagine for a minute that she could do that, and care a damn about the individual threads? No. Eventually, you would look up one morning, and realise that even while you were quite in love with her, and that you would sacrifice anything, you were just one of her threads, one that she herself had chosen and plied and dyed, and to which she had all the emotional attachment of a bobbin.'

'Well, I'm not in love with your kinsman, your Grace. This marriage is a business contract between friends,' Takiko said quietly. Even as she said it, she knew she wasn't quite telling the truth. 'I need somewhere presentable to live to host my more elevated patrons, and he wants to share the burden of his estate, which I believe he finds too large for one person.'

'Yes, one enters into contracts with husbands and lawyers, but other things too,' Choshu said, just as quietly. 'Things so old we cannot even call them good or evil, and which we do not ever expect to find introducing themselves in a good jacket at a matinee performance.'

She shook her head.

'Keitsune made him quite deliberately, you know,' Choshu said. He looked uncomfortably aware that the bar didn't suit what he was saying either, or the velvet upholstry. He glanced up at the sky-light like he was wishing for a thunderstorm. 'No one knows who the father was, but Keitsune disappeared for a week. One can only assume she was looking for the right ingredients. She killed herself on the day he was born.' He poured himself more tea again, even though the cup was in danger of spilling now. 'She was honourable about it; she said she was quite aware she had shamed her husband and she was paying with her life. Made us all vow to keep the child in the family.' He half laughed. 'I believe even that was a calculation. I think we would have found ways to chafe against that plea if she had lived.'

'That doesn't prove he's anything bad—'

'Miss Pepperharrow. Try to think past how wanted he makes you feel, and how necessary. Think instead how it is that he came to you.' He looked at her hard. 'You were on the point of despair. You would have crumbled, in some way or another, if he hadn't come into your life at the precise instant that he did.'

She bent her neck slowly. That was right, at least. 'I suppose.'

'And now, you owe him your soul.' The Duke sighed and drank some tea. He did it elegantly, she noticed; he wasn't as awkward as he seemed. In ordinary life, not trying to explain Keita Mori to an actress, he was probably a graceful man. 'Now tell me, what manner of creature is it that waits for a person's darkest moment, and then appears from the shadows, and says, I will save you; come with me?'

She stayed quiet. None of it seemed as stupid as it had a minute ago.

'You won't be the only one, you know. That poor fool Kuroda follows him around like a puppy; I guarantee Keita has plans for him and his certain brand of viciousness.' He paused, but he plainly hadn't finished. 'There are records, you know, of others. Like him. I looked into it, once I understood what Keitsune was doing. Folktales mainly, but the resemblance is uncanny. I was puzzled for years why there's nothing more obviously like him in anyone's mythology, and then of course I realised that if you are a thing that knows all the futures in the world, it's quite within your capability to ensure there's no record of you but murmurs.'

There was always some bored old bachelor in the audience who came up to Takiko or one of the actors after the show and talked earnestly about how the story was all real, and there really had been this or that princess, and she really had been seen floating through foxfire falling from the sky, and do you know, I'm related to her? She was pretty sure that there were stages of bored bachelorhood. First you played cards with yourself, then you cut your own ear off, and then you became a folklorist.

But the Duke didn't sound like those people. They never looked so resigned, or so aware that what they were saying sounded silly.

'You've heard the stories,' Choshu sighed. 'You remember the Winter King, and the two lovers?'

'No. I don't know many Japanese stories, my father was English.' She had a nasty dropping feeling. She hated talking about Christopher Pepperharrow. She didn't have many memories of him now and handing them out to strangers, like they weren't precious, felt horrible.

'Well, I'll tell it to you.'

It was an ordinary sort of story. There were two lovers who weren't meant to be in love and, one day, they ran away together through the forest. They didn't have any money, but they were cheerful. They hadn't gone far, though, before they saw lights behind them, and heard the voices of their fathers shouting. They were in real despair about what to do when a gentleman in white furs stepped out of the woods. He told them to turn back, but it was all right; he was the winter, and in three days, he would cast the deepest cold over the land for a generation. If they left on that night, the coldest and hardest for decades, nobody would follow them. So they agreed, and went back, apologised to their fathers, and tried again in three days. They were delighted to find that the Winter King was right; nobody followed. Once again they met him on the road, and he walked with them for a little while, and promised that he could arrange for them to be together always. They walked on, through the frost and the new snow, and at last, they came to a deep lake. Winter pointed and said, 'There is your eternity'. They killed themselves and their souls stayed together always.

'But that's just a story about winter,' Takiko protested. 'You know. Don't go out in winter. It's like Red Riding Hood. Don't trust strange men on the road, because they're wolves.'

'This story was real, in fact,' the Duke sighed. 'The couple in question died in sixteen seventy-two. Their deaths achieved a lasting peace between their houses, one of which happened to be the Shogun's family. It probably stopped a civil war.' He was studying her now, with no hope at all of convincing her.

'It happened at Hagi Castle. The familial seat of House Mori. A son of theirs was known very well locally to be a wonderful hunter. He had a knack for catching silver foxes. A gentleman in white fur; makes one wonder, doesn't it.'

Takiko shook her head. 'People spin magic out of real stories, it's what they do. It's what we do here. What are you saying?'

'That it is in Keita's nature to take desperate people, and lead them to a useful death. A death is a powerful agent of change, and whatever he is, he is in this world to change it. Are you absolutely certain he won't do that to you?'

She had to laugh. It was relief as much as humour. Just for a minute, she'd been standing on the edge of a chasm she had never known was there before, full of undefined things shifting in the deep – the way down into a place where there was a nasty kind of magic. 'Look, one story about a silly couple dying in winter doesn't persuade me that Keita is plotting my sudden demise.'

'He had five brothers, you know. They all died in battle. Supporting the Emperor. Their deaths were a great rallying cry, I tell you.'

'I know one of them shot him once, with an arrow.' She wondered suddenly just how much of Mori's never-spoken-of childhood had been coloured by people like the Duke, who thought he was something unspeakable. He had scars on his hands from sword-flats.

The Duke sighed. 'Just tell me – have you seen owls yet? Following you perhaps?'

'What? Owls?'

'They're lucky birds. He makes luck. They seem to know that.' He looked away at the bar and the lady there turning over the roasting chestnuts. He kept his voice arid and librarial. 'If you find that an owl takes an interest in you, then Keita will not be far behind. I suggest, madam, that at that moment, you walk firmly in the opposite direction.'

'Owls,' she said again, less flatly than she'd meant to. There were still talon marks on her old sewing machine.

Something came down over Choshu's expression. Pride; he couldn't keep going anymore in a subject that made him seem foolish. 'Yes, well,' he said. 'I'm sure you're perfectly capable of dealing with him. Good afternoon, Miss Pepperharrow.'

He left measuredly, and not at all with the awkward spring of the sort of person who usually said things like he had. Takiko sat back, not quite able to believe she'd just had such a mad conversation. It made her nervous; not about Mori, but the family. If they were all like that, then no wonder Mori wanted a normal person in his house.

———

She went round to Yoruji the next day, meaning to tell Mori all about the Duke and to have a good laugh about everything. On the way down, though, she realised that it would be downright cruel to remind him that his only living relative thought he was a witch. So she only said that the Duke seemed like a strange egg and that he'd said something funny about owls.

That did make Mori laugh. 'I'll show you.'

Yoruji had an aviary. She'd never seen it before, but it was big and spacious, full of interesting branches and hollows – and full of owls. There was no door; the whole front wall was open. But the owls all seemed to like it inside, and when they noticed Takiko and Mori, some of them glided across and hooted conversationally.

'We end up with dozens of them here, they seem to like us. They're all tame, look,' he added as one settled straight onto Takiko's wrist and consented to have its chest stroked. It was surprisingly heavy. It narrowed its eyes in an approving way when she rubbed her finger under its chin.

'I didn't know owls could be this tame,' she said, enchanted. The owl told her something in Owl. Her whole heart squeezed. They didn't seem like normal birds. There was something else in them.

'I think they fly all over, but they always come back here,' Mori said, half to her and half to an incredible eagle owl that had just soared across. It landed on the branch next to him, and then stepped onto his arm, looking carefully at its own talons as if it was trying to make sure they didn't dig into him too much.

That first impression of him she'd had at the theatre came back in force; that sense that he didn't belong now, but in some other place a thousand years ago. Holding the owl, he seemed medieval, and if Choshu had told her then that Mori had wandered the world since people had first been afraid of the woods, she would nearly have believed it. But it didn't feel like an ominous impression. The owl was stealing his watch.

'Do you tell them to visit people?' she asked. 'I think this one came to see me once.'

'No,' he said. 'But sometimes they seem to know where I'm going.' He inclined his head and the owl blinked slowly. 'Everyone says they know things, don't they?'

She grinned. There was a tug somewhere under her ribs, towards him and Yoruji. It felt slight but huge, and full of promise; like an anchor dropping at a home port after years at sea.

'Hey,' she said. 'What do you want for a wedding present? What do clairvoyants want?'

He looked around and went still. 'I'd prefer a favour to a present.'

'Favour?'

'In a while, I might … need your help with something. Maybe dangerous. I don't know exactly when yet, but if you'd consider helping me then, I'll very happily take that for a present.' He said it carefully, full of humility, as though the Duke was right there beside him hissing about witches and winter kings, and treating people like threads on a loom.

'Joy,' she said abruptly. That was what his name meant, in English. She'd started calling him that when he started calling her Pepper. 'We're not – talking about children, are we?'

'No.' He looked drawn, and his focus went far off. 'I'm in no hurry there.'

'Sorry,' she said, aware that she'd ruined what should have been a nice evening. 'It's just – an abrupt marriage feels like being hurried into cab with no idea where you're going. It's not good. Even if you – you know. If you like the person who's doing the hurrying.'

'Well,' he said, carefully, 'I'm going to England in a few years. And then I won't be back until … about eighteen ninety, I think.' He smiled a little. 'And then perhaps we'll be used to each other enough to think about it. I don't like being hurried either.'

'How can you ever be hurried?' Takiko said, a bit too high, because she wanted to cover over the sad flare of dismay in her stomach. Eighteen ninety; it was ten years away. 'You always know what's coming.'

'Yes. It's like standing on a conveyor-belt and watching the meat grinder get closer, and knowing already what life is like when you think it's normal to have no arms.'

She hesitated. 'Anything you need help with, in England? To ... redirect the conveyor-belt?'

'No.'

'So I'm here to fight the Duke off for you and then sit on a bench until eighteen ninety or whenever you decide you've got a use for me?' she said, puzzled. 'I'm sure there's more I can do than that.'

'No.' He looked worried. 'Pepper ... you needn't do anything for me. I think I know what the Duke said to you today, and he's right.'

'Mori – I do have to. If you hadn't come to sit with me in the theatre that day, Ayame would have swept me back onto the stage or boxed my ears until I did. I owe you everything. That debt is just going to sit on me forever unless I do something for you. You know that too.' She sighed. 'Don't – tell me it's frivolous or that saving me doesn't count just because you didn't do it on a battlefield.'

'I wasn't going to,' he said quietly.

'Right then. I have a debt, a genuine debt. Can't you let me pay it?'

He let his breath out slowly. 'Now this instant, it isn't possible to turn the world by much. I ... spend most of my time finding new half-formed Mozarts and Newtons and pushing

157

them along in the right direction, because given enough time, they bring about change in a way revolutions and guillotines can't. No one can help me with that. It's finicky. But in eleven years, there will be a window when we can do a lot of good all at once, without making reactionary factions of nationalists or tyrants. I will do it, and I'll need your help. But in those intervening years, you will see things that will make you wonder whether you should be helping me at all. You might very well come to the conclusion that I'm wrong entirely, and that your energy would be better directed elsewhere.'

She half laughed, because there were honest-to-God goosebumps prickling down her forearms. 'My very own prophecy.'

'Yes, we can frame it,' he said, with a muted sparkle that didn't have any humour in it at all. 'Pepper, I need you to understand. When I helped at the theatre, I knew it would change everything for you, I knew you'd feel a debt. What I want to do in eleven years will be dangerous. I can't pay someone to help me; a stranger won't be any good, it has to be someone who knows me and knows what to look for. But I can't ask anyone who actually likes me, either, because they would stop me doing it. What I need is someone who feels indebted to me but doesn't wholly like me. Which you won't, by the time it all comes around.' He lifted both hands a little toward her. 'So I sat down next to you.'

She snorted. 'I knew you'd have a reason beyond my superlative feminine charms. But that's not the point. The point is that I can't be unique. There must be other people you can annoy and manipulate, right?'

He nodded, unhappy and brittle at the edges. 'Dozens. So if you don't want—'

'Shut up. You didn't choose any of them; you chose me. I don't care if you decided on me because I've got a funny nose or you liked the candied nuts they were selling in the foyer that day: you still changed everything for me, and I owe it to you. Do you understand?'

'Yes,' he said.

'And a small service is still a service,' she finished quietly. 'So we will be getting married, I will see the Duke off for you, and I will be owing you that favour.' She hadn't felt awkwardness like she did around him since she'd been about sixteen. It was a sad little crush. But there was good, in doing something for someone so extraordinary. Honour. It was one of those words you heard men chuck around all the time and, until lately, she'd never thought it might be for her as well. It felt so good that all at once, even though she'd always thought they were fools before, she understood why soldiers would go into battle for a suicidal commander.

The Duke's voice was still there in the back of her mind, whispering about the loom and its bright threads: *Her great trick was that she would let you see just what she was, and you would want to do as she asked all the same.*

'Pepper, I don't want a servant,' Mori said softly. For the first time since she'd met him, he came right up to her. For a long second, he looked down at her like nobody had, like she was something precious. He touched his forehead to hers. 'I want someone to come back to.'

EIGHTEEN

Yokohama, 19th December 1888

The streets beyond Yoruji were exactly the tangled, cluttered kind that had looked so interesting in Tokyo. It was hard to tell what was a house and what was a restaurant, because all the windows were opaque paper, but as Thaniel walked – turning left at the man who did indeed have a cat on a lead – it became a bit clearer. You had to look for the steam. Tiny noodle shops that only seated a few people had opened their sliding doors out onto the street, and people in work clothes from the harbour ate fast at counters, or perched on old cargo kegs. Ladies in bandanas and aprons stood outside the bigger places, calling in the internationally familiar nasal tone of train announcers that people were welcome to come in. Thaniel nearly got herded into one just in time to see a chef swear and a basket of noodles go flying.

'Or maybe not,' the lady outside said cheerfully.

'Fucking ghosts!' the man yelled, and slung down his apron.

'I'm hearing about ghosts everywhere,' Thaniel said to her.

'I know, it's getting to be a real drag,' the lady said. 'All the exorcists are booked up. Come on in, everyone welcome ...'

He found the post office on the next street. A grumpy, solitary clerk absolutely insisted that Thaniel was speaking

English even though he never said a word of it. Overhead, the telegraph wires hummed busily. The package went safely on its way to Aokigahara.

Outside the post office, Thaniel almost walked straight into the man in the red coat, from Kuroda's retinue. The man broke into a smile nearly as bright as his Fabergé egg button.

'Ah, morning, mate,' the man said. He had a lovely warm Osaka accent and Thaniel felt involuntarily at home, because as far as he could tell, Osaka was the Japanese version of York. 'Going back to Yoruji? I'll walk with you.'

'No need,' said Thaniel, who didn't want to walk with someone who he'd last seen pointing a gun at Mori. 'I know the way.'

'Better safe than sorry. Things can be a bit rough for gaijin this near the docks. I'm Tanaka.'

'Steepleton.'

'I know. What did you send just now?'

Thaniel frowned. 'Who wants to know?'

'I do. I take an interest in what's going in and out of any house where Count Kuroda is staying.'

'Just presents home. Souvenirs.'

'And that's what I'll find if I go and get it, is it?'

'Good luck finding it,' Thaniel said. 'The clerk didn't even look at it, he won't be able to tell which it was.'

'Marked England though, right?'

'Nope,' said Thaniel. He looked down at him. Tanaka was tall for this part of the world, but it was still distinctly down. 'I'm not posting detailed reports on Mr Kuroda's security arrangements to Whitehall, if that's what you're worried about.'

Without any warning, Tanaka slammed him against a wall and held a knife half an inch away from his eye. He didn't lose the cheery manner. 'It's not the British I'm worried about, mate, it's Mori. What did he put in that package?'

Thaniel punched him in the ribs, which made the knife drop a bit, then caught the back of his head and thunked it into the wall. And then suddenly there were policemen on either side of him with batons.

Tanaka was laughing. 'You're spicy. That was assault, though, lads; you saw, right?'

The policemen had seen. They must have seen Tanaka pull the knife as well, but they said nothing about it. Thaniel sighed and put his hands behind his head. He got a baton in the ribs anyway, but he'd known it was coming and it didn't hurt as much as it could have. Twenty minutes later he was in a cold little cell at a police station near the harbour, feeling embarrassed.

————

He'd expected a wry-looking Mori to come and fetch him out, but it wasn't Mori who came. A strange nervous silence fell among the policemen when Takiko Pepperharrow walked in. She was wearing riding boots and a Western coat, only mutedly glamorous in comparison to the incredible clothes she'd had before, and she asked politely for papers without any kind of flourish, but the policemen nearly panicked; they had no idea what to do with a woman and they hurried around her like gorillas trying to look after a duckling. She paid the inspector and then shepherded Thaniel out.

'Just bribe them,' she said once they were outside. She was speaking Japanese. A couple of policemen had come to the door to watch them leave. English must have been suspect. 'You're going to be arrested all the time, just carry round a few yen in your pocket for it. I'm sorry about Tanaka, he's insane. Yakuza I think; you know, mafia. Kuroda collects insane people.'

'Thanks,' said Thaniel. 'What do I owe you?'

She frowned, looking like the question had nearly hurt. 'Nothing.' She paused. 'Are you all right? I expect they took the opportunity you give you a bit of a going over.'

'I'm fine,' he said, though his ribs did ache now.

'I know you don't like me, but let me make you a cup of tea. I knew we were all lunatic xenophobes but getting arrested in your first week for fighting back against a nutty yakuza thug is a bit much. It's embarrassing.'

He nodded a little. 'You're half and half. Do you … have any of this?'

'A bit. No one can say my name and people always worry I won't have proper manners and I won't know where to put my shoes if I visit.' She looked wry about it, without even a trace of irritability. 'But you'll do better in Tokyo. People will assume you're diplomatic staff. I mean, I expect you'll have a few nutters yelling "fuck off gaijin" every so often, but sticks and stones.'

'What does gaijin actually mean? The dictionary just says foreigner, but …'

'I'd say it's somewhere between "chink" and "mountain troll".'

He laughed. 'Thanks.'

She taught him more swearwords on the way back. He didn't want to find any of it funny, but she *was* funny, and it

163

would have been hard not to laugh with her. At Yoruji, she made the tea herself, and he started to see that he'd been jealously unfair to her before. The tea room – there was a whole room for tea – was a glass pagoda set on a little island in one of the bigger pools, warm despite the cool weather and riotously bright from silk rugs woven with chrysanthemum patterns. It was a gorgeous place to sit. He felt all his nerves unravelling after being wound up tight at the police station. Opposite him, Takiko cut an odd figure. She was wearing a man's suit; it was a costume from the theatre, but the props people didn't want it to look new on stage, and so she was stuck walking round in it looking like an idiot for two weeks while she persuaded some wear and creases into it. Kabuki, she explained, meant slantwise, queer; the entire idea was that it was weird, and so at the moment, they were casting all the women as men and all the men as women. She rolled her eyes when she said it, and he liked her suddenly for being embarrassed talking about art. He was exactly the same. He could barely say 'semi-quaver' to someone outside the orchestra without feeling like a pretentious twerp.

'Why were you out in the first place?' she asked at last.

'Oh. I was just going to the post office.'

'You know we've got a postbox here? They come at ten o'clock every morning.'

'No, it was a parcel, it needed weighing.'

'Presents home already?' She smiled.

He felt his shoulders stiffen, and shifted the teacup in his hands to disguise it. Kuroda's men rotated their posts at the sounding of those strange bells; and he had seen her putting up bells. And she must have agreed to have all the rest put up in the house, provided the servants with them, shown the soldiers the ways through the labyrinthine corridors. 'No, no. Although I should. Mori wanted something posting. Moths in cocoons.'

'Really?'

'For some collector in Kyushu,' he said, naming a random place that was not Aokigahara Forest.

'Kyushu?'

'I don't know, I just do as I'm told. Usually for the best.'

'I'd advise you not to do that,' she said.

'I know what you'd advise,' he said, angling for cheery.

'Did you ask him about Countess Kuroda?'

'None of my business.'

'Jesus Christ, you did and you don't care.' She shook her head once in a way that put Thaniel powerfully in mind his sister, when he was tiny and she could see he was about to fall out of a tree. 'All right, fair enough. But aren't you worried that that's you? You're ill. Have you asked yourself what your death might achieve, if he steered it into the right place at the right moment?'

Thaniel shrugged. 'If it's going to happen anyway then he's welcome to find a use for it.'

Her expression opened. 'How serious is it, at the moment?'

'I don't really know. The doctor said one thing, Mori said something else, but then he looks like he's seen a ghost whenever he bumps into me, which can't be very good. I don't feel right.' He hesitated, not sure why he was telling her of all people. But then, she was the only objective party he'd spoken to. He went into English, because he couldn't concentrate enough for Japanese past the rock forming in his throat. 'It's not a shock. My dad had this. We're pretty

165

short-lived, the men in our family. I hope it'll be all right, but …' He had wanted to say something balanced and cheerful, but it wouldn't come. 'But I don't feel right,' he said again, too quiet.

'There's nothing Keita can do?' she asked, in English too. The first time he'd spoken to her, her accent had been glassy, but it was less so now. She was copying him, in exactly the way he echoed the Japanese of whoever he was talking to.

'What's he going to do, cure tuberculosis? If we're not in sight of a cure, he can't do anything more than anyone else. If it's not there in the close future for him to remember, he can't know how to do it.' He put the tea aside. 'Like I say, it's not a shock. I think my lungs were buggered by the time I was twenty, if I'm honest.'

She had been nodding slightly while he spoke. 'Still bloody irritating though.'

He smiled. 'It is. I mean I might be fine, it might be fuss over nothing.'

'Well, I hope so.'

'Thanks.'

She leaned over and poked him. 'Get on with that music you were writing earlier. I was listening. It's gorgeous. I'm not having that go to waste just because you upped and snuffed it before you could be bothered to finish.'

Stupidly, even though he was almost certain she had only been kind to make him tell her about the parcel, being teased made everything seem a lot better. 'I will.'

She watched him for a moment as if she really was worried. 'Anyway,' she said. 'Are you all right if I abandon you? I'd better get going. I'm supposed to be at the playhouse soon.'

He nodded and promised it wasn't exactly a hardship, being abandoned in such a lovely place. He watched her go, waited til she was across the stepping stones, and then followed as quietly as he could. She was out of sight by the time he reached the corridor, but he could hear her on the nightingale floor, which was making its weird, starry squeaking off to the left. He walked right on the edge near the skirting board, and stopped when she stopped. She had tapped on a door. It was Kuroda's voice that called to come in.

He waited with his back to their wall. It was only paper, and he could hear straight through it.

'Moth cocoons to Kyushu,' she said. 'Have you got anything in Kyushu?'

'No,' Kuroda said gradually. 'Nothing. Might just be Mori being Mori.'

She might have said something else, but Thaniel didn't hear it, because Suzuki was coming down the corridor. Thaniel tried the door next to him, but it was locked. Suzuki looked shocked to find him there.

'That,' he said, as if he'd caught Thaniel in the ladies' cloakroom, 'is the old smoking room. We don't use it. Your room is this way.'

'What's wrong with the smoking room?' Thaniel said, puzzled.

'It's locked,' Suzuki snapped.

Thaniel inclined his head and wondered if Suzuki knew he lived in a gothic fairytale. A woman had been killed in the house, people saw ghosts everywhere, and now there was a mysteriously locked room. 'Better not be a dungeon full of dismembered ladies, that's all I'm saying.'

'I beg your pardon!'

Thaniel smiled. 'Where's Mori, do you know?'

'Not at home,' Suzuki said stiffly.

Thaniel would have laughed if he'd been less anxious. 'I'm not selling pins at the door. Where is he?'

'I really don't know,' Suzuki said, escorted him in silence to his room and then floated away again.

He was right; Mori wasn't here. Thaniel found Six playing with Katsu and Hotaru, the little gardener boy, and saw Lady Shimazu and some other women chatting over teacups in one of the hot pools on the lower levels, but no Mori. Out on the shore, the lighthouse flashed, and once again, little bells chimed and jingled through the house. Afterwards, listening hard, he could just hear the snackle and beep of Morse as Kuroda's men moved and exchanged notes. It was almost dark now. Thaniel hesitated on the verandah. His ribs hurt, and he was tired – exhausted – but he didn't think he could just sit still and wait for Mori.

He took a lamp and set out for the lighthouse. At least if he knew what the hell was going on there, he would have more to tell Mori than a vague accusation of nothing particular against Kuroda and Takiko.

NINETEEN

Tokyo, July 1881 (eight years earlier)

Kuroda thumped a journalist on the way out the office. It would, of course, only lead to another sketch of him as an ape or an especially fat catfish – he had never understood why the catfish joke had taken off so well in the cartoons. Politicians had whiskers and catfish had whiskers, but so did any number of things: rats, actual cats, raccoons. Beavers. Mori always said it was because nobody wanted to be accused of portraying government ministers as if they might be friendly or fluffy. Kuroda had wanted to ask what the hell kind of rats Mori had met, but Mori had a skewed idea of the world. If Mori ever came across a rat, it wouldn't give him the plague; it would make friends, give him an enchanted present, and arrange for him to marry a moon princess before the end of the fortnight. Mori always ended up with princesses where everyone else got plague.

———

Kojimachi glimmered. At a glance it would have been difficult to see the difference between now or a hundred years ago. Only from certain angles: if you didn't glance toward Hibiya at the be-cloistered atrocity that was the Rokumeikan, or the Foreign Ministry, or the new brick townhouses everyone seemed so keen about. The city Kuroda knew was fading away. It made him feel old, and stupid, and pushed out. He was forty-one. That was too young to feel evicted from your own country.

He didn't want to go home, so he bought another bottle of sake from the shop on the corner, and drank it on the train to Yoruji. It was only an hour's journey on the train from Shimbashi, and a portion of the track was by the sea, which was black and sighing.

Yoruji was at the top of a steep, uneven path from Yokohama's little station. He loved seeing it from below in the dark, lit up and warm, its lamps casting gold veneers underneath the old temple rooftops. It felt like home.

He let himself in to find that Mori was waiting for him in the smoking room, reading the *Daily*. All the doors and windows were open, the mesh screens shut to keep out the curious cicadas and let in the sea breeze. It was glorious after the sweating mess that was central Tokyo.

'Is that tomorrow's edition?' Kuroda said, roughly. He had never been nervous about what the papers said, but he couldn't remember them being quite so aggressive before, even during the Korea campaign.

'Yes.' Mori turned it around to show him the headline. Kuroda glanced at it. It was something along the lines of GOVERNMENT CORRUPTION SCANDAL SPARKS UNPRECEDENTED POPULAR OUTCRY. He took care not to remember it exactly.

'Popular outcry,' he growled. He poured himself some more sake. 'Most of those outcrying people have no idea what a land deal looks like.'

Across from them, beyond one of the little, dense gardens, Mrs Pepperharrow and Kuroda's wife were sitting in another room, all lit up, drinking tea at a table of their own. They were

170

watching; they'd seen Kuroda come in. Mrs Pepperharrow leaned over the tea table and murmured something that made Countess Kuroda nod seriously.

Countess Kuroda was at Yoruji more than she was at home. Visiting the Baroness, she said, but really avoiding him. He'd tried to make Mori send her home. Mori had said that Kuroda was welcome to take it up with Mrs Pepperharrow. Since Mrs Pepperharrow wasn't above running political satires at her extremely well-attended playhouse, he'd decided he probably shouldn't. So at Yoruji the Countess stayed. He was starting to wonder if she'd made it a permanent thing. Most of her clothes were here now, her jewellery, even the accounts ledgers.

The ledgers were a bad sign. She spent a couple of hours most mornings working on them, meticulous about the running of the household in Tokyo even in her physical absence, every sen and every bar of soap accounted for in her lacy handwriting. The steward sent her twice-daily telegrams. She kept them pinned together at the back of the ledgers, beside another pinned pile of right-angle-aligned receipts. He had thought it was forced conscientiousness for a long time, before he noticed how she ate. She peeled apples, always clockwise, and always in one smooth, perfect spiral.

He almost wouldn't have minded the under-handed little shuffle she'd done across to Yoruji – almost – but somehow everyone knew. Some of the gossip columns (they never named names, but they made such specific jokes that it was obvious who they meant) were even suggesting some kind of amazing, scandalous ménage-à-trois with Mori and Mrs Pepperharrow.

'Well, they do know that you probably shouldn't sell huge swathes of government land for tuppence to your definitely-not-mafia friends in Osaka,' Mori said fairly. Somewhere, the peculiar house creaked.

'What's this to *you*? It isn't as though someone handed me an envelope under a bloody table. It was put to the ministerial council and we all agreed.'

'The council knows how to watch you shoot yourself in the foot,' Mori said, amused. 'They're sending some accountants round tonight. Should be here soon.'

'So much for hiding out here. And I bet you find all this hysterical,' Kuroda snapped. He poured himself a third cup, then lost patience with the cup and drank from the bottle instead. 'You could have said something while it was happening. If there's one thing I'd bet my life on it's that you saw this coming miles away.'

Mori set the paper on his knee again. 'Why should I point out a pothole you can see perfectly well?'

Kuroda drained the last of the sake from the bottle and slung it at him. Mori leaned backwards without looking. It smashed on the wall next to him. Mori lifted a shard of it out of his cup and flicked it back. He didn't do it pointedly, only with fun in his eyes. Kuroda slumped down next to him. Mori gave him a cup of tea and watched too seriously as he poured a shot of brandy into it.

Kuroda smacked him over the head, or tried to, but Mori caught his wrist and bent it backwards until the bone creaked and he had to snarl and snatch his hand back. It hurt. But it was reassuring, too, wonderful, to smash up against a thing that wouldn't move even if he hurled his whole being at it. Abruptly he needed to test it again, to make sure. Before he had even drawn his fist back, Mori caught his throat and squeezed hard. His knuckles were criss-crossed with parallel white scars. He anticipated the coming punch in the gut, because he picked up the kettle with his free hand and tipped it until it was a fraction away from pouring boiling water into Kuroda's lap. Close up, he smelled of heat and the sea. He must have been on the beach before.

'Fuck you,' Kuroda wheezed, and kissed his cheek.

Takiko saw the men fighting through the two windows.

'It's like having dogs, isn't it,' the Countess said, and poured Takiko some more tea. She always took over the tea. Takiko, she said, was shocking at it. 'I think Kuroda's a bit in love with him, don't you?'

'He's fine, I'm not worried about Mori's honour.'

'So this play,' the Countess said. She was glittering in the lamplight. It was one of the things that Takiko liked about her, that she insisted on dressing for dinner and after-dinner tea in the evenings, even if nobody was around to see except Takiko and the owls. 'You'll start the new run when? Only you know Akiko, whose husband is that irritating education fellow who wants to abolish kanji? She's just started at *The Times.*'

'Isn't that in English?'

'One has to start somewhere.'

Takiko snorted and the Countess sparkled.

'But it would be good to give her an interview, give her a world of help. I thought we could invite her to court.'

'We? I don't get invited to court, I'm the scum of the earth,' Takiko laughed.

The Countess looked worried. 'No, but I thought you didn't like to go?'

Takiko had to smile into the tea. The Countess thought she wasn't a snob, because her father had been a lawyer and she'd married upward, but she was, and she had the upper-class habit of assuming that if you didn't do things, it was because they hadn't struck your fancy. 'I wouldn't mind if you'd put in a good word for me. Not that I – you know. I don't want to collapse at your feet and be all, please Lady Kuroda sort out my awkward social career, but ...'

'Oh, obviously,' said the Countess, who had a brilliant way of puffing up like a cross partridge when she was indignant. Takiko could never work out how she did it, because she was a very slim person. 'The Empress would be delighted. She's dull as bloody ditchwater, but she would be delighted.'

'Is she actually?'

The Countess inclined her head and gave Takiko a wry look. 'She has written,' she said, making an elegant, broad gesture with her tea that suggested some kind of art or ballet, 'a collection of poetry.'

'Is it good?'

'No,' the Countess said. 'It's a pile of absolute cack, Pepperharrow, you'll have to see it to believe it.' She straightened suddenly and preened. 'Oh, but we simply *must* support the young ladies of the court, even though life is simply dreadful for me, and look I wrote a poem, and I might have cut myself with a razor because of the dreadful anxiety of it all, but only a *teeny* bit because, you know, it would be dreadfully irresponsible, and this poem, well, it's about life and experience and by heaven if she wouldn't be improved with a chopstick in the eye. I mean I shouldn't say that, it's sad. She's got everything a person could possibly need, but she's got nowhere to channel herself, and it's making her peculiar and stupid. But the point is, don't turn all shy and working-class. You would be an edifying force in that room.'

Takiko grinned, feeling herself starting to colour. 'I don't know if I want to go now, thanks.'

'Tough it, you're going, and then I won't have to,' the Countess said firmly. 'I've been wanting to get away for a while now. She always has it in the mornings and I've been feeling ill in the mornings.'

Takiko edged the plate of little cakes over to her. She didn't know what to say. All her sisters had had children, but all she'd learned from it was that people with children turned inward. She didn't see any of them anymore. Congratulations would have been the right thing to say, but she couldn't bring herself to. She just felt lonely in advance. 'Oh, right. How are you doing with it?' she asked at last.

The Countess smiled, full of sympathy. 'I said I'm feeling ill, not pregnant. I've got this absurd hacking cough I never get rid of til midday, it's absolutely undignified.'

Takiko laughed and felt disproportionately relieved. She liked the theatre and the actors in their own tetchy way, liked talking to patrons, liked Mori, but Mori was more of a beautiful creature that lived in the same house than he was a husband. She saw him sometimes, and he still came up for tea in the attic at the Shintomi on Saturdays, but like he'd promised when they were first married, there wasn't much else to it. He could be sitting just opposite, but he was still as separate as a siren watching from underwater. She had been sad about that for a while, more than she had expected. It meant she never came first for anybody, least of all the people who she would have liked to put first. Until, that was, she got talking properly to the Countess, who had come backstage once and congratulated her and asked if could she possibly have a copy of the play script to read. Ever since, even though Takiko wasn't half as clever or half as funny, the Countess had shown every sign of putting Takiko first.

For the second time that evening, the Countess glanced down at the floor beside the table. Her accounting ledgers were there.

'Are you really going to do it?' Takiko asked. Mori had warned them earlier that the finance people from the Ministry were coming.

'Yes.' She paused. 'I'm tired of living with a drunk.'

'Well, cheers. To a long, long prison sentence.'

The Countess nodded and smiled, but she didn't repeat the toast. Later, when she looked back on that moment, Takiko had an unbearable feeling that the Countess had known full well it could never go her way.

The doorbell rang half an hour later. Kuroda's wife didn't give Suzuki time to go, and answered it herself; she had a habit of treating any house she was in as her own kingdom. Home Ministry auditors liked their late-night visits. Kuroda was tempted to go out to them and ask if they expected to find a smoking ledger called Naughty Deals about his person, but that would have been dignifying them with the time. His wife simpered at them in the hallway. The auditors kept their answers to yes and no.

'Just bring them in,' he snapped towards the corridor.

The auditors were respectful, but not as much as they could have been, emanating clerkly precision and faint distaste to be standing under the sword over the door, the one he had taken as a souvenir for Mori when the Koreans surrendered. They wanted to look at some records. He told them that obviously the records weren't here. They wanted him to go back to Tokyo. He said no. They wanted to talk. He said in the morning. But his wife hummed and hovered, and said 'I wonder if …' a lot, always trailing off into ellipses, and then produced the folders in a bundle and offered earnestly to make the auditors some tea while they read in the side office.

Kuroda wondered why he hadn't just locked her in the attic instead of letting her set up here.

'I don't suppose you charmed them into buggering off, did you?' he asked when she came out, trying to cover how much he wanted to demand why the hell she would feel the need to hand the ledgers over to Ministry auditors without a warrant.

'Oh, no,' she laughed, one hand over her mouth. She always pulled her sleeve well over her knuckles and it made her look like a schoolgirl. He didn't know why women imagined men found that appealing. He couldn't think of anything less worthwhile. 'They seem awfully serious.'

Mori stood up and started to get between them like he always did, lifting his hand to brush her sleeve. But before he could touch it, he stopped and clenched his fist, then sank back against the wall. He looked sick. He must have decided he was going to have to let them have it out at some point, if he didn't mean to spend the rest of his life shepherding them in opposite directions. The absence of the usual safety net made Kuroda feel odd.

'So you just gave them everything?'

'Well, it seemed much better not to try to hide anything.'

It was moronic even for her. 'Fuck's sake, girl – do you want to get me arrested?'

Her expression flickered, and then he understood. She did. Of course she did. She would love for him to be in prison and not blundering around her nice house, behaving like a commoner and trooping through with all his cheap, common friends.

Of course she didn't have the guts to tell him to his face to get out of her house. He would have, if she'd done that. It was her house. But instead she'd run here and cowered behind Mori and Mrs Pepperharrow, and now she'd come up with this slimy little slug of a plan to stab him in the back.

She ran like she walked, knees turned inward and pigeon-toed, because the hems of her kimono were all fashionably narrow. Any normal person would have just torn the dress to run properly, especially when he went after her. But she didn't. She kept on in that way and crumpled when she tripped. He picked her up again and banged her onto her feet and shook her. She wasn't stupid. She wrote poetry, beautiful poetry. But she always pretended to be brainless, and he hated it, hated it like everyone hated concealed weaponry, and he had never understood why she had to pretend and sneak when there were people like Mrs Pepperharrow who showed you all their guns and gave you decent warning before they blew you out of the water.

On the back of his neck was an awareness that Mori hadn't run out to stop him. All there had been from Mori's direction was a thump that sounded like he'd punched the wall.

'Don't run away from me, you little coward. Explain why you thought telling them everything would be the clever thing to do,' he hissed.

'Oh, but you see, I thought it would be for the best. After all we have nothing to hide—'

'No you didn't! Just admit it! Just say it, you bloody worm, tell me to my face!'

'I'm sure I don't know what—'

He only meant to give her a bang on the head. When he questioned himself later, again and again, usually in the middle of the night, he was certain that was true. He had not meant for it to happen. He'd meant to hurt her, yes, give her a shock, jolt her into some kind of common sense. But he was drunker than he'd thought, and the base of the tumbler in his hand was heavy. It broke her skull. After she had collapsed onto the floor, he stared. The blow hadn't knocked her out. She was feeling around for a comb that had fallen from her hair. It was right in front of her, but she couldn't see it.

He was turning around to go back for Mori when Mori came through quietly of his own accord. If he felt an iota of surprise, he didn't show it. He knelt down and gave her comb back, setting it into her hand, and then lifted her very gently upright. His knuckles were bleeding. He really had hit the wall, so hard the cuts were pale with plaster dust.

'We need to hurry to catch the post,' she said, sounding completely normal, 'or we shall miss the matinee.'

Kuroda stared at her. He didn't want to rage anymore. Instead he was seized with the need to get away from her. She wasn't a person now – she was a thing, a grotesque, wrong thing that was only human-shaped, except for the star-shaped dent in her skull where the likeness failed.

Mori inclined his head at Kuroda and watched him hard, and held her still by her shoulders, and Kuroda realised that this was the punishment. He couldn't blame it on rage in the moment or tell himself he had been drunk. He was stone sober now. Mori tapped her on the head. It wouldn't even have hurt her usually; it was the kind of strike you aimed at someone good-naturedly to make him look up and laugh with you. But something terrible must have gone wrong inside her skull already. She folded. Mori caught her.

'Send for the coroner,' was all he said.

Kuroda couldn't move. 'You let me do that,' he said, quiet at first, but then the enormity of it pumped a bellows and the anger roared again. 'You let me, you can't say you didn't see – you're just as guilty as I am, so don't get on your fuck-ing high horse now and—'

'I did let you,' Mori interrupted. He had put a hardness in his voice that Kuroda had never heard before from anyone outside the Admiralty. 'Now send for the coroner.' He lifted her onto the couch and arranged her hands into a modest clasp against her belt, around the gold comb.

'But – what will he find? There's a – damn it, Keita, there's the shape of a glass in her—'

'He'll find a haemorrhage,' Mori said. He looked to the side as his steward, Suzuki, arrived with new clothes and a sack. 'Get changed. Suzuki will get rid of what you're wearing.'

'You're helping me,' Kuroda said numbly. He heard the strength go out of his own voice.

'Yes, now go and fetch the coroner. And tell those two in the office that your wife is dead. Say something sensible. Unrelated to brandy tumblers.'

Kuroda took a breath to ask him to just explain what to say, but Mori gave him the look that sergeants give especially slow seamen. 'Either think properly and get through, or collapse and be executed. You're no use to anyone if you can't think. I'm going to sit here.'

The coroner, the auditors, and Kuroda had all gone. Everyone had seemed perfectly convinced the Countess had just fallen. Mori had told them so and that had been that. It had all happened before they had even touched the wretched ledgers, which lay unopened on a table still, someone's teacup still cooling on one. Takiko hadn't even seen bribes change hands; she didn't think there had been any. People just believed Mori. Even though Suzuki had gone right past the window with a sack full of Kuroda's bloody clothes and all the alcohol in the house, heading to the old sulphur well. She'd never thought she was naive, but it shocked her. She would have gone straight to the police station if she'd thought for a second that anyone there would pay her a blind bit of attention instead of just joking about Mori's mad foreign wife.

Instead, she went to find Mori in his bedroom. On the way, fury and fear roiled together right in the pit of her stomach. God, all that rubbish he'd fed her before they were married, about needing her help: she had been such an idiot that she'd never even considered that help might just mean being murdered at the right moment. The Duke had told her; he'd told her, and she had barely listened for long enough to write him off as a superstitious berk. Half of her wanted to bolt and never come back. It was idiocy to confront a man who had done what she had just watched Mori do. The other half screamed it was better to die fighting than live hiding. Countess Kuroda had lived hiding.

Mori was walking up and down by the verandah door, waiting.

'I know it was—'

She punched him in the head, a proper right hook. He went down hard on his knees on the floor. Knowing that he'd let her do it only made it worse. She'd never felt anger like it. There was madness in it, a raving howling need to go at him with whatever was to hand until his bones were powder. It was a colossal effort to lock her hands behind her back. She almost choked with it.

'You let that happen because you thought she was an idiot, didn't you?' she said. Her voice came out low and tight. She didn't sound like herself. 'You understand that she wasn't really like that? You know that *no one* is really like that? She was that way, she pretended to be stupid, because she's read Sung Tzu. Seem weak where you are strong. She was conducting her marriage like a war.'

'I know,' he said softly. He was still on his knees. He sat back on his heels. 'I know. I'm so sorry.'

'Why did you let it happen?' She snatched the back of his hair to force him to look up. 'What, you thought she wasn't worthwhile?'

'Because I need Kuroda as he is now, with this hanging over him.'

'That's ...' She had to open her hands, because there were words, but they were bandied around too often to have kept all their power untarnished by idiots and exaggeration. 'Evil. You're evil.'

'Yes.' He shook his head slightly. She wished he would just be obnoxious, because then it would have been fair to kick him in the face, but he looked haunted, and sad, as though evil was a border he had crossed a long time ago and he was so deep into the country beyond that he could hardly remember anywhere else. He got up gradually. 'Yes.'

'What do you need him for? What's so bloody important?'

He almost looked like he might explain, but then he seemed to put it all to one side. 'Does it make any difference?'

Without really deciding to, she picked up the sake bottle from the table and fully meant to slam it into his teeth – a savage fury voice right at the front of her mind wanted his teeth in a jar – but before she'd even swung it, he clapped both hands over his mouth and half collapsed. He let himself down the rest of the way to the floor slowly, breathing as though she had already done it, coughing through pain that couldn't possibly be real but looked entirely genuine all the same. She put the bottle down.

'What?' she said, confused.

Mori was shaking his head. He didn't try to talk.

'You feel it before it actually ... happens.'

He nodded.

Caught between indignation and guilt and deep, nasty satisfaction, she sat down on the floor too. 'But it wears off quickly?'

He sat back very, very slowly. He had gone white. He looked around without moving his head much, found a piece of paper and wrote, *Psychosomatic. Takes a while.*

'You bloody deserved it,' she said, uncomfortable now. His hand was shaking. She could see he would have liked to touch his own teeth, to prove to himself they were still there, but he couldn't.

Yes.

She sat in silence for a while, still too full of rage to ask if he was all right.

Mori was silent too. He was sitting back against the wall now, his eyelashes full of pain tears that didn't fall and his hands clamped together, but he was still shaking. With a little tide of disbelief, she realised he was going into shock.

'I didn't even touch you,' she snapped, and then went still when she heard herself. She was doing now what Kuroda always did. He was furious, he lashed out, he faded back and knew he'd gone too far, but he didn't apologise because he wasn't sorry, not really. And then, because he wasn't sorry, he was angry with whoever he'd thumped for being hurt.

It was different, obviously it was different, the fury voice snarled.

'Joy,' she said softly. 'Come on, let's … let's get you up. Come and sit down in the warm. You're cold.' He was. His hands were bloodless when she pulled him upright. She set him down again near the fire. She knelt down too and stoked it up, though she was too hot now. He made a sign to say thank you, and then let his head drop down on his knees. She sat looking at him for a long time, turning over and over the prickling realisation that, whatever he had just done, however bad, he was so utterly vulnerable that she was going to have to be more careful. All the anger misted into the awful bleak frustration of being the strongest person in the room by far.

She caught herself on the edge of apologising, understood just in time what he was doing, and almost punched him again. Fragile he might be, but Takiko was damned if she'd let him turn that fragility into armour when he had just used Countess Kuroda's to smash her to pieces. She didn't know yet how she was going to do it, but she was going to get a collar on Mori if she died trying.

TWENTY

Yokohama, 19th December 1888

The tide had gone right out when Thaniel stepped down onto the dark beach with a lamp. The lighthouse rock was on dry land now, or the nearer half of it was. The little boat that had been outside before was gone. So was the white shirt at the top. It was after midnight now, and for the first time since he'd been a child, he couldn't see street lights. Just the lights at Yoruji, and, in the lighthouse tower, a single point of candlelight. He trod over the crackly sand and started up the steps.

They were even and unweathered. At the top, the door was propped open, just, with a well-shined shoe. He tapped on the briny wood. Nobody answered. He pushed open the door. Inside was a spiral stairway that stretched up to the blackness at the top of the tower. He started up, slowly, because his lamp threw harsh shadows along the stairs that spun as he rounded the spirals, and soon he found why the lighthouse-keeper had propped the door open rather than take the keys. They were on a hook near the top of the stairs, big, churchy things that weighed hardly less than a metronome when he lifted them. They clanked as he let them go. There were four. That was a lot, he thought, for one door.

The lamp room was dark except for that one candle, which had burned right down at a desk by the window. He lifted his own little lamp, which was just bright enough to shine on all the machinery inside. Much more machinery than any ordinary lighthouse would have needed.

Parts of it in were wooden and glass casing, parts of it open strings and clockwork, some of which went up through the ceiling in exposed bronze mechanisms. The rest of the space, or almost all of it, was taken up by a table scattered about with papers, many of which were photographs. They all showed the same thing; mirror-twin zigzag lines, pale against dark backgrounds.

The machine, whatever it was, was working. Suspended inside a box, open at the moment but with a hinged side and a clasp that would lock it, was a fragile pair of metal prongs that looked like wishbones. They were moving; they drew together and apart, slowly, though the room was completely still. It was nothing to do with the wind. Beyond the big windows, the sea might have been a lake, and mist hung undisturbed at different heights above the black water.

He used to have a distrust of machinery, but he'd watched Mori teach Six, and when you were looking at something you didn't know, the principle was always the same; start with what you did know, and trust that the rest wasn't beyond the wit of man.

The only thing he recognised for sure was a clock. It was worked into the side of the machine, with a heavy counterweight and a pendulum that came to a precise point. The clock wasn't framed, and the workings were uncovered at the back. A wire led up from it. He climbed on a chair to see where it went. Inside were strings and pulleys, and a little clockwork mechanism.

'Right,' he said aloud, because the colour of the sound made tentative thoughts look more solid. 'So that regulates

– vertical motion, so it's pulling something up. In ... front of this lens here, which ...' He had to climb down again. 'Is a camera,' he said, puzzled.

There were photographs on the table. He picked one up and held it beside the camera chamber until he understood. If there had been photographic paper underneath them now, the tips of the two moving prongs would be making the same patterns as the pale lines in the picture. The point of the machine was to record the motion of the moving points on a photograph.

He looked up at the ceiling, where the stem of the prongs disappeared. He opened the little glass door out onto the gantry. On top of the roof, in line with the machinery inside, was a tall lightning rod.

It wasn't stormy now. Certainly there was no lightning. Inside, the prongs moved gently. He sighed. He never understood what was going on with electricity. Nobody had been able to tell him what was actually moving when they talked about electric current. Even Mori didn't know. He would, he said, be dead before anyone explained it, which meant he couldn't remember. Six said it might be ether, but nobody knew what ether was either. That wasn't quite true; his ex-wife Grace probably did know what ether was.

The door thunked closed downstairs. There was no use hiding. He went to the door instead. The lighthouse-keeper's steps were more than halfway up the stairs.

'Evening,' Thaniel called down. 'Sorry I let myself in. I'm lost.'

The steps paused, then sped up, and a man the opposite of what Thaniel had expected appeared on the landing. He was in a nicely ironed shirt and delicate spectacles, and his hair was neat and side-parted, Western style. He didn't look anything like a lighthouse-keeper. He looked like somebody from somewhere in the middle of the civil service. He looked flustered too. He was still tucking in his shirt in a way that seemed like he was hoping a bit desperately that Thaniel wouldn't ask where he'd been in the middle of the night. 'What? I don't speak English, what are you doing up here?'

'I was on the beach, but then the fog came in and now I'm lost. You don't happen to know where we are?'

The man blinked twice, then took off his spectacles and polished them on a fold of his shirt. 'In ... relation to where? I'm sorry, I'm really not very good at English ...'

'I'm not speaking English,' Thaniel pointed out, but patiently. He had a theory that for an oriental person to hear an occidental one speak understandably was a good deal like it would have been for an Englishman to encounter a talking horse who wanted to know the way to the tobacconist's. The best you could do was get in a chunk of clear grammar, so that people knew, at least, that you were a well-educated horse.

'Oh. Ah ... you're not, are you.'

'I was hoping to find Baron Mori's house?' Thaniel said, trying to seem as unhorsey as he could. 'I wouldn't have bothered you, but I saw the candle, so I hoped ...'

'Oh – oh. The house. Er ... it's up that way. You can go past the big gingko trees at the top there.'

'Thank you. So what's this thing?'

'Oh, heavens,' the man laughed. 'Rather complicated I'm afraid. It measures atmospheric electricity. We're a weather station up here, you see. It's called an ...' He said something Thaniel had never heard before, to do with electricity. 'Quite neat really, only about six of them in the world til recently.'

'Really? Beautiful piece of kit. What's it for?'

'Oh, you can predict storms and so forth. And we send random numbers to university mathematics departments and so forth.'

'Random numbers,' Thaniel said, and tried not to look too attentive. 'Why?'

'They use it for all sorts, I think. Codes and ... well, it's a bit beyond me. But atmospheric electricity is the best source of random numbers in the world,' he added, proud by proxy. He tapped the side of the machine, and then saw something on the strange photographic readout that made his smile falter. 'Anyway, as I say, the house is by the gingko trees.'

The lighthouse-keeper hurried Thaniel down. When the door shut, the keys clanked as he locked all four locks.

Random was random even for Mori. If Six could shock him with some dice and a firecracker, someone who had replaced dice with lightning would be able to do anything they liked.

Thaniel wondered what the firecracker would be.

———

Thaniel was just navigating back down the uneven steps when someone whistled at him quietly from just over the pebbles. He looked round. A dark shape resolved itself into Kuroda. Behind him were two of his men, walking at a respectful distance but not too far.

Kuroda smiled. 'Poking round, are we?'

'Just interested,' said Thaniel. 'They've installed some wonderful stuff up there. Random data generation, that's really something.'

'What, did you think we lived in mud huts?' Kuroda said with a sparkle.

'No, sir, but it's pretty impressive for anyone to come up with a system that allows his bodyguards to rotate at random intervals a clairvoyant can't predict. That machine up there generates the numbers, the lighthouse goes on when it hits – what, a particular range – and then anyone who sees it rings a bell; and your men change posts. That's right, isn't it?'

'Clever boy,' Kuroda said. It wasn't as patronising as it could have been. He had noticed Thaniel was having to walk slowly up the steep stretch of shale, and in a gentlemanly way that took Thaniel by surprise, held out one hand to help him over the last spray of rocks before the short stretch of flat sand. Thaniel felt himself bristle and then had to talk himself down. He was actually glad of some help, pitiful though that was. His whole chest ached, and it wasn't just the bruises from the policemen.

'The machine is called an … ah, you won't know it in Japanese. Electrograph,' he said, in perfect English. He had a precise American accent. 'Heard of that?'

'No, sir.'

'No. Normally we use them just to predict the weather, but it's good, isn't it, how you find other uses for things.'

Thaniel nodded in the dark. Behind them, pebbles squeaked as Kuroda's men followed. It was a horrible sound. He couldn't tell if he thought so objectively, or because they were sticking just a fraction too near now. He could smell them; one of them smoked.

'You know, when I took office,' Kuroda continued, 'I don't think I realised what an almighty fuckabout everything would become. I can't piss without these two coming with me. You should have seen the frothing the security detail did when I said I was visiting Mori. Clairvoyant? they said. Yes, I said. We're going to have to think about this, they said. Cue the installation of machines and bells and hell knows. Sorry about Tanaka, by the way, he's a bit direct. But you understand why he wants to keep an eye on everything. Mori's been in London for years, doing nobody knows what. Now Russia.'

'He didn't defect. He just makes watches.'

'You'd know, would you, if he had?' Kuroda said. 'Good spies don't tell their families, you know, never mind their geisha.'

'What?' said Thaniel, a bit flatly.

'Come on, lad, you're a musician. Don't get me wrong, you play beautifully and you're not bad-looking, but all this is a bit beyond you.'

'What the hell are you—'

'Christians; give me strength,' said Kuroda, as the muzzle of a gun pushed into Thaniel's back and a quiet voice behind him told him to calm down. The safety catch snicked white. He put his hands up slowly. 'Don't get angry, son, you're in a normal country now, no one's going to lynch you. You can put your hands down. Let him go, let him go.'

The gun lifted away. Thaniel let his arms sink. 'I don't know what the hell it is you think is going on, Mr Kuroda, but—'

'They really will have you face down in the sand; it's fun to watch,' Kuroda said mildly.

Thaniel put his teeth together and let his breath out, trying to get his heart back to a normal speed.

'They had a thing or two to say about a foreign diplomat breaking into government property, actually.' Kuroda nodded to the lighthouse, which was a gaunt, leaning silhouette against the moonlight now. 'I'll let it go this time, but do me a favour, lad. Don't do it again. Stick to your music. I know it's all interesting, but this lot will get tetchy if they think you're interfering with ministerial security, and then they're likely to want to interfere with you.' He looked rueful. 'I expect Mori will be pissed off with me if his geisha ends up in the sea tied to a brick, but he can always get another geisha. All right?'

There was nothing to do but nod and try to press down the shame and the helpless, pointless fury seething up through his ribs. A dark part of him he'd never known was there wanted to turn and punch one of the guards, because being shot and dead would be better than having to stand quiet.

Kuroda smiled. 'Good boy. Now come on, tell me about this music you're writing while we walk up. Mrs Pepperharrow's always telling me I don't get enough culture.'

Thaniel wondered if real geisha painted themselves white so that it was harder to see how angry they must be all the time.

193

Back at the house, Thaniel had to sit out on the verandah for a while, waiting to calm down. Sitting still, it was freezing, and he soon had to move to the hot slate edge of the closest pool. The steam eased the scratch in his lungs at least, and he wasn't alone. Katsu was floating origami boats on the pool, gleaming in the light of the bright crescent moon. The moon was tipped on its side here, so that it smiled. Once the boats had drifted out a bit, Katsu dived into the water and then engulfed one like a miniature kraken, making what might have been the clockwork octopus version of kraken noises.

After a little while, Thaniel got the uncomfortable feeling that someone else was there too. He looked round twice, thinking someone had just walked past, but the place was deserted. The only real movement was the spiralling steam.

The lighthouse came on again, and again, bells sounded in the house. Mori's door was open to the night. Thaniel looked back in time to see him jolt upright.

'They're random, aren't they?' Thaniel said, quietly, because Six was asleep in the corner. He paused, because his voice had turned smoky. His lungs still hurt, despite all the steam. 'This is dangerous. If someone can ring a bell and take you by surprise, they could fire a gun and take you by surprise as ... well.' He had to squeeze his eyes shut when he saw what was going on. Ministerial security; what bullshit. He couldn't believe he'd not questioned it before. Kuroda had come with a personal guard of – what? At least twenty men. Far more than even Queen Victoria had. All with guns. They weren't a security detail. Kuroda wasn't just visiting a friend. Kuroda had the Russian fleet floating just off his back porch, and now he had a clairvoyant.

'Mori,' he whispered, 'can you even leave this house?'

Mori got up fast and dropped onto his knees beside Thaniel on the warm slate. 'Don't get in their way,' he said quietly. 'I'm not doing this by accident. It's all fine. But no spanners in the works, all right?'

'Why won't you just tell me what's going on?' Thaniel demanded. His voice split over it and he had to look away, frustrated, because he sounded like a child.

'It's boring,' Mori said, smiling. He shook his head. He was starting to look worse for wear after what must have been a run of broken nights. It was the least convincing smile Thaniel had ever seen. When he tried to start saying so, Mori closed one hand over his knuckles, squeezed, hard, and flicked his eyes to the corner of the verandah, like there was someone standing there. There wasn't. Thaniel stared at him helplessly, trying to see what in God's name was going on. Mori was looking at him hard, every atom of him broadcasting a warning to shut up.

Thaniel felt suddenly like they weren't talking softly alone on the dim verandah, but floodlit on a raised stage, surrounded by people who were invisible beyond the lime-lights, but very much still there.

'I just want someone to invent an electron microscope a bit early, that's all,' Mori said. 'And in a very obscure and silly way, this will help.'

'A microscope.'

'Yes. It's a neat little thing, it's worth a few interrupted nights.'

'What's it for?' Thaniel said, losing steam.

Mori shrugged a little. The candlelight slung harsh shadows between the tendons in his throat. 'Lots of things. Generally useful. You know what I'm like, I get bored with waiting for things to be invented.' He bent his neck a little and his eyes bored into Thaniel's. *Just say yes, just say yes, let it go.*

Thaniel couldn't. 'Kei, I really think Mrs Pepperharrow means to be a rich widow pretty soon, and I know you've probably got it all worked out, but if they're pissing about with random data generation then you can't know what—'

'She doesn't,' Mori interrupted. 'She's doing what she's meant to.' It was terrible, basalt-hard certainty. If Thaniel had suggested to him that his own arms were plotting against him, he would have sounded the same way.

But Mori really didn't sound right. He hadn't since they'd arrived. The spotlight feeling had never gone away either. For all there was no light, and nobody nearby, Thaniel could almost hear the rattle of an audience.

He leaned close, lifting one hand to Mori's hair to try and shield them a little from anyone close by. 'Is someone watching?' he whispered.

He never knew if Mori heard or not. The bells had made him flinch, and he had looked haunted when he'd caught sight of Thaniel across the room before, but his hands came up now in the fastest block Thaniel had ever had come at him in or out of the ring. He barely had time even to see it before Mori had pushed him away, hard, one hand flat into his sternum. It wasn't designed to hurt, but he was springcoil-strong and it almost knocked Thaniel over backward.

There was a hanging moment of silence. All Thaniel could hear was his own heart and the awkward catch in his lungs. He'd never been shocked from taking a hit before, not once, or afraid, and certainly never from anything that hadn't even hurt. But he'd never come up against anyone who could have killed him without trying. Mori almost had. It hadn't been a considered lashing out; it had been panic. If he'd punched Thaniel in the throat, he would have broken his neck.

'I'm sorry,' Mori said softly. He was holding his hands up, absolutely still.

Thaniel shook his head once. He wanted to vanish. He hadn't listened properly, before; he hadn't bothered to imagine what it must be like for Mori to remember someone wasting and weakening, fading into nothing but sickness and then, at last, like a mercy, the shrouds and the finality of a graveyard; the house finally without anyone coughing or dying in it, waking without worrying about looking after the wreck of another human, airing away that rank chemical smell of antiseptic medicine, settling down with a brilliant, laughing wife – only to jolt back to the present and find it was all ahead and that person, that thing, was leaning up close.

'No, I'll go. I'll go. I'm sorry.'

Mori was quiet at first. 'Are you all right?'

'I'm fine. Christ, it's not your fault. I'll get on in the morning. And then ...' He had to fight hard for something

197

that sounded almost natural but non-binding. 'I'll see you when I see you.'

'Thaniel … I've never been more ashamed of anything than this.'

'All right, calm down. It's not the end of the world, is it.' It came out rougher than he meant, but that was worlds better than weeping.

Mori tilted his eyes down. 'Right. Well; night.'

'Mm.' Thaniel waited for a few minutes after Mori had gone, crushing his fingernails into his palms, then cried until he could think again.

———

He was surprised when, as he was putting his things together the next morning, Six announced that she was coming to the legation too. When he asked if she was sure, she nodded and said that the generator here was very unreliable.

'We're not going to see much of Mori,' he said. It was a shock to hear it aloud and he had to scrabble for a lie. 'It's too far to come to and fro, and the train's too expensive.'

'Mori's optional,' she said.

He pulled her close. She didn't like it and squirmed away, but a few minutes later she came back in holding a huge, fluffy owl that didn't seem to mind being carried round.

'Six,' he said, somewhere between laughing and terrified. 'They bite, put it down.'

'He doesn't bite. He's called Owlbert. He's coming too.' She held it out to him, looking awkward, and he realised she was trying to make up for not being as companionable as she thought she should be. Owlbert hooted, a deep smooth purple.

Thaniel had to swallow hard. 'All right, petal. Let's go and find a cage then.'

For his part, Owlbert seemed so tame that Thaniel suspected he was probably considered a bit of a holy fool in the owl world. Thaniel took him carefully and held out his arm to see if he wanted to fly away, but the owl only shuffled up closer and pushed his head under Thaniel's chin.

'Owlbert loves you,' Six offered mutedly, not looking at him.

He knelt down to see if he could catch her eye. 'You know it's all right to do things a bit differently, don't you? You don't have to touch people if you don't want. Your way's not wrong.'

She nodded once, still at the floor. 'No, but yours is, you're extremely peculiar and trying. You really do take it out of me.'

PART THREE

TWENTY-TWO

Abashiri, Hokkaido, 10th January 1889

Takiko slid the door open a few inches and then jerked back when a lot of snow tried to come in. Her uncle – not really her uncle, more like someone's second cousin, but they had never quite worked out what – leaned back from the table in the next room when she picked up the spade. She glanced back and he gave her a guilty give-it-a-try motion with one small fist. She made a face at him to make him smile. She had tried to explain that you couldn't feel guilty about helping less when you were eighty-four, but he wasn't convinced.

The packed snow was printed perfectly into the shape of the door. She shoved the edge of the spade into it. Like she'd hoped, most of it collapsed, nearly all air and powder, but at about waist-height, it crunched with unpromising solidity. She dug slowly, not wanting to end up tired before she even started work. When she reached the end of the little path and broke out onto the main road, which had been cleared by the early prisoner detail, she heaped up a bit of snow at the edge of the path where her uncle would see it and gave it stick arms, and a face with bits of gravel. After some thought, she gave it a stick headdress as well, since there was no reason you couldn't have a Mohican snowman.

203

Her uncle hurried out with a little bento box. In it was a square of shepherd's pie to heat up. He had heard from some relative or other that she was foreign, and yesterday he had spent four hours looking at an ancient English recipe book he'd sent for from Tokyo, and put together with alchemical precision a perfect shepherd's pie, because he said she ought to feel at home, and he wanted to feel useful. She squeezed his hands and did her best not to cry.

When she had arrived last week, the days were still clear enough to see Mount Shari. It was a long way off, miles over the marshes, but the peaks had been crookedly white against a blue sky. This week, though, the snow had fallen and fallen, and the murmur at the fish market that spring might be coming early had thoroughly died. Even indoors, her uncle had tied tiny hessian bags around the four pears his pear tree was making. It still looked worse for wear.

Takiko had never been in cold like it. She hadn't even known that this kind of cold existed in Japan, but that might have been because she had never really thought of Hokkaido as Japan. The island was a great manta-ray shape, and in the northern part of it – Abashiri was right up near the manta ray's left antenna – you were closer to Vladivostok than Tokyo. It was, everyone said with some pride, the southern-most point in the world where the sea froze.

The cold was convenient, though. It was easy to stay locked indoors going slowly mad with cabin fever, so her uncle hadn't seemed surprised when she'd suggested she start working at the prison. They lived right next door, her uncle knew the guardsmen, and they had been looking for a cleaning woman for weeks. When her uncle took it up in his shy way with the warden, the warden had said hallelujah, the last girl had fallen in a ditch and frozen to death, and could she start tomorrow.

She stood in the road, holding the spade and looking up at the hill and the prison's high tower. The cold was unbelievable, the shredding kind, and when she tried to put the spade down, it had stuck to her glove. She unpeeled herself.

She had never been inside a prison. Her uncle said this one was run well, though with fewer staff than it needed. People escaped every now and then, but not from inside; they ran when they were out building the new roads, in the forest where it was hard to see. The warden had solved that problem by dressing them all in bright red.

The main road was ridged with tracks, perfect half-sphere lines that cut through the snow in snaking patterns. Outside the prison gates, the prisoners all wore chains and a heavy iron ball around one ankle. One of the guards had come round for dinner last Wednesday and brought an iron ball for her to try on. She could move it, and it didn't hurt, not with the thick leather straps that spread the weight, but it would have been impossible to go fast.

Takiko hadn't gone far when she caught up with the prison detail. The prisoners were a brilliant red splotch in all the white, their guards mounted on either side. One of them saw her coming.

'Move for the lady!' he called.

'It's all right, it's easier for me to go around you,' she called back. He nodded, looking relieved, and she climbed on the hard-packed verge of snow.

'Eyes front,' the guard said tightly.

The prisoners were all quiet. The winter was too hard for anyone to think about anything but not freezing to the spot.

Having tried the iron ball, she wouldn't have been afraid of them even if they'd laughed and hooted. She could have outrun them hopping. They weren't serious criminals, either. The serious ones were marched out at one o'clock in the morning. All last week, she'd woken in the night to the eerie labour song they sang as they trudged to the forest in the coal-pit dark.

The prison was at the top of the hill. On the north side, it overlooked the village and the sea; to the south and the west, there was forest, and to the east, the marshes and the fang of Mount Shari. Over that way, the dead reeds had buckled under the weight of the snow, and that whole stretch of land was a decaying colour almost the same as the strange brown sand on the beach. With the plunge in temperature, the trees were contracting still, and now she was close to them, she could hear their weird laughing, a guttural noise that some prehistoric instinct wanted to get away from.

Snow had blown up against the prison walls like buttresses and settled along the tops of the gates and the watchtowers. It was a vast irregular place. Between the long frozen winters and the warm summers, wood crumbled fast, and so some pieces of the structure were always newer than others and some were rotting. It smelled of fresh-cut wood and mould, and moss, and the sharp salt zing of the sea.

At the little side gate beside the main one, she looked back down the hill. The sea was frozen. It was still moving, just a tiny swaying, crunching bits of ice together in ridges and chunks. She banged on the door.

'Hey, Mr Horikawa! It's me.'

The door creaked open and Horikawa, the gate keeper, stepped back with his hands cupped over his cigarette to keep them warm. He spoke round it rather than move it. 'In you come, girl, before the prisoners.'

She ducked in and he clanked the door hard behind her. The way in was a short tunnel under the watchtower above, open to the weather on the other side. A tiny staircase led up on her left. She stopped. 'Do I just go to the main ...?'

'Expect so,' he said, lifting his eyebrows to ask why she didn't know. 'Whatever you're doing, do it before the detail gets in.'

She crossed the main courtyard, expecting someone to shout that she wasn't meant to go that way. Something scratched at the door of what she had thought was a shed. It made her jump.

'Can I come out yet?' a voice whispered, nearly lost on the wind. There was no glow of a light or a fire from under the door, and no windows. It was only wood.

'Sorry,' she said. 'I'm not a guard.' She stared at the door. 'Sorry,' she said again, and crossed the courtyard as fast as she could, feeling dirty all the way. It was enough to make her want to turn around and leave. But she had promised not to.

───────

A couple of nights before Christmas, coming back from a ride with Kuroda, whose horse had thrown him and who was limping back a fair way behind them on Tanaka's arm, Takiko and Mori had followed the steep hill path up along the southern edge of the Yoruji graveyard. The horses were trotting parallel a short way off, playing and looking pleased with themselves. She was certain Mori had persuaded Kuroda's to buck, although she hadn't seen how.

The lighthouse flashed; from here, it was only possible to see the glow above the crest of the hill. Mori slowed and looked across the cemetery. He had an inhuman way of moving, fast and then slow.

Like silver cicadas, the bells in the trees and in the grave-yard began to sing. Even though she knew just what it was, and that the lines were all connected back to the lighthouse and the machine there that generated random intervals, it was eerie. Near the gate and up by the house, dark figures moved; Kuroda's men, changing their positions.

Mori pushed one fist hard into his chest, and by the uplight from her lamp, she could see the pulse in his wrist pounding far too fast. She'd seen people have nervous attacks before, actors mainly, but it seemed different on someone who was normally so calm.

She took his arm, pushed his sleeve back and then slapped his wrist, hard. His hand flickered and he nodded.

'Thank you,' he said quietly.

Caught between exasperation and guilt, her voice came out with a sharp mix of both. 'Why are you letting Kuroda do this? He's got you trapped here. What's in it for you?'

He shook his head slightly. 'I don't remember why. I can't remember anything very well at the moment, not really past next week. Then it's only snatches. There's a strong chance I might be dead soon. It makes things foggy, because having a future at all is unlikely.' He sighed. 'It's why Thaniel left. I kept walking into rooms and seeing him and thinking I was seeing a ghost; I was convinced he was already ...' He shook his head once. 'I don't know what's wrong with me. I've nearly died before, it hasn't been like – it hasn't made me feel confused. But I keep waking up and not knowing when I am. It feels like being drugged, I … well, maybe they will give me something and my useless brain is reacting beforehand.'

Quite gradually, the long nerve down her back shrank and pulled all the bones together. It hadn't occurred to her until then that he was really risking anything at all. 'If Kuroda could kill you, why is he still walking about?'

'Because I need all this to happen.'

'Why?'

'I told you, no idea anymore. I just know I got myself into this on purpose. So it must be necessary.'

'And you haven't written anything down for yourself?' She couldn't keep all the incredulity out of her voice. 'No instructions? At all? You're walking through fire with no idea why?'

'I had this done in Russia.' He turned back his sleeve. Just under his elbow was a small, neat line of text.

Make Kuroda fight, but let him win.

'What the hell use is that?' she demanded. Without meaning to, she brushed the tattoo with her fingertip. Mori hated tattoos. They made you look, he said, like you were in the yakuza, and only teenagers and people who lived with their mothers wanted that.

Horribly, he relaxed when she touched him; as though it was all just Kuroda, not her too. Something deep in her gut twisted. It was easy to talk about Mori like a force, something terrible. It was easy to forget he was just a person too, with light bones and a deer's shyness even around people he knew quite well.

'Well, useful enough,' he said. 'It's much better for me not to know in any detail.'

She didn't understand.

He smiled. 'I'm the easiest person in the world to interrogate. You don't even need to hurt me, you just need to intend to and there I am writhing around on the floor like an idiot feeling ghost pain from a finger you haven't even broken yet.' He didn't say, as you know. Her insides shrank up with guilt anyway, and a rotten sort of anger that he'd brought it up. She pushed it down. She had seen it too much in Kuroda now to imagine there was a single righteous thing about it. 'Listen, Pepper ... we talked a while ago about how I might need to ask you to do something for me one day.'

She frowned. 'I asked what you wanted for a wedding present.'

'Yes. It's now.' His eyes were serious and quiet, and like he always had when he fell still, he looked like something older than human beings. 'I know you aren't sure about me anymore. I know that what I did to Countess Kuroda was terrible. I'm not asking for a promise, just ... some consideration.'

'Why would I even consider it? I stopped feeling obliged to you the moment she hit the floor.'

'I'll give you anything you want.'

'What? I don't want money—'

'I didn't say money, I said anything.' He shook his head once. 'Anything. You want to keep me locked up forever, I'll do it. You want Kuroda dead, I'll do it, or ironclad women's rights, or universities in Countess Kuroda's name, a family; anything.' He didn't touch her, but his fingertips were an inch above her arm. 'No tricks.'

She stared at him for a long time. She should have said no, she could feel it, but it would have been right on the line where prudence became cowardice. 'Kuroda faces real justice for what he did, and you never manipulate anything ever again if it's more significant than a pet rabbit.'

'Done,' he said softly. He looked fragile in that desperate, terrible, composed way he had on the night the Countess died.

She swallowed. He had killed the Countess, he was by every measure in the world a murderer, and God knew how often he'd done it when Takiko wasn't there to see, but she had an awful sense that she had just slammed a beautiful wild animal, one that had always trusted her, into a cage. When she spoke, her voice came out too harsh. 'So what is it you want me to do?'

'There's a prison camp in the north, in Hokkaido.' He paused as if it was hard to make himself say the words. 'Abashiri. You have an uncle who lives there; I sent him there years ago. Get inside the prison. I can't remember now why you need to be there. But I do know that you need to look for something …' He was staring hard into the middle distance. 'Strange,' he said at last. 'Anything that doesn't belong. I know that's counterproductively vague.'

She hesitated. She'd heard about the prisons in the north. Everyone had. But only in general terms, because nobody ever came back, and they didn't let journalists in. 'Mori, you were in Russia for six months. And now the Russian fleet is here. What if you did that? What if what you've forgotten is that in the long run, you think Japan will be better off if it's part of the Russian Empire, and you're arranging the war?'

He nodded a little. 'Yes. I sent them, yes, I told a friend in the Okhrana to send them before Kuroda's new ironclads arrived. I don't know why, though.' He paused. 'I told him something about wars and Americans, but I think I was lying.'

The honesty set her off balance. She had expected excuses or denials, not just a frank owning up. 'If they fire on Nagasaki,' she said slowly, 'they'll murder tens of thousands of people.'

'I know,' he said. 'I don't know why I'd risk that. Can you think why I'd do that? I didn't – tell you, somehow?'

'No.'

He nodded again. He was holding himself steady and still now, but the edges of the panic from before were still there. He was looking past her, not at her.

'Hokkaido,' she said after a long time. There was nothing in Hokkaido but endless forest, bears, and those labour camps. It was exactly the kind of place Mori would send someone meddlesome to get her out of the way. 'I'll think about it.'

He hugged her, hard, and not like he was worried he could hurt her. It was a thump of bone on bone. When he kissed her forehead, an ashamed part of her was glad he was unhappy.

Another part, one that whispered in the Duke's paper voice, wondered if that couple hundreds of years ago in the woods had thought they'd made a clever deal with the Winter King too.

———

She was too anxious to go to bed. Instead she sat by one of the hot pools with a view over the bay, her ankles in the water, and tried to calm down. If Mori knew she was helping Kuroda and he was angry, he had no need to send her to Hokkaido on a wild goose chase. He could just arrange for her to be arrested for something vague right here, or for her to break a leg falling down the stairs.

And he wouldn't have made a promise like the one he had if he'd any intention of keeping it, surely. Surely.

She wondered what it looked like when a fleet of ironclads shelled a town. She knew what it looked like after; when she was little, they used to go on holiday to Kagoshima, which the Americans had blasted to kingdom come not that long ago. Her father had put her in one of the craters in the castle walls to take a photograph. She asked Kuroda when he came out.

'It's beautiful, actually,' he said. When he sat down, he kept a tentative distance. Ever since that night with the Countess, he had been anxious around her. She didn't know if it was because he was genuinely frightened of himself now around women, or because he was scared of what she might put on the stage. 'Like God's own firework show. I'll take you on a ship one day, you can see. Are you worried about the Russians?'

'Not worried, I was just thinking about it.' She sighed. 'Abashiri prison. Mori wants me to go there. Does that mean anything to you?'

Kuroda frowned. 'Abashiri, no. Well, it's a labour camp. It's one of eight or nine up there. Did he say anything else about it?'

'I'm worried he's sending me because he knows I'm talking to you.' She was almost sure Kuroda was lying. His eyes had sparked when she mentioned Abashiri. It was such a benign-sounding word; it meant 'netting-run', so it must have begun life as a fishing village and not a labour camp, but already it had more gravity than it should have. 'To get me out of the way. If you know what's there and why he might want me to go, I'll go. If he's just getting rid of me — the winters are hard up there. It might be a death sentence.'

Kuroda smiled. 'How do I know you're not in cahoots with him and you're not going to do one of your Kali manoeuvres and screw me utterly? You're only talking to me at all because I'm the lesser of two evils, but he's a charming bastard. He could have talked you round.'

She shook her head. 'You are the lesser of two evils. You're a vicious idiot with a drinking problem, but he ... isn't. He's entirely sane, and very clever. And he watched you drink, and drink, and then he watched you kill your wife. Maybe it was you who hit her, but only like it's the bullet and not the man behind the gun that hits someone. And now, he's watching the Russian fleet get closer, and closer. If there's a choice between loyalty to my charming husband or serving my country, I'll serve.'

'Well, you're a samurai now,' he said gruffly. 'Obviously you want to serve. Basic chivalry.'

She sighed. Probably it was a decent translation of what she'd said into Hopeless Posh-Boy, but it made her fingernails itch. 'Chivalry — Kuroda, you know when women put vegetables on a spoon and zoom it round so their kids think it's a magic butterfly or something? Chivalry is just what your mum called being a decent human so you'd feel like a really good boy when you were nice to people. Don't say it to grown-ups.'

He snorted. 'Like I say. Samurai.'

They were both quiet for a while.

'At Abashiri,' Kuroda said at last. 'If you see that he's set up something — dodgy. Put a stop to it.'

She nodded. God knew what was really going on in Hokkaido. The only thing to do was go to the north and see, and make sure that somehow or other, she got a collar on Mori and Kuroda both, before either of them could do anything too nasty.

Although she had sturdy boots and two pairs of socks on, and thick trousers under the rough work dress, Takiko's feet were numb by the time she reached the prison's main doors. One stood propped open. Inside was a broad entrance space, and in the middle of it, boxed off to keep in the heat, was a tiny office. It was all wood, except for a small paper shutter, which was open.

'Hello?' she said, feeling like she was looking into a dolls' house.

The guard hunched up at the kotatsu looked up from his newspaper. Despite the warmth inside, he had a scarf muffled up over his ears. She wasn't surprised. He looked ill in an unspecific, long-running way; too stringy, too sore-eyed. 'Who are you?' he asked indignantly. He sounded like he had a cold.

'I'm Mr Tsuru's niece, the new cleaner.'

'Oh!' The guard looked startled, then laughed. 'I was expecting an old lady.' He stood up, and the little paper hatchway proved in fact to be a tiny door. The hatchway slid sideways and the lower part opened outward like a gate. He looked pleased to find he was a head taller than her. The smell of smoke had drifted out with him. She pined. 'Right, come with me, Miss Tsuru. You'll need to get started right away.'

TWENTY-THREE

Tokyo, 10th February 1889

The morning was cold and dim under gathering storm clouds, and the floating market on the Imperial Canal gave off such a beautiful glow from its red lamps that even people who had imagined they were in a hurry for work found themselves coming down from the bridges, onto the jetties cobbled together from apple crates and parts of old carts, and into the warmth under the bright canopies of the boats.

Thaniel put Six in front of him on the way across to the first boat. The man who owned it was selling chicken skewers from a big open grill whose frame he'd hung about with paper lamps, the tops spotted with grease. Every boat in the market had red lamps, but all different sizes and all different shades of red, with black characters painted down the sides to say what the stalls were selling. Six shot across the gangplank and vanished out of sight. Thaniel had decided to stop worrying someone was going to steal her or that she would fall in the river. They came to the floating market every morning, and every morning she was fine. She had bitten people before, probably more often than she would have if he hadn't given her a sugar-mouse every time she did.

The next boat sold fresh lobsters and the one after that had tea and stronger things. Five men were sitting along the tiny makeshift bar on stools of mismatched heights.

Nothing was in a straight line and there was music some-where, but it was too early for crowds. Snow feathered in and disappeared in the heat from the big grills and braziers. Thaniel walked over the gangways with his hands in his pockets, passing between clouds of lovely heat and gusts of river cold.

There was ice around the hulls of the boats, and a veneer just forming over the wider gaps. It was not the morning to fall in.

He found the chestnut boat a good way further downriver than usual. Six wasn't there, but the chestnut man had just added a bag of new nuts to his grille, which was a caramel-ised, amber mess from the honey he put over everything. The hot smell of burnt sugar drifted between the boats.

'Have you seen …?'

The man pointed next door. Thaniel leaned around the corner. It was a lamp shop, all kinds, but mainly paper with little designs, and a few fittings for gas outlets. Up high on one shelf, wrapped in cotton and paper and tied up with string, like bombs, were lightbulbs. The lamp-seller sat at the back with a newspaper. There was a sign up on a chalk-board on the counter, advertising a half-price sale for something called highly perfumed water, exclamation mark, which Thaniel mulled over for a while before he wondered if it meant kerosene.

'Morning,' he said.

'Morning,' said the lamp lady. She was in her eighties at least, bundled up so well that she was spherical. 'Would you like some kerosene? Half price. Won't be able to give it away if this keeps up.'

'If what …? No, thank you. Have you seen a little girl?'

'I'm here,' Six said dutifully. She was looking at some tiny candles. There was a Catholic mission not far away and they were souvenir versions of gilded altar candles.

'It really is very cheap for kerosene,' the lamp lady added.

'I know, but it's all right, thank you.' Thaniel glanced down at Six, who never asked for anything. 'Do you have any lightbulbs?'

'Lightbulbs! No, no, no, nasty silly things, you don't need lightbulbs,' the lamp lady said quickly.

'She collects them,' he explained.

'No lightbulbs here.'

'That box on the shelf behind you has "lightbulbs" written on it,' he said after a moment.

'No it hasn't,' she said. 'Kerosene is much more useful, you know.'

'Chestnuts,' called the chestnut man.

'See you,' said the lamp lady, and nodded approvingly when Six bowed.

Thaniel went away none the wiser, which was how most conversations ended now. There was an English way of thinking and a Japanese one, and although he was fluent enough to step over the gap, he still fell into it quite a lot too.

He gave Six the chestnuts and helped rearrange her scarf once she had tucked them down her front for heat, then followed her back through the market and out into the sharp daylight. The sky was gunmetal and grainy with snow. The bell above the Dutch legation tolled eight. Six waited for him at the side gate to the British one.

When he looked back the way they had come, the bridges over the canal – which was actually the moat around the Palace – were vivid with deep purple banners. The parades would be tomorrow; the Emperor was announcing the new

Constitution. It was going to be huge. Everyone was getting a day off work. It was making Thaniel wish that people in England would see a way to caring so much about politics.

'May I go over the snow?' Six said, looking at the pristine white roll of the lawn.

'Better had, or someone else will.'

She didn't run, or make shapes; she only walked and watched the marks her shoes left.

Thaniel went on the path, because it was shorter and his lungs hurt already. The borders, bare now, were still spidery with old vines. The gardener had hung labels from parasol handles, and now they and their strings were all frozen perfectly, marking patches where the flowers would be in spring.

'Morning, Mr Fukuoka,' Six called toward the tents set up on the lawn. Between them, drooping now in the middle because a fold in the canvas was weighed down with snow, was a protest banner that said in tall kanji, *Respect the Emperor, Expel the Barbarian.*

'Morning, love,' Fukuoka said, tired. He was scooping snow into a kettle, looking worse for wear. He and his mad friend Yuna had been camped out here ever since the junior diplomats had shooed them away from the front door last month, and they had a few more friends now. It was, technically, part of Thaniel's job to make sure the legation premises were not full of nationalist protesters, but it felt like bullying to call the militia for five miserable men and a sign.

'How's it coming?' Thaniel said.

'Got some more lads coming soon, for the Promulgation tomorrow. Hoping to get a few journalists up here.'

'There will be. But don't get too cold; come in for tea if you want. They've been baking a bit over-enthusiastically

219

this week, so there's plenty of leftovers. If you don't mind everything in Imperial purple.'

'I've got some already,' Fukuoka said in a guilty hush. 'But don't tell him.'

'Barbarians go home!' shouted the tent.

Thaniel bowed slightly to Fukuoka, who bowed back. He went on up the gentle path, feeling grateful he wasn't living in a tent. As he came up the legation steps, something gave him a vicious static shock through his sleeve and he swore, but when he looked around there was nothing it could have been. The steps were stone. Lightning flickered between the Palace buildings, but there was no thunder. He rubbed his arm and wondered if it might just be the air in general. It tasted of iron. Storm weather; he hoped it would break soon.

'I thought I might build an igloo,' Six said quickly before he could tell her to come in.

He wanted to say no, and to keep away from Fukuoka's friends, but it was instincts like that – people deciding that locals weren't to be trusted with children – which had made everyone angry in the first place.

'Come here.' He knelt down when she did. 'Let's see a left hook; right hook; uppercut, uppercut – good. Do it again and move your feet properly. Faster. Good girl. All right, go on.'

In the spacious hallway, the butler must have had some shocks of his own, because he was tying tea-towels around the handles of all the doors. Halfway inside, Thaniel caught another one off the lion knocker on the front door, stronger this time, and heard himself make a resentful noise. The butler nodded sympathetically.

'This weather – do you normally have electrical storms?' Thaniel asked, and noticed too late that he was making it sound like the butler's own personal fault.

'No, sir, it's all very singular.'

It was still early and downstairs was quiet, although the ceiling creaked as people moved to and fro upstairs. He took off his coat gradually, because his shoulders ached, but then thought better of it. It was incredibly cold even inside. He could see the current of his breath.

Vaulker shot out of his office waving a piece of paper. 'This is your department!'

'Morning,' said Thaniel.

'It's the bloody kitchen staff. They just left me this bloody note. Apparently they're leaving. Blackmail for another bloody raise like the grubby little Arabs they are.'

Thaniel took the note. 'This isn't from all of them, it's only Mrs Nakano's girls. They say their mother is bringing in her friend Mrs Enno and her daughters, who are ...' He turned over the page, which smelled of Mrs Nakano's sinus-destroying cigarette smoke. 'Thick in the head.'

'Tell her that if I hear one more squeak about ghosts, I shall sack them all. It's not New Year anymore. I'm sure I can find other less neurotic people.'

'Vaulker ...' Thaniel picked up a spare tea-towel from the butler's basket and tucked it into the letterbox, which had just sparked. He tipped his head to look at it properly, nearly convinced somebody must have posted a sparkler through it, but no. He was going to write his sister a letter about the weather. She'd love to hear about a place with worse weather than Edinburgh. 'There's a nationalist protest on the lawn. If we sack our entire staff for no reason, the first thing they'll do is go out there and join in, and probably bring all their friends, and probably egg anyone who tries to come for an interview.' He'd enjoyed it at first, but the shine had worn off arguing with Vaulker. They should have been friends and they weren't. They were the same age, they were in the same place and they knew all the same people at the Foreign Office. But Thaniel could never put aside the certainty that Vaulker was lazy, and Vaulker made no secret of worrying that Thaniel might lose his civilised veneer one day and punch someone. If they had talked about it early on, it would probably have been all right, and they would have forgiven each other a lot, but they hadn't, and now those little dislikes had solidified into a cement block.

'Damned if I shall be frightened of a protest,' Vaulker said, but glassily, with cracks in the surface.

Thaniel didn't say it would have to go into dispatches, and that Fanshaw in Whitehall wouldn't be impressed to hear that they'd turned a small, pathetic protest into a full-blooded one the day before the new Constitution was announced and government dignitaries were in and out at all hours, along with journalists. It would probably be one of those invisible-ink marks against Vaulker's name when the next Berlin posting opened. 'I'm not saying we should be frightened. I'm saying that it will be a long while with-out cooked food.'

Vaulker seemed to ease. There was a tiny moment, not the first one, during which Thaniel felt like he and Vaulker were both holding chisels, but neither of them knew where to begin chipping, and neither of them wanted to get dust on the carpet. Instead they went into the translation office to fetch the morning papers.

As they came in, Pringle was building a tipi of firewood, his sleeves already sooty. He flushed when Vaulker asked what on earth he was doing.

'The staff won't lay fires, sir, they say it brings the ghosts.'

Vaulker made a noise like a disapproving horse and looked at Thaniel. 'You were saying?'

'It won't light,' Pringle said miserably. He was bundled up in a scarf.

'I'll do it,' Thaniel murmured. Pringle's tipi was all heavy pieces of wood, no kindling, and no sawdust.

It was a relief to sit down on the hearth and do something practical. Vaulker leaned against the chimney, the back of his paisley waistcoat crackling where it caught against the brickwork. He gave Thaniel a brief, disapproving look; Thaniel had a feeling that Vaulker thought doing anything useful was a sign of bad breeding. Pringle flopped onto the nearest chair and hunched over, rubbing his hands together.

'I've never been so cold in my life.'

Thaniel bent forward over the grate and blew softly on the little flame he'd just coaxed to life in a new nest of sawdust. It caught and clicked, and then snackled over the kindling. Pringle edged gratefully closer. Thaniel showed him the sawdust bag for later, and the little kindling sticks.

'Ooh, fire,' one of the other juniors said from behind the door, and hurried in.

Only a few seconds later, Mrs Nakano's daughters stopped in the doorway. Thaniel thought at first that they wanted to come and get warm too, but when they started across, they came much too fast. They ran. One of them snatched the tea-towels off the cupboard door handles. The other pushed Thaniel aside hard, and together they plunged their arms into the grate and smothered the little fire.

'Hey!' Pringle squeaked, sounding very young in distress.

'What in God's name?' snapped Vaulker at the same time, and then everyone was shouting at once in a blinding salvo of reds and indignant blues, and Thaniel couldn't make out anything from anyone. Vaulker snatched the older girl's arm and began to shake her.

'Tom! Jesus Christ.' Thaniel caught Vaulker's wrists to stop him and the look he got for it was hotter than anger. 'Let her go,' he said quietly. He put himself between them, which forced Vaulker to step back.

'What is going on?' Thaniel asked her in Japanese.

'We've been telling everyone all morning!' she said, nearly as angry as Vaulker. 'You can't have fires! They bring the ghosts! Why do you think we're leaving the kitchens?'

'They bring the ghosts how?'

'How should I know? But the ghosts like fire. Don't light fires. Tell everyone. It'll all be worse than ever in this weather.'

'What's she saying?' Vaulker asked.

'I don't know.' Thaniel shook his head once and switched to Japanese again as the butler came in, alarmed. 'Mr Ueno, I think Miss Nakano needs a cup of tea and ...' He stopped, because Ueno was shaking his head.

'She's right, sir. It's the fires. With this storm, I really don't think we ought to light any more.' He swallowed, and looked agonised to be arguing. 'I had a nasty scare myself this morning. I believe if we want the legation to run smoothly, it would be best ... that is to say, if the gentlemen will insist on lighting fires, I'm afraid we must all leave you to it. Even the stable-boys agree.'

While he had been talking, some of the other servants had materialised too. They must have been waiting all morning for this argument. Everyone was nodding. Not a single person looked uncertain.

'They say they'll leave if we light fires,' Thaniel said at last to Vaulker. 'They say the fires bring the ghosts.'

'Oh, for—'

'Just for now,' Thaniel interrupted. 'We'll have to put up with it for now. We can hire new people but not everyone all at once.' He felt the servants watching him. None of them really spoke English, but they were fluent when it came to tone and posture.

Vaulker studied him and the chisel went down. Thaniel didn't think he would be picking it up again soon. 'Very well then,' he said. 'No fires. Someone do alert Dr Willis, however; I can see flu and lung disorders hoving in force over the horizon.' He left, and his office door clicked once as it closed, then again as he locked it.

Pringle and the other juniors looked worried. Ueno the butler had melted away already, and most of the other staff were on their way out too, but the Nakano girls were both still standing in front of Thaniel.

'Whatever you mean by it, I wish you'd just say,' he said.

'Fire brings the ghosts,' the eldest girl said solidly. 'I'm sorry, Mr Steepleton, but it does, and I for one can't bear to see any more of them. Do you know who the last one was? A little boy who had fallen in the oven. I don't think you would like to see that twice either.'

He sighed. 'Come and talk to me if you think of anything I can do.'

'You can keep the fires out,' she said.

Her sister smiled. 'We know you're doing your best,' she said as the older girl turned away. She was softer-spoken, less like their mother. 'But your best would be better if you'd listen to us.'

Once they had gone and the argument was over, Thaniel felt how cold it was again and tucked his hands under his coat sleeves to warm them up on the insides of his elbows.

Pringle squeaked. 'Why is it always me?'

'Another electric shock,' one of the juniors explained when Thaniel looked back. Three of them were huddled together on the dead hearth, in a miserable row like winter ducklings.

'Silk shirt?' Thaniel asked.

'Yes.' Pringle brightened. 'New, actually. Got it for an absolute steal at a charming little place in Kabuki-cho. You must go. If you mention my name you might get a discount, the store girl seems rather keen on me.'

Thaniel had to concentrate not to interrupt him. He did like Pringle, but it was difficult sometimes to separate Pringle himself from Pringle's packaging. He had differently coloured handkerchiefs for every day of the week, ironed between two sheets of crepe paper into origami tulips. Thaniel's soul cramped whenever he thought about paying so much attention to something meant for sneezing on. 'I mean you're a conductor. Better change into cotton.'

Pringle smiled and nodded too much. 'Ah! Yes, sir.'

Thaniel nodded once, slightly, to make him do it less. Pringle copied him. Thaniel felt proud of him. However badly Eton and Oxford had tangled him up, Pringle did try hard.

'Sir?' Pringle said. 'Is there anything in the papers about the weather?'

'Is there?' Thaniel said to them all, because they were meant to be learning Japanese too.

'It's too hard to read,' one of the others mumbled.

'Anything about science is deuced difficult,' Pringle put in.

Thaniel relented. It was too cold to be a school-master. 'Everyone's saying it's the mountain,' he said, motioning towards the window where Fuji would have been visible in clearer weather. 'Something about iron in the rock.' He picked up one of the ironed newspapers and flicked through to the weather section. 'Yes. The Met Office says—'

'Our Met Office?' Pringle chipped in.

'No, the Tokyo Met Office.'

'They've got one here?'

'No, they've got a shaman who forecasts the weather with a special dance.'

Pringle looked uncertain, then laughed experimentally. Thaniel smiled to show he'd got it right.

'The Met Office thinks that in the right conditions you'll get this kind of thing every so often within a certain radius of Fuji.' He scanned the dense print. 'Increased electromagnetism when the volcano is active. They're not too sure.'

'I can't believe you know the kanji for electromagnetism,' Pringle said.

Thaniel showed him the article. Pringle giggled when he saw that the sign for magnet was just the sign for stone with wiggly lines coming off it. Behind them, the ashes smoked sadly. The tea-towel was a black web now.

The butler leaned in. 'Sir, there's a gentleman to see you. He says he's misplaced his wife.' He spoke quietly, exuding apology for interrupting again.

'A gentleman? Ah – he needs Mr Vaulker, not me.'

'He asked for you by name.'

Thaniel stood up, puzzled, because he didn't know anyone in Tokyo who would come to see him here. His heart tightened wondering if it was Mori. He stopped still when he saw his ex-wife's new husband studying the paintings in the hall.

'Matsumoto.' He hadn't thought he'd expected Mori enough to feel disappointed, but he did. It felt like being punched unexpectedly, when you were still tying on your gloves. 'What's happened?'

'Oh, hullo,' Matsumoto said. He was handsome and impermeably cheerful, and exactly the same as he had been the last time Thaniel had seen him four years ago. He always wore beautiful suits from Paris, pitch-perfectly chic, and he always had shoelaces that were a different colour to his shoes. Today, they were a pleasing shade of kingfisher blue. They sounded like a girl singing a high note.

When the question arrived, it was a peculiar one. 'You haven't seen Grace, have you?'

'What? No, we're not really … on speaking terms. Why?'

Matsumoto hung his hat on the banister of the stairs while he took off his scarf. He smelled, even a few feet away, of vanilla. 'I seem to have lost her. Or put her somewhere, I really don't know. But never mind. She's not turned up here?'

'No,' Thaniel said, bewildered. 'Sorry, how can you lose her?'

'Oh, you know what she's like. One minute she's at the university and then she's gone off to the States to talk to Tesla about his magic tower. I lose track.' He paused. 'She thinks it's nosy if I ask what she's doing too often.'

'I haven't seen her,' Thaniel said again. He frowned when he remembered that her father had been asking after her at the Foreign Office.

'Never mind,' Matsumoto said, still cheery. 'How are you? You look ghastly.' Now Thaniel was scrutinising it, the cheer had cracks in it. Something like hysteria winked through. No, not something like. It was. Matsumoto was scared out of his mind.

'Do you want to come in for some tea?' Thaniel said. 'Tell me more about it?'

'No, no, I'll be on my way,' Matsumoto said quickly. 'Thank you. Didn't mean to fret at you. I guarantee she's gone to Colorado and I forgot to put it in the diary again.'

Thaniel moved towards the door to block the way without getting right up close to him, very aware of his own size. 'I can start a missing persons file, that's what we're here for—'

'God, no, she'd go spare,' he laughed, looking like he might break in half.

'No, you're coming in,' Thaniel insisted carefully. 'Matsumoto – what's going on?'

'No, I ...' Matsumoto snatched up his gloves.

Thaniel caught his arms. He didn't like doing it. Like Mori, Matsumoto was delicately made, but, unlike Mori, he had not been born into an era of sickening violence. 'Please. This is my job. You came here for a reason.'

'If anyone comes asking,' Matsumoto said softly, 'you can't tell them I told you. This was just a social visit. We like each other, don't we?'

'Of course.' It was true. He'd been glad when Grace and Matsumoto announced the banns in the newspaper. The two of them had gone to Oxford together; they were a damn sight better matched than Thaniel and Grace had ever been. 'Who would come asking?'

Matsumoto shook his head. 'Don't know. A government man,' he said, but he didn't look one. I thought he was from the mafia at first, they all dress like demented actors. But he had a court injunction ordering me to speak to no one about Grace. He wouldn't tell me where she was.' He swallowed. He was speaking much too fast. 'I ignored it, of course, it's absurd. People can't go round kidnapping a fellow's wife, can they? I asked some people in the cabinet, you know, my father's friends. Next day the same man came back with a baseball bat.'

'Jesus Christ. Come in and sit down. I've got brandy.'

'No. No, this was a bad idea. Look, you can't open a missing person's file. Her name's been tagged, or something. I just wondered if you'd – heard anything.'

'No,' Thaniel said, and couldn't quite believe it was true. There were so few British people in Japan that it seemed ridiculous they could lose one and not know. 'But Matsumoto, I can open that file. I'm diplomatic staff, if someone comes after me with a baseball bat then it's a major international incident.'

'Yes,' Matsumoto said, not sounding sure at all. 'I see.'

'Please stay.'

'No, I think someone's following me.' He hesitated, and then set his teeth together. 'Could you ask Keita Mori? It's true about him, isn't it, that he knows ... things?'

Thaniel shook his head, feeling pointless. 'I'm sorry. I haven't seen him since before Christmas, he's ...' Not coming back. Absurdly, even almost voicing that solidifying certainty growing like a cancer at the back of his mind made his eyes start to burn. Mortified, he coughed to hide it. 'I don't know where he is.'

'No. No, of course,' Matsumoto said, and left.

Thaniel stood in the doorway for a while, wondering what had just happened. He looked over the morgue reports for the last few weeks, but there were no unidentified white women in any of them.

He wired Tokyo University, just in case.

While he waited, he pulled across a few newspapers, meaning to do a quick translation of the headline articles so that Vaulker would have no excuse not to know what was going on. The Constitution parades tomorrow featured a lot, along with a good few little asides about the weather, and precautions about binding horses' hooves, and brief cheery theories about the electromagnetic properties of Mount Fuji. The Russian fleet was now floating in plain view of Nagasaki.

He couldn't concentrate. Seeing Matsumoto had spun him around.

He had known, when he left Yoruji, that whatever fragile bauble of a life he and Mori had in London was broken. It wasn't anyone's fault. But it was like Six's lightbulbs. The filaments were delicate things, and if the electrical current surged by even a couple of volts, they snapped, and the feedback shorted the circuit. You couldn't go round blaming the filament, or the electricity. They were just two things that any sensible person recognised might destroy each other if conditions were anything less than perfect. Thaniel liked to imagine he was a sensible person. God knew a sensible person would just get on with life, without sulking about broken lightbulbs.

He'd done quite well consciously. He'd been busy: even ordering dinner at a pub was a major intellectual exercise now if a person were to avoid cartilage in disguise as real food or a bartender who thought it would be funny to recommend raw whale. Finding out how bank accounts worked on diplomatic papers alone was mad; learning how the legation worked was even harder. He'd got into a new rhythm that, because Mori had never been part of it, didn't feel the loss of him.

Otherwise, he hadn't done so well. It was the oddest reaction to anything he'd ever had, but he'd stopped dreaming. Sleep took much longer to arrive than it ever had before. He'd lost the direction of it; he could lie down, but he couldn't turn towards it anymore. There was a broken compass somewhere in him. He was so ashamed that he couldn't come anywhere near speaking it.

If he sat still and let himself think, he could feel all the snapped filaments and cracked places.

The telegraph rattled. The overhead, which came through first in a brief clatter, was from Tokyo University.

Dr Grace Matsumoto on research sabbatical.

He snorted and answered straightaway. *Back when?*

There was another long pause. Then, finally, *Uncertain. Perhaps next year.*

I know she isn't on sabbatical. Where is she? Her family in England have reported her missing.

The reply was only one word.

Classified.

There was no diplomatic trick to get around that. *Unacceptable to have no information whatever about a British citizen,* he tried.

Can confirm Dr M alive and well.

Provide proof or I'll open a murder inquiry.

The line went silent.

Bizarre. He pulled a pen and a pad over to write Matsumoto a quick letter, to say what had happened. He was halfway through when something brushed his sleeve and made him jump. The curtains were silk, and they rippled towards him like something alive and hopeful.

TWENTY-FOUR

Abashiri, Hokkaido, 10th January 1889 (one month ago)

The prison was simple.

Upstairs, in a sparse office, were the warden and the warden's secretary. Below were the guards. There should have been thirty. There were only ten. Then there was Horikawa, the gatekeeper; the cook, whose name nobody knew; and now Takiko, to clean. In the cells were nine hundred and seventeen prisoners.

It was easy to get lost. The four wings, arranged like wheel-spokes connecting to the entrance hall, all looked identical. From that midpoint, they were long, dark, quadruplet corridors whose length she could only make out from the specks of lamps burning at the ends. High, high windows, darkened by the snowfall, let in some light from above the rafters, but only just enough to cast shadows. The guard told her not to talk to the prisoners, and certainly not to say her name. A man – and as he said it, he pointed out to the miserable wooden shed in the courtyard – had escaped and killed one of the guards.

Once she had found a brush and a bucket, Takiko edged downstairs to investigate the kitchens. There were taps close to the door and no sign of anyone else. She filled up the bucket, tipped in some cleaning salt, and struggled back upstairs with it, then along the long wing to start at the far end. It was difficult to see into the cells. Most of the doors were only bars, but all the light, what there was of it, was from the corridor. The men inside must have been able to see her, because some silhouettes came close to the bars as she went by. At the end, a friendly voice said,

'Make sure you keep rubbing your nose.'

'My nose?' she said slowly.

'Or you'll get frostbite. Shame if it were to fall off.'

'It would be a shame,' she agreed. 'Thank you.' She turned away from him and lit a cigarette so that she would have a clear excuse not to speak.

'Who are you, then?'

'I'm not meant to talk to you, I'm sorry.'

'I'm not a murderer, don't worry. I'm here because I wrote rather an ill-advised book.'

She kept a few feet away from the cell. The bars were wide enough for a slim person to fit their arms through. 'And how long have you been here?'

'Nine years. It wasn't even that interesting a book. One wishes one could at least go to prison for something spectacular. Do you know who the Marquis de Sade was?'

'I'll stop you there,' she said.

'I didn't mean that,' he protested. 'I meant he went to prison for a spectacular—'

'Stop scaring the girl,' a rougher voice said.

'I was just telling her about the frostbite—'

'She doesn't look stupid, she can probably work it out. Miss, you wouldn't have got any of those cigarettes spare, would you? I'd bloody kill for one. We can never get them in winter.'

'Don't tell her you'd kill someone!' the Marquis de Sade man squeaked.

She smiled. She could envisage a moment when knowing two sort-of-friendly prisoners might be a good thing. 'I really don't think you'd kill me, either of you.' She set two cigarettes on the ledge of the barred part of the door, at arm's length, so neither of them could grab her, but neither of them tried. The cigarettes disappeared inside.

'Thank you, miss,' the second voice said, with feeling.

'Hey! Is that a girl?' someone called from further up.

Takiko started with the brush while the wave of catcalls wore themselves out. She decided before long that the edges of the corridor would have to stay dusty. Someone put a part of himself he shouldn't have through the bars, so she hit it with the broom and carried on on the other side, and smiled as a shout of laughter went around the cells. The guard from the office came running. She inclined her head, because it seemed like a very specific kind of policy, to come when the prisoners were laughing rather than yelling. She explained, but he ignored her and unlocked the cell, and disappeared inside. She stood up slowly after a minute or so.

'Excuse me,' she said over the noise. 'Excuse me,' she said more loudly when he didn't hear. It had gone quiet on the rest of the wing. A slim shadow and a big one had come to the bars of the cell behind her, the one belonging the de Sade enthusiast. Both of them were holding the bars hard. She could see enough of them to make out that their knuckles were tight.

'What?' Some of the rage was in the guard's voice and it came out snappish.

'Suppose I make you a cup of tea? It's nearly ten o'clock,' Takiko said.

He came out unrolling his sleeves. 'Oh. That's kind.'

'Do you have cups of your own or shall I go on a thieving mission to the kitchens?' she smiled. It was amazing what a protection it could be, being little and a bit stupid-looking.

'Oh, no, no, we've got our own. I'll show you.'

More than anything, going into the guards' office, which had a small set of creaking steps down to its sunken floor, felt like being a miniature thing going inside a warm tree trunk. When the kettle was half boiled on its own little heater, she poured some water out into a bowl and gave it to him.

'Hm?' he said.

'You've got blood on your face,' she explained, and pattered her fingertips over her own cheekbone to show him where.

'Oh, right. Thanks.'

When she tucked herself under the table, the heat from the stove underneath washed round her legs and made her feet prickle as the feeling came back. Once she had made the tea, she held her cup to warm up her hands and then pressed one palm flat to her nose. It was absolutely glorious.

'You make tea very beautifully,' the guard said. And then, obliquely, 'Accomplished sort of thing for a cleaning girl?'

She smiled and pretended not to have understood what he was really asking. 'Cleaning girls who would like not to be cleaning girls one day ought to cultivate useful skills, don't you think? One must have ambitions. One might even work at a proper restaurant one day, should anybody ever build one here.'

He laughed, because she had said it in her princess voice. 'That's a thing! Can you teach me?'

'Of course, darling, you must pretend you're half Chinese and half English, it's the most fabulously easy thing.'

'Stop, I'm going to spit tea everywhere.'

'Sorry,' she said. 'Normal voice.'

'Can I ask how old you are?' he said.

She was the only woman she'd seen here. She had a depressing vision of being raped behind the solitary confinement shed.

'Forty-two,' she lied.

'What! You look much younger.'

'Thank you. How old are you?'

'Twenty-one,' he said shyly.

She patted him on the head as she got up. He had soft hair, too thin. 'Lie to the next person, will you? It isn't polite to make ladies feel old. Dear me. Well, I'd better get on, hadn't I.'

———

She soon found that the best part of the day was cleaning the warden's office. It was beautifully warm, with a fire burning in a real Western-style grate and lamps everywhere, even in the gloomy daytime. He had glass in the windows and furs on the floor. There was a big desk, full of good pens and paperwork, but at the other end of the room was a littler desk and a young man with glasses and a typewriter, and a telegraph machine whose wire came in through a tiny hole in the wall behind him. He typed all the time, but only numbers, which he was reading from graph axes drawn onto dozens and dozens of peculiar photographs. They were all the same, more or less; two pale, fluctuating patterns, traced out on a dark background. There was nothing more to them that, but they were unpleasant anyway, in a way which scratched at a nerve in the back of her mind, like a razor blade just catching on your knee.

So they had an electrograph. Mori might be here some-where. She had an uneasy stir. If he thought she'd feel guilty and break him out once she actually saw the place, he'd miscalculated. A prison was where he belonged.

The warden snapped his fingers at her. 'Less staring, more work. Come on, girl.'

'Sorry, sir. Shall I do the desktop or are you too busy?'

'No, on you go.' He pushed his chair back to watch her work. He relented after a second. 'It's a kind of experiment,' he said.

'Oh. It looks complicated.'

'It is,' he said, with feeling. 'Electrical. I wouldn't even like to say.'

'I wouldn't understand even if you did,' she said, and real-ised wryly that she was doing her best Countess Kuroda impression. It gave her a spike of sadness. Everyone always said, well, you find other friends to fill the gaps the old ones leave; but she never had.

Behind the warden, on the broad window sill, a snowy owl landed and peered in through the briny glass. The warden saw and shooed it off.

When Takiko had finished in the office, she carted everything back down the steep stairs, into the dense cold, then tapped on the window of the guards' office. 'Is there anything else?' she said to the young guard.

'No! No, that's you done for the day. The forest detail will be back soon,' he said seriously. He checked his watch.

'Actually, they should be back already. It's better if you're safe at home when they come in.'

'I see. Thank you.' She paused when his hand skittered on the desk in an involuntary-looking way, so violently he had to catch it with the other. 'Are you all right?'

'Oh, it's nothing,' he said. 'Just palsy.'

She tapped her fingers against her thigh and didn't point out that that was only a way of saying shaky, not a why or wherefore. 'Well, see you tomorrow, Mr ...'

'Tanizaki. See you.'

The snow was falling again, thick and spinning. There was at least another few inches of it in the courtyard, enough to have covered over the tracks of the day. The cold was so dense it felt solid – it was a shock to walk into. She rubbed her nose and bounced twice on the spot to try to get the blood flowing. Her legs were stiff. Out on the dim shore, the sea had stopped moving. She looked at the padlock on the solitary confinement shed. The chain would probably have broken with a good enough smack from a spade. But there was a light in the window of the gatehouse, and, inside, Horikawa was watching her.

Just before she passed beneath the gatehouse, he opened the window.

'I know your game, girl. Think you can make money out of the lads, do you? It's not decent.'

'I'm just doing the cleaning.'

'My arse,' he said, and didn't shut the window. He only looked down at her, chewing the side of his tongue. After a while, he scratched his neck with his whole hand, making a claw.

She dropped her eyes so he would think she was upset, and jumped when something clanked into the snow beside her. When she picked it up, it was a bell, the kind you put on cows and oxen.

'Ring it if you walk back after dark,' Horikawa said. 'There's bears. Don't want to take one of them by surprise, do you?'

She didn't say that the bears were hibernating now, and carried on. Down the hill and right to the darkening horizon, there was nothing but the creaking forest, and the powder snow streaming where the wind blew it from the canopy. There was no sign of the late forest detail.

She wondered if she was going to have to do something about Horikawa.

TWENTY-FIVE

Tokyo, 11th February 1889

There was someone else in Thaniel's bedroom. For a
sliver of an instant he saw it: a grey thing hunched over
on the hearth with its back to the grate.

And then there was nothing. The room was ordinary,
the door was shut, and he would have noticed the latch,
because it clicked such a bright shade of yellow. His heart
was heaving.

It was the third or fourth time he'd had the same nightmare. He had to go to the hearth and stare at it until the
absence of a person sank in properly. The chimneys all went
down through the house, this one having its base in Vaulker's office. In defiance of the staff, Vaulker had his fire lit, and
so the grate was smoking. Thaniel could feel the warmth if
he held his hand above it. He stood there for a couple of
minutes, soaking in the borrowed heat, even though the soot
dusted his palm.

In any case, nobody was lurking halfway up the shaft. It
must have been the stormy weather that was niggling at
him. The electricity in the air was a background scritching, hardly noticeable, but it had a sound, God knew how,
and it tinted everything the colour of tin. It tasted of
metal, too.

The nightmare figure didn't feel like something in his own mind. He saw things that weren't there all the time. If somebody played a rich enough E flat, the whole world went purple. There had been someone there.

'Look …' He sighed, feeling ridiculous. 'You're scaring the hell out of me, is the thing. If there's anything I can do to help, tell me. If not – I need to sleep.'

Silence. Of course there was. But he felt straightened out for having said it.

Away from the second-hand heat of Vaulker's fire, the air was freezing. There had been new snow. Down on the lawn, two more tents had arrived in the night. Fukuoka and his friends had cleared a space and lit a fire, which made one orange point in among all the white. Thaniel paused. Although he had tipped the jug at more than a steep enough angle, the water wasn't moving. The surface had frozen. He smiled and cracked the ice with the handle of his razor. It wasn't really winter until you'd done that at least once. When he was little, his sister had always laid a fire in the bedroom on the first day there was ice in the jug.

There was a polite tap on the window. It was Owlbert, who to Thaniel's enduring surprise had decided to stay. He'd made a nest above the window of the doctor's surgery, but when he was cold, he came up here. Thaniel opened the window and the owl shuffled in. Thaniel stroked him carefully, hoping he was all right. Owlbert hooted his deep purple hoot. His feathers were full of snow particles. Thaniel put a spare jumper around him. Owlbert shuffled about and then went to sleep.

'Sleep well then,' Thaniel said. He smiled. There was something lovely about a wild animal that came to see you to borrow your jumper.

He took his good shirt down from the hanger and basked in the feeling of cotton that was both good and well-ironed at the same time. He meant to put on proper cufflinks, but when he touched one, it sent out a static shock so hard he actually saw it, a crackle of blue. He put on ribbon ones instead and then paused tentatively over his watch before he brushed his fingertip over it. It didn't shock him, but it was warm.

Sheet lightning flashed above the deep clouds. His wisdom teeth stung.

When he went out into the little living room, he found Six bundled up on the cold hearth like an owl. He bent down and made a fuss of her. She didn't giggle, but she jigged a bit.

'Who were you talking to before?' she said.

'Owlbert. He's in there.'

'Mm, he's helping me keep an eye on you. May I show you something good?' she said.

When he said yes, she hurried into her own tiny room across the corridor, which she shared with the stable-master's twins, and came back holding one of her lightbulbs by the glass. She gave it to him and when he touched the stem, it lit up in his hands. It was the one Mori had made for her in Russia. The filament octopus rippled different brightnesses, so it looked like it was furling about in a bubble.

'H … ow is it doing that?'

'They just work,' she said, pleased. 'There's electricity in the air. It's not enough to light anything by itself but once there's something conducting it a bit, they do. Look.' She pointed. The leather top of her desk was tooled in a gilt pattern. All the lightbulbs scattered across it were lit. 'That's like a big circuit board now. I get shocks if I touch it.' She smiled suddenly. Some of her new teeth were too big for her. 'It really hurts.'

'Well, that's – unusual.' In its bulb, the octopus floated on, serene. Thaniel had to look away from it, because, just for a second, he was back at Filigree Street, Mori a warm weight against his chest with *The Tale of Genji* propped on his ribs for Thaniel to read for Japanese practice. 'Listen, let's get all those together and put them in that bowl, before we set fire to something. They'll look better all together anyway and I think you have to fill out a lot of forms if you electrocute children on legation premises.'

'All right,' she said, and together they gathered everything up, tiny bulbs and big, apple-sized ones, and put them all together into the pottery fruit bowl that never had any fruit in it. Even there, the filaments kept up a small, zithering glow. 'It's probably the storm.'

He glanced outside and paused when he saw how black the clouds were. Lightning flickered away in the distance again. It was snowing in spinning eddies, and cold emanated from the window pane.

Six tapped his arm. He hadn't been looking impressed enough with the lightbulbs.

'In the *Daily* a man said he was electrocuted by a weather-vane,' she said. 'I cut that one out in case you could read it to me later.' She looked worried that it was presumptuous, even though he had never once said no.

'I will. Right, that all looks safe enough, doesn't it?' he said, wishing, not for the first time, for a sheet of rubber. It was one of those things he always meant to find and never got round to. The idea that a person ought to properly insulate his daughter wasn't one that many shops had taken up. 'Do you think they're all right?'

Six put her hand over the bulbs. 'They're not hot.'

'Good.' He lifted her up. 'Come on. Let's find some breakfast.' He felt depressed about the idea of a cold breakfast. No fires; no coffee.

She nodded again. He opened the door onto the back stairs. 'Why are we going this way?' she said, with an edge of panic in her voice.

'Because I'm forgetful.' He let the door swing closed again and went on, towards the main staircase. He always went the back way by himself, because it was quicker and it meant you didn't walk the length of the house twice, but the butler had taken them up the big staircase the first time they had come, and that was the only way Six went.

He rapped his knuckles on Vaulker's door as they passed. 'Constitution ceremony today, remember,' he said. Vaulker threw a shoe at the door. 'And I need you to sign the forms for the investigation into the disappearance of that Englishwoman I told you about.'

The other shoe.

Six knew whose door it was. 'Mr Vaulker tried to get out of paying me for fixing his phonograph,' she said, 'but I did my sad face and then he said all right and I could have *all* the cherry bakewell as long as I didn't cry.'

Thaniel snorted. 'Well played.' He said it in Japanese in case Vaulker could hear.

'And he doesn't seem to know very much about Tesla,' Six added. 'But I'm not altogether certain that I can consider that to be a reflection of his moral fibre.'

He put his cheek against her hair. It was a bizarre way of talking, that catch between very simple and completely adult,

245

but he knew exactly what it was. It was how Mori talked to her, and she was only copying his voice in her head. She hadn't asked him about Mori.

They were passing right above the kitchen, and from that direction came shouting. Six twisted her nose.

'Ghosts again.'

'Mm, the exorcist didn't help. He gave us a refund.' Thaniel wondered hopefully if someone had lit a fire down there after all. He was starting to find he could live without all sorts of things – Mori, a piano, working lungs – as long as there was a decent supply of coffee.

'The second law of thermodynamics suggests it probably isn't ghosts.' She studied her own buttons, looking like a baby. 'Have you explained to them about that?'

He sighed. 'No. I don't know it would be right to. This isn't our country, people see differently.'

'No they don't. Thermodynamics aren't geographically specific.'

'Blue and green are the same colour here. What if, when someone here says blue, they mean what I'd say is green? What if ghost doesn't mean ghost?'

She frowned. 'What else could ghost mean?'

'I don't know. That's the point.'

He saw her decide to be kind to him, even though she didn't believe it. 'That's fair.'

They reached the dining-room door. He set her down on the threshold so that she could go on ahead. She always sat with the stable-master's twins, girls about her age and nicely calm. They were doing her good.

The dining room was full. The chatter gave it a party feeling. There were Imperial purple runners along the tables and at the serve-yourself counter at the far end, little cakes iced with the symbol of the royal household sat in stacks. He went over tentatively. There were cafetières. He put his hand on the side of one of them. Hot. Thank God. He made off with it and claimed the empty end of a table, feeling gleeful.

The coffee cups always came paired with a silver bowl of icing sugar. Mrs Nakano had said once that she'd heard how foreigners put milk and sugar in coffee, but sugar hadn't really caught on here yet and he doubted that many people knew there were different types of it. No one had mentioned it to her. It would have been ungrateful, and it was too much fun to play with. He dropped the spoon in it to make a mushroom puff of powder that tasted sweet when he leaned over it.

There was no cutlery anywhere, except chopsticks. Even the teaspoon was porcelain. He wondered at first if it was some kind of subtle revenge against Vaulker, who thought chopsticks were heathen, but then realised that it was probably the electricity. If his cufflinks were getting too hot to wear, the silverware would be too hot to use.

With the cup warm between his hands, he watched the stablehands in the courtyard fitting out the good carriage with ribbons for the occasion. Once the coffee had wound up his springs enough, he fetched the paperwork about Grace Matsumoto. A single form to launch a full murder inquiry was forty pages long. He'd done most of it now, but he was having to come up with some creative lies to keep Matsumoto's name out of it, and that had involved telegraphing Grace's father, Lord Carrow, in London. The reply wouldn't come for a few hours yet at least, with the time difference. Thaniel had signed it just as 'British legation, Tokyo'. His own name wouldn't do any good.

Hands landed on his shoulders. He jumped.

'Easy! I hate to interrupt you with sublunary considerations, but is that a murder investigation? And is it someone delicious and interesting?'

'Standard practice for when a citizen goes missing,' he said, as someone with a carnation in his buttonhole sat down and stole the rest of the milk. Feeling grateful for the interruption, Thaniel decided it probably counted as an honour to have your milk stolen by the Minister for Education.

Arinori spent a lot of unnecessary time at the legation, which he used like a gentlemen's club; he'd been the ambassador in London five years ago and he had a horror, he said, of letting his English slide. Thaniel thought he did it mainly to annoy conservatives. Kuroda hated the Anglicisation of hats, never mind the government. 'You know,' Arinori said, 'you could be handsome if you didn't cut your hair like a sailor.'

'What are you doing here?' said Thaniel, who cut his hair like a sailor because it meant having it cut less often.

'I stayed the night. I was writing a speech.' Arinori dipped his fingertip into his coffee, then into the icing sugar, and sucked it pensively.

'Oh, a speech. Abolishing kanji still?'

'I'd have thought you'd be for the idea.'

'What, because I'm a stupid gaijin?'

'Well, yes,' Arinori said. 'You have smaller brains. Look at you, you weren't made to write, you were made to nut a mammoth.'

Thaniel stole the milk back. 'But it wouldn't help foreigners or anyone learn, would it, to write Japanese in Roman letters? Niwa niwa niwa niwa ga iru.' In the garden are two chickens. 'How are you going to know if you're talking about

248

a garden or a chicken if you don't have the pictographs? Or tell the difference between jishin like confidence and jishin like an earthquake, or your nose or a flower … or any of the other fourteen million identical words you never phonetically differentiated because the entire language is nicked from Chinese but you couldn't be bothered with the tones?'

'That was quite a good rant. Did you practise on the mammoths?'

'The speech isn't about kanji, is it.'

'No, it's about the sovereignty of the Emperor.' Arinori smiled. 'Anyway. How are you?'

'Not bad,' Thaniel said. 'What about this weather, though?' Now that he'd said it, he wondered what was going on in the kitchen. They'd been so adamant about the fires that he couldn't imagine the ovens were running. But here they were with hot coffee and pastries.

Arinori moved his cup to one side and collapsed face-first on the table. 'I've died of boredom. You'll have to apologise to my wife.'

'I'll send some flowers,' Thaniel said, starting to laugh. Arinori made friends with the lower orders like other people kept hamsters or songbirds; he looked in on them every now and then to see if they were doing anything interesting, and if they weren't, he tickled them.

'I'm determined to get to the bottom of you and your mysteries.'

'I'm not mysterious,' said Thaniel, surprised.

'Where did you learn Japanese then? Your gorgeous, Imperial, courtly Japanese which you could have learned only from one of a handful of people who both speak like that and have been to London, all of whom I know?'

Thaniel smiled. 'I think I'd better protect him from you, don't you?'

'You are No Fun. That can be your Chinese name.'

There was a skitter against the window. The snow was coming down fast now, and even since Thaniel had sat down, a new layer had sifted over the courtyard. Thunder rumbled from the south, over Fuji, a deep snarl that came up through the floor as much as down from the sky. Everyone looked around and up at the big windows over the garden.

Arinori made an unwilling sound. 'I'd better get changed. Many unearned medals to put on before the whatsit.' He looked nervous, and Thaniel realised that he had been trying to distract himself. The cabinet had been compiling the new Constitution for years, but in the last few months there had been shouting matches at the Palace if even half of what the papers said was true.

'You'll be fine,' Thaniel said. 'Although — careful of the medals. Anything metal is getting a bit hot.'

'Oh, hence your boring poverty-stricken cufflinks on our day of constitutionally significant days, I see.' Arinori pursed his lips and ran his tongue over his teeth. 'I must say, this electricity is passing beyond the bounds of fun and into inconvenient.'

Thaniel agreed and went to see what was going on in the kitchen. Looking cheerful, Mrs Nakano pointed out the heap of cutlery glowing in the open stove, the kettle nestling among it, steaming. Thaniel went out to buy some blank bullets and spent a happy ten minutes with Pringle tying them up in handkerchiefs. They were heavy, but they made excellent hand-warmers.

TWENTY-SIX

When the carriages arrived, they cut black lines through the snow. Arinori came down nervously early to watch the stable-boys putting the last fittings on the horses, a heavy coat on over his state clothes. Thaniel went to wait with him and persuaded him to come just inside, into the empty office. The junior diplomats had the day off and everyone was still taking their time over breakfast.

While they waited, he composed the weekly telegram to Fanshaw in his head. Yes, they're still seeing ghosts, no they still won't tell me if something else is going on; meanwhile, we're using hot cutlery for cooking now and I'm imagining people sitting in my fireplace.

He looked back, surprised, when Mrs Vaulker touched his sleeve and drew him aside.

'I'm afraid Tom's ill,' she murmured. 'It's the cold. You won't mind going instead?'

'He's not ill, is he, he just doesn't want to go,' Thaniel said, a little irritated and a little amused that Vaulker felt the need to deploy his heavy guns.

'He's too proud to admit that he has bad nerves,' she said, inclining her head, unimpressed. 'He served in Africa, you know. He's been fretting all night. The fires debacle hardly helped.'

251

Thaniel lifted his eyebrows. 'It wouldn't really matter if he'd just lost an arm; he needs to turn up to this thing. People will notice if he's not there. And I notice you did light a fire this morning.'

'Well, he isn't going, I've forbidden it, and if you don't go, then nobody will.'

Pringle appeared in the doorway of the translation office. 'Ah, sir, I wonder if you know how to tie a—'

'Pringle, it's a tie, not atomic theory,' Thaniel said, because Pringle knew exactly how to tie a bow tie but asked unnecessary questions when he was anxious. Thaniel didn't like answering them seriously. It seemed patronising.

'Sorry sir,' Pringle said, looking soothed. He was going out to see the parades with the lady who'd sold him the silk shirt.

'I think that boy might have your name tattooed on his chest,' Mrs Vaulker said sweetly.

'If Mr Vaulker doesn't go,' Thaniel said, trying to scrub the image off his mind and failing completely, 'the second page of all the papers tomorrow will be about how the British missed the ceremonies. All he needs to do is sit in a carriage to the parade, stand for an hour and then come back. I'll go with him if that would be better, but—'

'If it's so easy then you'll be perfectly all right by yourself,' she interrupted.

'They'll notice at Whitehall. He wants Berlin, doesn't he?'

'Carriage's here,' Arinori said. He had kept a polite distance, but he must still have heard everything, despite having pretended to be concentrating on his cigarette. The smoke drifted towards them in the draught from under the door, woody and warm. 'Where's – aha,' he sang, because his wife

Akiko had just come around the corner. She had a camera with her; she was a journalist for *The Times*.

'Unearthed that actress from the coalshed?' Arinori said cheerfully.

'You're sneering,' his wife said, 'but I guarantee Kuroda's murdered both of them.'

'What are they saying?' Mrs Vaulker asked, a little sharp. 'Are they talking about Tom?'

'No, they're talking about a ...' Thaniel stopped. 'Arinori. What was that about Kuroda?'

'Oh, we think he might have vanished an actress and a glamorous nobleman, but there's a press embargo and obviously Akiko is now only all the keener,' Arinori said wryly. 'I don't believe I've had a single conversation at home since New Year that has not in some way involved Takiko Pepperharrow.'

'Like it or not, my dear, famous actresses and their husbands vanishing is news much more than ministers huffing at each other,' said his wife. She had a fur coat over a gorgeous kimono, but Western boots, which she was tapping together now to knock off the snow.

'Sorry,' said Thaniel, 'but I – you said Kuroda might have killed them both?'

'Yes,' she said, 'It's all very hush-hush and no one's admitting anything, but—'

'I know them.' Thaniel interrupted without meaning to. 'I mean – I know her husband. I came here with him.'

Arinori pointed at him. 'Scoundrel. He taught you Japanese. I knew it was someone good.'

His wife sharpened, attentive. 'How do you mean, you came here with him?'

'What in the world is going on?' Mrs Vaulker demanded.

Thaniel should have been dragging Vaulker down the stairs by the back of his shirt, but he had no idea when he was going to see Arinori again.

'Sorry, yes. I'm going,' he said to Mrs Vaulker, who looked suspicious to have such a sudden and unexpected victory. 'See you in a few hours.'

As they left the embassy district, the buildings became more and more traditional, all wood and paper. Open doors let out cooking steam and light into the deep gloom of the morning, and tiny snatches of the people inside. The roads followed a long curve, skirting the Palace moat. Every now and then the water gleamed black through a gap between houses. There were rivermen out despite the holiday, poling barges beneath single paper lamps. Under the storm clouds, the dark hadn't quite gone away. It felt like evening. Purple banners hung everywhere.

'How could they have disappeared?' Thaniel asked Arinori's wife. 'People would know. She's – quite famous. Isn't she?'

'Well, the actors at her theatre say she's on holiday, but no one knows where,' she said. 'When you say you know Keita Mori …?'

'But then why don't you think they're on holiday?' Thaniel pressed.

'How much do you know about what Mori used to do here?' she asked.

'Um – he was civil service. An intelligence officer.'

254

She and Arinori both laughed.

'No, he ran every intelligence officer in Japan. And then he went to live in England. Everyone thought he defected. And then back he comes, just as the Russians begin to look like they might invade. Now, call me cynical, but no pragmatic Prime Minister – and Kuroda is the most pragmatic man I've ever met – would let such a person wander about free to chat to whoever he likes. Either he's dead or Kuroda has him somewhere,' Arinori said.

'Could I interview you, later?' his wife asked Thaniel.

'What? No,' said Thaniel, with a shot of fear that he had to scramble to cover over. 'I don't know him that well, I just rented the spare room. Has Kuroda said something?'

'No. And he hasn't started any kind of investigation. If he didn't already know what was going on, he would have started a manhunt.'

'But really it's the fact that Takiko Pepperharrow has vanished too that persuades me,' Arinori said. 'She owns the Shintomi-za. That's like our version of the Royal Opera House,' he added when Thaniel looked blank. 'If she thought anything had happened to Mori, it would have been on a stage inside a week. She doesn't care about injunctions.'

Thaniel hesitated. In the small quiet, the driver's voice reached them, trying to soothe the horses, whose hoofbeats were getting more and more skittish. The carriage bobbed, and slewed them to the left. 'Well – all right, but even spies and actresses go on holiday. You still haven't said why you think they haven't.'

Arinori glanced at his wife.

She nodded. 'Because of their house. You can't get in. Can't get near it. There's a police cordon, and when I tried to go, I was firmly escorted away by a man who said he was with a gas company. Some kind of problem, dangerous, they're fixing it, but I went to see the gas company. Yoruji isn't even connected to their lines.'

'That hasn't been in the papers,' Thaniel said incredulously.

She drew an imaginary needle through her lips. 'Court order. We can't print it. A man barged into the office to tell us so.'

Thaniel could only stare at her. If she'd told him that somebody had stolen his own left arm, it wouldn't have been much stranger.

'Did you notice anything strange, when you were with Mori?' she said.

'He and Kuroda were fighting. I couldn't tell why. He made out like it was nothing, but ...' Thaniel shook his head. 'He looked scared, but he wouldn't tell me what was happening. Then my contract at the legation started. I've not seen him since.'

'You know I really would like to hear what was going on,' Akiko said. 'I don't have to use your name, you can be an anonymous source.'

'I can't, I'm diplomatic staff. Anyone who was there would work out who I was. Kuroda included.'

'We could pay.'

'I can't,' he said again.

'Only you seem very worried, for someone who claims to hardly know the man. If something bad is going on and we print this, it might help. The injunction won't hold if Kuroda's using it to cover something illegal.'

Thaniel had to clench his hands. She was right, perhaps it would help, but Kuroda would know who the source was instantly. One telegram to Whitehall, and Thaniel was in an asylum forever, and Six would be sent God knew where. 'I don't really know him,' he said. 'I'm just surprised.'

She leaned across and gave him her card and an encouraging look, but she didn't push any more.

'What I find interesting is that it's not just Keita and Takiko,' Arinori murmured. 'People are disappearing all over the place. Half the pamphleteers in Tokyo are suddenly missing. A shedload of scientists, too. There are injunction papers everywhere.'

'I had someone come in the other day looking for his wife,' Thaniel agreed, desperately glad to be even slightly off the topic of Mori. 'She's a physicist.'

'A woman physicist?' Arinori said doubtfully. 'Like a pretend one?'

Akiko hit him.

'A rich white woman,' Thaniel explained.

'Oh! You mean Grace Matsumoto, don't you? I didn't know she'd gone missing – what's happened?'

'Her husband doesn't know. Someone came after him with a baseball bat when he tried to find out.'

'Someone went after *Baron Matsumoto* with a baseball bat?'

Thaniel nodded. 'He was shaken up.'

'Kuroda's going to go full tyrant any day now,' Arinori growled.

Thaniel had to look out of the window. His reflection was older than he was. A police cordon and a court order. They couldn't be dead. Mori wouldn't have done that. Not without saying something.

Only, if he were going to do something like that, he would absolutely do it without saying anything. Thaniel would have lifted him bodily back onto a ship straight to England if he'd got so much as an inkling of it.

He didn't know he had been sitting with his hand pressed over his mouth until Arinori leaned forward and brushed his arm.

'Are you all right?' Arinori said quietly.

He said something incoherent about the electricity hurting his teeth.

They were rounding a bend, which brought the horses into view through the window. One of them was chafing. He frowned when he saw a spark. Blue light trailed from the tips of their ears and the edges of the reins. He watched it for a while, not sure if he was seeing a reflection or something real.

One of the horses reared and the carriage swung hard.

The door snapped open by itself and flung him out. He landed in the road, which hurt less than it could have, because they hadn't reached the cobblestone stretch yet, but his head smacked into the base of a telegraph pole. Through bursts of white, he saw the carriage jack-knife. Everything seemed to hang still for a long time. Later, he could remember how the silver studs on the harnesses were winking in the blue fire that trailed the horses' ears and tails, and the odd stormlight behind the clouds that wasn't quite lightning. He dragged himself up and ran to catch the nearest set of reins. The driver yelled at him to get back, but though he saw it, a flash of orange, he didn't hear it. He didn't remember hearing anything. He put his arms up to catch the horse's blinkered eyes and then snatched the reins to drag it back down. He pulled open the buckles on the harness until the first horse was free to run, then the other. They crashed past and charged down the road, hooves still sparking, blue fire in their tails. He stood still in the road and began to feel the bruises down his side and the sting in his hands. When he looked down, there were strap marks across his palms from the reins. A silver noise was still whining inside his head.

The carriage was on its side. The door was facing upward opened and Akiko climbed out, then turned back to help Arinori. They both looked all right, if thrown about. Arinori scooped her close and breathed through her hair for a moment, his gloved fingertips on the nape of her neck. Thaniel looked away.

'So we're all walking from here then,' Arinori said cheerily, though there was a brittle edge in his voice. 'Honestly, Steepleton you idiot; what sort of madman runs towards a panicking horse?'

Thaniel shook his head, because it had been pure force of habit. For years, if anything dangerous was even in view on the horizon, Mori had navigated it to one side. He had gone towards that horse as if it couldn't kill him because he had been certain that it couldn't, even with its hooves six inches away from his face. But it could have. Mori wasn't watching him anymore.

He wanted to go straight to Yoruji. But his head was still ringing, something had cracked unpromisingly in his shoulder, the trains wouldn't be running today, and his lungs would not last the long walk to Yokohama. And there was Six; he couldn't just vanish. She would tear herself to pieces.

'Coming?' Arinori called from ahead.

He hurried to catch up. Even that set his whole chest on fire.

TWENTY-SEVEN

Tokyo, 11th February 1889

The road up to the parade route was straight, so they could see the purple bunting from a good two hundred yards away. Someone else had noticed the lightbulb trick, and all along the final section of the parade's path were strings of lights, wired to nothing but iron pegs in the ground and starry in the storm, which was getting darker and darker. Thaniel couldn't look up at them for long. After the accident, something in his neck felt wrenched. A fever ache was coming back into his joints.

He decided he was going to have to see the others to the parade, and then go home. He was going to keel over otherwise. And then at the legation he could wire – someone. Matsumoto, at least, to say that Mori was missing too. Fanshaw; no. It wasn't Fanshaw's job to care. Mori wasn't British. He tried to rake over his memory for someone whose job it was to care. He didn't know Mori's family, except that he had a cousin who was Duke of somewhere. Choshu. He had no idea how you contacted a duke. 'Look,' Arinori said.

Away in the distance, at what must have been the foot of Mount Fuji, there was a deep red glow. It glittered. 'That – is the volcano going off?'

'Maybe a little.' Arinori knocked him lightly. 'Rare to see it, it doesn't erupt often. Lucky.'

'Right,' said Thaniel, not convinced that an erupting volcano was ever going to be lucky.

More men in smart suits were joining their road from either side, too smart to be going anywhere but the parade. He ducked his nose into his scarf and watched the electric lights above them flicker between their usual brightness and brighter flares. Lightning moved nearly constantly overhead, but the snow had stopped. He had hoped the storm would break, but it was showing no sign of that.

Another man in a guard's uniform joined them off a narrow side street, only about a yard in front. He was uncomfortably close and Thaniel caught the smell of him, damp, like his clothes never had a chance to dry properly after being laundered. Rather than speed up to get ahead of them, the man kept perfect pace.

Because Thaniel was watching the man, trying to decide if he was being purposefully rude or if he was only absent-minded, he saw him touch the handle of his gun before anyone else noticed.

He drew it fast. He shouted something that Thaniel didn't catch – it might have been 'traitor', but maybe not – and aimed at Arinori. It was an awkward lunge to get in front of him, and then both he and Arinori tumbled together onto the ground. The gunshot turned everything blinding white and at first Thaniel couldn't see at all. When he'd blinked it away, the man was running, but a pair of guardsmen had taken off after him.

'You're all right, you're all right. Get up.'

There was a pause. 'You know, I don't believe I am,' Arinori said softly.

His black suit had hidden how much blood there was. It was only a small rip in his jacket, but he was already pale, and they were kneeling in a dark pool. Arinori stared at it. Thaniel caught his chin.

'No, look at me. Calm down.'

'I'm going to die!'

'I think so. Better get it done properly.' It was the worst thing he'd ever said.

Arinori let his breath out, and smiled, just about. 'Yes. Good idea.'

His wife skidded onto her knees beside him. The cobbles put ladders through her stockings. Arinori smiled at her, just, and died there with the electric lights in his eyes.

The world spun and then vanished.

Thaniel opened his eyes in a room he didn't know. It was plain and pale, but there was a silk rug on the wooden floor, and it didn't smell like a hospital. When he sat up, he felt tired and shivery, and fogged. He stretched his shoulder back and then found that his left arm was strapped to his chest. It hurt. Someone had put him in a different shirt. He touched the top button. It felt much more disturbingly personal than whatever had happened to his arm.

'Hello?' he tried, then frowned into the echo of his voice, which had sharp edges in the bare room.

He had a crackling sense of being in a crowded place. If he'd woken blindfolded, he would have said the room was full of people. It wasn't. He was alone. But he felt sure that some-one brushed past him while he was listening, sure enough that it made him jump. He twisted around as far as he could. Nobody.

An incredibly tall man came in. He had to duck the low door frame. The legation doctor, Willis; which meant this was one of the downstairs front rooms whose windows just peeped above ground. Thaniel had never been in the surgery before.

'Good. You're awake. I'm afraid you've got a fever, but it's to be expected.' Willis seemed irritated that Thaniel had done something so stupid as to hurt himself significantly on a holiday. 'Your body's had a shock, that's all, and you didn't start out at full steam. It's nothing to worry about; nothing important hit.'

'What happened?'

'You were shot. Went through your upper arm, nicked your collarbone. It'll hurt like buggery but with any luck you'll keep the use of the arm.'

Thaniel sat still while that filtered down. He couldn't remember a bullet.

Willis sat down awkwardly in the chair by the bed. He didn't quite fit. The back was wicker and squeaky. 'What's your diagnosis? If you have one. You have trouble breathing. It's very noticeable when you sleep.'

Very noticeable. The skin down Thaniel's shoulder blades tried to crawl. There was something uniquely horrible about being told a thing about yourself you didn't know. 'Lungs, something. I never found out properly. If it kills me it does, I don't need to call it by its first name.'

Willis lifted his eyebrows and made no effort to disguise that he considered such an approach to be stupid. 'Well, let's see.'

Thaniel turned his head away as Willis twitched the edge of his shirt aside with a cold stethoscope. It made him shy.

Willis looked annoyed and listened for what felt like an unnecessarily long time. When Willis sat back, he inclined his head.

'Well, it's not going to kill you quite yet. If you look after it,' he added from under his eyebrows.

Thaniel nodded.

'How's the symptoms?' Willis asked.

'I'm fine. Bit slow sometimes.'

'And?'

Thaniel hesitated. He didn't want the conversation to last any longer than it had to – he didn't like Willis or his patronising sharpness – but it would have been more stupid not to mention it. 'I'm seeing things. You know. Dreams, ghosts. Like the staff.'

'Are you indeed,' Willis said, looking disgusted.

'I don't believe in it. Is there anything you can give me?'

'Short of laudanum, not really. I'd suggest you spend less time going native. It's admirable, naturally, but it can cause one a certain flabbiness of thought. The Japanese are essentially pagan, you realise; they exist rather in the state Europeans did some three thousand years ago.'

'Japanese isn't witchcraft, Willis, and it is definitely not making me see anything.'

Willis opened his hands to say, well, there's your problem.

Thaniel shook his head once, too tired to point out that not that far down the road at the Palace was a good collection of Japanese men who felt exactly the same way about English, and that most international treaty problems would vanish overnight if everyone would just get over their snobbery long enough to sit down, have a cup of tea together, and recognise that they were all exactly the same person in slightly different hats.

'Do you know where my daughter is?' he asked instead.

'No, I've no idea,' Willis said, as if Thaniel had asked what all the names of Saturn's moons were. 'Don't try to get up. Get some rest and read the newspaper. You ought not wear yourself out with visitors. If you get up I will tether you to that bed,' he added.

Thaniel was certain this advice had less to do with rest and more to do with Willis's unwillingness to have children in his surgery.

'This came for you,' Willis added, and handed him an envelope.

Thaniel waited, and then had to say, 'Could you open it for me?'

Willis did so, and handed him the single sheet inside. It was a photograph of Grace Matsumoto. She was standing against a white wall, holding a newspaper from the day before yesterday, and a small sign that said:

AM NOT DEAD STOP MAKING A FUSS.

'Well, that's that then,' Thaniel said, puzzled. The sign sounded exactly like her, but the tone didn't match the way she was looking into the camera. She was just like he remembered her, pointy and boyish, but she looked exhausted. There were marks under her eyes. He sighed. However she looked, he couldn't open the inquiry now. Something brushed him again. It didn't touch him quite, but he felt that pre-touch along the fine hairs on his arm. 'Can you feel that?'

'Yes,' Willis said unexpectedly. He breathed out loudly through his nose. 'This place is rather creepy. It's the weather, that's all.'

Just for the barest second, right on the edge of his eye, he saw Mori. Not in clothes Thaniel had seen before – a lovely evening suit – and he was holding something he never once had at Filigree Street – a cigarette and a book of Lucifers. Just a brief shape in the dusty air and then vanished. Thaniel sat frozen, searching for the shape again.

'Don't let it get to you,' Willis growled.

Once Willis had gone, he felt too tired to pick up the newspaper. The shade of paint on the wall opposite, a pale cream, was the colour of the scritching noise that cheap phonographs made when violins lifted too high for the wax to record properly. He drew his knees up so that he could look at the blue blanket instead, and sat still, his free hand on the back of his neck where the nerves ached and his hair was growing through softer where it had been shaved up. The bruises from the carriage crash were starting to throb.

He could feel Arinori's blood still; it was sticky over his good hand and both knees, even though when he looked, there was no trace of it. When he thought of what he'd said to Arinori, he wanted to scream. Get it done properly: it flamed and burned through everything else, each word a lump of charcoal.

Christ, and Mori.

There was every chance he was all right. He was under no obligation to look after Thaniel now, after all. Maybe this vanishing was just part of his fight with Kuroda.

Willis's voice came sharp from the next room. 'Miss Steepleton – you can't come in here, you must leave him alone—'

'He said he would read,' Six's voice said, unmoved.

'For heaven's sake, girl—'

He straightened up. 'Willis, let her in.'

'You shouldn't pander to this sort of thing,' Willis said crossly.

Six appeared in the doorway, looking at him like she might drop him in the sea one day.

'It isn't pandering—'

'No, I forbid it. Miss Steepleton, on you go, if you please. This isn't the place for little girls.'

'Willis—'

'Now come along.' Willis caught her arm and tried to steer her out, back towards the stairs.

Six screamed. It wasn't how children usually screamed. This was primal, funnelled up from some interior inferno, and it didn't sound human. Thaniel struggled upright but couldn't stand. He hadn't felt it lying down, but Willis had given him something, opium or laudanum, and the room hammocked. Willis yelled as Six banged both fists into his stomach and took a chunk out of his hand with her teeth. He dropped her and she shot into the corner, under a side table on which a potted fern sat.

'What in *God's name*—'

'Touch her and I'll break your nose,' Thaniel managed. 'Get away from her. Now.'

Willis backed off, bewildered.

'She's made differently, you fuckwit, any idiot can see that. Leave her the hell alone.'

For all Willis was a foot taller, he looked frightened. Not quite for the first time, Thaniel felt wearily glad that he looked so much rougher than he was.

'What on earth is going on?' Vaulker demanded, halfway down the stairs.

'I had no idea it was quite like that,' Willis murmured. 'She should be in an asylum, Mr Steepleton—'

'Over my dead body,' Thaniel said flatly.

'Steepleton!' Vaulker snapped.

'Look at her,' Thaniel snapped back.

Vaulker looked and faltered. 'Is she all right?'

'No.'

Vaulker glanced up at Willis, then back at Thaniel. 'I see. Well, Mr Steepleton, perhaps you'd agree to not shout obscenities at the good doctor. Dr Willis, I'm entirely convinced that your intentions were excellent as usual, but I don't believe that any little girl would maintain perfect equanimity should a man of your stature lay hands on her. Might we consider a pax?'

'Yes, naturally,' Willis murmured, and then hissed as he poured iodine over the bite.

'Should she be in an asylum?' Vaulker asked Thaniel.

'No! She's not insane, you know she isn't.'

'Contain yourself, please! For the second time!'

'No, sir, she's wholly sane, but she was very ill treated in the past. She was born in a workhouse.'

He paused. 'Very well. Miss Steepleton?' he added, in the patronising tone of people who hadn't met any children since they were children themselves. 'What do you say to Dr Willis?'

'Don't attack me again please,' she said in her emotionless way.

'I didn't attack her,' Willis protested. 'I only said—'

'Perhaps we ought to draw a line under the thing,' Vaulker said, looking unsettled. He studied Thaniel. 'Get some proper rest, please, Steepleton, you look terrible. And if I ever hear you speak in such a vulgar way to anyone again, you're sacked. Do we understand each other?'

'We do.'

Vaulker waited for him to say 'sir', and Thaniel waited until Vaulker had to look away.

Vaulker trooped back up the stairs. Willis went into his office without saying anything else and shut the door. Slowly, because the room was still swaying, Thaniel went around the bed, keeping one hand on the mattress, and then eased down onto his knees on the silk rug a short way from Six.

'That was really good, petal. You did exactly the right thing, all right? Are you hurt?'

'No.'

'Will you come out?' he tried quietly.

'No.' She put a piece of paper – it was a cut-out of news-print – on the floor beside her, seemed to screw up the kind of courage it would have taken him to catch a spider in both hands, then pushed it, fast, over the boards. She couldn't reach far enough and edged it further towards him with the toe of her boot, before snatching her leg back under the shadow of the little table. Thaniel took it gradually. Leaning made all the muscles howl down his strapped arm and on that side of his chest.

The article was about a spate of electrocutions, all at blacksmiths' workshops. He read it aloud and saw her ease a bit, but she didn't come out.

'I found out what that blue light is,' she said into her knees. 'It's called St Elmo's fire. Usually you only ever see it at sea, before a storm, on the masts of ships. It's to do with static electricity and vapour in the air.'

'Why do we have it here?'

She didn't seem to hear. 'We've got scrap iron in all the fireplaces now instead of fires. Mine is full of old bed-knobs. I fried an egg on them.' She was looking into the deep distance. 'I made them put the horseshoes in yours because you need some luck.'

'That's kind,' he said helplessly. Out of bed and calmer now, he was starting to feel the cold. He could see that Willis had something glowing in the grate – it might have been a length of heavy chain – but it wasn't anything like as warm as a fire. 'Will you show me?'

Six was quiet, then nodded and crawled out. She straightened up and brushed off her dress, and waited for Thaniel to stand as well. It was difficult. He swallowed. The air tasted so dry it was sandy.

'Can you hold my hand? Or I'll fall over.'

She did think about it. 'No,' she said.

'Let's – just go slowly then.'

'You shouldn't be going anywhere,' Willis said from the office. 'Don't be surprised if you collapse.'

Thaniel shook his head at nobody and couldn't think of anything to say that Vaulker wouldn't mind.

'He's a prick,' Six said sombrely. 'Pay no attention.'

He laughed, which hurt. She kept pace with him as he inched up the steps, one hand on the wainscoting. When he half fell, she waited but didn't touch him. In the porcelain bowl in his room, Six's lightbulbs were still alight. They were brighter than before.

'Where are you off to?' he asked, because she had picked up the octopus lightbulb and now she was heading back for the door.

'To show this to Mr Fukuoka.'

270

'Ah – hold on, petal. Why?'

'He's my friend. He gave me half of his jam thing.'

He bit the end of his tongue. Fukuoka was a kind man, Thaniel was nearly sure. 'All right,' he said at last. 'But don't stay with him too long, he has plenty to do.'

'How long is too long?'

'More than half an hour.'

'Half an hour,' she repeated, and took out her watch to set the bell.

The door clicked shut. He listened to the brown thumping as she went downstairs and wanted to go out after her, but standing up was too difficult. He waited at the window for a little while, leaning hard on the sill. Fukuoka was at the edge of the protest camp, and he bent down and made a fuss of her when she tumbled out, then picked her up to show her what was going on. Everyone had crowded together; they were burning a big, floppy doll made of white bedsheets and stuffed into a Western-style suit, complete with necktie and pocket watch. Fukuoka put Six on his shoulders.

Mori would have said that the worst really hadn't come to the worst if people were still doing that sort of double-thinking. She was fine.

Owlbert surfaced and pecked the window latch. Thaniel let him out, and watched him swoop down to the protest camp to land on the crossbar of a half-constructed tent.

Thaniel crumpled onto the hearthrug and stayed sitting up for long enough to make a fire among the warm horse-shoes in the grate, because it was so cold the lenses of his eyes felt like frost and he had a distinct feeling he would never wake up if he let the temperature drop any more. The second the little flame caught properly, he dropped down sideways. He lay with his cheek flat to the sheepskin rug, still too cold, breathing the smell of lanolin. He felt ill enough to spark a lick of panic. If he died and if Six came back in and assumed he was asleep, which she would, no one would find him until the steward came in mid-morning tomorrow.

After a heavy while, he forced himself half-upright and pulled the side table nearer. It was where the phonograph sat, well away from the fire to save the cylinders. He put it on loud, so that if it carried on late into the evening, someone would come in. Putting the needle onto the cylinder was as much as he could do. He snagged the blanket off the chair and fell back onto the rug. He felt victorious about the blanket. The fire roared through some pine needles.

He fell straight into nightmares about being lost on roads he didn't know, with something following him. He kept waking up, but every time he went back to sleep, the thing was closer.

TWENTY-EIGHT

Abashiri, Hokkaido, 17th January 1889
(one month ago)

Takiko had gone to the edge of the forest early for firewood. They were running low at the prison; apparently it was one of those things the previous girl had done, but nobody had known. It was a novelty to collect wood for fires. She was used to coal, and as she picked up promising twigs and little branches from the dry powder snow, she quite looked forward to lighting them. Burning wood was a gorgeous thing, especially when it was minus fifteen in the sun.

There was a big snowdrift by one of the trees just a little way into the woods, suspiciously big. Hoping it was a stack of wood that the last girl had collected, she brushed some snow aside. She found the head of a horse underneath. She stood still for a while. The cold had desiccated the horse's eye and turned it glaucous. She brushed off more snow. The rest of the horse was there, saddle and all. When she straightened up, she saw there were snow mounds right back into the woods. She chose one at random. Under it was a dead body in red. It was peculiarly less than upsetting. She'd never seen a dead person before, but, blanched in the cold, the body didn't look like a person at all anymore, just a clumsy impression of one; as though something lonely had tried to make a man from frost and shards of birch bark.

When she hurried into the warden's office, she recoiled at the heat inside. It wasn't that hot, but after the gnawing cold outside, it was as bad as charging into a sauna in a fur coat. She had to catch the door frame, feeling sick.

'Miss Tsuru,' said the warden, surprised. 'We're in a meeting.'

He had called together all the remaining guards. Only eight. She explained what she'd found. Nobody looked surprised, only gloomy.

'Yes, so,' said the warden, 'that's two more guards gone. Consider the timetable changes permanent, gentlemen.'

'Are we to expect any new staff from Tokyo, sir?' Tanizaki asked, looking drab. He had his palsied hand strapped to his chest today, but it was still trembling despite the binding. She couldn't see the timetable, but she could imagine it landed everyone with more night shifts for which the pay did not entirely compensate.

'Not until March, I'm afraid. The sea's impassable for now. On you go.'

It wasn't until she had been going to the prison for a week or so that Takiko really noticed the big central tower. It didn't have any windows. Its single feature was a lightning rod on the roof. She wondered if it was one of those odd government building projects that happened for no reason except to give restless people something to do. Whatever the reason for it, she had never been up there, though it must have sat right above the warden's office. In fact the office, up its little stairway, must have been in the base of it. She frowned when she thought of that, because there was no stairway leading

274

upward from the office. It could only be one tall, empty attic space. The electrograph had to be up there.

There had been a lull in the snow and the guards had taken advantage of it. The prison was almost empty, except for the high-security inmates. Everyone else was out in the forest, building the new road, the cell doors left open. She swept inside, took out blankets for laundry, and put new ones in. It didn't feel like going into anyone's private space. There was almost nothing else inside most of them. It wasn't, Tanizaki pointed out, the kind of place where there was ever such a lot available on the outside to smuggle in. She stoked the braziers in the corridors and had to keep going back to them to warm up her hands. It had been cold before, but there was a miserable, permanent quality to it now.

The edges of her hands felt rough when she pressed her palm against her nose. The cracked skin was starting to look like burn scars. She sat looking at them, aware that the cold was coming up through the floor and seeping into her knees. Whenever she went to town to buy food, she saw fishwives her age who looked old. Even the Ainu women, who had been made for the cold, were grown up at fourteen and elderly by thirty. It wasn't about quality of food or exercise, or any of it. It was just the weather. It was too cold to wash properly, too cold to sleep properly, too cold to eat anything fresh and not hot, too cold to ever get more sun than a ten-minute snatch on the way to somewhere else. For every day you were in this winter, you were three days older.

The warden had said the sea was too frozen to sail on now. Whatever happened, she was stuck until spring.

'Tea time,' Tanizaki called down to her.

'Right, coming,' she said.

When she came into the little office, the tremor in his hand was bad. He couldn't pick up a cup and had to use his left. He was pinning his right down with his knee, but the next spasm was so strong that it knocked his leg upward into the underside of the table. The teapot juddered.

'You need knee pads,' she said.

'I do. Like those things gaijin wear to play cricket. You couldn't run down to the kitchen and fetch up some more water, could you? We're running out and I think I'd ... spill it,' he said bleakly.

'Should you be at work today?'

'It never lasts long.'

She nodded and went downstairs, into the steamy damp of the kitchen. When the cook saw her, he pointed at her with his ladle. There was something wrong with him or, if not wrong, then at least irregular. His eyes were too small and his tongue was too big. She couldn't always understand what he was saying, although she did now. No stealing. She said yes. He said no. She took the water anyway.

He grunted and put a tray into a dumb waiter, and pulled a lever. It went up geriatrically. She looked up at the ceiling and bent her mind round the angle of the stairs. The warden's office was right above them. It was a piece of special laziness not to come down and fetch your own tray, but then, given the choice between having a dumb waiter and not, she would have wanted one.

She lingered as long as she could decently stretch a tea break with Tanizaki in the warm guards' room, and then took the cleaning things upstairs.

'Miss Tsuru,' the warden said when she came in. 'I don't suppose you might make us some of your famous tea. We're feeling rather envious of Mr Tanizaki downstairs.'

'Yes, of course,' she said.

'Might help with my headache.'

'Headache, sir?'

'Oh, don't be sympathetic, I'll collapse. Wretched things. I see starry lights when they're on the way and you're looking sparkly.'

'No one here seems to be very well, sir.'

'Well, it isn't the most healthful place in the world,' he said. He rubbed his temple while he watched her lift the little iron teapot from the fire. 'Quite weak, please. Nakamura?'

The typing man said yes please. When she handed over his cup, he looked apologetic and turned away coughing. He did as he was told when she said that breathing the steam might help.

'The fireplace is getting ashy,' Takiko said. 'It won't be doing him any good. I meant to ask, sir, if I could have the key so I could come here early and clean it out while you're not here. It would be a terrible disturbance if I were to do it now.'

The warden was quiet for a long moment, and she had a nasty certainty he knew exactly why she wanted to come in early. 'Yes,' he said at last. He took a key from his desk drawer. 'I'm trusting you with this. You mustn't touch anything but the hearth.'

'Yes, sir. Of course. I would never look at any documents, or – I hardly know how to read,' she said.

'No, of course. You're a good girl. The last girl was rather nosy. I know you'll not be like that; you're quite a different class of person altogether.'

She nodded once, almost before she remembered that the last girl had frozen to death in a ditch. 'I hope so, sir. It would be unconscionable.'

She wondered what the last girl had seen.

He relented. 'I don't mean to frighten you, I'm just antici-pating this headache. After you've done the window sill, that's all I think.'

'Shall I take the tray down too?'

He looked up. 'Tray?'

It was instinct, not a decision, that stopped her mention-ing how she had seen the cook put a whole meal into the dumb waiter twenty minutes ago. She had a powerful feeling that it would be very stupid indeed to say anything about it. She did look round, though. There was no hatch in the walls, not anywhere.

'Forget my head next,' she said. 'I was so sure you were eating when I came up.'

He flapped his hand towards the window. 'It's this place; you lose track of things. Perhaps you were thinking of yes-terday?'

'Must have been. Sorry, sir.'

So someone was taking meals up there. She scrubbed at an old stain on Nakamura's desk so that she wouldn't just stand and stare into space, listening to the mechanical clicks inside the wall. Nakamura smiled briefly and moved some of the pattern-photographs from the radius of her brush. When he paused, so did the clicking in the wall.

She concentrated hard on the stain. The clicking sounded like clockwork. It was operating something; a lock, a door, something. It had been a passing thought when she first had it, but she was beginning to feel creepingly sure that Mori was either up there, or would be soon.

'Oh, my head,' the warden mumbled. He sank down on the desk, his head in his arms. Across from him, the typist coughed into his sleeve but kept on with his keys, his nose pink despite the waving heat of the fire. She could hear the wheeze when he breathed. As she went back down the stairs, the cold coiled up to greet her. Tanizaki was still huddled miserably at the table, holding his skittering hand flat to the wood while he talked to another man, newly arrived, with snow on the shoulders and sleeves of his greatcoat and a damp sheen on his riding boots.

'... dropping like flies,' the other guard was saying. 'Two this morning. And there's another blizzard coming this afternoon, you can see it on the mountain. I'm bringing them in for the day.'

She tapped on the door. 'Afternoon all. Shall I see about some lunch?' It was only half an hour since she had fetched the water for Tanizaki, but the cold was so dragging that she was starting to feel hungry all the time. Everyone seemed to need more fuel just to stay awake.

'You're spoiling us,' Tanizaki said happily.

'Of course I am, look at you, you're falling apart. You look like you've frozen to the floor,' she added to the other guard. He was so tall and spindly that one of his parents must have been Chinese. It was very noticeable next to Tanizaki, who was short and stocky. When he folded down at the kotatsu, he looked ridiculous, because he was too tall for it and he had to hinge all his joints down into the right places one by one like a giraffe.

They both looked pleased when she came back with fish and onigiri. She sat down with them and lifted the spine of her salmon from the rest of it without thinking before Tanizaki laughed that her table manners were too good. He was yanking his fish apart with one chopstick in each hand. His bad one had stopped shaking so much.

279

'Mr Tanizaki,' she said, once they had joked a bit about geisha. He had said it too suggestively, and so she had said she couldn't possibly be a geisha because the last time she'd played a samisen the cat had run away and been hit by a cart. She made up an unnecessary bit about its guts for good measure. If she could only train him to associate her with disgusting things, he would stop leaning so close when he spoke. 'You know the big tower, above the warden's office?'

'It's called the Oracle. It was only built last year. Year before?' He glanced at the tall man, who shrugged. 'I forget.'

'What's it for?'

'It was meant to be a watchtower. Some new prison regulations came in, everyone had to have a watchtower of a certain height. But it's never been used that I know. Piece of bureaucratic rubbish, I think. They've put in some kind of electrical equipment now, something to do with the weather.'

'Ah,' she said, and pretended to lose interest. She sipped her tea.

'We are a weather station actually,' the tall man put in suddenly, in the quiet. 'They send all the readings to Tokyo. There's no better place to gauge south-coming storms. You know what Shiretoko means, in Ainu?'

She shook her head. Shiretoko was the name of the whole region, their manta-ray antenna at the top of Hokkaido.

'The end of the world.'

'That's accurate,' she said.

'You made that up, Oemoto,' Tanizaki laughed. 'Unless you've been hanging round with the Ainu on your days off.'

'No, they told us at school. I had a Russian science teacher. It's like Russian, Ainu—'

'Oh, the famous science teacher!' Tanizaki grinned and thumped him. 'He fell in love with a Russian science teacher, it was very sad,' he explained to Takiko, then giggled when Oemoto thumped him back. 'Get off, it's not slander if it's true—'

Tanizaki collapsed. Oemoto only stared at first. 'Hey – stop pissing about – Tanizaki …'

When she came around the table he was seizing. She dropped down and held him still as best as she could. Oemoto knelt beside her to help.

'Is there a doctor here?' she said.

'Gatehouse – yes. Dr Fujiwara.'

By the time she had run back with the doctor, the seizure had stopped and Tanizaki was picking himself up slowly, white and shaken. The doctor listened to his heart and looked into his eyes and said he was as all right as he was going to be, though he didn't look convinced. The seriousness was noticeable, because it didn't suit him. His name, Fujiwara, meant wisteria, and he had a bright purple cravat on to match. He must have been quite a flamboyant person normally.

It wasn't only the staff who were ill. As Takiko let herself out through the delivery gate, which she was using on her way home now to avoid looking at the solitary confinement shed, she saw, just down the hill, that there were bodies with red clothes in the long rubbish trench, dozens and dozens, not quite covered by the snow. Not far away, the birch woods creaked and groaned, white on white, and from somewhere inside came drumming. When she looked that way, an Ainu woman was watching her. She was holding a rich bundle of sealskins, and she looked unearthly, because she had a solid

281

black tattoo right across her mouth like a gag. Her clothes were all bright colours; it must have been one of their ceremony days. Their festivals had been banned, technically, but as far as Takiko could tell, the Ainu ignored mainlanders as a passing nuisance and went on like they always had. The woman turned away and disappeared into the birch wood.

The drums had disturbed half the birds in the woods. An owl soared right over Takiko's head and fluttered up to land on the eaves of the Oracle tower. There were six others already there.

TWENTY-NINE

Tokyo, 13th February 1889

Thaniel snapped awake. Someone was leaning right over him. Their noses were almost touching. He could feel that tiny electric warmth that came a fraction of an inch above human skin. It smelled of ash. The taste of it settled right in the back of his throat.

He couldn't open his eyes or move. He lay exactly still and had to tell himself it was a nightmare while he screwed together the courage to sit up.

The person, the thing, grabbed his shoulders and squeezed. He spun over to the side and bumped the hearth, on his hands and knees and with all his tendons singing with the urge to run.

No one was there.

The fire was smoking badly and the room had filled with soot. Thaniel pitched the water jug over the grate, then pushed open the window as wide as it would go. He was choking now, the ash like cement when he swallowed. Once he was calm enough to listen, he heard how his lungs were wheezing on deeper breaths. He crossed the room and bent to see the door latch. He could sleep in the translation office. There was a couch down there and the air would be better. His shoulder hurt and hurt. Lying on the floor hadn't done it any good.

It wasn't until he had opened the latch that he saw his own shirtsleeves. When he did, the strength went out of his hands. Across his shoulders, very clear in black soot smoke stains, were two handprints.

Thaniel checked everywhere – under the bed, in the wardrobe, behind it, outside in the corridor – but there was no one. The legation was silent. Not even the servants were moving about now. He stood in the open doorway, waiting to calm down.

He eased across the corridor and opened Six's door. She was asleep; so were the twins. He closed it again and didn't want to go back into his own room. But he couldn't wear this shirt either, so he left his door open and changed, painfully slowly because he could only move one arm, looking around all the time, his heart straining, and came straight back out again. Absurdly, crossing the threshold and onto the differently coloured wood of the corridor floor felt like reaching safe ground. Still no sign of anyone else. Despite the new shirt, he couldn't stop rubbing at the places on his upper arms where the black handprints had been. He stood out in the dim corridor, lit by nothing but snowy moonlight, trying to decide what to do with himself. He couldn't imagine sleeping.

There was no reason he couldn't do some work. It was sedentary and boring, two things that would probably be quite helpful.

Light spilled reassuringly from the translation office. Mrs Nakano had forbidden Kelly lamps, because of the flames, but she had provided lightbulbs. They were tied onto the metal pipes now with neat little coils of copper wire, and they worked perfectly. He sat down at his desk and felt much easier bathed in electric light. It was shocking how fast he'd got used to the dim whale-oil lamps here, with their greasy smell that put him in mind of an oven that needed cleaning. The brighter light made everything clear and ordinary. The stacks of newspapers, the two telegraphs, Pringle's little geisha doll, the clean papery smell of any office where nobody smoked. He sat still for a while and let it soak in.

He translated a few bits and pieces from the Foreign Ministry. Telegraph messages had come in through the day. The first wave were party invitations; the second, sent in the afternoon, more sombre congratulations that everyone had carried on through the ceremonies despite the disruption.

His stomach snapped itself into a knot when the telephone rang. The bell was deafening white in the silent office. He snatched it up. He hated the telephones and on principle he never used them. Vaulker had had them installed because he said it was civilised, but Thaniel couldn't think of anything less civilised than making a terrible noise at somebody until they answered you. Everyone else on the Tokyo lines must have felt the same, because nobody ever telephoned unless they wanted to be rude.

'Hello?' he said.

'Prime Minister's office,' said an exhausted clerkly voice in Japanese. 'Is Mr Steepleton there?'

'Speaking. You know it's two in the morning?'

'Hold for the Prime Minister,' the clerk sighed.

Thaniel pushed his hand over his forehead. There was a click, and then Kuroda's shale voice said, 'Did I wake you?'

'No, sir.'

'Shame. Just calling to make sure you know you're a fucking useless sow. Mori must have put you there because you were supposed to save Arinori.'

'Yes, it's definitely all my fault. What have you done with Mori and Takiko Pepperharrow?'

'I haven't done a damn thing. I thought you'd got jealous and murdered them both.'

'I'm pretty sure you're the one with that kind of record. Where are they? Are they all right?'

'Take that tone with me again and I'll tell your Foreign Office you got your insipid little heart broken and now I'm missing a high ranking samurai and his lady. No? Didn't think so. Coward,' Kuroda said, and banged his receiver down.

The bullet wound was burning as if someone had washed it out with vinegar.

Kuroda was lying about Mori. Arinori and his wife had been right; if Kuroda really hadn't known where he was, he would have turned half of Tokyo upside down. Thaniel sat looking hard at the telephone, thinking about how you went about finding someone who the Prime Minister didn't want found.

He'd go to Yoruji in the morning. Diplomatic immunity was handy when you had to duck a police cordon. He wasn't going to think about what he might or might not find there. He was no use to anyone if he let himself turn into a hysterical mess. Least of all Mori, who was probably fine, and who would probably consider any effort to be found by some hulking gaijin he used to live with barely more acceptable than stalking.

Mrs Nakano must have heard the telephone, because she came in with coffee and the silver bowl of icing sugar. In place of the lid, she'd put a lightbulb on the kettle. It cast a friendly glow.

'Did you see one?' she said.

He looked up. 'Did I wake you up?'

'No, no, lad, I was watering the door-hinges.' She didn't pause to explain what she meant. 'You had a fire lit. Did you see one?'

'I … no, I just had a nightmare.' Which he must have. When he went back upstairs, there would be no soot hand-prints on his other shirt. He was ill, injured, and someone had been killed in front of him yesterday. It had been a night-mare.

She gave him a schoolmistress look and left. The floor-boards squeaked something savage, because at some point through the day, the nails must have overheated. Someone had taken them all out and put them in a glass vase on the floor, over which there was now a heat shimmer. As she passed through the dining room, she picked up a watering can from the corner, and watered the door-hinges. They steamed.

———

It was possible to make quite a good coffee-flavoured icing in the saucer, so Thaniel tipped out some of the coffee and then sprinkled the sugar into it as softly as he could with his left hand. Some of the sugar missed the plate and snowed onto the desk instead, exactly where the draught could catch it. It skittered off the edge and into the air. He watched it twist.

But the ordinary twisting was disrupted before it could fade off to nothing. It was outlining the perfect shape of a hand, in nothing but the air. He could even read the manu-facturer's mark on the button in the sleeve. It was from

Shirokiya's, the big department store opposite the bank in Ginza.

Thaniel flinched back but it only hung there. The sugar fell gradually and the image faded.

He took the silver bowl up again and blew over the surface of the sugar, then held his breath so that he wouldn't disturb it while it fell. The sugar billowed into the air and showed other buttons, a waistcoat, a watch chain, hands hidden in trouser pockets and then the neat sweep of Arinori's hair. He was looking out the window. As Thaniel watched, the sugar ghost sighed noiselessly and turned away. He stared at it, then threw another spray of icing sugar at it. It seemed not to see him at all, and only stood propped in the doorway, reading over ghost papers.

Thaniel snatched up the telephone. He plugged in the wire for the line to Vaulker's room. While it rang – he could hear it upstairs – he watched the space where Arinori was fading again. He had never gone cold with fear before, and he'd always thought it was just a figure of speech. But he could feel the blood creeping away from his fingers, which were white around the receiver, his nails an unnatural, dead grey.

'Hello?' Vaulker sounded puzzled, but not like he had been asleep.

'Can you come down to the office a minute?'

'Steepleton? Do you know what time it is?'

'It's quarter-past two in the morning,' he said, still watching the icing sugar. The ghost was still there, just. He could feel his pulse squeezing right inside his skull, but the instinct to get out was fading more the longer the ghost did nothing sudden. 'There's something here you should see.' He had to swallow, because he could taste the icing sugar, sweet but dry. 'Right now.'

Vaulker came down still fully dressed. 'What's going on?'

'Hold on, let me – find it again,' Thaniel said unevenly, because he had just seen a flicker in the sugar. He tipped the rest of the bowl into the air. It furled at once around a shape. Arinori was still looking through the papers. They were government memoranda. The icing sugar clung more to the white of the paper than to the black ink, so the letters were outlined strangely. 'Can you see that?'

Vaulker stepped around to see it better. 'That's ... what in God's name is that?' He glanced at Thaniel. 'Can it see us?'

Thaniel shook his head.

Vaulker clenched his hands, but he went up closer to it. 'Hello?'

The ghost didn't say anything, or show any sign it knew they were there. Thaniel and Vaulker glanced at each other, both of them waiting for it to turn and scream at them.

Thaniel blew softly and watched the sugar particles spin. The patterns were natural until they reached the ghost, when the motes veered across the outlined surface like they had been magnetised. He drew his fingertips through the shape and looked away to see if he could feel it. There was a tiny, tiny crackle. He wouldn't have noticed it if he hadn't been concentrating. They both jumped when the ghost moved, but not towards them, or not as if it knew they were there, only to the desk.

'I should fetch my camera,' Vaulker said unevenly. He didn't move.

Thaniel drew his hand through the ghost again. The sugar parted and then moved straight back again into shape. It was hypnotic. 'No wonder they were seeing things in the kitchen. Flour everywhere.'

'But this can't have been happening for months. We would have noticed,' Vaulker murmured.

'Would we? How often do you throw powder into the air?' Thaniel had never felt so stupid. At Mori's house, the little gardener, Hotaru, had seen ghosts in the particles of quicklime. The salt burners saw them in the smoke. 'Jesus, and the fires. It's the smoke. The servants lay the fires, of course they're the ones who see what's in the smoke.'

Vaulker drew his teeth over his lower lip. 'What the hell do we do? Go to the mission church?'

'I don't ... think it's that kind of ghost.' He brushed it again, and this time it gave him a static shock that made him clench his hand.

'What was that?' Vaulker asked tightly.

'Electricity.' Mori had said Yoruji was haunted in bad weather. Christ. 'How long has the weather been stormy? Since November?'

'Yes. Maybe the middle of November.'

'Which is when the staff began to complain.'

Vaulker lifted his eyebrows. They both glanced at the window where the fire on Mount Fuji was still clear.

'Iron in the ground all around Fuji, isn't there?' Vaulker said. 'Was it you who said that was why this weather is so electrical? Something to do with electromagnetic something-or-others when the volcano's active?'

'The Met Office says that. I don't know if iron in the ground could really cause all this, though, no matter how stormy the weather is. It would have happened somewhere before, wouldn't it?'

'Perhaps it has, perhaps that's why some places are haunted and others aren't.'

Thaniel dug his fingertips into his own shoulders again. Black handprints. One of them had touched him – shocked him awake with that static snap. His skin, all of it, as one organ, prickled.

'Dad,' Six said from the door.

He paced forward, into the ghost, to displace the last of the sugar. He would have shown it to her in daylight, but however clockwork-minded she was, it wasn't sensible at two in the morning. 'Nightmares, petal?'

'No. There's a fire outside.'

'It's on Fuji, it's miles away.'

'No.' She pointed towards the canal. It was hard to tell quite how far away the fire was, but she was right. Vaulker's reflection came up behind them too.

'One of the warehouses on the canal?'

'Must be.' Thaniel lifted Six up, less because she needed any reassuring than because he did. Like always, she didn't lean against him and only sat girder-straight.

'Look how bright the city is,' Vaulker breathed.

He was right. The whole city was alight, so bright that there were orange reflections on the undersides of the clouds. It looked unlike itself. At night Tokyo was usually a place of leaning wooden gates half lost above the lamps, and then sudden, new stone places. There were great dim expanses that were the parks, points of candlelight moving on the river where the night bargemen arranged cargo crates ready for the morning. But now it was brilliant. Thaniel could see the shapes of the streets swooping along-side the canals. Half of Tokyo must have bought lightbulbs

in the last couple of days. It looked like the inside of a phos-
phorescent hive.

Something exploded in the building that was on fire. The
bang rattled the windows and they stepped back. As they
did, some of the junior diplomats came down the stairs in an
anxious, excited cluster.

'There's another fire on the other side,' someone said. 'Ow,
Jesus!'

'What?' said Thaniel.

'The – bloody door handle. It's red hot. Even through the
towel.'

'Is there … not a cotton factory down there somewhere?'
Thaniel said slowly.

'The tea-towel is smoking,' the junior diplomat reported.

'The cotton factory is next to the building on fire,' Six said
to him in the quiet way she had when she was worried she
wasn't meant to be speaking.

'Christ – get back from the windows. Everyone. Now.'

There was a rush for the back rooms just before a much
bigger explosion blew the windows inward. He snatched
Six up again and looked back in time to see the silk curtains
catching fire on the in-furl. They went up like they were
soaked in oil, still swimming in the hot air and the floating
cinders. Blackened rags frayed away and settled over the
papers on the desks. He saw a sheet begin to burn, still upright
in a Corona typewriter.

A quarter of an hour later, they were sitting in raggy groups
in the dining room of the Dutch legation, while the Dutch

diplomats' wives came round with hot drinks and blankets, and sweets for the children. Six seemed to think it was an interesting variation on an ordinary night. Thaniel didn't understand why that was all right but going down the corridor the wrong way wasn't. She'd got the other children together and now they'd made a fort under a table. He was still seeing after-flashes of the explosion, and as they popped and spun on the edges of his vision, they sounded like xylophones.

The Dutch had listened to their servants a lot earlier than the British. There was brand new linoleum on the floor, lightbulbs looped around the rafters, and rubber stitched over all the door handles and hinges. Buckets of sand waited on either side of every door and window.

'Steepleton,' Vaulker said, and then stopped short. Thaniel was sitting with the Dutch doctor, who had made him take off his shirt. The doctor was lifting bits of glass out of his shoulders with tweezers. 'Christ, you're black and blue. Did you – fight the man who killed Arinori?'

'No, the carriage crashed, before. The horses spooked.' He hadn't noticed before – he hadn't looked at himself – but he was bruised right down what he'd been thinking of as his uninjured side. With the twang and burn of the bullet wound, he hadn't felt any other pain, not even from the glass shards.

Vaulker looked like he wanted to say something, but another explosion went off close by and they both jumped. 'What the hell was that?'

Much longer than the explosion was the crash of a falling roof. It took whole seconds.

'The fire crews demolish houses to stop fires. All the houses are wooden. There's no other way to control a fire until it reaches one of the canals. Are you all right?' Thaniel added, because he was starting to think that neither of them was. He didn't usually startle easily, but the noise just then had fired a jolt right up and down his spine. He was shying at smaller sounds than that too, as badly as a hare. 'Have you even sat down?'

'What we saw ...' Vaulker began. He crumpled down beside Thaniel, all the creases in his skin and his clothes outlined in soot smudges. 'If it's caused by this weather – well. We need to know if it's going to get worse. And particularly if it's to do with Fuji. If this is a sign the volcano is about to go off, we have to evacuate.' He was speaking very quietly. He glanced around the room after he'd finished, and when Thaniel followed his eyes, he saw that some of the Dutch diplomats were talking in the same way, low, heads close. Nobody wanted to say volcano loudly. The room was full of children. 'The Dutch Minister has just sent someone to wake up that fellow who runs the Met Office, but I don't think they'll be allowed to say even if something was about to happen. Chaos at the docks.'

Thaniel nodded. 'You want to go, in case?'

'Francis Fanshaw will have my head on a plate if I evacuate everyone and nothing happens. I haven't got much goodwill capital with him at the moment, I suspect.' He flicked his eyes up at Thaniel.

'I haven't told him anything,' Thaniel said. 'If no one's noticed you weren't at the promulgation, good. What are we doing, then, if not leaving?'

Vaulker looked taken aback. 'You haven't told him I didn't go?'

'No. Why would I?'

'You don't like me.'

'I do not,' Thaniel agreed, smiling.

'Well …' Vaulker stopped to laugh. 'Thank you. No, so. We need to send someone to Fuji to see what's going on.'

'Foreigners need papers to leave Tokyo. They'll never issue them if they think we're poking around.'

'I think any police along the way will have other things to consider.' Vaulker hesitated. 'Look, I can see you're in a state, but I've got a nasty feeling you're the only one fluent enough to go. We'll ask the Chinese and the Dutch, but – be prepared.'

Thaniel nodded slowly. He wanted to say no, he had to get to Yoruji, now even more than yesterday. Something had happened to Mori. That was the only explanation left. He could accept that Mori might let a carriage crash and a minister be murdered, but it was stupid to imagine he would let Six drift into harm's way. The windows had exploded. She could have died. If Mori had been able to stop that, he would have.

But if the volcano was going to erupt, getting Six away was going to have to come first. Not to mention everyone else's children, and the juniors, who were still boys themselves.

'I can get on a train in the morning.'

Vaulker sighed as if he'd thought Thaniel might refuse. 'Listen,' he said suddenly. 'I know I was the one who sent you in that wretched carriage. Don't imagine I don't know it should be me sitting there with a bullet wound.'

Thaniel had to lie. 'I hadn't thought about it.'

'Well, that's very …' Vaulker shook his head, which shimmered his light hair. He must have run water through it already, because it was clean even while the rest of him wasn't. The effect was odd, like he was made of two photographs of the same man in different lights. 'I'd better make my obeisances to the Dutch Minister. Do your best not to swear at the Dutch translators, won't you.'

It was nearly reassuring to see him return to his usual self.

'What's that racket?' Vaulker added.

Now that he'd pointed it out, Thaniel saw the staccato white raps that were banging over the low murmurs in the hall. They sounded like telegraphs. In an office just off the hall, five telegraphs were indeed going mad by themselves, spooling spirals and spirals of transcript paper right over the floor. Some Dutch clerks were trying to make them stop, but pulling out the electrical wires hadn't helped.

'Excuse me,' Six said carefully.

Thaniel stood aside for her. She ignored the alarmed yells when she dipped her hand past the hammering key of one machine, and pulled out the spark gap. It died. The clerks all looked surprised.

'They're electric,' she explained. 'Dot dash is on off.' She studied all the men. 'I don't speak Dutch,' she added into the quiet.

'Where did you get her, did you say?' Vaulker asked. 'And ... do you suppose there are more?'

Six looked between them. 'Is he being horrible or good?' she asked Thaniel.

'He's being good,' Thaniel promised. He wanted to pick her up, but she would hate it. He was surprised when, without looking, she patted him absently. He looked out at the city instead of at her while the Dutch clerks set about dismantling the telegraphs. Away towards the canal, the smoke had made huge clouds. The air was full of cinders that might have been great swarms of fireflies. While they were watching, something further away went off with a colossal bang and fireworks exploded every which way. People laughed and oohed, and Six rocked happily. It was beautiful. But it rocketed the fire over the canal. The trees on the other side were starting to burn. The next building on from those was the Palace.

Towards dawn, the Dutch Minister's man came back, ash-covered, to report that the Met Office were issuing a statement to the morning papers. It would say that while the weather was alarming, it was definitely nothing to do with any volcanic activity under Fuji, and the city was, except for the hazards of increased electricity, quite safe. They were forecasting an end to the problem once the storm blew over.

Thaniel didn't know what the Dutch for 'absolute bollocks' was, but he suspected it was what went around their staff. It was certainly what had gone around the English, and the visiting Americans who had come to see if they were all right. The Chinese diplomats didn't look convinced either. They had brought food for everyone.

The American Minister came across to say he was inclined to give it another couple of days. The Dutch Minister came too, and then the Chinese. It was difficult, because some people had no English and not everyone had Japanese, but after some translation, the Chinese Ambassador, who was the oldest and most senior, sat back in his chair.

'Of course we need to send somebody to Mount Fuji, but Mr Steepleton here is in no state to go. There must be other translators.' He looked round them all expectantly. The Dutch and the Americans glanced at each other, guilty, and admitted that they only had badly paid freelancers who would laugh in the face of anybody who tried to make them go to Fuji on no notice.

'What about you?' Vaulker said, a little accusatory. 'Chinese is much closer to Japanese than English; don't you all speak it?'

'It is about as close,' the Chinese Ambassador said, slow and flat, 'as English and Norwegian. Naturally we have a translator, but he is from the royal family, and I'm afraid I can't conscience that risk.' He pointed with his eyes to a very young man huddled over a cup of tea not far away. The boy was a perfect Chinese version of Pringle. The Ambassador sighed. 'Mr Steepleton, I really hate to ask this, but will you be all right?'

'I'll be fine,' said Thaniel. He didn't feel too certain, and he was still seeing the xylophone flashes, but hell would freeze over before he let any iteration of Pringle anywhere near anything dangerous. He folded his arms and tried to stifle the noise of all his paternal bells going off at once.

The Chinese Ambassador didn't look very convinced. 'I suppose that's that, then. We shall wait for Mr Steepleton to come back from Mount Fuji, and if it's bad news, my government will host you all in Peking.'

'Steepleton,' Vaulker murmured as they all separated off. He put his hand on Thaniel's back to make him incline his head down and close. 'Listen. Whatever you find up there: I think it would be wise to report back officially that it's dangerous.'

'Why?'

'Because the FO got a message to us last night. Prime Minister Kuroda made the official and final order on a fleet of ironclads a few weeks ago, but the contract had been in place for years. The damn things had already been built, on the understanding that the Americans would buy them if Tokyo's funds fell through. They're being brought here from Liverpool now.'

Thaniel leaned back. 'So ... whatever is going on here with Mount Fuji, we've got the Russian fleet just off Nagasaki still, and now there's a British fleet sailing to deliver new battleships to Tokyo.'

'Mm. They'll literally have to shove the Russians out of the way to get here. I think there's going to be a firefight one way or another. Whatever you see — find a way to make it into a reason to get us out of Tokyo before the world and his wife tries to flee the start of a war and there are no more bloody ships to flee on.'

PART FOUR

THIRTY

Aokigahara, 13th February 1889

Travelling to Fuji in as straight a line as anyone could, you came first to Aokigahara Forest. It really did look bluish in the deep mist and shade of the mountain, which took up the whole sky in one titan wall of white snow. The taste of iron had grown stronger the nearer to the mountain Thaniel came. It stung his teeth, even though Willis had given him morphine for the journey.

He had a stagecoach to himself. Everyone else, the driver said, wanted to go the other way.

On the other side of the road, people were moving north in a great caravan, carrying bundles and children on their shoulders, or on oxen. Everyone was smoke-stained. A lot of them had noticeable burns, and they all stared at the stagecoach. Someone shouted, wanting to know if Thaniel was from the government. Someone else saw that he was white and slung a melon at the side of the coach, and yelled something about fucking Americans. Other people realised and yelled too, and more things thumped on the door and the window. He put the blind down. It had to be the volcano; but nobody could blame Americans for the volcano. When he asked the driver if he could get out and ask someone, the driver told him that he did not refund the families of those lynched in his coach, thank you.

Soon, the road emptied. Everyone who was leaving had left, and the way turned quiet. Thaniel put the blind up again. The trees that flanked the road were grey now. He thought at first that it was snowing, but it was ash. The land, which had been lush before, had faded and deadened. Nothing was bright but what had been left on the side of the road.

Some of the abandoned things were big, like oxen har-nesses or cartwheels. But mainly it was jewellery and money. People had just flung coins and watches away, and the verges, ashen and colourless, glittered with a jetsam of gold and silver. Someone had left a collection of rings on an old tree stump. They had become so hot that the stump was smoking.

The coachman had to stop well before the forest. The roads were shut. Had been for months; something to do with the army, he said. Thaniel walked the last mile – very slowly, and not too steadily – and when he reached the barrier, he could see why the driver hadn't wanted to go any nearer to it.

Across the road, and in both directions on either side, vanishing into the woods, was a tall fence. Copper wires stretched between posts about nine feet high, whickering with electricity. Thaniel lobbed a stick at it. The stick caught fire.

A klaxon went off. In the silence of the forest – and it was silence, because no animals rustled and no birds clipped among the pines – it was shockingly loud. The whine was deafening, and the whole world exploded into white, which greyed and then brightened painfully and greyed again as the klaxon lifted and fell. He got off the road, fast, and ran to the darkest patch of woods. There must have been a seam of iron just underground, because the frost had melted in a swathe, and the trees smelled cloying with sap and warm needles.

'Fucking kids,' someone complained, a man. 'Oi! You little pissheads, I know you're hiding out there somewhere!' he shouted into the trees.

Thaniel didn't breathe while the soldiers stood and listened. In the warm patch, the white blanket of the road had turned to snow bones and dead earth. He could feel himself sinking in the mud and he had to shift onto the roots of a tree instead. It wasn't the kind of tree that had grown with hiding people in mind; it wasn't tall or broad or straight, but narrow and crooked, and he had to crouch.

Once the men began to walk away, he straightened, agonised for a second, then tucked his bag into a dry hollow and followed them. There was a small watchtower not far away. It didn't look new; it was the ruin of something else, part of an old temple or something that someone had only reroofed. He paused at the door, told himself to calm down, and knocked.

'You've got some nerve, you little – oh,' the soldier said. The surprise had nearly made him squeak. He frowned. 'Who are you?'

'I'm from the Ministry,' Thaniel said. He could imitate Mori exactly when he concentrated. It hurt to do, because he had to listen to Mori's gold voice in his memory, but it was courtly, and never the voice of someone who was not who he said he was. 'You'd have been expecting me, but the telegraphs in Tokyo are out and you know what happened when we tried the bloody messenger pigeons.'

The soldier paused uncertainly. He was just young enough to want to say yes, he did know things, even when he had no idea about any pigeons. 'Right, of course. You don't look like you're from the—'

'Says everyone; it's a drag. You haven't got some tea, have you, before I have to slog up the mountain?'

'Um – sorry, may I see your papers?'

'Afraid not.' He tipped his shoulders back and concentrated on looking rueful, and embarrassed. 'You try swimming upstream in a nice coat when everyone and his dog is running the other way with nothing but what he can carry. It provokes people.'

'Sorry?'

'I was mugged,' Thaniel said. 'Papers, money, the lot.' He held his arms wide to show he wasn't carrying anything. Stretching made the gunshot wound zing nastily, and the bruises down his ribs ached. He felt light-headed and promised himself more morphine once he was through the fence. 'You're not going to send me all the way back to Tokyo now, are you? The Minister will be livid.'

'Well …'

'What's your name? Private …?'

'Oh. Oh – of course, no, just come in,' the young man said, looking like he might be about to suffer some kind of internal collapse. 'We've got tea. Come in.'

———

The soldiers were local, recruited especially, and they seemed relieved to chat to someone who didn't want to throw things. After the tea, they directed Thaniel up along the road, and warned him that it might be different to what he would have seen on previous visits.

Once he was out of sight, he took some more morphine and leaned against a tree until it kicked in. He'd been worried when Willis gave it to him that it would make him hazy and heavy, but in fact all it did was take a lot of the pain away and fill him with a gentle sort of optimism.

He walked slowly to the village that lay at the foot of the path up the mountain. His watch was getting warm in his pocket. He'd already wrapped it in a handkerchief, but if it kept heating up he would have to leave it and he didn't want to think about that. Mori had made it. Everywhere, the ash drifted on thermals. It was turning the real snow a dead, cement grey.

Despite the morphine cheer, he was starting to feel the same unease that he'd had at Yoruji. That weird certainty that, for all he could see he was alone, he was being watched not just by one person, but a legion.

He paused when he came to a herd of goats scattered across the gravel road. They were nibbling at the grass growing up through the muddy patches. No one seemed to be with them. He walked around them rather than through, aware that one of the older nannies was watching, horns tipped down and ready.

When he pushed his hair back from his face, it crackled with static. The dark was coming down now, earlier than it would have in Tokyo. The sky was very clear, and cold.

Up ahead were other lights. He thought it was the lamps in the village, but then suddenly he was in the village and the lights looked no closer. The buildings were dark. The ash was very thick now, gathering along the folds of his coat sleeves.

In fact the lights were only about fifty feet away, and they weren't lamps, but sparks smouldering in a thatched roof.

The thatch must have been damp, because it was smoking like hell, but it was still burning, some sections duller, some deep red and sparkling. The ashes floated and spun. There was no one to put it out. Other roofs were burning too, and even other houses. It was slow; some of them must have been burning for days. The smoke made a deep fog. He pulled his scarf further up and tied it tight. In places, the smoke sketched the ghosts of people doing ordinary things – leading cows, talking, scrubbing doorsteps. But there was nobody real left.

There was something in the road, something big and blackened. He slowed down as he came to it, his throat tight with the almost-certainty that it was a person.

It was too big to be a man. It was a cow; a dead cow, almost completely burned up from the head to its forelegs but whole after that, except for where the ravens had got at it. Something glinted in the shrunken bones. It was steaming. He didn't touch it, but he knelt down and leaned nearer. It was a bell. Just an ordinary cow bell. He leaned back again and waited to stop feeling queasy. Even a hot cup of tea would burn right through you if you held it long enough. The cow must have gone mad with the bell getting hotter and hotter. He touched his watch again. Already warmer, even through the handkerchief.

It wasn't until he'd picked himself up again that he realised he'd been relying on staying the night here. Not sure what to do, but very sure he needed to get out of the smoke, he trudged on, past a place that had been a neat little inn. It was a burnt husk now. Up ahead, a wooden sign, smouldering around the edges, pointed uphill and said, *To the mountain.*

By the mouth of the path was a shrine. The trees were much bigger here, great pines whose heights faded into the smoke and the mist. Little fires snickered high in the branches and sometimes there was a sudden static clatter of burning pine needles, but the trunks hadn't caught yet, too soaked from the wet winter. Between two of them, up its own tiny set of steps, was a wooden cabinet with a statue of the local spirit in it; and beyond that, through a curving temple gate, the shrine itself, hardly bigger than the cabinet. One miniature window was open, so that it looked more like a souvenir kiosk than anything very religious, and through the spaces between the planks, it glowed.

When Thaniel got close, he saw that it was filled with lightbulbs. They were different shapes and sizes and none of them seemed to be wired to anything. They were hanging on strings, in clusters, like fishing floats. He wished Six could have seen. The air by the hut was warm from the heat in all the filaments. They lit up shelves of other things, prayer cards and ribbons, lucky charms, rice cakes. Thaniel looked up when he felt water mist over him. On the roof of the hut was a motor, turning a sprinkler that sat above a generous bucket of water. It was keeping everything too damp to burn.

There was a monk inside, reading a newspaper.

'Light the way,' the monk said happily. He was miniature and ancient. 'Scare off the ghosts. Oh, goodness, you're a foreigner, um …'

'It's all right, I understand,' said Thaniel, confused. If someone had said he was dreaming, he would have clapped them on the shoulder and said yes, of course.

'Oh!' The monk looked delighted. He had a lamp on the end of a slim pole, a lightbulb with a paper cover over it, and now he poked it out to light up Thaniel better. 'How in the world did you learn Japanese?'

'Um, excruciatingly. How come you're still here?'

'Someone has to look after the shrine.'

'Right, right.' Thaniel looked at the bulbs for a second longer before he remembered what he was meant to be doing. 'Listen, I wonder if you could help. Er … with two things actually.'

'Oh, yes, yes. Thing the first?'

Thaniel smiled. 'How long has there been electricity like this? Enough to …?' He motioned back at the village. The motorised sprinkler misted his sleeve.

'Oh, on and off for months,' the monk said cheerfully. 'Them on the mountain of course. If you want to kill yourself, you can find rope in there somewhere if you look about a bit,' he added, waving at the forest. 'The rangers leave it up. Would you like a lightbulb?'

'Thanks.' Thaniel passed the lightbulb between his hands twice. It stayed lit all the while. 'What do you mean, them on the mountain?'

'The scientists. Whatever they're doing, it's been very pronounced lately. The ghosts seem terribly flustered by it; there are a lot more of them than usual.'

'So it's not the volcano?'

The monk laughed. 'How in the world could the volcano make ghosts? No, no, they've got machines, great big things. They're doing it on purpose. I quite like it.' If he was angry that the village was on fire, he didn't mention it. He only pointed down, to where the ghost of a cat was curled up asleep close on Thaniel's left, and then, anticipating the probable question, lifted up the real cat to show that it was all right. It had tiny rubber boots on.

'They're not always dead, the ghosts?' Thaniel said, taken aback.

'No, no. Sometimes, sometimes not,' the monk said.

'But then ...' But he couldn't think what that meant. He couldn't think what the hell kind of machine would generate free electricity across an eighty-mile radius. All at once he didn't much like the idea of going up.

All around them, the ash was still falling, and it was hard to think through; it looked like white noise. Quite often, it became too heavy for the pines and they tipped a lot of it down all at once into soft piles around the trunks. Where it puffed up, there were maddening half-shapes that didn't look like people, but not like animals either. It was making Thaniel more jumpy than ever. He had never minded crowds, but these were crowds he couldn't see or name, and a horrible tight dread was building in his ribcage. 'Then what are they?' he said.

'Pssht,' said the monk, not bothered.

His nonchalance made Thaniel feel better. 'Is it far up the mountain? To where the scientists are, I mean.'

The monk looked anxious now. 'You mustn't walk in the dark, it's bad at night. You'd better stay with me.'

It would have been much more polite to go back and forth a bit, and pretend at least twice that he was fine, but suddenly he was so tired and so grateful he would have handed over anything for the chance to lie down. He said so, worried the monk would think he was being rude, and offered to pay.

'Rubbish,' said the monk. 'I shall be glad of the company. You can play Go, can't you? Oh, I'll teach you, it's easy,' he added, with a wicked little spark. 'Don't worry, I've put up rubber everywhere. Safe as you like. I'm Daichi, by the way. You know, like Great Help?' He traced out the kanji in the air. 'Though really I'm Medium-sized Help now, on account of my age.'

Thaniel laughed and introduced himself. The monk thought about it, said he wouldn't be able to say Nathaniel in a million years and would he mind awfully if he just called him Natsu. Thaniel didn't mind. It meant summer, and he liked the idea that the man thought he was summery.

Thaniel lost four games of Go, slept unexpectedly well on a mattress on the floor, thanked the monk again and set out at half-past six in the morning. The monk made him take a lightbulb and wouldn't let him pay for it. When Thaniel put it in his coat pocket, it stayed lit even with the insulation of the fabric. It looked like he'd picked up a star.

The mist was dense, and the great pines were close-set, so the glow of the lightbulb didn't reach far. Sometimes it was stronger and sometimes weaker, and then, suddenly, it went off altogether. The difference was amazing. The air felt light and clear. The pain in the roots of his teeth vanished. He could smell the pines, that lovely, resin freshness, and the soft saltiness of wet stone from the path. He sat down in the roots of a tree to enjoy it, and to get his breath back. The horrible foreboding feeling went away.

When the electricity came back, it was sharp, a nasty twang that made every cell in him squeeze. He took another morphine tab.

Something cold traced a soft, barely perceptible arc across the top of his spine. When he looked back, it was someone's toenail.

He almost dropped the lightbulb as he spun away from the tree. The body was hanging from one of the lower branches. There were others too, perhaps two dozen, all a good way apart from each other. Some were clear and some were only shadows. It took him a minute or so, standing and waiting for his ribs to unlock, to see that they were all shapes in the mist. None of them was solid. When he moved the light towards them, they had no colour. The mist had only furled into the imprints of people, like plaster into fossils. The nearest one swayed, but the rope made no sound. Very slowly, he touched its ankle. His hand passed straight through. There was only the dampness of the mist – just enough resistance to suggest some unusual quality of the air, just enough for him to have felt it when it brushed him.

He stood for a long time watching the ghosts, but none of them did anything sudden. A long way off, crows hooted – they didn't caw here – but that was all. His breath helixed away from him. He didn't want to carry on. But going back would mean going past the hanging ghosts. He felt tight and anxious again, in a way he hadn't since having nightmares as a small child. Maybe it was the altitude – altitude made you panicky, Mori said – but Thaniel didn't think so.

Eventually, he started along the path again. Once he was on the upper track, the lightbulb shone brighter. Steadily, over perhaps seven or eight hundred yards, the glow strengthened, and so did the sharpness of the ghosts. They weren't all hanging. He saw a man in the mist spooling out a long string between the trees. One end of it was still tied around a tree beside the path, though the length of it had fallen and rotted away a long time ago in the damp.

A flash of blue light flickered right across the sky. Thaniel was still wondering what it was when he felt something hot in his pocket. By the time he remembered his watch, it was burning. He pulled it out by its chain, his sleeve over his hand. It was too hot to hold. He put it down on the ground and knelt still. Where the chain sat over the damp moss, it steamed.

It would have been sensible to leave it behind. But the watch was a little cache of old happiness, and while he should have let it go, even without any electricity, he couldn't.

Carefully, he tucked the watch into his wallet and waited to see if he could smell anything burning, but it seemed all right. It was hot, but only like a hot-water bottle. He slid it into his breast pocket to have the warmth over his lungs. Ashamedly, he decided he would rather burn than leave it.

THIRTY-ONE

Abashiri, Hokkaido, 19th January 1889

Horikawa the gatekeeper was taking pot-shots out of the gatehouse window with an ancient rifle, aiming at the forest. Takiko arrived just in time to see an Ainu man jerk behind a tree.

'Bloody savages,' Horikawa said. 'Bloody bear ceremony. What did the bear ever do to them?'

She pushed the gate open with her shoulder and decided life would be much pleasanter if she just pretended he didn't exist from now on.

The owls were still on the roof of the Oracle tower. She stood and looked at them for a while. Yesterday she had walked all around the tower, but there were no doors. There must have been a cell up there, but whichever way they had taken Mori up, she couldn't find it. She had a heavy feeling that they'd walled him in. Today, she was here half an hour early to see if she could find a way in from the inside of the warden's office.

Just to make sure Mori was all right. If he was, he was staying put.

There was no one at the desk in the guards' office. Tanizaki had died in the night. A seizure. She heard it from the prisoners. They were chanting it on the fourth wing.

'Well?' Oemoto snapped. He was the tall man who Tanizaki had been teasing, and now he was prickly with anxiety. There were so many prisoners to so few guards now; he looked hunted. 'Are you going to do the tea or was that only so you could make eyes at Tanizaki?'

'I do it at ten o'clock,' she said. 'Keep yourself busy another couple of hours.'

'Damn it, you'll do it now! Do as you're told!'

'Ten o'clock,' she said, and looked at the whip in his hand when he twitched it.

She turned away from him, knowing he was going to hit her. When he did, it hurt incredibly. It felt like a hard smack over the back of the head. She didn't feel the slashing sting of it until a moment later. She pushed her hand up through her hair. Her fingertips came away sticky. She looked back slowly. Oemoto's expression was caught exactly halfway between shocked and brash.

'No more of that,' she said quietly. She had to concentrate hard to keep calm. She had known it was coming, but she hadn't realised how furious she would be, or how powerful the urge to punch him in the face. She had to summon up everything Ayame had hammered into her for the stage. He had once screamed into her face to make sure she could stay as calm as a princess should. Even knowing it was pretend, it had been difficult at the time not to nut him. You had to put yourself behind a glass pane. 'You can make your own tea.'

The back of her skull still howling, she carried the bucket and cleaning things up to the warden's office. She had a sharp sense of being a small person in among a lot of big, frayed, angry ones on short fuses. Of course, it didn't change anything. What she had to do was the same. Find whatever it was Mori needed, decide whether or not she should help, find a ship, and bugger off home. It was simple. But it seemed further away than before.

The key to the office was stiff. She expected the room to be empty, and she gasped, surprised, when she saw a man at Nakamura's desk, typing. He lifted his hand and ducked his head, and then went back to the photographs and the numbers.

'I'm just going to clean out the grate,' she said.

The man touched his own ear and made a slicing motion with one hand. Deaf. She pointed to the grate and mimed scrubbing. He nodded.

Her knees cracked when she knelt down and pulled out the grate to look up into the chimney shaft, hoping for steps up. Nothing. It was far too narrow to fit a person.

But, she could just make out another grate, well above this one.

She glanced back at the man at Nakamura's desk. He was typing again, not looking at her.

'Hello?' she called up the shaft.

There was no answer. But after she had sat back on her heels, there was a crackle of paper, and then a paper crane fell down the chimney. It puffed into the ashes in the grate in front of her. She lifted it out slowly. There was writing on one of the wings. It was shaky.

Help me

Behind her, the door opened and the warden came through. 'Morning, Miss Tsuru.' He waved at the young man, who must have been here overnight, and motioned that he could go. The young man looked grateful and hurried to fetch his coat.

She crushed the crane and dropped it through the spaces of the grate into the dark ash pit below. 'Morning, sir.'

'Oemoto's in a terrible fluster downstairs. He positively burbled that you've been asking questions. About the tower.' The warden pointed upward, and lifted his eyebrows. 'I told him that was unlikely, since you and I had such a clear agreement about minding your own business.'

She stood up carefully and brushed the ash off her knees. 'He's lying. He just hit me over the back of the head with that whip of his. I imagine he was afraid I'd tell you.' She put her head down so he could see the blood, which had seeped stiffly into her collar.

'Why did he hit you?'

'I wouldn't make the tea quickly enough.'

'Is that really so? Because Mr Horikawa seems to think you took this work in order to garner ... other kinds of business.' She'd heard people say 'whore' with much less force. 'And I know Mr Oemoto to be a very upright man.'

'It is really so, sir, and Mr Horikawa is mistaken. All I do here is clean. And look at me, I'm old enough to have grandchildren.'

He watched her for a moment. 'I respect Mr Oemoto's opinion a great deal, you understand; his father was very highly thought of in the army in his time.'

'Yes, sir,' she said, and didn't ask what magnificently stupid thing Oemoto had done to end up posted to the arse end of the Arctic.

'Another word from him and I shall have to dismiss you.'

'Yes, sir.'

He paused, awkward. Sternness didn't come naturally to him. 'If he did hit you for nothing but tea, that's dreadful.'

'All the guards are feeling very strained, I think.'

'Well, I'll … overlook this claim about your nosing around if you'll forgive him.'

'How kind of you, sir.'

'Well; off you go.'

Takiko bowed her head and hauled the cleaning things downstairs again, even while the greater part of her howled to get up into that tower room. That trembling handwriting had stirred something slithering in her gut. Mori's writing didn't look like that – but no one's did. It was how you wrote if you had to do it lying down, feeling sick. It was how dying people wrote.

Mori had said he might die. He deserved to be in a cage, but he didn't deserve to die in it.

There had to be a way up, but she was never going to find it with Oemoto looking for an excuse to get her sacked.

Down on the misdemeanours' wing, the first one she'd seen on her first day, she counted along the cells until she found the door of the two men who had spoken to her about the cold and the Marquis de Sade. She tapped gently on the bars.

'Hello, miss,' the bigger man said, wary.

'You know you said you'd kill for cigarettes?'

She pushed her hand into her sleeve pocket and held up the new pack she'd brought from home today. It was a wrench, because she had wanted them a lot, but she'd live.

He gave them a longing look. 'What's the plan then, ma'am?'

'Well, if you could grab me and we'll both scream a bit. And then if you could put Mr Oemoto in the infirmary for me when he comes to break it up, these are all yours. He's just sliced my head open with that poncing whip he carries around.'

The man had come to the bars to look at the cigarettes. He must have been mafia, because he was missing the ends of two fingers – they did that, if you didn't do a job properly – and he had a tattoo on his arm. He looked puzzled. 'Trust me to do that, do you?'

'Course I do,' she said. She didn't, but just occasionally, trust was a force in itself. 'I think we all know which side of these bars the psychopaths are on.'

She saw him warm, just fractionally. She put the cigarettes down by the stove where no one could snatch them, went to the bars, and helped him find a way to grab her hair without hurting the new cut too much.

———

At ten o'clock, she took Oemoto some tea in the infirmary, where the doctor was dabbing at the puffy mess that was one side of his face.

'I'm ever so grateful that you rescued me,' she said, making serious eyes at both of them. 'I made you that tea. Good thing you like it so much really; you don't look like you'll be able to manage anything *but* tea for quite a while.'

THIRTY-TWO

Aokigahara, 14th February 1889

After a long uphill climb, the path came out on the bank of a reservoir. The water was silent, and on the far side, a gaunt metal tower hummed and sparked with blue coils of static. Thaniel had to sit down for a while and watch it, because his chest hurt. He didn't want to think about going all the way back. The walk up had taken hours.

He hated reservoirs. He had grown up in woods that flooded sometimes into pools and ponds that had no clear edges, and after seeing water free to do as it liked, something felt wrong about a dam. The quickest way to the tower, though, was to walk across on the dam, so he did, feeling taut with the awareness of the weight of the water on one side and the huge steep drop to the river on the other. Somewhere, he could hear turbines. Below him, the water roared. It went into a narrow river, all white over rocks and falls until it evened out much lower down into a silver curve. On the other side it was dead quiet. There were no birds. Ahead, there was a much louder snap, and the air crackled.

There was a gate at the end of the dam, and a gatehouse. Because it was the only tall thing but the mountain itself, there was an optical illusion around the tower from further away that made it look smaller than it was. It was colossal.

'Stop!' someone shouted. It made Thaniel jump. 'Don't cross the white line!'

He looked down. Someone had painted a thick white line across the way in. Up in the gatehouse was a soldier who was pointing a rifle at him. He put his hands up.

'I'm from the Ministry,' he called back. 'I'm here to see the director.'

'I've not been told to expect anyone.'

'Of course you haven't, all the bloody telegraphs are down.'

There was a pause. From the gatehouse, even in the mist, it would be obvious that he was a foreigner, but Mori's imperial Japanese did its job and the soldier stepped back to talk to someone else.

'He's coming,' the soldier said when he reappeared. 'Don't move.'

'May I put my hands down?'

'Keep them out of your pockets.'

Thaniel crossed his arms and paced to try and keep warm. Now that he was waiting instead of walking, the gunshot wound hurt a lot more. It was a blessedly short wait before the soldier came down and unlocked the gate.

'He says you can come in.' The soldier watched him curiously but didn't say anything else.

The door at the base of the tower opened and a smart man in a suit leaned out. 'Sorry to keep you waiting in the cold; we've had a few people try to wander in lately – ah – you're not from the Ministry?'

'Says everyone I ever meet,' Thaniel said. When he stepped over the threshold, the air smelled of metal and damp like before, but now it had a steel-string hum in it. It was dim inside from the frost that clouded the small windows. It had made fantastic patterns, like pine trees.

'Oh. Half and half?'

'Yes, but citizen and all.' It was parachuting across the face of the obvious truth, which was that there were moon rocks more Japanese than he was, but sounding right counted for much more than looking right.

'I see. How curious. You know, I thought you were a ghost.'

'I saw plenty on the way in.'

'Yes, yes; very clear in the mist, aren't they. What can I do for you?'

'Tell me how you're getting on, if it wouldn't be too much trouble.'

'I was told I had wholly free rein,' the man frowned.

'Well … Tokyo is on fire.'

The director bristled, but then nodded. 'Yes, of course. Naturally I don't have an enormous amount of time to spare; you don't mind being briefed by one of our scientists? You'll get on. Foreigner too.'

'Thank you,' said Thaniel, wondering how long he could keep it up. It was ridiculous, but they had no way of checking who he was; if he didn't lose his nerve, it would be all right. And he only had to hold his nerve long enough to find out what they were doing. With any luck, it would only be about twenty minutes.

The director led the way down a flight of wooden stairs, below ground, to a broad, heavy door clad in rubber. From beyond it leaked a sound, deep and thrumming, and purple. When he opened it, the door swung on hydraulics, too heavy to move by hand, and as soon as it was open, the purple noise was everywhere.

Thaniel only knew what a generator looked like because Mori had one at home. Theirs was small, easy to take apart. This one was a hundred feet high. The heat it gave off was so intense he had to take off his coat. A lance of static snapped out and touched his sleeve. It made him jump and he expected a horrible shock, but it was only a breath on the back of his hand. He felt a bit wry as Six's voice in his head reminded him that you only got a shock if you touched a charged *object*, not just static.

The electricity flickered at him again as he moved away from it, following him, and, for all he knew what it was, he couldn't shake the feeling that it was a sort of bright animal, trying to work him out.

Although they were indoors, it was snowing.

It wasn't until he rubbed his sleeve that he realised the white particles weren't snow but chalk. The air tasted dry from it, and, when he looked down, there was a thick layer on the floor. They had made perfect powder footprints in it, and with each step, it puffed. It was falling in curtains from great fans turning ponderously in the roof.

Standing there, he could feel the bulk of the steel tower above him. Static brushed at him again, very gently, though the noise it made was infernal. He wanted suddenly to get out. Deep under the floor somewhere was that earthquake-purple thrum. It made him nervous even after he reasoned it was just the water moving through the dam, and perhaps other machines buried under the generator.

He didn't see the ghost at first. It was crisp and perfect, but despite all the chalk, still only as solid as a moonbeam.

'What the hell is that?' he said quietly.

'Extraordinary, isn't it?' the director said. 'We have no idea. But it wanders in and out, so its territory must have been fairly small.'

The ghost was a monster four times the height of a man. It had a cruel thick beak and a birdish look, but though it had glorious long tail feathers that swung right round the generator, it didn't have wings but strange, small forearms and claws. It was pacing gradually to and fro, looking at far less substantial shapes that might, at a stretch, have been trees. As they watched, it stretched right up onto its hind legs and reared up to snap at something. At its full height, its neck stretched up, it must have been upwards of fifty feet tall.

'Here be dragons, hey?' the director said, pleased. 'Anyway, I'll leave you with Baroness Matsumoto.'

Thaniel spun and then had to keep a vice on his expression. He recognised her well before she turned around. She managed to keep her face completely neutral when the director pointed him out. She came towards him on the very edges of her shoes, like she was tightrope walking, to keep from exploding chalk dust all around herself.

He felt like he'd swallowed a mouthful of sand. He'd forgotten how frightened of her he was. It wasn't the kind of fright that came with ghosts, or being made to jump. It was an unpleasant background tang, just like the taste of the electricity. She was the only person in the world but Mori who knew why they had got divorced.

He tried to keep his expression friendly and to stave off the unpleasant truth, which was that she was the worst possible person he could meet here. Not only could she have him thrown out straightaway for illegal nosing about, she could smash him to pieces with an accusation that would send him to an asylum.

She shook his hand as if they had never met, smiling. 'Keep pretending you don't know me. Someone's always watching. Understand?' She said it in a bare whisper.

'I understand,' he said, and had to rearrange what he thought of her and the world.

'I'm afraid the director didn't tell me your name?' she said, over-politely, at normal volume.

'Compton. I'm from the Ministry.'

'Pleased to meet you, Mr Compton. I'm Grace Carrow. What do you need to know? Apart from what on earth this lizard thing is. We don't know. It's very, very old, though. Millions of years. Someone has an interest in prehistoric flora and apparently that fern over there hasn't existed since the Jurassic.'

She was no different. She was little and sparse, and she still had short hair, though it was in a sleek neat bob now, and she had the glow of someone very well kept. Because her dress was grey, she could have looked like a governess from a distance, but close to, it was beautifully made. The creases were too white; chalk dust.

'What the hell is going on?' he whispered.

'A progress report,' she said loudly. 'Yes, of course. Come up to the office with me.'

She led him out of a side door that looked like it belonged in a bank vault. She sealed it after them and nodded him up a tiny narrow staircase with its own door, which she thumped shut as well, and then sagged.

'Thank Christ,' she breathed. 'I've been waiting for you to turn up for months.'

'What?'

'You have to believe me. I didn't know it was about Mori til we got here, and then it was too late. We're stuck up here. They've got our papers, they lock the gates, there's no way down. The guards shot the ornithologist when he tried to escape. I mean an ornithologist, Christ's sake! He was studying owls!'

'Sorry, sorry,' Thaniel said quickly. 'Mori's here?'

'No, God no, they wouldn't risk it. I don't know where he is, but they have him somewhere. I'll show you. How did you find this place? Did Akira ask you to come?'

Akira – Matsumoto, of course. 'He reported you missing. Tokyo's gone mad, there's electricity everywhere, everything's on fire – everyone thought it was something to do with the volcano, so I came up to see if it was erupting, and then I found all the ghosts and a monk who said there were scientists up here— what did you say about Mori?'

'This is all here because of him. It—' She glanced up, because someone had opened another door at the top of the stairs and footsteps were coming down. 'Come up, I'll show you,' she said, falsely bright again. Another man passed them and nodded. 'Dr Shirakawa.'

'Mrs Matsumoto,' he muttered.

She made a brittle effort at wry. 'I think the university only sent me and not the head of department because they knew it was shifty,' she explained.

'Morons.'

She laughed. 'Entirely,' she said, and clipped up the stairs. After the bizarre testing room, the little stairway was ordinary. It had a grey carpet, and the edges of the steps were lined with fresh strips of linoleum.

At the top was a gallery office whose window overlooked the chalk-dusted testing floor. A few people were there, but no one paid them any attention; they were watching the testing floor, making notes, beside bulky things wrapped up in rubber and mounted on tripods. Cameras. The room was full of other devices too, but Thaniel couldn't have got close to naming most of them. Something that might have been a telescope was pointing out the window, but it was made mostly of cardboard, and wires flooded around one side. There was something complicated going on with paperclips and scavenged bits of clock. On a desk in the corner was a weird mutant of a microscope with a lightbulb burning underneath it. It might have been going for a while, because there was a smell of hot metal coming from that direction.

'Damn,' Grace muttered, and slung a tea-towel over the lightbulb. 'People keep using it and leaving it on.'

'What is it?'

'I'm trying to see if it's possible to see ether particles – it would help a lot – but normal microscopes don't have anything like the magnification. I'm focusing down electron streams instead of visible light ... no, it's boring, you don't care,' she finished, and then scuffed her hand through the back of her hair and scanned the ground as if her thoughts had just rolled off in different directions. 'Sorry. I'm going to bits; nobody up here believes in sleep. I was going to show you ...'

She went to a filing cabinet and took out a heavy folder. The hum of the great generator was low and nagging in the background.

'Every day all through January,' she said, very low, 'we sent information requests to a research facility whose location we don't know, via the Home Ministry. Every day, we received answers to the requests of two days before. These are the records.'

Thaniel looked down the page she had opened. It was a zebra-striping of telegram transcripts pasted on black paper. She cleared aside odd bits of mechanisms and cardboard stencils to make room for them to lay out some of the pages.

Q: Please place the Subject in total darkness. Set out in front of him three coloured sheets of paper. Allow nobody, including yourself, to tell him which colours they are. Ask him to identify the colours. Is he able to do so?

A: No.

Q: How does the Subject respond to the THREAT of corporal punishment if it is a) fully intended and b) unintended.

A: a) Subject reacted as though I had removed his first two fingers, although I hadn't yet picked up the chisel. Subject assured me in no uncertain terms that he would make me kill myself before too long.

b) Subject didn't register that he was being spoken to.

Q: Please place the Subject in a vacuum, with breathing apparatus, in total darkness. Is he able to predict how many times you mean to tap his hand?

A: Yes. We're not doing this one again. He got a match into the room and set the oxygen tank on fire. I no longer have the use of my eyebrows.

There were pages and pages, double-sided. Thaniel turned them over, not breathing. The final page was from the end of January. The transcript only reached halfway down the page.

'They stopped,' Grace said quietly. 'We've had nothing since. I tried to ask why, but the Home Ministry only told us to make do with what we have.'

He lifted his eyes slowly, because they felt heavy. 'What's it all for?'

'This place was built,' she whispered, 'to discover what Mori does, and to reproduce it. I'm not even meant to know his name. He's just Subject A in all the official communications.' She flicked a glance towards the big window, but the men there still weren't paying them any attention. 'But it must be him. When did you last see him?'

Thaniel shook his head slightly and turned back to the beginning of the folder. The first date was the second of January. He clenched his hand when his eye caught on 'chisel' again. 'Christmas. Grace – why the ghosts?'

'Mori remembers the future. He can tell you what it looks like, what it sounds like.' She coughed. It sounded bad. She must have been breathing chalk for weeks. 'So we knew there must be visual information to be had. We knew that any perception of future events must be happening at faster than light speed, and – God, you don't care,' she said, shaking her head. 'What we found very quickly is that if you electrify the atmosphere and introduce a fine medium – chalk, sugar, flour, smoke – it will outline imprints. You know what the luminiferous ether is. Immensely fine, subtle substance that permeates everything, and through which light moves.'

'Like sound moves through air.'

'Well—' She looked pained, then seemed to let it go. 'Yes, fine. It turns out light makes prints on it. The ghosts are light fossils. The marks made by visible light on the ether. Which is like the bedrock of the universe. Unmoving, but like real bedrock, possible to imprint.'

'But how is that anything to do with …'

'If you can have past ghosts,' she said softly, 'and if you can have a clairvoyant who recalls every possible future, then there must also be future ghosts. We're trying to find a way to see them.'

'Christ,' Thaniel whispered.

She nodded, very slight and tight. 'I've been trying to say we haven't got enough data to produce them,' she said softly. 'But – we have.'

He looked across. 'What?'

'Someone else here is going to realise …' She shook her head. 'I've been sending everyone down as many wrong tracks as I can, but I can't keep doing it. You have to find out where Mori is and get him out. I don't think anyone else can stop this now. Imagine Count Kuroda with the ability to accurately tell the future. It would be the last weapon human beings ever built. And, once they have the ability to do it, they'll kill Mori. I never thought I'd be scared of that, but at least he's sensible.'

'But the telegrams stopped coming at the end of January.'

She nodded fractionally. 'Perhaps they're moving him, perhaps someone decided after the oxygen tank incident that it wasn't safe, perhaps he's refusing to cooperate.'

'Or he's dead,' Thaniel said. He felt like his logical facility was ticking without the rest of him. The rest was in a sealed cork chamber, screaming.

Chisels. Vacuums. And he'd let Mori walk into it.

'I hope very much that he isn't.'

He swallowed. 'What makes you so sure they're close to finding future ghosts?'

She leaned down over the table as if she were poring over one of the documents, and nodded for him to do the same. He did, and she put their heads close together. When she spoke, it was barely audible, even so close.

'Because you can already see them.'

The director breezed in then. 'Ah, Dr Matsumoto! Looking after our guest, I hope?'

'Certainly,' she said brightly. 'I thought I'd show him the ice caves. Good show down there.'

'Excellent, excellent,' he said, and went straight to the scientists at the window, who he plainly thought were more important.

———

At the foot of the stairs was another door. It led to a deep cellar room full of huge machinery. Beside an enormous steam engine, whose belly glowed red and waved a gorgeous heat everywhere, there were stairs again. They led down a subterranean tower, bricked roughly all around like the inside of a well. It went deep, lit at insufficient intervals by bare electric lights. The heat didn't even reach a quarter of the way and soon it was freezing. Thaniel followed Grace. The way the hem of her skirt trailed on the steel steps was hypnotic after a while.

'Ice caves?' he asked when he was sure no one else was here, and that nobody could hear.

'Ghosts are easiest to see in a place that sees very little traffic in the way of living things,' she explained. Her voice echoed blue, up and down. 'And we've only got owls down here. Owls are – well, I'll show you.'

When they reached the bottom, there was a long, narrow corridor, only just wide enough for one person. It put Thaniel strongly in mind of a mine. The walls were raw rock, seamed with iron. The iron was warm. He couldn't hear the generators anymore, or the thunder of the dam. They were somewhere below the waterfall now, perhaps even below the river beneath.

More steps down, uneven and rough-hewn, and then suddenly they came out on a brand new wooden gantry that still smelled beautifully of fresh cedar.

They were in a low, broad cavern, where ice curtained the walls. It had formed huge stalactites, which glittered blue by the glow of the lightbulbs someone had hung on string from the gantry rails. There were thick pillars of ice on the ground too, as tall as a man. In the middle of it all was a deep pool. The water was so clear it didn't look like water. Rocks lifted from the bed. No weed, though, nothing. Just tiny fish. Thaniel was still looking when a grey owl soared down and snatched one from the surface. It landed on an ice pillar and blinked at them.

'Before they started building generators or anything like that,' Grace said quietly, 'they had a whole team of people researching old stories about anything that could have been − whatever Mori is. There's a good few. Fairytales mainly. There's a winter king who leads people to their deaths in the woods, or death gods who mark out particular people, or half-devil figures who you can make pacts with for unnatural good luck. The stories are all remarkably similar. They all seem to describe a person, and not an actual god. They're all tricksters − you never get what you expect from them. And, they are always attended by owls.'

While she was talking, she was opening a box. Thaniel wanted to ask if she could hurry up. His shoulder hurt with a bright fresh pain that felt like the stitches might have come undone, and thinking of all those stairs back to the surface made it worse.

'It's a really common thing to hear here, superstition about owls. Some people think they're lucky, some people think they mean you'll die soon. But they definitely indicate some kind of change.'

Thaniel nodded. Grace's box was full of chalk dust, and a little pair of bellows. She pressed them together, and dust blew across the pool.

'What the researchers found in the trickster stories was that owls always preceded the appearance of the trickster. Obviously it could just be a narrative device, but I don't think it was. I don't think our ornithologist thought so either.' She sighed. 'I think he found something. I think that's why he tried to run away.'

There were clouds of chalk over the water now. The chalk plumed and danced. He wanted to say he would help her with the bellows, because she looked thin and exhausted, but he was fighting off a wave of dizziness. He could feel his shirt catching on all the glass cuts.

She pointed. 'Watch the chalk.'

It was forming patterns. A network of lines outlined themselves in the white dust, quite broad, like owl-sized tunnels. For a while nothing moved but the dust. Then one of the strange air-tunnels sharpened, and an owl ghosted down exactly through it, took a fish from the water, and flew back up through another.

'What was that?' Thaniel said.

'That,' Grace said, 'is what a future ghost looks like. That tunnel in the air, that line. It's where the owl will fly. You see?'

Thaniel thought about it, then decided that in five seconds' time, he was going to reach out and touch her shoulder. A very thin, feeble little line appeared in the chalk dust between them. Grace nodded.

'Yes. We can do it too, but not half as clearly as the owls do. I think it's because we decide things vaguely, most of the time. But say you could perceive the future – even just the immediate future – you'd know what you were doing far more precisely. You'd know the variables. You wouldn't just decide to cross the road, you'd know exactly when and where you'd cross, because you'd know where all the carts were going to be. Much more specific, much clearer. A much more definite future. I think the more inevitable the future, the clearer the future ghost. Look at this.'

She flicked a sovereign coin. It fell down a very clear coin tunnel in the whorling chalk, and then, right at the last second, the tunnel split into two fainter ones. Heads and tails. The coin landed heads. The ghost trails all vanished.

'Gravity. Certain. Always,' she said. 'Followed by exactly even chances, which are fainter because they have only a fifty per cent chance of actually occurring.' She sighed. 'This is exactly how Mori works, isn't it? He perceives possible futures. This is what he's seeing.'

'Yes.' He hesitated. He had conditioned himself so well never to talk about Mori that it was a struggle now. 'Sometimes you can ... Six was angry with him not long ago. She threw a dice, and if it landed on a six, she threw a firecracker. But even when the dice didn't land on a six, Mori still heard the firecracker. The – potential firecracker.' Prising the memory away and giving it to Grace left him feeling hollow.

'Because the dead future takes a little while to fade,' she said. She was watching him ruefully. They hadn't divorced just because Thaniel had fallen in love with a watchmaker. It was as much because Grace had always thought – as far as he could tell – that it should have been her Mori was intrigued by, not some nobody from the civil service.

Thaniel looked away at the owls. They were mesmerising. Some were grey, but some were a deep, coaly black. They might just have seemed unusual out in the forest, but in here, beside the ice and the deep, silent pool, they couldn't have looked more preternatural if they'd tried. 'But how are they so clear about where they're going, then?'

She nodded a little. 'There's no light at all in this cave without the lightbulbs. So how do they know ...'

'... where the fish are,' Thaniel finished. Another owl swept down, though another chalk tunnel. It caught its fish so neatly that it only just disturbed the water.

'Exactly. What if it's not that the owls hear their prey extraordinarily well – what if they can sense where the fish intends to go? Like Mori would do?'

'Christ.'

She glanced up, tentative. 'Of course nothing is proven yet, but what if all those trickster figures in the stories were people like Mori, and what if the owls follow them because they mistake a clairvoyant's very clear, very defined lines of intent for those of another owl?'

'God, you're right. There are always owls at Filigree Street. I always thought it was because we were near Hyde Park. Mori never said anything.'

She tipped her head, philosophical and tired. 'It's only a hypothesis. Owls, for Christ's sake.' She looked up at him properly for the first time. 'What happened to him? How did they get him? I've been thinking about it for months, there's absolutely no way he wouldn't know what Kuroda intended for him. Unless he walked into it willingly.'

Thaniel nodded a little. 'He walked into it. He knew something was wrong when we got here. I tried to ask, he said it was fine. He sent me away.' He had to cough, and tasted iron this time as well as chalk. He hoped it wasn't blood. He had to get down off this mountain and back to Tokyo before he keeled over. The morphine seemed not to be doing anything much. 'And I went, like an idiot.'

Grace drew her teeth over her lip. 'He didn't tell you anything.'

'No. But something's gone wrong. He wouldn't let anything happen to Six, even if he was away. I've seen men who were looking at her too closely get run over by horses. I'm not joking.' He told her about the carriage crash and Willis, and the windows exploding inward at the legation.

Grace had been nodding gradually while he spoke. 'You think he's dead.'

He couldn't say it. 'I think none of this feels like him.' He turned away, coughing again.

He must have looked bad, because he saw real alarm go across her face. 'Christ, you're ill ... come on, enough of all this. No more chalk.' She took his elbow. 'We've got staff cabins. Let's get you fed and settled for the night.'

THIRTY-THREE

Yoruji, 15th February 1889

That morning, Kuroda had been at a coal warehouse. It was empty because the labourers had fled, but haunted with black ghosts formed from the pitch dust. The Ministry had organised the trip to prove to the increasingly skittish general public that the ghosts, in themselves, were harmless. Photographers from the newspapers had come to take pictures, and everyone had been laughing and cheerful. It was the most haunted place Tanaka could find, with about ten ghosts. Even the journalists who'd so enjoyed laying into him when he was in the Navy had said, not even grudgingly, that it was a good thing to do for people. Kuroda had been having a good day.

Once the photographers had gone, Tanaka had taken him quietly to one side, and said that they had a problem.

'So the lads are keeping an eye on Yoruji,' Tanaka said, uncharacteristically oblique. He looked grim. 'They've been noticing ghosts in the snow. Like a lot.'

Kuroda frowned, because he had never known Tanaka fuss before. 'Well, that's to be expected, isn't it? Yoruji is closer to the mountain than Tokyo—'

'No, but like *a lot* a lot. The men are getting nervy. So I went up this morning to have a look round, just to reassure them, sort of thing. Just chucked a bit of flour around.' He paused. 'There's fucking hundreds of ghosts. I think – for some reason, that place is recording pretty much everything that happens there. It's not just the odd random thing. I looked round for fifteen minutes and I saw ... well. It's like a giant sodding ghost phonograph. I think it might have recorded things we don't want people to see.'

'How clear?'

For the first time since Kuroda had known him, Tanaka looked uncomfortable. 'I can't describe it. I think you need to see, sir.'

So Kuroda had cancelled the afternoon's appointments.

Tanaka had set up little fans and chalk packets in the ceilings all through Yoruji. They feathered down a soft snow of chalk, outlining any ghosts and falling in a strange, soft blanket on the nightingale floors. It held the marks of everyone's bootprints beautifully. Someone gave Kuroda a cotton mask on the way inside.

Like Tanaka had said, the ghosts were everywhere. In every corridor, at every corner, by every pool and balcony, they overlaid each other in silent crowds. The same people appeared again and again, Suzuki and Mrs Pepperharrow, Mori; Kuroda even saw a glimpse of himself, walking the other way. Every single one was a perfect recording of a lost instant months ago, years ago, all overwritten across each other. The more recent ones, or what he thought must be the most recent judging from the way people's haircuts and clothes changed, were the clearest. That made sense. New recordings over the top of old ones.

Kuroda's stomach clenched. He walked carefully through the chalk, through two of the little gardens, and to the old smoking room. The smoking room Mori had locked up, ever since the Countess had died. It was still locked. He kicked the door in. Tanaka followed. Silently, he threw a new packet of chalk into the air.

The Countess was there. Running, like she was chasing him down the halls of the years.

Kuroda slammed the door shut. 'He knew,' he said softly. 'He fucking knew, Tanaka, he kept that room locked so nothing else could overlay it.'

Tanaka put one hand on his arm, very carefully. 'All respect, sir, but that isn't our biggest worry now.'

'What?'

'The most recent thing that happened in the dining room,' Tanaka said softly. 'It's there. Clear as the morning.'

'But muddled up with everything else that ever happened in that dining room, surely?' Kuroda said, sharper than he'd meant. A foul tattoo needle of panic was starting to prick at his lungs.

It was ridiculous, how easy it had been to convince himself that he had outgrown fear. Of course he hadn't. He had just grown so big that there wasn't much in the world to fear anymore, but here was one of those things. He felt as though Mori had dumped him back in time to that first shameful morning he'd gone into battle in the Navy, white and sweating and absolutely certain he was going to be blown to pieces. That terrible fear, the one he'd convinced himself was childishness, was just as vivid now as it had been then.

Tanaka was shaking his head. 'It's blasted everything else. It's like – it was so violent or so important it formed much clearer—'

Kuroda pushed past him and strode back to the dining room. The chalk dusted down, and showed everything that had happened to Mori. Kuroda had ordered it, but seeing it gave him a nasty twist. Tanaka was right. Those ghosts were clear, and the ones they overlaid had faded to a sort of white noise crackle in the background.

'What the hell has he done to this place?' Kuroda said at last. 'How did he do this? How did he make it record everything like this? Nowhere else is like this, not even in Aokigahara.'

Tanaka was nodding a little. 'I don't know. But the thing is, I don't think he did it on purpose. It records him even when you wouldn't want to be recorded.' He paused. 'Come and look at this. It's – peculiar.'

'Tanaka, I don't know how much more peculiar I can look at today.'

'Please,' Tanaka said, unexpectedly humble.

Kuroda set his teeth. He had thought the most difficult, nervy part would be taking Mori, but he was wrong. He felt like a spring deep in his gut was winding tighter, and tighter. He kept expecting something to explode in his face. He hadn't slept for days. It was the owls – the bloody owls were there always. They sat on all the window sills, tearing into little mice or squirrels, watching him, as if they expected something interesting.

Tanaka led the way through the labyrinthine corridors, among the crowds of ghosts, to a room that looked out over the hot pools. There, right in the doorway, were another pair of ghosts, and again, they had impressed themselves more strongly somehow than anything else. One was Mori, and the other was his musician. They were just talking, kneeling close together.

'I really don't need to see him have sex,' Kuroda snapped.

'No,' Tanaka said. 'He doesn't. Watch.'

Kuroda could already see what Mori was saying. You learned to lipread quite quickly on the deck of a ship.

—*boring. I just want someone to invent...*

They argued back and forth a bit, something about microscopes, and twice Steepleton glanced around as if he could feel someone looking, but that was just Yoruji, or Kuroda thought so, until he saw him say,

Is someone watching?

And then Mori looked right at them. It was unmistakeable.

'Does he know we're watching?' Kuroda said slowly. 'Can he see us?'

'I can't tell,' Tanaka said, very quiet. 'They reckon future ghosts are possible, though, don't they, up on the mountain?'

Kuroda nodded.

'We could be making ghosts in the past now. The electricity's cranked up pretty high, and this place ... seems to be a hell of a lot better than anywhere else at taking an imprint.'

The silence crackled. The chalk sifted down, and Mori's ghost got up and went away. Steepleton stayed still for a while, and then curled down small as if Mori had punched him in the gut.

Kuroda knew the feeling. He had increased his security detail at home, at the Ministry, everywhere, and he had four bodyguards with him now, but, like an imbecile, it hadn't even occurred to him that he might just have walked smack into a trap here.

'If,' Kuroda said softly, fighting hard to keep his voice level, 'he's been seeing us all along, if our ghosts were visible to him in the past, then we are not safe. He could have set something up. We have to get out. He's a watchmaker, for fuck's sake; what if there's a clockwork bomb in the cellar?'

Tanaka shut his eyes for a second. 'Yes. Right – everyone out.' He raised his voice to carry through the house. 'Everyone out now!'

Two of Kuroda's bodyguards caught his shoulders and hustled him fast towards the front door. Tanaka ran to keep up.

There was no bomb. Nothing exploded. No one was hurt. They all stood out in the snow, and the house stayed just as it had been, the timbers cackling as they settled in the cold.

'Burn it down,' Kuroda said at last.

'We don't know if fire will destroy the ghosts—'

'Then at least it will be harder to look for them.' His heart was cantering. 'If one single fucking journalist takes a photograph ...'

'We've not let anyone in. Just in case.' Tanaka looked wearily glad he'd got that right, at least. 'Problem with gas lines, we said.'

'Perfect, then no one will be surprised if it burns.'

Tanaka hesitated. 'People will start asking questions, though, when Mori doesn't turn up to ask where his house has gone. The Duke will know something's happened to him.'

'Yes, I know. Where's the body?'

'In that graveyard in the woods. No one would look in a grave.'

'Good. Let the fire die down, then take it to the Duke. We found it here when we heard about the fire. Let him come up with his own theory. Then keep this place cordoned off. Gas leaks, investigations, whatever.'

Tanaka nodded. 'One thing though.'

'What?'

'Mori's gaijin. He's a diplomat. He could come in here and ignore any police, any cordon, and we can't touch him. He's going to hear about this. He'll come looking. He knows it might be us, as well.'

'Hit him over the head with a brick and drop him in the sulphur well, then. Bloody hell, Tanaka, have some initiative,' Kuroda said, knowing he was being unfair. Tanaka was built of initiative.

Tanaka was shaking his head. 'Sir, we can't risk killing a diplomat. The British would come here straightaway with cameras, looking for any ghosts that might show what happened to him, and we wouldn't be able to do anything to stop them.'

'No, you're right.' Kuroda sighed. 'Fine. Keep up the cordon. If he comes, you go straight to the Duke. Tell him we think Steepleton did it. Jealousy. He went back to Yoruji to move the body when he realised the place had burned down, in case people started looking too closely. He might be a diplomat, but he looks like he'd mug you and steal your shoes. The Duke isn't going to listen to a word he says, even if he has it all bang on.'

Tanaka puffed his breath out, relieved. 'Yes, sir.'

Yoruji burned fierce and brilliant once Tanaka's men set the fires. Kuroda stood watching at the edge of the woods. After a while, he caught himself knocking his hat against a tree over and over again. He'd begun to do it to dislodge the chalk dust in the brim, but never stopped. His internal spring was wound up more tightly than ever. Something was going to happen, and Mori was just making him wait, and wait, and wait.

THIRTY-FOUR

Aokigahara, 15th February 1889

The cabins were tucked along the tree line, just on the far bank of the dam. A soldier opened one and gave Thaniel the keys, and a wooden box full of rice and vegetables.

The cabin roofs, heavily insulated under thick sheets of rubber, went down almost to the ground. Thaniel had expected an empty room inside, but there was a futon and blankets in the cupboard, a piano, phonograph, and shelves of books, all about bird-watching. The only thing to say that nobody had lived there for a while was a deep dusty smell, and the wallpaper that was peeling near the door. He pushed the paper down absently, then paused when the wall underneath felt too springy. It was insulated with a thick sheet of rubber too.

He went to see what was in the phonograph. He wound up the handle and waited. Handel bloomed out into the little room. It wasn't until he saw how bright the colours looked that he noticed how dark it was getting outside. He took the monk's lightbulb from his coat pocket and set it on the low kotatsu table. The filament made a gentle buzz, which haloed the glass. It was homely.

He settled back against the wall. The air was still mountain-thin and electric-coppery, and it was still hard to inhale all the way, but apart from that, it was a nice evening and the sun was going down. After he'd eaten, he felt better.

He got up again and brought in some wood from the pile by the door, and lit the old-fashioned stove under the table. Once it was going, he put the grate back over it, a blanket over the table, and tucked himself under the edge of it to catch the heat, basking in how good it was to have stopped walking and to be warm.

A tiny sound uncoiled somewhere on his left. It was so faint that it was on the edge of being imaginary, but he straightened up and heard it again, a slightly different shade of red. It was just the pitch of a man's voice.

He stood up again, trying to hunt it out. At the right distance, running water – gutters mainly – had the colours of a human voice. He opened the door. There was a faint chattering somewhere outside and if he'd heard it blind it could have been a stream or children talking, but he could see the water from here, or rather, he could see something like a stork walking in it, just through the trees.

When he pulled the door shut, he heard it again, a bloom of gold off to his left. There was a deeper, dark red under it. Piano strings, but only the thrum they made when you blew on them, nothing stronger. He strayed across and put his head against the top panel. It was a fraction stronger there. It wasn't a tune, but it didn't quite sound random either. It was snatches of something, too quiet for him to catch and fill in the gaps. He listened for a while before opening the lid. The hinges squeaked.

He didn't understand what he was seeing at first, but when he did, he jumped and the piano lid banged shut, which juddered the strings and made the ground look like it was casting a rainbow mist as the reverberation hummed up through the floorboards. From inside the piano came upset, disturbed skittering. He waited for it to stop before he opened the lid again.

The strings were covered in moths, a whole colony of them. They were shuffling over the entire sounding board, their wings and legs just heavy enough to sound the strings. He stared down at them and wondered what the hell to do about them.

He took the monk's lightbulb outside and propped it on the bough that stooped down just outside the window, then pushed open the window, which was uneven and warped on its runners. In the dimness, the moths were only a shifting shimmering over the strings. Not wanting to hurt them, he eased the damper pedal down and then rippled the keys to make them move. They lifted from the strings and hovered, disorientated, and then began to falter out towards the light.

One of them landed on his knuckles and paced about – it was very soft – then bumbled away again. He was no entomologist, but it seemed like too much of a coincidence to meet some winter moths only two months after Mori had asked him to post a package of them to this same forest. But even if they were the same moths, he had no idea what they were supposed to mean.

The crawling, slimy thought he'd had after the explosion in Tokyo, and with Grace, crept through his head again. Something had gone wrong. None of this felt like Mori's plans did when they were going well. There were too many gaps and broken pieces.

On their way out, the last moths avoided a distinct space in the air, like they were hitting the edge of an invisible thing. It was only for a second, but they outlined the shape of a person. Then they were out and coiling around the lamps.

He watched the place where the ghost had been, unable to shift the creeping sense that it was watching him back.

He couldn't sleep. Whenever he was close, there was another flash from the electricity tower, or a clatter outside that might have been a bat or something else, and he jerked awake again. All the while he couldn't stop feeling like there was someone in the corner.

He pulled the blanket further up his shoulder and curled forward against it. It felt like one of those makeshift nights when something had gone wrong and everyone ended up camping on the floor instead of in their usual places. It had happened once at Filigree Street; they'd given up the bedrooms to Dr Haverly and his youngest boys, because Mrs Haverly was in a difficult labour. Sometimes over the patter of the hail outside it had been possible to hear the midwives talking, urgently, through the chimneys, and so Mori had kept the phonograph going on the hearth to send the music up the chimney shaft to the boys upstairs. It was Christmas, and he'd put on carols, because Mrs Haverly would be all right in the end and so would the baby.

Between them, they had a candle and a game of backgammon, where the lacquer counters winked.

He couldn't remember who had won or lost, but after the game, Mori had pulled him back to fit them together under the blankets. Thaniel caught his hand and pulled it down, not quite all the way, and pressed his knuckles to ask him to keep it there. He did, and didn't move except to stroke the edge of his thumb against Thaniel's last rib, like it was made of something much more difficult to come by than bone. From outside somewhere came the bright clatter of breaking glass. It didn't even occur to him that their own windows might be in danger. He had fallen asleep listening to the carols and the hail and the bang of the wind hitting the side of the house.

There was still some leftover calm in the memory, enough to rub off and catch a silvering of it, at least. He lay holding it until he could sleep. In the dark, the room strobed every so often as the tower fizzed and flashed.

The next morning, everything outside was invisible in glowing white fog. Wisps of it had come in where he'd left the door a fraction open for air. He lay watching it, only half awake, and thinking distantly that the weight of his hands on his chest was uncomfortable. A new arena of feebleness. He didn't move, not wanting to get up straightaway into the cold, but he could tell that if he stayed where he was, the background panic under his ribs was only going to get worse and worse. He hadn't completely relaxed at night since the ghost had caught his shoulders at the legation.

He shifted as an overture to getting up, and froze when he realised that it wasn't his own hands on his chest.

He couldn't see it properly without turning his head, but there was something beside him, formed of small moth bodies and shifting wings. He jerked away from them and ran to the door. The second he moved, the form dissolved, but he saw it, just; a man kneeling down. The moths burst away in all directions.

He stood frozen on the doorstep, waiting to see if it would come back.

The moths started to come together by the wall. He leaned back in. Gradually, enough of them gathered to form the person-shape again. It was doing something; writing, or painting. Then it stooped down and seemed to unroll something invisible down the wall, and mimed out nailing it up. The rubber: it was the workman who had put up the insulation.

The ghost looked right at him and pointed urgently at the wall, then dissolved again. The moths edged towards the window.

Very slowly, Thaniel stepped back inside. He had to look around for a bit before he found a hammer, but when he did, the nails in the rubber insulation slid out easily enough. The rubber fell off. Underneath, the wall was bare wood. The writing on it, in white paint, was in big clear Japanese letters.

DO NOT GO BACK TO YORUJI.

He stared at it for a long time. A flutter in his chest buzzed with joy to see some sign from Mori, but it was very small. Mori had gone to a lot of trouble to make him see this. Something horrible must have happened at Yoruji.

Thaniel stared at the block letters. Yoruji was cordoned off, Arinori's wife had said. No one had heard from Mori for months, except Grace and the scientists, who didn't know where he was being held. Somehow everyone had assumed Mori was somewhere far away, but Kuroda had set everything up perfectly at Yoruji itself.

Kuroda could have kept Mori there all this time. Or at least until the end of January, when Grace's telegrams had run out.

He didn't have to be dead. Anything could have happened; he could have been ill from everything they'd done, or even from something they hadn't even done yet. He felt the pain before he knocked into things.

And he was too bloody stubborn to ask for help. He was doing what he always did; tidying people out of the way. Thaniel had had enough of being tidied.

Thaniel nailed the rubber back up, packed and locked up, leaned into the office to say goodbye to the director. He wished he could say it to Grace too, but he didn't want anyone to notice him paying her any more attention than a Ministry clerk would have to. He was feeling as strong as he was ever going to, so he set off back down the mountain with his whole mind churning so much he barely noticed the hanging ghosts on the way.

———————

He couldn't really believe it when he saw the glow of the little lightbulb shrine. The monk was there too, cheerful as ever. Thaniel thanked him for everything again and then paid him to fetch in a horse ready to go, and then to go up the mountain if he could and tell the white lady there that she could get out as soon as she needed to, even without money, and without papers if she could keep to the back roads. The monk promised he would.

He went back through the burning village, back through the fence, past the crooked tree to fetch his bag, and out to the road, to find out if there were any stagecoaches going up towards Tokyo.

His memory kept replaying every conversation they'd had at Yoruji, how nervous Mori had been, how wary. If he had been watching a future of imprisonment, maybe even his own murder in that godforsaken house slink nearer the whole time, in silence, he had done well to stay standing up.

Thaniel had to punch a tree when imaginings of black rooms and chisels seethed up too far. He should never have left Yoruji. He had to go back.

THIRTY-FIVE

Yokohama, 15th February 1889

The tiredness caught up with Thaniel on the last leg of the long stagecoach run. The journey back had been much more crowded than the way out, so he was propped against the window in order to give a lady with her baby and two chickens space on his right. Despite the cramped awkwardness, he fell asleep against the glass and woke, disorientated, to the comb pattern his hair had made in the condensation. The lady prodded him and said they were at Yokohama.

There was a rope barring the gates at Yoruji. On it was a sign that said *Home Ministry: No Entry. Danger of Death.* A policeman clipped over and told him to move along. Thaniel knocked him out, put him under a hedge, and ducked the cordon.

The path up to the house was a ribbon of undisturbed snow. Pheasants ducked about under the trees, tail feathers trailing blue fire. It was eerie quiet, because any seagulls that might have cried over the sea had long since flown away or flown into something. The snow was packed and slippery where the way was steep. There was no sign of anybody, or

any attempt to keep the paths open. Just a spade leaning
against a tree, four inches of snow piled up on the handle.
The wind ruffled the graveyard bells. Nothing else. The
Ministry must have sent the servants away.

He stopped dead when he reached the top of the hill. It
should have had a view of the whole of Yoruji, all its roofs
and balconies. But the house was gone. Instead there was a
blasted black mess, with snow dusted over ruined, warped
crossbeams and the charred husks of fallen gantries. It was
gone.

THIRTY-SIX

Abashiri, 20th January 1889

The warden's secretary, Mr Nakamura, had become steadily more ill since Takiko had first met him. She found him one afternoon not long after Horikawa had been killed by an angry Ainu man who had finally decided to shoot back. Nakamura was just outside the warden's door, coughing into his sleeve. He lifted his eyes apologetically. He had a scarf tucked under the collar of his kimono jacket and his hair stuffed up in a rag, even scruffier than it had been last week.

'He says I have to cough outside,' he explained, and motioned at the door with his elbow. 'He says he can't cope with his headaches and me making disgusting noises.'

'Can't you go home?' Takiko said. Her voice was starting to come out strained. She still hadn't found out how to get into the tower. The handwriting on the paper crane had stuck with her in a way the frozen bodies in the woods hadn't. Mori could have been dying up there from something they hadn't done to him yet; it would be wholly counterintuitive for anyone talking to him, or at least, anyone who didn't know him. If she could just get up there and make sure he was still in one piece − temporally, physically, whatever − then the painful tightness right in her chest would ease. She had not − *had not* − signed up to hurt him.

In her head, a wry voice that sounded an awful lot like Ayame's wanted to know just what she thought she'd been doing.

'No,' Nakamura said miserably. 'The electrical readout has to be inputted constantly.'

'Why?'

'I don't know, I'm only paid twenty sen a day.' He broke off coughing again and looked significantly at the door. He smelled of damp and unwashed clothes when he leaned nearer to her. 'It's for a lock,' he whispered. 'A special new kind. Super-secure. The combinations change randomly. Something to do with the numbers on the readouts.'

'You go home,' she said. 'I can do it. It's just numbers, isn't it? Even I can do numbers.'

'You would? Really?'

'Go, go. Do first, apologise later.'

'Bless you, miss,' he said, heartfelt, and went downstairs still coughing.

Takiko thought the warden would need some persuading, but in fact he was slumped over his desk with a migraine and only waved vaguely to her to get on with it.

'Type the values from the graph into the typewriter there. New graphs come down into that little postbox next to you. You can read numbers? Get going. I couldn't be more delighted to explain it to you in more detail but the room is literally splitting in two,' he said into his arms.

She lifted her eyebrows and sifted across the cluttered desk. It was full of photograph after photograph, all showing the same thing: a grey background with two strange, waving white lines, mirror images. Each photograph had been printed onto paper with the axes of a graph already marked onto it, and so the waving white lines made coordinate points with their peaks and troughs. Now that she was listening for it, she could hear a scritch somewhere above them. It would be the electrograph, ticking.

'Which line should I—'

'Either, don't care.'

While she was still looking at one, another slid into the letterbox built into the wall beside her. It had a glass compartment you could draw down with a lever. She took it out, and held it with her left hand while she typed coordinates from the top line with her right. As she did, something deep inside the wall began to click. When she paused, it stopped. When she found a rhythm and went faster, it whirred. It sounded like clockwork.

The warden waved at her vaguely. 'Never stop for more than ten minutes. Got it?'

'Why, sir?'

'Just say you understand.'

'I understand, sir.'

'There's a good girl. Excuse me while I die,' he said, and curled up in a ball under his desk.

So she typed, and every half-hour, just before she could finish each graph, a new one shucked down into the glass postbox. None of them were ever exactly the same. The white lines were sometimes jagged, sometimes almost straight. Towards mid-afternoon, one arrived with the lines all over the place, veering wildly right from the top of the graph and right into negative numbers at the bottom, and no sooner had she picked it up than thunder rolled around the sky and snow swirled down, so thick it hid the view of the town and the sea. She looked out at it for a little while to give herself a rest. The whip bruise over the back of her head was blooming a thick ache all around her skull now, even down to her eyebrows.

'I told you not to stop,' the desk said. 'It's a lock, girl. If you stop then it won't be bloody locked anymore.'

Nakamura, it turned out, had an especially horrible kind of flu, and so Takiko kept on as the warden's secretary. The time dragged and then melted in irregular chunks. She typed the coordinates from the graphs into the typewriter, and listened to the parts of whatever mechanism it was attached to turn and click inside the wall beside her. After a while, she made up maths games with the numbers. By the end of three days, she could multiply by twenty seven without straining.

There was never a chance to talk up into the tower room. Every night, the silent night-shift man came to take over, and every morning, he handed over to her just as silently. The warden said he'd hired a deaf man because deaf people couldn't talk.

But on her fourth morning, there was a crane in the hearth when she came in. The young man, of course, wouldn't have heard it fall, and the fire had burned right down. Horribly aware that the paper wings were smoking, she waved a cheery good morning to the young man, who smiled and bowed, and mimed how cold it was. She agreed. In the hearth, the crane shifted in the ashes.

Finally, he left.

She snatched the crane out. In handwriting that was even worse than before, it said *are you still there?*

It made her think of the whispering voice in the solitary confinement shed and she wanted to shriek. She was about to call up the chimney when the warden clattered in with a rush of cold air, stamping snow off his boots and frost off his coat. All she could do was light the fire to show that somebody was there. She flopped hopelessly back into her own chair.

The prison had a small shrine. It was a sorry affair, with a horrible little pottery statue of some kind of fishing god, and Takiko wasn't religious. But at six that morning, before she had opened the office door to find that the warden had taken to sleeping at his desk, she rang the bell and put a cigarette in the offerings box, because she didn't have any money left but what she would need to get home. She didn't say the prayer aloud, in case someone heard. She said in her head, as clearly as she could: *Let Mori still be alive.*

Being locked up in a tower explained why he hadn't known what she should look for when he told her to come. He had been remembering forward to a time when he was too isolated and too ill to know much of anything, except, maybe, that the place was Abashiri.

Furious with herself, she clanged the shrine bell again, hard. Probably the fish god would be offended, but that couldn't be worse than being so generally stupid. She didn't know now what she'd thought would happen, once Kuroda had Mori. Some gentlemanly confinement with the scientists at Aokigahara; academic questions, perhaps some threats to make him come out with something useful about the Russians, but really, just a stranger sort of da Vinci in a secret workshop.

Idiotic. Kuroda always went too far. She knew it; everyone knew it.

At her desk in the warden's office, on her left, was a telegraph machine. She had noticed it before, but it had never moved and it made her jump when it bumped to life now. The warden swung around and waited by it to catch the tape. The machine clacked as the code transferred itself into writing. She could see where its keys were inside. The long steel tines they hinged on moved like piano strings. The warden's expression clouded.

'There's been an avalanche,' he said quietly. 'They're evacuating Kabato prison.' He lifted his eyes. 'They're bringing them here.'

She frowned. 'How many prisoners at Kabato, sir?'

'Nearly a thousand.'

She looked down at the desk and wondered how she was going to get Mori out with double the number of prisoners and guards. It would be barely possible to move without bumping into someone.

She sat back slightly when she overheard her own thoughts. She hadn't been aware of deciding to break Mori out. At some point in the last few frozen days, though, the resolution had solidified. If she could get into the Oracle, she wasn't going to be able to leave him there.

The warden sighed. 'With any luck, most of them will die on the way.' He made a small sound and touched the side of his head.

Takiko looked up. 'Sir, if all that's coming – maybe you really ought to go home and have some rest? You won't get any once they arrive.'

She couldn't credit it at first when he said that she was right, and picked up his coat. As he trudged out, he said to stay until the night-shift man turned up again.

'And don't tell a soul about this machine or I'll put you in the solitary confinement shed,' he said, and left.

She looked at the patch of air where he had been. She didn't think he was joking. It seemed to take a long time for his steps to fade away.

———

At last, though, Takiko stopped typing and went to the wall, where she tapped along the wainscoting. When she finally found it, the hollow place was right by the hearth, about a foot above her head. It was tiny; just a little panel the size of a plate that hinged outward. The panel exposed the wheel of a vault door. She had to shove hard to spin it open, and when it did, she understood why the rest of the wall had sounded so solid. It was solid. A whole section of it, bricks and all, swung just far enough inward for someone to slide through. Inside was a tiny staircase.

Because it was right next to the chimney flue, the steps were warm. She snatched up a lamp and eased the wainscoting door to behind her, but not shut. It had no inside handle. The lamp fluttered in the pitch black. As she climbed the stairs, the air took on the warm smell of dry wood. Something scuffled in the roof.

At the top of the stairs was a door that shone. It was fitted with a clockwork panel the size of a person, and eight different locks, built into mechanisms whose motion was dying down now. She waited for them to stop, then released them all one by one. They were heavy.

When the door opened, there was no daylight in the room beyond. There was an oil lamp, which made the golding of a perpetual evening, and a fireplace just beside her, lit, miserably, with only a few pieces of crumbling coal. What she could make out of the floor was bare. A ladder led up to a tiny loft space up in the tower rafters, where she could just see the coverlet of a neatly made bed.

'Mori?' she said quietly.

'Who?'

The man had been sitting with his back to the hearth, in plain view but very still. He was reading a book, or he had been; now he was looking at her, full of surprised interest. He was old, with a neat beard and warmer clothes than the other prisoners, but he was still wearing red.

Takiko realised her mouth had fallen open, and clamped her molars together for half a second too long, trying to make sure it wouldn't happen again. 'I'm sorry – who are you?'

'An obscure prince I don't expect you've heard of.' He looked hopeful. 'Who are you?'

'The cleaner. Sorry, I … thought you might be someone else.' She swallowed. Her throat was suddenly scratchy. 'Sorry – what are you doing up here, why are they keeping you like this?'

'I don't think they wanted to put a prince in with the other prisoners,' he said unhappily. 'I should have liked the company.'

'What did you do?'

'Disagreed with the Emperor once or thrice too often. Wrote a pamphlet.'

'So what's this palaver with the door?' she demanded, and then held her hands out to show she wasn't angry with him, only the circumstances.

'I'm not sure. It was there when I got here. Rather clever, isn't it? But will you sit with me a bit, since you're here? I only ever see the warden and he is – desperately boring.'

'I can't. If anyone catches me they'll put me in the solitary confinement shed.'

'Yes, I see,' he said, with a terrible docility. Now that her eyes had adjusted, he looked much too intense and his friend-liness had a hysterical edge. 'But perhaps for five minutes? Or even four?'

'I'd really better—'

He caught at her hem. 'Please—'

He was just an old man left alone too long, but she lost her nerve. She pulled away and shut the clockwork door, locked all of its unnecessary locks, and stood with her head against the warm bronze, listening as he cried on the other side. With a creeping, seaweed cold, she realised she had no idea what to do. This was a cage for Mori. But no Mori. The more she tried to tell herself it was a good thing that he wasn't locked in that terrible, perfect, efficient cell, the louder she heard him say that he didn't know what was going on because there was a heavy chance he would be dead.

When she reached the base of the stairs, there was another telegraph message. This one was from Hakodate prison. There had been a typhoid outbreak. They were evacuating surviving prisoners to Abashiri.

Very slowly, she straightened up and folded the message into as many tiny sections as it would go. Kuroda had let her come here, knowing fully well that Mori wasn't here. Mori, perhaps, had been confused, but not Kuroda. The only reason to let her come all this way for absolutely nothing was to get her the hell out of his way. Maybe with any luck she'd even die here, in the prison or just the pounding cold.

She should have known, of course.

Meaning to leave right then, find a ship, go home, she swung towards the window and then stopped. Of course she couldn't. The shore was a deserted white stretch, and beyond it, the sea was frozen – an unnavigable mess of pack ice and snow. The ships in the bay were all stuck in place as firmly as they would have been in tar.

THIRTY-SEVEN

Yoruji, 16th February 1889

Something bumped into Thaniel's ankle.

He thought for a split second that it was a horribly deformed cat, but then he realised it was gleaming, and the bizarre shape resolved itself into Katsu. The little octopus backed up a bit, tried to shuffle through Thaniel again, then seemed to give up and coiled away at an odd angle. Thaniel dropped onto his knees again and pulled his sleeve over his hand. Even so, Katsu was hot to touch. When Thaniel picked him up, he only waved drowsily as if he still thought he was on the ground.

Thaniel couldn't keep a proper hold on him. Usually Katsu would furl up round your arm and get on your shoulder, and it was the devil's own work to prise him off again if he wanted not to be prised, but if he didn't hold on, he was heavy. He writhed out of Thaniel's hands and bumbled away over the same tracks he had already made, cutting them new again through the fine dusting of snow that had blown over them. But it was only a dusting. Under that was clear ground. He must have been going round the same circuit since the snow started. Whatever catch between clockwork and life there was in his mechanisms, none of it thought Thaniel was there.

Hating the idea of leaving him behind, Thaniel set off after him, down towards the ruins. There were no bodies, at least. At a distance, a good many things looked like wrecked skeletons, but they were only burnt furniture, collapsed doorways, floorboards that had warped right upwards into the shape of ribs. Katsu trundled through everything. Thaniel had to climb sometimes, half looking, too, for any surviving tablecloth or scrap of sacking to scoop Katsu up in. There was nothing. It had been a very thorough fire.

Katsu disappeared down a set of stone steps Thaniel had never seen before. The way down was completely dark. Thaniel stopped at the top. There were burnt floorboards all around, and jagged edges around the stairway. It had once, he realised, had a trap door. He gazed around, trying to work out where he was in the house. It took him a long time before he understood that he was in front of the same hot pool he had been when they first came to stay. He was standing in the room Mori had slept in.

Somewhere in the darkness, Katsu clunked down more stairs. Thaniel hesitated, because the daylight was failing, but Katsu was noisy on the stone. He could navigate more or less by the sound colours and the way they rang off surfaces, if he had to.

It was a long way down. The stairs went beneath the hot pools, and after a few yards, the air was warm. When he reached the bottom, he almost fell over the lamp someone had left on the last stair. It was an oil lamp, and beside it, a little box of matches. The gunpowder fizzed as he struck the match on the wall.

He didn't know what he'd hoped. The light edged over arches carved in the stone, and marks that looked old, very old, the rambling, weird, characters that had been writing before someone sensible standardised them. Generation upon generation of novice monks must have practised on them, for whatever reason, in the house's monastery days. It was hard to tell what the place had been meant for. The walls were rough-hewn and irregular, lined now with shelves. The light was only just enough to brush them. The flames from the lamp rippled red and blue at first before they balanced.

In the ceiling, an odd, soft clicking began. It tinted things a dim yellow.

Every shelf was lined with dozens of glass bulbs, but not for lights. Rather than filaments, they housed miniature black windmills. Some were turning, and more began to turn as he watched. He leaned down to see one. It stopped when his shadow fell over it, then began again when he let the light touch it. The little set of sails was winding a tiny, fragile mechanism in the base of the bulb. From the base ran a hairline thread. It was real thread, not copper wire.

The walls shimmered, because similar threads, all different colours, stretched up from the light mills. At the top, worked into the ceiling, were little vials. The threads were pulling springs there, which spun the vials, and now, they were beginning to fan down a soft snow of something white that hung in the air. He put his hand out to catch some. Chalk.

'Hello.'

He swung around, because it was Mori's voice, and Mori was there too, just behind a desk tucked into an alcove behind the stairs. He looked exhausted.

'I couldn't leave a note out on the desk here, you might not have found it. Sorry it's so obscure.'

'I don't understand,' Thaniel began, and then did understand, because he had gone nearer to the desk.

Mori was only half as solid as he usually was. He sounded wrong, too far off. It was a phonograph. It was clearer than any phonograph recording usually could be, and the phonograph itself, which was right next to him on the desk, had been altered. The cylinder wasn't wax but something else that sheened strangely.

Outside, the electricity waned. The blue fire in the trees stopped spilling down the stairs and Mori vanished into the falling chalk. The phonograph was still going.

'I'm ... leaving this here in case I didn't work up the nerve to ask you for help in person. I mean to try, but I know what I'm like at asking for help.'

Thaniel went nearer to the desk, his throat closing.

The St Elmo's fire came back. So did the ghost. He was packing away the machinery scattered over the table, ghost things that weren't there anymore. Close to, Thaniel could see how the figure affected the chalk. One mote might drift about normally in the air, then snap across to make part of the shape. It was pin-sharp in here. Mori had been wearing a threadbare jumper and through a loose part in the knit, the chalk had even outlined the stitching of the leather patch on his waistcoat shoulder underneath. He had sewn that on himself, because he always put clockwork pins through it and he'd wrecked the tweed.

'What shows up in the ghosts,' said the phonograph, and Mori, 'are moments where there are several possibilities depending on them, so I should be making one now. The greater the dependent possibility tree, the better the ghost will imprint.' He swallowed and looked at his watch again. 'It's why a lot of the ghosts you're seeing are caught in the moment they're dying. Death generates massive possibility trees; one

368

person's death affects dozens of other people, thousands of other decisions. And that's why Yoruji has been so haunted since I've lived here. Because I know everything that might happen, everything I do is always – in aid of what I want to happen. I end up doing a lot of small things that will affect a lot of larger things later. What that really means is, I'm going out of my way to create big possibility trees. Forests.' He sort of laughed. 'You can always tell when someone like me has lived somewhere; it'll be the most haunted place for miles around. In order to see the ghosts, you need a lot of electricity in the air, so they always show up in stormy weather. And there's a lot of electricity now because it's artificial. There are generators at a station in Aokigahara. The scientists there are under orders to work out what I do, and reproduce it. They run the electricity strongest at night, I think so it will disrupt Tokyo less. Nothing mystical is going on, if you were worried. I'm rambling,' he said, and stopped for a few seconds. 'Anyway. I'm hoping the ghost upstairs will still be visible now. They replay themselves whenever the electricity becomes strong enough.'

'Upstairs,' Thaniel murmured.

Mori nodded once as if he'd heard him. 'I'm going to be arrested and taken away by Kuroda's men. It's important that they do it, so I'm not going to stop them. I don't know where they'll take me, they're deciding randomly, but that doesn't matter. Or I don't think so. I think I've arranged it properly. All I need is someone to go to Abashiri and ... something.' He had been leaning forward against the desk to speak into the phonograph. He looked ill. 'I'm sorry. I have no idea what I'm doing anymore. I can't remember anything after next week. Or not really. Snatches of – the most likely future as it stands just now.'

Thaniel stared at him. There was an electromagnet behind his heart, tugging uselessly towards the ghost. It was so strong it hurt and he had to close his hands over the edge of the desk and press his fingernails into the leather top, which put half-moon dents into the filigree edging. Mori was quiet for a moment, too still, catching the rhythm of his own breathing again. Thaniel wanted to reach out, for all it would have been pointless and trite. He kept still and waited. Under the electromagnetic ache was something better. A sort of slow, tentative happiness. Mori hadn't forgotten about him.

Behind him, Katsu bumped into his heel.

The phonograph crackled.

'If you could go and see what happens to me, that might be useful,' Mori said. 'It will be in the dining room. As I say, it should be clearest at night. I'm sorry. I wish I could be more specific, I wish I could tell you what to do. But all I know now is that this has to happen and that I'm going to need some help. It's something to do with a place called Abashiri.'

Thaniel had thought he'd been relieved when he got down from the mountain safely, but it was nothing beside the wonderful, luminous relief of finding there was something good he could do.

'Thank you, Pepper,' Mori said, belatedly.

Thaniel looked back. Mori switched off the phonograph. It clunked as the recording stopped, which was eerie because it made it seem like a ghost had moved it, though of course he hadn't; it was only running parallel.

The ghost didn't disappear straightaway. He faded once he was away from the chalk, but some of it clung. It took half a minute or so for the last line of his shoulder to dissolve.

Thaniel turned away and walked out too fast, then folded down on the stairs, pulled his sleeves over his hands and pressed them over his eyes, shaking with the effort of trying to keep at least a little calm, because every jolt of his shoulders hurt the bullet wound. It didn't work.

THIRTY-EIGHT

Thaniel waited in the relative warmth of the stairwell for the night to come down fully, and for the electricity to wax. Like Mori had said, the power strengthened a lot just after nine o'clock. The wind lifted and blue fire sighed through the gingko trees as the electricity surged. There were ships leaving the docks, two huge liners, and their funnels trailed brilliant aurora sheets of blue.

The snow had stopped. The ruins of the house were sparkling under the blue light from the trees, and the air was frozen and pristine, with the faint salt clarity of the beach. Not sure where to look for the ghosts, or even if they would appear on what was now the ground, he gathered up pieces of half-burned wood and set fires all around the footprint of the house. The wood was damp now, but he doused it with lamp oil and soon there was smoke everywhere.

When the smoke reached what used to be the dining room, the ghosts turned nearly as solid as real people. Breathing into his sleeve, he navigated through the burned remnants of the corridor to see them better.

Mori was sitting by what had been the window, holding a watch formed partly of cinders, waiting. Thaniel brought some spars nearer to make a new fire up close. Despite all the heat, the blood had gone out of his hands and he could hardly grip. He'd never felt so cold.

A whorl of sparks spun through Mori's ghost. It ribboned up his arm at first, then up behind his eyes and into his hair. The bright pinpoints followed strands of it, fading as they reached the tips, turning to red and then grey ashes. Thaniel almost didn't notice when he lifted one hand, the ends of his fingernails bright with rising cinders. He was counting down; five, four, three, two, one.

Ghost men burst through, silent and smoke-roiling. Mori didn't move. He let the nearest man pin his hands behind his back and didn't bother even to turn his face away when a second man held something that must have been chloroform over his mouth. When he collapsed, they only looked shocked he hadn't fought, and the man with the chloroform didn't move for a long time before he remembered that too much killed you and jerked the cloth away. Someone else, a giant who looked like he might once have been a wrestler, lifted Mori away. It was all soundless, but one of the others waved at him and held him back as if that was wrong, to leave already. The cinders glimmered on the Fabergé egg button on his coat.

The ghost took out a pair of dice and a piece of notepaper. Thaniel turned away, breathed in deep from the clearer air, then went closer to see. The ghost threw the dice and consulted the paper, but the smoke wasn't clear enough to show anything written on it.

They seemed decided. The big man hurried out, carrying Mori. He let Mori's wrist bang against the phantom door frame, and then disappeared into a clearer patch of air where the smoke didn't reach.

Thaniel went out onto the lawn to breathe. He went too fast, though, and at first all he could do was cough, until he felt dizzy and noticed, distantly, that he'd gone down on all fours. The snow soaked through to his knees, and all at once he felt again how horribly, miserably cold it was. There was nothing clear or fine about the air anymore. It felt like trying to inhale razors. But when he shut his eyes, he kept seeing Mori's wrist bang against the door frame.

When he could stand up again, he looked around for Katsu, but there was no sign even of any tracks. He started back down the hill towards the railway station. There was nothing he could do officially, but he had a pretty strong feeling that now there was proof of an attack and arson, the head of Mori's house would have things to say.

As he ducked back under the Keep Out rope at the gate, he saw a man across the street, watching him from below a street lamp. The man was wearing a bright red coat with a Fabergé egg button on it. The man waved easily and stepped into the carriage beside him, which took off fast before Thaniel could follow.

THIRTY-NINE

Tokyo, 17th February 1889

The huge redbrick terminus of Shimbashi station was deserted. Snow blew along the road in writhing patterns and caught in the shirts and coat hems of the ghosts there. There were hardly any real pedestrians. The electricity was weaker here than in Yokohama, but as the train pulled in, the smell of burning haunted the carriage and a fire crew hurried everyone off at the platform. Theirs was the last train. Once everyone was out, firemen closed the station. They put a thick, official-looking rope over the broad doors, and a sign that said *Closed until further notice.*

The station clock tower was striking midnight. There was one last cab, the driver hunched over a cigarette. Thaniel had no idea where the Duke of Choshu lived, but the driver did, and seemed warily impressed that Thaniel was willing to interrupt such an important person at such a late hour.

The Duke of Choshu's townhouse was so close to the Palace that it was possible to see into the windows of the buildings above the curtain wall. On either side of the gate-posts hung the Mori house banners, lit from below by brilliant electric lights. The symbols of the noble houses looked odd, coming at them from an English point of view – a view which

375

usually expected lions couchant or a fleur-de-lis, something recognisable. Here they might have started out as a picture of something, but they were so old that they had been redrawn and simplified, until they used the smallest number of marks possible. The Mori sigil was nothing but three circles arranged in a triangle above a straight line, black on red.

They did colour well here. He'd seen samurai sigils in photographs and they were nothing frightening, but the red and the black flying above the gates had been made for battlefields.

A steward answered the door, unsurprised to find such a late visitor on the step. He looked sceptical, but eventually he let Thaniel in.

It was a pidgin of styles inside: as traditional as you could get away with without being trite, and as Western as it could be without looking imitative, sitting balanced on the scales between two worlds that hated each other. The balance was diluted and insipid, and completely sensible.

The sliding doors were mainly closed, but he caught a glimpse into some of the grand rooms. There was a library, and some women talking over tea at a low table. The floor creaked and above them hung banners with different sigils – other smaller houses that served this one, maybe, but he didn't recognise them.

The house was laid out in a way Thaniel couldn't follow. By the time they reached the Duke's study, he couldn't have found his own way out again and he didn't recognise the view from the window. The Duke was waiting at an austere desk, full of papers. He was a delicately ugly man with gold-rimmed spectacles and a manner like a banker. His clothes were beautiful but plain. It was half-past midnight now, but he didn't look tired, just as crisp as he must have been at nine o'clock in the morning.

'You have news pertaining to the disappearance of a bannerman of mine, I hear,' he said. He had a parchment voice.

Thaniel nodded. 'Yes, sir. I've just come from Yoruji. I saw ghosts there. They show some of Count Kuroda's men abducting Keita Mori. The whole house has been burned down.'

The Duke lifted one eyebrow, which shifted his spectacles ever so slightly. He moved them back and pursed his lips. 'And why might they have tried to abduct him, do you suppose?'

'They wanted to take him somewhere. He left a phonograph recording in the cellar; he mentioned a place called Abashiri.'

'I believe you know the Baron quite well, Mr Steepleton?' He enunciated quite. Thaniel swallowed, because although he'd told the steward his name, he hadn't said who he was, least of all who he was to Mori. 'You are familiar with his particular capabilities?'

'I – yes, well enough.'

'Then I wonder if you would be so good as to explain why in the world he might allow himself to be kidnapped and taken to Abashiri prison?'

'It's a prison?'

'It is a labour camp of over a thousand inmates in the far north of Hokkaido, where, because there is a constant threat of invasion from Russia, all prison details are devoted to clearing roads through the forest, to allow the movement of our troops when they are, inevitably, required.' He spoke slowly, and so clearly that Thaniel could hear the punctuation. 'In the winter I believe the death rate is one in six, daily. Not the sort of place I can imagine Keita allowing himself to be taken.'

Thaniel shook his head, which panged his shoulder. He'd taken some more morphine in the cab here and it was keeping him upright, but nothing more. 'I watched them take him.'

The Duke moved his head just enough for the reflection of the window in his glasses to obscure his eyes. 'And how would anyone keep him in a cell?'

The Duke was unsettling him in a way that Kuroda never had. Choshu sounded different. He was measuring every word on some internal accounting scales, and the books in front of him were ledgers. He didn't sound like he had politics. He sounded like he had money. There was nothing to prove, nothing to want or strive for, only maintenance and the deep indifferent calm of a caretaker.

'A constant supply of random data,' Thaniel said. 'He can't predict random things. Dice, or atmospheric electricity. You feed those numbers into ... maybe they have a combination lock that they keep changing, or something that rotates.' He could hear how unlikely it sounded, but he ploughed on anyway, even though he could feel the ploughshare grinding. 'It would be hard work, but it's possible if you have enough numbers. I've seen it done, Kuroda had something like it set up at the lighthouse in Yokohama. Does Abashiri have an electrograph? You know, a machine to—'

'I know what an electrograph is. All Hokkaido prisons double up as weather stations,' the Duke said. He didn't seem to have an opinion about what Thaniel had told him, one way or another.

'I've just come from a research station in Aokigahara. They're generating all this electricity, and until the end of January, someone was sending them experimental information about Mori, they have transcripts of it, they're calling him Subject A—'

The Duke's eyes flared at the mention of Subject A and Thaniel had a tiny flutter of hope.

'You'll excuse me a moment,' the Duke said. He got up without letting his spine bend, and left.

Thaniel waited again, staring at the Persian rug on the floor. There was a cat sitting on it, a beautiful grey one with huge green eyes. The quiet went fathoms down. Somewhere through the walls, he heard an argument break out, two men, but he couldn't hear what they said. The quiet came back. The snick of the door was loud when the Duke opened it again.

'Come with me,' he said. He stood back and seemed wholly unworried that Thaniel was nearly a foot taller than him.

They went through to another room, much bigger and full of old, beautiful maps of the city, and then outside, across a snowy courtyard, to a shrine. It was beneath a huge pine tree whose trunk was tied with thick red rope. Thaniel had seen those at other shrines but he had never found out what they meant. The pillars inside were hung with prayer cards. It smelled of fresh-cut wood, which seemed always like a warm smell, even now when there was snow floating in with them. Under the bell was what he would have called an altar but probably wasn't, and on the altar was something the size of a man, covered with a shroud. Someone else was there too, a broad man in a Western suit facing away from them. A priest beyond the barrier read out the day's prayer cards. After each prayer, the bell tolled. Thaniel felt something under his ribs slither.

379

'Keita Mori isn't at Abashiri, Mr Steepleton,' the Duke said. 'He's here. Or what's left of him is.'

Everything spun without moving. When it stopped, he felt like panels of glass had thunked down around him. The world was still there and he could still hear it and see it, but it was muted and he might have been watching a play. He had started towards the altar before he had decided to move. The man standing there turned back. Thaniel only just had time to recognise that it was Kuroda before he was smacked flat on his back in the snow. Kuroda clamped one hand round his throat to keep him there.

Thaniel couldn't talk, or breathe. Of their own accord, his hands had jolted up to catch at Kuroda's wrist, but he stopped himself in time. He could think just clearly enough to see that if he touched Kuroda now he would end up in a Japanese prison for the rest of his life. The scar on his shoulder seared.

Kuroda let him go like touching him was repulsive.

'Your Grace,' Kuroda said to the Duke, 'you'll excuse all this, I hope. I'll get him out of your sight now. Mr Steepleton, you're under arrest. For murder.'

'No!' Thaniel said over him, jerking onto his feet again to turn to the Duke. 'It was Kuroda's men, the ghosts are still there! You can go and see!'

Kuroda nodded at someone and two men came up on either side of Thaniel. One of them was the man in the red coat with the Fabergé egg button. 'You can indeed go and see if you like, your Grace, but what you'll see is this parasite murdering your bannerman and setting fire to the place in a fit of jealousy. Found out Mori was married, you see. Look at his eyes now, he's off his head on something. He got scared when he realised the ghosts would have recorded what he did, he's taken something and now he's come raving to you.'

'Go and look for yourself,' Thaniel begged the Duke. 'You'll see what happened.'

'I should be gratified if you wouldn't take it upon yourself to give me orders,' Choshu said, as cool and quiet as he had been throughout. 'And I shall not do the Prime Minister the indignity of doubting his word because some foreign troglodyte tells me so.'

'Take him back to the British legation,' Kuroda said to his men. 'Make it clear to Secretary Vaulker that if he strays from British soil, he will be delivered back again in pieces. I want him deported and tried in London. Choshu, thank you for having invited me, it was very kind.'

The Duke bowed slightly and Kuroda bowed deeper. Two men pulled Thaniel away. He didn't feel it. At the door he twisted back against them to see the shrine again, willing there to be some sign it wasn't Mori, but the form under the shroud was the right size.

Thaniel didn't remember the journey back to the legation. The first thing he remembered was ridiculous: he had to explain in third person what they had against him because Vaulker didn't speak Japanese and Kuroda's men refused to speak English, and no one else was good enough to translate well.

Vaulker wasn't surprised. He directed them up to one of the diplomatic guest rooms at the top of the house. The men went away. Vaulker followed him inside and shut the door.

'I didn't,' Thaniel said, but mechanically.

'Well, let's have your version then.'

He shook his head. Maybe he could have had a stab at explaining about a real clairvoyant and all the rest of it if he'd been feeling normal, but he wasn't. It was half-past two in the morning.

Six had to be on the edge of blind hysteria by now. He couldn't imagine anyone had taken the time to explain anything to her. They would all just be telling her no, she couldn't see him, and to stop being a nuisance and go and play.

In the distant sort of way he recognised from fevers, he noticed that he couldn't hold a thought for very long before he skipped onto the next one. They were skipping fast, all over the place, except to the memory of the shroud and the chapel, and the delicate bones; it was like trying to catch a swarm of frogs jumping away from a cat.

'I'm sorry,' Vaulker said after he had let the silence go on, 'but I'm sending you back to England. This is far too sticky. You'll be on the next ship out.' He blew his breath out in a near-whistle. 'If you want my advice, I'd tell them that you ought never to have been put into a position of responsibility in the first place. You weren't educated or brought up for it, naturally it went wrong. Clearly you haven't killed anyone, you've just been mixed up in something you don't understand. Not your fault.'

Thaniel smiled a little. 'You know it's not just London and then a big wall and then Pandemonium. I didn't get much school but I remember they were pretty solid about not killing your child's godfather. It isn't like getting the dative and the locative confused if you don't learn your declension tables properly.'

Vaulker stared at him. When he spoke, his voice broke. 'I know that. I'm telling you what to tell those fossils at the FO. There are men there who still disapprove of people who only have money because their grandfathers were promoted from the ranks at Trafalgar. People like … but you think I'm like them, of course, just because I bothered to learn to speak properly. Steepleton, I don't know why you did it, and per-haps – God knows perhaps you didn't – but I can't do anything else, except what I'm doing. I'm going to lock you in now. Kuroda's men are staying outside and … if you try to escape, I think they will shoot you. For God's sake, think of your daughter.'

He let himself out. Thaniel watched the door close and heard the green clank of the lock, and felt nothing for a long, long lag before it broke over him. He pressed his hands over his mouth to keep from making a sound.

PART FIVE

FORTY

Abashiri, Hokkaido, 19th February 1889

Kabato prison was two hundred miles away. Most of the way was roadless through the forest, and it took the prisoners thirty days to arrive.

It was a very, very long month. Takiko had no idea what to do anymore. She'd never had no idea what to do, and she was so angry with the helplessness of it that she stopped being careful. She snatched five bewildered prisoners from in front of a firing squad – including the yakuza man who had beaten up Oemoto – and said she needed help cleaning if so many more people would be coming from Kabato. She'd been watching firing squads for days. They were trying to clear space in the cells. They let her have the five prisoners. The warden stirred himself enough to say it was irregular. She said it was free labour. That was that.

And all the while, the owls stayed on the roof of the Oracle tower.

———

The first column arrived early in the morning on the thirtieth day. Takiko saw them from the prison gates. The prisoners were in bright red, just like the Abashiri men, but theirs was weather-faded and frosted now. They'd come through the forest, not along the coast. There could only have been roads for a tenth of the way, and they looked exhausted. Only a few guards rode up and down the lines. More than anything, they looked like a defeated army trailing home. She was too far away to see properly, but the stiff way the men at the front moved made it clear enough that they were chained together.

Gunshots rang out inside the prison. She glanced back and hoped they were shooting the cows. They had a herd of their own, because people in town charged mad prices for cheese, but in all the time she'd been here, the cows had proven themselves to be nothing more useful than grain-eating machines. She wasn't usually much of a beef or milk person, but for the whole of the last week, she'd been craving a proper English Sunday lunch so badly that she'd made herself a meticulous menu for when the spring crept round and the boats ran to Tokyo again. She was getting to the point where she would have cheerfully murdered someone for some proper roast potatoes, the kind they'd made at the old legation when her father had been the translator.

It wasn't the cows. The guards were shooting men straight over a big open grave. Takiko watched for a second and thought absently that everyone was going to get cholera when the ground thawed.

'Fuck!' someone yelled from inside.

It sounded like the warden. She went inside, in case he had finally collapsed, but in fact he was standing at the top of the stairs, in the doorway of his office, holding another telegram.

'It's Kushiro,' he said. 'The mines have flooded. They're closing too. The survivors are coming here. As well as Kabato, and bloody Hakodate. Where do they expect me to put them, in a box? We're going to have to build a new wing – oh, my *head*,' he said, and bumped it against the wall. From the window, she saw the gates open, and the first men come through. The warden sighed, straightened again, and seemed to remember something. He patted himself down, went to the hidden door in the wainscoting, opened it, and disappeared up the stairs. She frowned and strayed to it, only to almost bump into him coming back down, leading the old prince by his arm.

'You're free, now bugger off,' the warden said.

'I'm what?' the old man said, bewildered.

'Free! Go away! Make friends with some fishermen or something.'

The man looked helplessly at Takiko, so she gave him directions to her uncle's house and hoped they would both be as pleased with each other's company as she thought.

She should have kept quiet, but it was too much. Part of her had swelled up like a hot-air balloon, just ready to float. They needed the cell free. 'What was it all for, the lock and …?'

'Oh, every prison in Hokkaido has to have one,' he said. He glanced down at her. 'Regulations are to keep it running. Why are you asking me questions? I'm busy. You're busy. Go away.'

The warden from Kabato was the first through the gates. He looked terrible. He had black frostbite on both hands and across his face, but he bowed stiffly all the same and thanked them for taking his men. Two-thirds of them, he explained, had died of the cold on the way, and so the situation was not as drastic as it might have been. He would have joined them, but he had a prisoner to explain. He glanced bitterly back to the gate, where men in red were trudging through. They all had sacking tied over their boots and the same exhausted hunch.

389

'It's all rather strange,' the Kabato warden began.

'It's all right, you need not explain,' said the Abashiri warden. 'I was briefed months ago.'

The Kabato warden shrank by three or four measures. 'Well, that's something. In that case, I should be obliged if you would shoot me, sir.' With some difficulty, he handed over his revolver. 'I'll lose both hands and half my face. I shan't be anything but a damn drag on my wife.'

'Naturally,' their own warden said gently. He looked sad, but he was too polite to say anything so patronising as, are you certain. 'Let's go outside and find you something nice to look at.'

They went away together and left Takiko watching the men file in. There were so many. She wasn't used to seeing crowds anymore. The Abashiri work details were only a few dozen. As the courtyard filled up, the guards began to herd prisoners inside, Kabato guards sharing ragged clipboard papers with Abashiri guards and pointing out, she supposed, different varieties of criminal. The murderers bound for the high security wing had come in first.

And then there was a strange hollow in the caravan. People had hurried or lagged to avoid a particular space. In the middle of it was a tall, broad guard who looked like a bear in his winter furs, leading a much slighter man on the end of a chain. Takiko realised suddenly that she was going to go mad if it wasn't Mori, if she had to wait anymore, and so, ridiculously, to delay the moment she would have to find out, she turned away fast, trying to think of chores. Tea; yes. She ducked into the guards' empty office to make some tea, six pots so she and the five prisoner-helpers could take enough round for a decent number of people.

'There's so few of them,' one of them said quietly.

When they came back out, the big guard was unlocking the chain around the smaller man's hands. She knew it was Mori even before he turned around; she didn't know anyone who moved quite like he did, quick and then slow. He must have had something over someone, because despite all the precautions, he was clean-shaven.

'Hello,' she said to the guard. Her voice sounded amazingly steady. The cups on the tray shook when she held it out, but she nearly convinced herself it was just the cold. 'You look like you've had a hell of a time. Tea?'

Attracted to the clink of china cups and the wisps of steam, some of the mounted guards drifted across too. The five tea-bearing prisoners started to hand around cups. The guards only stared at them at first as though tea were an imaginary thing from a story.

'Oh, lovely,' said the big guard. His sleeves were covered in frost, but he took the first cup and put it between Mori's chained hands. He did it with a kind of shy reverence, and a flicker of his eyes that made her wonder if he was anxious to make up for something, the chain maybe.

'Who's that?' she said. There was a lump in her throat. Mori had looked at her, but his eyes had gone straight through and then sharply down at the unexpected heat in his palms. It had made him jump and he frowned. He seemed like someone coming partly out of a dream, and as he stared around, it was plainly the first time he'd been entirely aware of what was around him.

'Our lucky charm,' the guard said, smiling over his cup as the others came for one too. 'He got us all the way through them woods without a scratch on us.'

'How?'

'He knows the future. Hey,' he said gently to Mori. 'Say hello to the lady ...? Sorry, miss, he can't always tell what's what in the here and now. He's not trying to be rude.'

'Hello,' she said tentatively, hoping Mori was acting, and absolutely, coldly certain that he wasn't.

The warden stamped back in then, by himself this time. 'Aha. You must be Mr Nishi?'

'That's right, sir.' The guard bowed. 'Is the warden ...?' His eyes flicked out to the side gate through which the Kabato warden had not returned, and then, just for a skitter of a second, back to Mori.

'Yes.' The warden sounded weary. 'And while is it very proper and socially responsible and upstanding and so forth, I do wish I weren't obliged to shoot people in front of my favourite view. Puts one off. Anyway. Right.' He studied Mori, curious and wary together, then glanced around the emptying courtyard and the men holding Takiko's teacups. In a gesture of real decency Takiko had not expected, the Abashiri guards had taken over from the Kabato ones without a murmur. 'Prisoners all tucked up, gentlemen?'

There was a murmured chorus of yes-sirs.

'Well – up to the tower, then. I think you fellows deserve to drink your tea in the warm. Miss Tsuru will look after you excellently.'

Takiko went up with them and made another round of tea. More wood went on the fire, and soon the warden's office was full of the animal smell of damp fur drying, and sweat. Dr Fujiwara had come up to look at the Kabato men, several of whom had frostbite. When the warden took a cup, he paused and massaged his temple with the hot rim, wincing.

'Are you all right, sir?' she murmured, half to cover over the thud of her own pulse in the long vein in her neck. It was so hard she was sure they could all see it.

'Oh, I'm fine, the splatter missed me rather,' he said. 'Although I think I might be dying of a brain tumour. You're all swimming in sparkly lights.'

'You need glasses,' Mori said.

'Sorry?' The warden frowned. And then, as if a bird had spoken to him, he looked to the kind guard for translation. 'What did he say?'

'You need glasses,' Mori repeated. 'It's not a tumour. You have headaches because your eyes are straining.'

'What?' the warden said slowly. 'But I can see.'

Mori had already lost interest. He looked at the kind guard and handed over a tiny paper crane, which he'd made from a scrap of paper he'd picked up from the desk. The guard laughed gently.

'Tsuru, that's right. There you are, miss, I expect that's for you.'

She took it gradually. She couldn't tell if it was just that some half-wakeful part of his mind had put together the word and the meaning, or if it was the closest he could come to hello in front of everyone. She tucked it into the top of her belt. The warden was still staring at him.

'My dear fellow, are you serious?'

'Oh,' the guard said suddenly, and produced a pair of spectacles. 'He gave me these ages ago, said to keep them. I had no idea what he was on about at the time, but, you know. You get to trust him. Must be for you.'

The warden took them slowly, put them on, and read a note he had written on the back of his hand. He looked like he didn't know what to do with himself.

'I think,' the warden said finally, 'that we all deserve something a bit stronger than tea.' He was watching Mori still, rather than the room generally. 'And I think we can afford to unchain this gentleman, just for a few minutes.'

After perhaps half an hour, the courtyard below was as still and quiet as it had been this morning, and the snow began to cover over the tracks. Sitting still with wine and a fire, and looking out at the white gatehouse and its little lights, the whole thing felt like Christmas.

A bell on the kind guard's watch dinged. Everyone looked around, except Mori, who had his hands flat on the floor as if it was moving.

'Ah,' said the warden. 'That means a new dose?'

'Yes, sir,' said the guard. He looked uncomfortable, but he took a neat medicine box from his pack. Out of it came a delicate vial, and a syringe. Mori's arm was already a mess of needle scars. He frowned when the needle went in, but then, horribly, his expression faded down to nothing, and his focus moved a thousand miles somewhere beyond the floor.

Dr Fujiwara pursed his lips and held Mori's wrist, looking to one side while he counted. Despite his seriousness, his purple necktie made him look festive. Before enough time had passed for him to have taken any kind of average, his eyebrows lifted, but he seemed not to see the point in saying anything to the warden, who was conscientiously ignoring him.

Takiko couldn't watch any more. 'What is that stuff?' she asked.

'Oh, it's clever. Chinese,' Mori's guard said, with muted cheer. 'It makes him remember better. That's what he calls it, remembering, but forwards instead of back. Only there's quite a lot more future than past, it looks like, and – well, lately, I don't know if he can tell what did happen from what might have, or what could happen from what is. Here and now looks a bit remote in all that. I think.' His eyes flickered back to Mori, who still hadn't moved.

'He's getting worse,' someone remarked.

'It's the same dose,' his guard murmured.

'Yeah, but he's getting worse.'

'Can I see that?' Dr Fujiwara said, holding his hand out for the case. When Mori's guard gave it to him, he took out one of the glass vials. The label was in dense Chinese. He frowned. 'This is for patients with hysterical disorders.'

'I don't know the details, sorry,' the guard said.

'Yes – it induces high blood pressure,' Fujiwara said, frowning. 'Which is fine for hysterics, because there's an imbalance to even out; the effect is to allow them to sit still and regain calmer cognition by slowing the blood supply to the brain. But give this to a healthy person and you'll eventually induce ... well. Stroke, heart attack, dementia.' He lifted his eyes on the last one. 'Students take this all the time as a studying aid – it gives you huge concentration, you never fidget or get bored. Marvellous til you keel over. Headaches, sudden spinal pain, dizziness, any of this familiar?'

'He wouldn't have said if he'd had any of that,' Mori's guard pointed out, frowning too. 'Our doctor said – well. It was orders from on high, you know?'

'Bloody Tokyo. Trust them to find a piano and decide that the best way to play it is to hit it with a sledgehammer.' Fujiwara had gone down on his knees to look into Mori's eyes. 'Can you tell me if you've been having headaches?' he said carefully.

'Of course I've been having headaches,' Mori said, sounding, more than anything, amused. 'What d'you expect?'

'Oh, glorious,' Fujiwara said. He gave the guard a black look.

Mori was looking out the window, down into the courtyard, as if he expected something to be happening there. Takiko glanced down too. The courtyard was empty.

'Well, I received orders from Tokyo,' the warden chirped, in a way that was clearly meant to put an end to any debate. He brought out a telegram and unfolded it to show them all. 'The Russian fleet is still very close to Nagasaki, but, thank heaven, our new fleet is nearly here. We are to ask Mori here exactly how to form up the battle in order to see the Russians off. The Prime Minister wants every single one of their fleet sunk.'

There was a flutter outside. The owls were flying away, towards the town and the sea. Takiko looked at Mori, but he was still watching the courtyard.

FORTY-ONE

The warden opened out a maritime map on the floor. The land was marked on it – Korea, China, and Japan – but the details were about the sea; the shoals, currents where they whirled around the Sea of Okhotsk, wind direction. Its scale was big, and it took up most of the broad space by the hearth. The paper crackled, razor-sharp along its folds. It was brand new. It had come from an envelope, now open on the warden's desk, labelled 'The Weather Station Project'. Because the map was so big, it took four of them to flatten down the corners with cups and books.

'Right,' said the warden. 'Now what does he do?'

Mori's guard moved him carefully, tugging him down from the hearth to kneel on the floor at the edge of the map. The edge of Takiko's skirt covered Siam. 'You have to ask him. But – you have to be careful how you ask. It has to be precise or he doesn't understand.' The guard hesitated. 'Odds are he might not anyway. You have to make sure you've only got one question in mind at a time. Otherwise he'll answer what you might say in ten minutes' time. You can't … be in a hurry, sir.'

'I see, I see,' the warden said. The other Kabato guards had gathered around too, interested to see what would happen. 'How does he know? He sees the future, yes? But not the objective future, *his* future. So how in the world would he know what's going on in Busan or out to sea if he's here with us?'

The guard nodded. 'Newspapers. We bring in hundreds and hundreds of newspapers. They're always old, but as long as we order them in, he can remember reading them.'

'Miss Tsuru,' the warden said to Takiko. 'In that envelope is the exchange number for the department in the Home Ministry running all this. The contact is a Mr Tanaka. Get on the telegraph and ask them to send copies of every daily paper, immediately.'

Takiko nodded and found the paper that outlined how to reach the Home Ministry department. It was complicated. There were three passcode words. Everyone watched her as she sat down at the telegraph. The clattering chink of it was loud in the silent room. The buzz that came from the operator at the other end was much faster and more professional than her hesitant code. Order confirmed.

The warden nodded for too long, nervous now. 'Let's give it a stab, then, shall we? Mr Mori ...' He hesitated while he put together the words. 'Show me the coordinates that must be occupied by the Japanese fleet, in order for you to read of the sinking of one hundred per cent of the Russian fleet.'

The guard put a pencil in Mori's hand. The pencil began to move over the map while the warden was still talking, and then the room faded into a deep, attentive silence. Mori didn't do what Takiko had expected; he didn't just mark on some crosses straight off. Instead, he took the pencil by its very end and held it loosely, like he was scrying with it, and moved it gradually up and down the map, starting on the Korean side and moving east. His hand hitched halfway up the Sea of Japan as if he had felt the pencil lead bump something invisible on the paper. He moved the tip to and fro three or four times more, and then marked the place. It was the first cross of twenty-five, across the west side of Japan. Some of them were in a cluster off the coast of Nagasaki, and some were very close to Abashiri, hardly a mile out to sea. It looked very much like the Russians had staged a large distraction off mainland Japan to make every-one look at Nagasaki, but a wholesale invasion of Hokkaido in the north.

'Good grief,' the warden said quietly.

Mori was still writing. He was annotating the crosses with the names of battleships. *Takao-maru, Katsuya-maru, Heian-maru.* She knew most of them, from Kuroda. Mori put smaller battleships and frigates off the mainland coast. The dreadnoughts, the city-sized ships crewed by a thousand men, he stationed off Hokkaido; right by Abashiri.

'Good thing so many prisons have had problems,' Mori's guard said once it was done. He sounded a little awestruck. 'We've got practically our whole labour force in just the right place, if the Russians do manage to land here. Do you think … he did it on purpose, to make sure we'd be able to defend the coast?'

The warden was studying the map still. He snapped his fingers suddenly at Takiko. 'Back on the telegraph. Send them those names and coordinates. Someone write down the coordinates for her,' he added.

There was an unobtrusive clatter as Mori dropped the pencil. He was kneeling already, but he leaned forward with his hand flat to the floorboards again, looking dizzy. His guard looked uneasy.

'What's wrong with him?' the warden demanded.

'He … this happened before the avalanche in Kabato. He got all dizzy if he tried to walk on the north side of the cell.'

'Why?'

The guard hesitated. 'Well, the avalanche … it tore off the north side of the cell.'

Everyone looked round. There was no obvious avalanche coming, though, and after a moment they all laughed. Takiko sent off the coordinates and sat back in her chair, uneasy, because Mori's guard hadn't laughed, and he hadn't said how far in advance Mori had felt the absence of the floor.

'Hey,' someone said, and nodded at the window. 'Look.'

She looked, half expecting to see a tidal wave or Mount Iou erupting, but the man hadn't meant that at all. The sun had come out, sudden and bright, in a patch of vivid blue sky. The snow had stopped. She must have been imagining it, because there was no way in the world she could have heard it through the glass, but perfectly clearly all the same, she caught the minuscule popping of ice melting.

'Another round,' the warden decided. 'To spring, gentlemen. That's the first blue sky we've had since October.'

Mori was the only one who didn't join in. He was still bent forward, his breathing visible. His guard tried to coax him into taking a sake cup, but if he heard, he didn't show it. He still hadn't made a sound. She wished he would; the others might have understood better that he was dying, inch by inch, in front of them.

Something thumped into the window right by her. They all jumped, except Mori.

But it was nothing awful. Someone had thrown a snowball. In the courtyard below was one prisoner, unwatched, standing there bright red in the snow. He smiled at her and threw another snowball. This one hit the pane above her head.

'Er, is he meant to be ...'

'Why are there unaccompanied prisoners throwing snowballs at my bloody office ...' The warden was already on his way downstairs.

Little thorns pricked along the back of Takiko's neck. All the time they had been talking, there had been a strange quiet from downstairs. It didn't sound like five hundred men were trying to settle in or jostle for space in the cells, or telling their stories to another five hundred. There hadn't been any shouting among the guards either. She looked down into the courtyard again. The man was still there. So were three horses, new ones from Kabato. They were ambling about unattended. They hadn't even been unsaddled.

'Say,' she said. 'How many guards did you come with?'

'Only about fifteen of us in the end. But all the men were too cold to do much about it.'

The doctor was trying to talk to Mori, who still couldn't hear him.

A gunshot exploded at the base of the stairs and the warden yelled. It electrified everyone and there was a rush for the stairs, for guns, for gloves in the bitter cold. Something smashed and a horrible, mechanical klaxon whined deafeningly across the courtyard. She caught Mori's hand, meaning to go after the others and get out through the front gate, but the courtyard burst into red with running men. They were all out of the cells. She pulled the hidden tower door open instead.

Mori wouldn't move, or couldn't. Takiko had to lock one arm around his ribs and lift him up the first step to make him go. He must have been starving for all the time he had been in prison, because it wasn't difficult.

The second they were through, she tilted the door shut. The dark was complete, except for one tightrope line from the keyhole, barely broad enough for a grasshopper to walk. Only a few seconds later, men bounded up the stairs and laughed in the strange hyena way of people who want to destroy something when they found the warden's wine. She drew back from the door, horribly aware that she couldn't close it completely without being locked in.

Although Takiko wanted desperately to watch, and know if anyone noticed the door, she stood back from it so that the light couldn't catch in their eyes or their clothes. She could hear the men prowling and smashing just beyond it. Beside her, Mori swayed queasily, as if he wasn't sure about the floor in here either. She held his shoulder. She could feel the bones underneath. Her mouth had gone so dry it felt like she'd drunk a whole bottle of vodka.

If she left him here now, he would be dead in five minutes. The men outside would kill anything that didn't run away. They were feral now, she could hear it in their voices, and so abused that they were owed some killing. She could get out on her own, she was pretty confident of that. She was fast. It would bloody hurt if she smashed the window and jumped through it, but she'd be alive, and they'd be distracted by Mori.

And then: she'd be free. Free from that rancid fear she'd carried around ever since she'd seen Countess Kuroda smash into the floor at Yoruji.

She would be mistress of Yoruji, and free to marry again; more sensibly this time. Nobody would be surprised to find she had managed to shed an inconvenient husband. Kali the Destroyer.

Mori was watching her, almost formless in the dark except for the shine of his eyes. He didn't say anything, but he was frightened; and not as if he were worried she might decide to leave him. He thought she already had. There was no hope in him, and when he looked away from her, his eyes filled with a sadness she'd never seen in anyone before. She could almost see all the stars of his already-faint possible futures winking out. She saw him accept it, too. He didn't try to argue.

The room beyond the heavy door had gone quiet. She caught his hand and edged out. The men had gone. Takiko hurried them both to the stairs. This time, at least, Mori moved with her.

Downstairs, more men were raiding the guards' lockers for coats and scarves, at least thirty of them, and already small fights were breaking out over the supplies. Takiko snapped back behind the corner of the stairs, one arm flat to Mori's chest to stop him moving.

'No,' she hissed when he ducked under it.

There was instant silence when they noticed he was there. Everyone got out of the way. He looked back for her and she had to go fast to catch up, willing no one to attack him for his coat.

One of the five prisoners she'd snatched from the firing squads came up to her and for a second she thought he was going to hit her, but he only fell in alongside.

'On your way out?'

'Very much so. Do you want to come? I've got to get this man to Tokyo.'

'Who is he?'

'My husband, and like an idiot he's let them drug him to the eyes. I'm going to steal a ship if you're up for it.'

She had a flare of relief to see that the other four were with him. They closed around Mori and her in a protective semicircle, and nobody even tried to stop them.

The courtyard was chaos, but none of the prisoners knew about the delivery gate behind the kitchens. The little road down to the town was quiet, even though, around the other side of the hill, there were yells and shrieks. Takiko had no coat and the air was bitter, but the town wasn't far, and bobbing on the gradually melting sea, right by the pier, was a small but sturdy ice-cutter called *Narwhal*. They were the first there.

Mori stopped on the jetty. The others ran on ahead. She shook his arm.

'They'll leave us behind, move.'

It was a clear struggle for him to talk. 'This … jetty will be burned down soon. I can't really see. I can't …'

'Shut your eyes. Hold my arm.'

By the time they reached the ship, one of the men had already got the engine going. The yakuza man helped Mori over the rail, then lifted Takiko. She thanked him and locked her face into a smile, so that no one would see she was almost certain they would steer the ship wherever the hell they wanted and pitch her and Mori overboard if they complained too much.

When she looked back the way they had come, the prison was burning.

FORTY-TWO

Watching Mori felt like living in the lag of someone else's déjà vu. Whenever the boat rocked as it struggled through the ice, Mori leaned into the corner where his seat met the wall a second before he needed to. It was maddening, because it wasn't enough warning to copy him, and so Takiko found herself jolted about, always knowing fully it was about to happen. Mori watched her as if he couldn't quite see what the trouble was. He didn't eat when someone brought in some fish, just caught from over the side. The others were ravenous, and so was she.

'Not hungry?' she said. She couldn't believe it. The bones in his hands showed too much.

'What?'

'You haven't eaten yet.'

Mori moved the bowl toward himself and picked at it, slowly, as if they had just eaten and nothing but good manners had persuaded him to even look at it. Before long he left it again and ignored her when she tried to tell him to have more. He was looking over at the far corner, at a stack of newspapers.

'Do you want …?'

'No. Someone's left some French pornography over there, it's horrible.'

All around the ship, the ice broke and clunked, groaning. Sometimes she couldn't tell which noises were from the ice, and which from the hull. One of the men knew how to steer a boat, and they were all keeping pretty jolly, but everyone was staying very quiet about how rusty the hull was, and how the *Narwhal* had probably been docked for repairs.

Takiko nudged Mori and gave him some soup – it was just miso boiled up from an old cube someone had unearthed from a cupboard, hardly more than flavoured water, but it was better than nothing – hoping that having to hold something liquid was a better anchor than a bowl of sashimi he could ignore without burning himself. Mori touched the edge of the cup, but then stopped and looked out of the window, where there was a sea eagle on the ice. She saw him forget about the soup.

Someone came in and rifled through the pile of newspapers. 'Ooh, nice,' he said, over something with a black cover.

Mori pushed his hand over his eyes, then seemed to forget. 'I miss radio,' he said. 'What do people do on long journeys?'

'What's radio?' Takiko said. She sighed. 'No, I don't care. Look, I know you're not hungry, but you haven't eaten. Think about it. Please.' She picked up the bowl and put it in his hands again. He put it straight down.

'I can't read books, I always know what happens.'

'Unless you eat that,' she said experimentally, 'I am going to punch you in the eye.'

He pressed one hand over his eye, and took the bowl.

She sat back once he had got a respectable way through it, feeling like a bully. 'What will happen when we reach Tokyo?' she said.

He ran his fingertips over a few inches of the window pane, exactly level with his own temple. It was where he would have hit his head, if she had knocked him hard enough. 'Say again?'

'Has – something gone wrong?' she said. She hadn't meant to say it, but it was self-preservation; if she hadn't asked, she would have drowned in it. 'You're not – well.'

'The legation might be difficult,' he said quietly. 'There's trouble …'

She felt like she was trying to swallow her own heart. It was torturous to see him like this, such a ruin of himself. 'Hey. Do you know me?'

Nothing. She unfolded one of the blankets on the shelf behind them, because he must have been cold, even though the part of him that should have known to shiver had gone wherever the part that should have been hungry was. He was just present enough to hold it when she put it around him, but after a while, his fingers slackened and the blanket fell.

'Hey, miss,' the yakuza man said from the doorway of the little bridge cabin. 'You should come and see this.'

As she got up, something huge boomed, a long way off. It still shook the whole ship. She had to hold onto the door frame as she ducked into the cabin, and then she stopped dead when she saw what was beyond the windows.

Arrayed in a vast line over the icy water was a fleet of ironclads. Each one might as well have been a black floating castle. Although they must still have been three or four miles away, she could see their water wheels, and the smoke rising in cathedral pillars from the funnels. They were exactly where Mori had said they would be; stationed just off the coast, blocking any possible shipping route round to Abashiri and beyond. She looked round and snatched up a pair of binoculars to make absolutely sure. Yes; the names of the ships were all in Russian. Every few seconds, huge, beautiful arcs of smoke soared out from their guns. They were running drills.

'Wonder where our boys are,' the yakuza man murmured.

'I think they're coming,' she said. 'They were gathering intelligence at Abashiri – I telegraphed the Navy about this half an hour ago. We should go right around. I think this is all going to be a battlefield by tonight. Hold on, I think they're signalling us. What does that say? Does anyone know Morse?'

One of the Russian ships was flashing its fog lamp at them.

The man who had used to be a fisherman peered at it, then smiled. 'They say they're about to stop firing. We can go straight through.'

So they did, and sailing between two battleships was like sailing on a little stream at the bottom of a canyon. The steel hulls towered above the trawler on either side, so big they made the sounds of the water and the crackling ice echo. The gun ports loomed, crawling by. Some of them were still steaming. She glanced back into the other room, to where Mori was sitting exactly where she'd left him, and hoped to God he hadn't been lying about how to win.

'Are we definitely sure we want to be in Tokyo when all this kicks off?' the fisherman said, and Takiko set her teeth. 'I mean really. We haven't got a chance in hell against Russia—'

'We're going to Tokyo,' the yakuza man said flatly. 'The lady says so, so we're doing it.'

She must have looked shocked, because after a while, he nudged her.

'Miss. You literally walked in front of a firing squad for us. We can take you to Tokyo. People aren't always shit, you know.'

It was two days' sailing to Tokyo, even with the engine. They came into the bay in light that looked like dusk, but really it was storm dimness. The city was brilliant, and for a good while Takiko couldn't understand what she was seeing. It was an electric glow that turned the undersides of the snow clouds orange. The others watched it too. It looked like the end of days.

As they turned into the great harbour, another kind of light, blue foxfire, followed the angles of the prow and the bridge cabin. It brightened and brightened, shining up the mast. She started to get a strange, metallic headache.

Mori hadn't moved from his space by the window in the little communal room for the whole journey. He was struggling to stay upright; he wasn't aligned enough with the immediate present anymore to move with the bob of the sea. Instead he pressed back against the cabin wall. He could talk when he was lucid, which was intermittently, but she hadn't been able to make him eat properly, or sleep. His mind was working, but the clocks in his organs and bones had stopped.

'I'm going to take you to the British legation. I'm a citizen and Kuroda can't get you there.' She glanced up, because the tip of the mast was tracing a beautiful line of blue fire at least forty yards behind them now. That happened in the famous scene in *Princess Yaegaki*, when the princess was taken over by the spirit of a fox and flew to stop a fight in among little falling fires. They did it with tiny paper lamps on stage, charged with baskets of kerosene. She hadn't known foxfire was real.

Mori hesitated, worried. 'Takiko,' he said, and she frowned, because he had never called her that. She was always Pepper. He didn't say anything else, lost.

'It will be all right,' she tried. 'We'll be safe.'

He looked down at his hands. Something in him faded. 'Are you sure about Eton?'

She touched his arm. 'Can you try and hold onto now for a bit longer? Just for another few minutes. Joy – look at me. Can you?'

He heard something else, from some time else. 'He's so little. He's only seven. It just seems awfully ...'

She couldn't move or speak then, because she could nearly see the future he was talking about sketched between them. A little boy. When she realised, she was paralysed; she smacked the back of her own hand to bring herself up from it. It stung enough to work. She opened the door and guided Mori through by the small of his back.

She had never thought about children. There had been no point. When her sisters asked if she wanted any, she had never been able to say, because hers had never been that kind of marriage, so there was a dam across the idea. It had never been worth knocking through. If she'd found that she did want children, it would have been horrible. She would have turned into one of those middle-aged people who collected dolls, and ended up with a room full of bright glass eyes in porcelain faces, all lined up on shelves pegged to walls painted in nursery colours. She couldn't think of anything more disgusting.

'Nearly there,' the yakuza man called. 'We'd best all go in different directions once we dock. Good luck, miss.'

FORTY-THREE

Tokyo, 22nd February 1889

With the storm and the electricity, all the ships back to England were booked up for the next week, and so Thaniel had spent four days locked in the visiting diplomats' room with no company but the grand piano. They let Six in for an hour a day. He knew he ought to have been angry about that, but in fact he was grateful, because it would have been difficult to pretend to be cheerful for longer. Outside, the protest camp was much bigger. Someone with a good arm slung a wine bottle through the window in the middle of the night, but he couldn't remember which night now. He had taped a newspaper over the hole, sheet by overlapping sheet, so that the articles about him were all overlaid in a meaningless blur. It was still cold, because the stewards wouldn't come in to bring firewood, but whenever Six came, she smuggled in more lightbulbs, and the combined heat was enough to keep his corner of the room warm. They were shining more brightly than they had before, and there were more fires in town. The newspapers were full of a rush of solved crimes, and the big debate across the middle pages was whether the ghosts were admissible in court – whether a witness was enough or whether you had to have properly photographed the scene. But his own name came up too often and he had to stop looking at anything except the weather forecasts.

He couldn't sleep. He had to take the newspaper off the window at night because as soon as it was dark, a wrenching claustrophobia he'd never had before settled over him and tightened until he couldn't breathe. It was freezing with the hole in the glass, but it was better than suffocating. He couldn't do anything but lie there, exhausted and awake, watching his own breath whiten just above him and listening to the protesters' storytelling outside. Trapped. He'd always been able to sit happily in small spaces, but this was different.

Snatches of the newspaper headlines kept catching his eyes. *Murderer – court – Duke of Choshu to speak at the funeral.*

He'd had to tell Six before she read about it by herself. She hadn't believed him. Owlbert, she'd insisted, was here because he was waiting for Mori to come. Owls did that. Thaniel had tried to tell her that owls were just owls sometimes. She had gone quiet after that. He had no idea how she was taking it.

On the first night he had tried to think about that old memory of the Christmas carols in the hearth and sleeping with Mori on the living-room floor, but it had turned to cinders in his hands. He'd picked it up too often. All the calm had worn off. He couldn't bring back what it had felt like, or even which carols they'd been. When he tried to remember, the part of him that had felt it didn't work.

All he could do was listen. The protesters all sounded normal, individually. Sometimes they took water from the outside tap under the window, so he heard them talking, and they were all carpenters and schoolteachers. The teachers had only come for this week, because of the national holidays around the Constitution ceremonies. Fukuoka's friend Yuna, the one with the mad gleam, was an accounting clerk.

Thaniel felt like he knew them. It was feverish and ridiculous, and he hated it, because he could feel his mind escaping through his fingers. He hadn't known that all it took was a few days locked in a room alone.

On the fourth day, Six was anxious and brittle.

'The diplomats say no one's allowed outside. Nobody will say why.' She went naturally into Japanese now. English was for school. 'They say we should keep quiet. Mariko says the men outside want to kill me. Not her, just me.'

'They don't want to kill you personally.' Thaniel lifted her onto the piano stool beside him, though he wanted to put her on his knees. He had a feeling she needed the dignity more than a hug. She was carrying a bag of flour, and her sleeves were already white with it. Like everyone else, she'd spent the last few days casting it around. Everybody wanted to know whose ghost they were sitting in. He brushed it off her. 'It's all of us. We're British. The men outside are angry because people like us have done terrible things here before.'

'What things?'

'Bombs, warships. Treating people like they're less good than us. You can't blame them for feeling like we shouldn't be here.'

'But we haven't done anything—'

'No, no, no, no,' he said over her, wanting to nip that sentiment before it could grow any more. 'Doesn't matter. You know that story about the trolls under the bridge who eat people? You couldn't really blame anyone who rushed up and chased them out instead of waiting around to be eaten. Even if those particular trolls didn't hold with eating people at all and just handed out tea to anyone who stopped by. They'd still look just like the dangerous trolls.'

414

She smiled.

He squeezed her gently. 'We're like the nice tea trolls. This is the price we pay for looking like something evil. Even though we're not. You just have to be a bit patient with it. I don't think we'd help anything by getting angry. What do you reckon?'

'Yes,' she agreed. And then, solemnly, 'Rar. Arg. Tea troll.'

He grinned. 'But we'll be going home soon, so it won't matter.'

'To London.'

'Yes.'

She frowned. 'But we have to speak English there all the time.' She was looking into the middle distance in exactly the way Mori did when he could remember a future he never wanted to see. 'There are things it's hard to think in English. There's not a word. You can think them but you can't explain properly and the thought just fogs away because you can't call it anything. What if we forget how to think properly?'

'We won't. We'll still speak lots of Japanese. We'll still see Osei.' He bit the end of his tongue. 'Anyway, you can't say everything in English, but that doesn't stop you thinking it.'

'Makes it harder though,' she murmured.

'Help me with this,' he said quietly, because he wanted to distract her, and because he needed to look away. He showed her the music on the stand.

'What is it?'

'You know how I told you about the moths in the piano, at Aokigahara? This is what they sang, more or less. But I don't know how it goes from here. You're in charge of the left hand, mine hurts.'

She wasn't that musical, but she did it with a deep concentration now, frowning. The notes furled woodland colours round everything in the sparse frozen room and made it warm-looking, at least.

'I like that,' she said at last, puzzled. 'That's different to normal music.'

'Thanks.'

'Dad,' she said slowly. He could tell she'd been working up to it for a while and braced himself for something difficult. 'How come we've got so many ghosts?'

'How do you mean?'

'Well, they had three at the Dutch legation. But we've got them everywhere.' She pointed to the floor. 'It feels crowded in Dr Willis's surgery. If you put flour around, there's loads of ghosts there. It's like a party.'

'I don't know, petal. Maybe we've got the best view.'

'That's facetious,' she sighed.

Someone tapped on the door. 'Time's up.'

He touched her back. 'Six. What you were saying about speaking. That's what music is for. Anyone can understand.'

She looked up. 'No. Numbers do that. That's why scientists from different countries talk in numbers. They don't talk with pianos.'

He took care not to laugh. She would have thought he was laughing at her, not at the idea that there was a human being of nine years old who would say that. 'It's for the things numbers are less good at.'

'You can talk about anything with numbers,' she said, confused.

'Well, never mind it, then.' He gave her a soft push towards Vaulker, who must have been getting used to her, because he looked warmer with her now.

'We're trying to hurry it along,' Vaulker said quietly. His eyes moved down and up Thaniel once. He looked tired and crumpled, and like he had never felt more weary of anyone. 'Board up that window, God's sake.'

Thaniel nodded. The door snicked shut and locked. He bent forward and watched his hair fall down by his eye on the right. He knew exactly why Vaulker had no patience for him. Music and playing with little girls were supposed to be things good and useful people did, not idiots who caused international scandals.

He let his head rest against the wall. There were pipes right behind it and they conducted sound very well; he could hear everything going on in the translation office clearly, though it came with a coppery tint. He didn't pay attention until raised voices carried up.

'What do you mean, they can't send the militia?' Vaulker sounded frayed.

'They're saying that with the fires everywhere, they haven't the men, sir.'

'This is about Steepleton. They won't send anyone to protect us while he's still here.'

'Well, sir, unless we float him off on a raft there isn't much we can do there.' The second half of the conversation was Pringle, who had turned out to be unexpectedly loyal.

'Those men are about to storm this place, they've been working up to it for days. Look … tell the glaziers to go home. We need to put boards over the windows. And – telegraph the Navy. This is ridiculous, we should have been evacuated days ago. They'll be here soon anyway with Kuroda's new fleet.'

Thaniel nearly called down that the British Navy were exactly who shouldn't cruise into Tokyo Bay just now. The Russians weren't going to view the British warships escorting the new Japanese ones as a special sort of postal service. If the British escort – and there would be an escort, to take back the temporary English crews on Kuroda's ships – sailed ashore to evacuate British citizens, no number of white flags would convince the Russians not to fire.

Hooting and shouting rose up in a wave from the driveway, like it always did now when anyone tried to drive towards the legation. Thaniel thought it was only the post at first, but the pitch of the yells was different and he realised they must have found a cab with a girl in it. He went to the window and looked out through the small part that wasn't smashed or covered over with newsprint. He was in time to see Takiko Pepperharrow climb out. She went round to the other side, ignoring the protesters so completely that she didn't flinch when an apple burst against the carriage door.

'Oh, gentlemen, do settle down,' she said. It worked. Thaniel wondered if it was just that the protesters didn't really want to hurt anyone, or if she had managed to trick them into being the audience in an involuntary pantomime. It had been a stagey thing to say, but perfect. She was tiny and fragile, but there was power in that. Nobody wanted to throw anything at her. She smiled at them all. 'I wonder if you'd be darlings and let us through?'

It was a kind of magic. Men shuffled back for her.

She opened the other door and handed down someone else. There was an odd quiet.

'Isn't that the man from the papers?' somebody said.

'Would you let us by? Thank you.'

Thaniel stared until he was sure, then looked towards his own door. It was Pringle who opened it, looking flustered. They were at the bottom of the stairs, a tangle of people.

Takiko was asking for a doctor, and Vaulker was trying, in a way that sounded like he didn't know what he was saying, to argue that it couldn't be who they thought. Two of the younger translators were trying to tell him that it was.

'Keita?' Thaniel ran down the stairs.

Mori looked shattered and thin, but he brushed Vaulker out of the way and made it to the foot of the stairs before he collapsed. Thaniel caught him and had to buckle down onto the floor, because Mori was heavier than he looked. It was like seeing a light turn off; the last glow in the filament lasted a while in his eyes before it was gone.

FORTY-FOUR

Willis was always big, but he looked monstrous when he held Mori's wrist. He frowned while he counted his pulse against a watch. They were in the airy surgery, with a proper fire burning in the grate. Takiko was pouring them all a generous tumbler of Willis's apparently medicinal but very expensive brandy. She had brought a sample of the drug that had done the damage. Willis had recognised it almost straight off. Normally it was to help you think. In big doses it was to treat blood clots. It could cause strokes, but it didn't make anyone catatonic.

'Well,' said Willis, standing back. 'If I didn't know I was looking at the effect of a drug, I'd say he was sleep-walking. You can move him, he can see you, you might even talk to him and get something of a reply, but he's not conscious.'

'Is there anything you can do?' Thaniel said quietly. His voice sounded wrong after having been underused for the better part of the week.

'No.' Willis paused. 'It's a standard drug but I can't quite tell what it's done to him. I'd be wary of trying to give him anything else, but we're in no immediate danger. His heart is slow; he could sit there all week like this without eating and he wouldn't be particularly the worse for wear. It's almost stasis. I think this is nothing but an allergic reaction.'

Thaniel swallowed, not wanting to argue it now. 'But – if he's awake, why won't he talk? He's not sleep-walking.'

'I really couldn't say,' Willis said, looking annoyed with the whole problem, as if he suspected Mori was just being perverse. He sighed. 'Well. I'm starving. You too, I suppose, ma'am?'

'I am,' Takiko said, in her fine English that was completely different to her Japanese.

'I shall scavenge,' Willis said. He had taken to her straightaway and he went up the stairs looking cheerful. Thaniel watched him go, then studied Takiko and wondered if she just thought the world was full of well-dispositioned and helpful people, in the same way the Queen thought everything outside the Palace smelled of fresh paint.

He moved across to the window to sit with Mori on the sill. It was colder, but Mori had gone there naturally when Willis tried to set him near the fire. He was looking out across the lawn, which, being downhill, was all in view despite the lowness of the windows. The protesters had gone back to their tents. It looked like a tent village now, and cheerful, hung about with lightbulbs on strings and dotted with fires. New banners were going up. More expel-the-barbarians, but other things too, fiercer, less official. The noise had been rising since yesterday.

Mori wasn't looking at them. He was looking at a point in the air directly above a tiny sapling cherry tree. He wasn't staring either; he was only watching the garden, his eyes moving, but always much above where any of the plants or the people were. Thaniel leaned close to him to try and follow his eye line, in case there was something in the air he hadn't seen before, but there wasn't. There was only the snow.

'You were at Abashiri prison?' Thaniel asked Takiko at last.

She nodded. 'And he was at Kabato prison.' She made a sound somewhere been a snort and a hum. 'He got himself to me, so I got him here.' She didn't sound like she thought she had managed it very well. She looked bad up close. Her knuckles were cracked from cold, and the glow of wealth that had haloed her at Yoruji was all eroded away. He thought there were lines across her forehead that hadn't been there before.

'Are you all right?'

She lifted her eyebrows at him as if he'd called her a silly bitch. 'What?'

Thaniel smiled. It was exactly the way Mori answered questions like that. 'How do I say that in samurai? Buck up, horse-face?'

She laughed. 'You should write a dictionary. I'm all right. Sorry.'

He shrugged to say he didn't mind. Between them, Mori was as still as the trees.

'I don't think he can find where now is,' Takiko said.

'Sorry?'

'He's been getting it wrong by … a few minutes at first, and then he was hours or days out, and by the time we arrived at the dock, I couldn't have a conversation with him. I think he's off by much more now.' She swallowed. He heard it. She sounded ill. 'Years I think. He was talking about our son, going to school.'

A child. Thaniel couldn't speak for a while. Then he never wanted to speak again. He wanted to find a snowdrift and die in it – just get out of the way, out of the life Mori was supposed to have.

He'd been wondering for weeks now what the point of all this was, why Mori had come to Japan at all, knowing what would happen to him. But a child was a very good reason indeed. Maybe even a child who could do what Mori could do. Maybe that child would change the world, or maybe it wasn't that, maybe it was just about having someone who understood – someone who was Mori's own, not a glad-rag family he had pulled together from a place so far from home that every single conversation had to be signalled across the oceans that separated how they thought.

'He killed a woman,' Takiko said abruptly. 'I saw it. Kuroda was drunk, and angry, and he killed his wife. She was my best friend. Mori stood back and watched. When I asked him about it, he said he needed Kuroda, and she had been about to send Kuroda to prison. That was all. He had plans, so she died. I think he's here with us because we're supposed to help him, but – I don't want to. Do you honestly think he should be free to do that? Because that seems to be what we're saying here. Either he stays like this, or … we let something dangerous and inhuman back into the world.'

Thaniel drew both hands over his face. 'He's not inhuman. It's for something.'

Takiko turned sharper than usual as she lost another few motes of patience. 'Yes, obviously it's *for* something. What if, in the really long run, it's better if thousands of people die now and Japan folds under Russian rule? What if it turns out that insane nationalists like those pricks outside end up being the deciding vote in everything, and a powerful Japanese Empire now means atrocities later?'

Thaniel nearly laughed. 'If he wanted to stop that, he wouldn't use a war to do it. Some minister somewhere would trip over a screw and change his mind about what to have for dinner and the world would turn.'

'You sound a lot like someone hearing hooves and scrabbling for reasons it might be zebras and not horses.'

Thaniel shook his head. 'And you sound like someone who hears ticking in a watchmaker's shop and thinks it has to be a watch, and not a clockwork octopus.' He sighed. 'He's a zebra person, is all I'm saying. I just ... he's good. He is. Whatever your friend died for, it will be something good.' He glanced up. 'And you must think so too, or you wouldn't have rescued him from Abashiri.'

She was pushing her hands together. 'I owed him that one thing. No more, though. If he'd just told me what it was for ... but he didn't. All he would say is that he needed Kuroda.'

'No, he wouldn't tell me either, but he wasn't being difficult when I asked. I think he was ashamed.'

'What's shame got to do with it?'

'Shame shuts you down, doesn't it.'

'Does it?'

'Does it?' Thaniel echoed, not quite able to believe she was asking, but then, she had nothing to feel shame about. 'I wake up in the night trying to think what I'd tell my sister if she ever found out about ...' He could only bring himself to nod at Mori. 'And I still don't know. Nothing, probably.'

Takiko was quiet for a long time. 'He let me hurt him. Quite badly. I hit him. He didn't even put his hands up.'

'Why do you sound surprised? He wasn't going to hit you back, was he? Christ, he wouldn't hit me back.'

'But people hit me all the time.'

He didn't know what to say to that. He had to let his neck bend and stare at the floor. He didn't think there was anything to say. The world had been pretty savage to her and a few words from some gaijin musician weren't going to convince her that Mori was any different.

'The hell is he looking at, anyway?' she sighed. She was right; Mori was watching the far corner as though something were going on there, but there was only a bookcase.

'Something that might happen there in ten years' time probably,' Thaniel said heavily.

She nodded. 'This isn't the ideal place to bring him. We were in and out of here all the time years ago. He probably can't tell which occasion it is.'

'Why were you here?' Thaniel said, without really caring.

'Well, he was Home Ministry. Half the job was to turn up to the British and American parties. We all used to go, the four of us. I mean Countess Kuroda and ...' She shook her head and waved her hand once, like she was clearing a ghost that had wisped too close in front of her. Her eyes ticked around the room. 'They used to use this as the cloakroom. When you got sick of the ambassador you ducked down here, had a cigarette, bitched about gaijin and then – once more unto the breach.'

Thaniel nearly laughed. They'd all been wondering why the legation was so bloody haunted, but Mori had said it, in that recording at Yoruji; wherever there was a clairvoyant in and out, there were plenty of ghosts.

'He needs – a flare. Something to show him when now is,' he said instead. 'Something to stand out.'

Takiko only glanced at him and shrugged a little to say she wouldn't be helping him to think about it. Her eyes slipped away, full of sadness, but he could see that being sad wasn't going to change her mind.

425

Six came down not long later, taking the stairs carefully because they were steep. Thaniel went to her and picked her up before she could come too near. She stiffened. 'Put me down, I'm busy. Good evening,' she added to Takiko, and didn't seem to find it irregular that she should be there. 'Busy,' she said to Thaniel, who set her down.

She had another packet of flour, and as soon as she was on her own feet again, she feathered little handfuls of it into the air and watched intently as the ghosts formed.

'Why did you say Mori was dead when he isn't?' she added.

'I thought he was.'

'Hm,' said Six, and hurried after the coat-tail of a half-formed ghost.

'What,' said Takiko, who had stood up. She was staring at the ghost.

'We have ghosts now,' Six explained. 'Where have you been?'

'Away,' Takiko said, looking shocked.

Half-heartedly, Thaniel told her about the engines at Aokigahara, the scientists, the electricity, and what Mori had said about ghosts and clairvoyants.

'Six, petal … can you stop doing that?' he had to add. He could taste the flour. 'I can hardly breathe as it is.'

'No. You said he was dead and he wasn't.'

He bent forward and pushed both hands over his face.

'Six,' Takiko said. 'What's over there?'

'A bookcase,' said Six, a bit flat.

Takiko lifted her eyebrow. 'You're not little enough or strange enough to get away with being obnoxious. Look where Mori's looking.'

Six looked, then frowned and bumped across to strew flour into the air there. She could only do a bit at a time, and it was a broad space. It would keep her occupied for a bit. Thaniel nodded ruefully to Takiko.

Willis came back with a tray full of sandwiches and onigiri, and tea.

'This might be the last food we get for a while, so set to,' Willis said, a bit gruffly. When she went up to him to see what there was, Takiko looked quail-sized. 'The kitchen staff have run away. They saw the translators boarding up the office.'

'Oh, real chicken,' Takiko said reverently. Willis laughed. She took two sandwiches and gave one to Six. Six looked up, surprised, then took a bite out of it while Takiko was still holding it. Thaniel hated them both in an awful little spike for that. He wanted to remind them that he was still here, Six was still his, for now. He squashed it, appalled with himself.

'Vaulker's hovering at the top of the stairs, by the way. Probably trying to work himself up to an apology,' Willis said.

'No need.'

'How magnanimous.'

'It's just translation,' Thaniel said, wondering if there might be a way to persuade Mori to eat something. He didn't look too thin yet, but he had turned fragile. 'Translating Eton to Lincoln is harder than London to Tokyo, stupid not to expect problems. You didn't believe me either, did you?'

'No. I always did wonder why you didn't just change your accent. Save you a deal of bother.'

Thaniel didn't have the energy to point out that there were some guns you had to stick to, if you still wanted to be you.

'I imagine he'll come out of this by himself sooner or later,' Willis added into the silence.

Thaniel nodded. Mori had better do it quickly, before he starved.

The telegraphs had gone haywire again. Some of them were sparking and juddering of their own accord. As Thaniel came into the translation office, the juniors were pulling the wires out with their hands over their sleeves and getting shocks anyway. One of the translators had just volunteered to go north, wherever the electricity was weaker, when they all noticed Thaniel and went quiet.

'Mr Steepleton,' Vaulker said, too briskly. 'You can go. We need to find a working telegraph and arrange a Navy ship.'

'We can't ask the Navy,' he said. 'We'd start a war. Pringle, get down to the harbour and charter a ship. The problem is getting places on board a liner but we don't need a liner to get to Peking, just a clipper. Whatever they ask, give it to them, there's no point haggling when everyone else will be doing the same thing.'

'Hold on,' Vaulker said.

'Go on, Pringle, through the stables.' Pringle went.

'No – no, I said, the Navy—'

'This will be quicker and quieter than the Navy,' Thaniel said when Vaulker caught his elbow. He waited and looked down at his arm. After two ringing seconds Vaulker let go and kept his hand open above it, conciliatory. He looked frightened.

'But not safer,' Vaulker said. 'There are women here.'

'It is safer. No one's going to open fire on a chartered clipper. And we need to go before everyone outside realises the militia aren't coming, whatever the protesters do. Speaking of families – are people packed to go?'

'Not yet.'

'Better get together what they can carry. And tell the women they need to be in flat shoes.'

'Flat …' Vaulker nodded and went to the stairs, more slowly than usual, as if they were between earthquakes and he was waiting for the floor to ripple.

A flash went off in the camp, but nothing explosive. It was silver, magnesium, from a camera. Then another and another; there was a whole firefly swarm of journalists just beyond the gate. Thaniel bit the tip of his tongue. The whole government would know Mori was here in a couple of hours. After that, there would be nothing stopping them telling Vaulker to hand over Mori or enjoy the incoming mob.

Vaulker turned away to tell some of the juniors to make sure the women were ready. Everyone else went back to what they'd been doing before – fighting with the manic telegraphs, or else nailing boards up over the windows. Thaniel wanted to help, but he could barely lift his arms. The bruises and the gunshot wound had stiffened. All around him, the hammer blows shot unpleasant green stars over everything.

The other door banged open. Pringle came through, out of breath and frightened. 'I couldn't get through,' he said. His eyes were streaming. The others had paused to listen to him and after the hammering from before, everything was very quiet. The shouts from the camp seemed much closer. 'They saw me. Some men chased me. They had – they had knives. I'm sorry, sir,' he said wretchedly.

Thaniel put him in a chair and gave him some of the plum wine they usually saved for diplomatic guests. It was as strong as rum. Pringle scrubbed his sleeve over his eyes. The wine danced in the glass when he took it.

The quiet in the room lasted a long time.

'If we're trapped and we can't even use the telegraphs,' someone said eventually, 'what do we do now?'

'Keep nailing those up, for a start,' Thaniel said. 'And then – might as well crack open the good wine. Not going to be a better time.'

That got a half-hearted little whoop. Pringle popped the cork on another bottle and took it round, and people started to make gallows-humour jokes. Because the wine was strong, it didn't take long before the laughter wasn't forced. Everyone's wives came down too, and the children. Six came up to see what the noise was about. Thaniel gave her some wine to try. Pringle asked awkwardly if Thaniel wouldn't play something on the piano, so he played something he would have done at a pub, the sort of song people could sing and clap to even if they didn't quite know the words. Mrs Vaulker turned out to have once been a professional singer. They shook hands over the piano top.

'We ought to have had a glass of wine together before now,' she said wryly. 'But I was taken up with drumming classes with the girls, and I believed Tom when he said you were an awful prick.'

Thaniel started to laugh. Vaulker looked mortified, but then laughed too and toasted her forlornly with his nearly empty glass.

Thaniel went downstairs to tell Willis and Takiko what was happening, and to bring them some of the wine. Mori hadn't moved an inch, and Willis looked more worried than he had before, even while Thaniel was still explaining.

'Under siege, how droll,' Willis said, but distantly. 'Listen … I'm worried I was wrong about his being stable. His heart is slowing down. So is his breathing.'

'Why?'

'It might be nothing more complicated than a kind of catatonic state brought on by trauma or shock,' Willis said uncomfortably, plainly unsatisfied with it. 'Honestly, I don't know. I've never seen a damn thing like it.' He lifted his hands and let them thump again onto his knees with more of a bang than most people's would have. He was more than twice Mori's size and Thaniel wished, however gentle he was, that he would sit back.

Takiko caught Thaniel's eye and asked with her expression, shall we tell him? Thaniel shook his head. Willis wasn't the kind to believe in clairvoyance even if it was dying in front of him.

Thaniel sat down on Mori's other side and folded his arms to keep from touching him. Panic was starting to flutter under his sternum. There were too many things he couldn't help or change, and they were all closing in, and there was nowhere to go.

'I must have a book that has something to do with this,' Willis grumbled, and went back out to his study.

If Mori knew they were talking, he was ignoring them. A shard of gravel pinged off the glass and a shatter-spider cracked over the surface. Mori didn't move. Some boys outside cheered.

'We need to get him to another room,' Willis said from behind them. 'They're going to smash that.'

'They're not,' Thaniel and Takiko said at the same time. A faceful of glass would be very memorable, even twenty years away.

Fukuoka shouted something at the boys and they went to throw stones at something else. He glanced towards them – he must have been able to see them clearly with the lights on inside – and bowed awkwardly and quickly, looking worried someone else would see. Thaniel nodded back to him.

Upstairs, someone turned up the volume on the phonograph. Some joker had put on the 1812 Overture, and the cannon blasts were drowning out the little bottle-bombs that were smashing against the walls now. The crashes made him study the window. If it had exploded inward, Mori would have felt it. Even if he was so lost that his lungs and his heart didn't know how often to beat and breathe.

Willis retreated to his office again.

Thaniel stared at the floor and tried think what he remembered clearly from ten years ago, the things that stood out and acted like lighthouses and landmarks. He'd been twenty; just moving to London for a job in the telegraphy department at the Home Office. He could clearly remember moving into a small flat in Pimlico, overlooking the Thames. But everything after that was a just a grey haze of day shifts and night shifts on a complicated rotation. Nothing that shouted out a particular moment. Moving, getting married, and dying: those were the days you could pinpoint exactly from years away. Nothing he could very well recreate here for Mori.

432

'This isn't you,' Six observed from the bookcase. She was talking to Takiko. She had managed to highlight a whole pair of ghosts, talking over cigarettes. One was Mori. The other, as Six said, was a little woman, but not Takiko.

'No, that's Countess Kuroda,' Takiko said quietly. She was watching the cigarette smoke wisp. 'I forget when that was. One of the parties nobody wanted to go to.'

'That's really clear,' Six noted. 'They're deciding something that matters.'

Thaniel watched them hard. He could read lips, always had done; you had to across orchestras. When he understood what they were talking about, he caught Takiko's hand and pulled her across to make her see.

———

'—says I've got a year maximum. Then it will all be rather unsightly.' The Countess paused, and lit a new cigarette, which she gave to Mori. The flour grains clustered whiter where her silk dress shimmered. It made her look luminous. 'Takiko tells me you know things.' She smiled. 'And you're not surprised, are you?'

'No. I'm so sorry. It's … Midori, it's a bitch of a disease.'

'I've always had the constitution of a damp cobweb, I'm not shocked.' She studied him quietly. The cigarette smoke wisped, perfectly clear in the flour. 'Listen. The stories about people like you. Are they true?'

Mori flicked his eyes up. 'Which ones?'

'You can change things. Given the right leverage, you can … do something decent. Kuroda thinks you're a death god. Or something.'

He was quiet at first. He sat back from the smoke as though it had made him feel queasy. 'Yes,' he said.

She straightened, pleased. It made her look like a very cheerful, very beautiful pheasant. 'Well then. Let me give you a present, then. I am not going to die coughing out my lungs onto your beautiful nightingale floor. I meant initially to have a nice walk on the cliffside and then jump off it when I started to feel bad, but that's rather stupid. I'd rather give my death to you. What can you do with it?'

Mori watched her for a long time. When he was entirely still, it was easy to see he wasn't altogether an ordinary human. There was something else in him. 'Could I have the cigarette packet?'

She gave it to him. He tore open the packet so he could write on the inside with a pencil. It was impossible to see what he was writing – the flour ghosts didn't show up the lead on the cardboard – but the way his hand moved implied lines, and numbers; maybe a kind of chart. He gave it back to her without saying anything, in the way serious traders handled balance sheets.

Her expression changed as she read it. When she looked up, the balance sheet might just have told her that, after a lifetime of penury, she had inherited millions of pounds' worth of holdings. 'How do we do this?'

'Kuroda. If we can make him kill you on this day, at this time, we'll get that end result within ten years.'

'That's hundreds of thousands of people.'

'Yes.'

She started to laugh, and then suddenly she caught the side of his neck and dragged him close into a hug. 'This isn't a trick, is it? This isn't some Winter King semantic rubbish?'

'I don't really do semantic rubbish, I've not got the right sort of brain,' Mori said. He kept his hands in his lap rather than touch her.

She held his shoulders for a little while. She still had a vestigial smile around her eyes. 'Well; let's go back up and get howling drunk, shall we? Can we tell Takiko?'

He looked past her, terse now. 'I – no, she'll … I think she would kill me before we managed any of it.'

The Countess frowned. 'You don't sound like you're joking.'

'I'm not.'

'Mori, this is – rather a personal question, but she's pretty rough and people have never hesitated to be rough with her, and I can imagine she doesn't really see any reason not to take it out on someone else. She's like Kuroda that way.' She paused and tipped her head to catch his eyes. 'She hasn't hurt you, has she?'

'No.' He didn't laugh.

'But she could.' She frowned. 'You must feel it already.'

'I'm not who you should be worrying about. Come on. I want to get drunk too. I'm a funny drunk, I go round prophesying at people I don't know. I nearly caused a trade war with Holland last time.'

The Countess laughed. As a couple of hulking white men blundered by on the way to the stairs, she put herself between him and them.

———

Takiko had had one hand clamped over her mouth all the time they watched. When she took it away, she'd gone so

435

white Thaniel thought she might collapse. He put his hand out in case she needed it, but she knocked it away and crossed her arms tight as if she would have liked to crush her own ribcage inward.

'He didn't tell me. He didn't ...' She looked at Thaniel with drowning eyes. 'What are we going to do?'

There was no time to say anything, because yells and barked orders filtered in from outside. Someone was shouldering a way through the protesters.

FORTY-FIVE

Kuroda's men had come with twelve soldiers, with rifles, and the protesters let them through without much argument. Thaniel was surprised to find that in charge was the man in the red coat, although he didn't have the red coat now. He looked different in an austere morning suit. He shook Thaniel's hand once the door was shut.

'Phew. You've got a crowd out there now, haven't you? Afraid I've got some bad news for you. The Prime Minister is ejecting you all from the country. He's breaking off diplomatic links with Great Britain.'

'But Mori's alive.'

'Can't have foreigners wandering around Tokyo burning down people's houses,' Tanaka said easily.

Thaniel thought about punching him.

'I'm in charge here,' Vaulker put in.

'Who's this?' Tanaka said.

'What is he saying?' Vaulker demanded.

Thaniel took a deep breath, waiting to be able to switch easily between English and Japanese. It was like trying to come into a piece of music just off beat. When he did explain, Tanaka waited, listening rather than idle, and Thaniel had a powerful feeling that his English was as good as anybody's. It would have been difficult to do his kind of work without it.

'We can't go anywhere,' Vaulker said, frowning. 'Mr Tanaka, you walked past that mob outside, they're out for our blood. We've been trying to evacuate the legation all week.'

'Not really the problem of the state,' Tanaka said drily, 'and I don't think we owe you any favours.'

'You've just handed us a death sentence then,' Vaulker said, incredulous.

Thaniel was starting to ache from standing so tense. He knew exactly what Tanaka was going to say. It was a small relief to finally get there.

'But,' Tanaka said, cheerful again, 'luckily, you do have a prisoner who's escaped from state custody here. If you'd hand over Baron Mori, I'm sure we can come to an agreement about getting you all out of here safely.'

'Tom,' Thaniel said quietly, even though he could see he was on sinking ground. 'They'll kill him.'

'This is the job,' Vaulker said, hard. 'What would you say to me, if I had an old friend in our cellar and a mob at the door? Those men outside are going to kill us all. And him, if they get in.'

Thaniel nodded. He heard it all, but at a distance. He didn't understand how things could have gone so wrong, with all of Mori's foresight.

Something banged hard on one of the new boards over the windows. It was small and the noise was white, followed by tiny sigh that might have been fire.

Tanaka lifted his eyebrows. 'What's it going to be?'

Vaulker nodded to Pringle and then at the stairs. Pringle glanced at Thaniel, then quickly down again, ashamed, but did as he was told.

A vicious static snap whipped round the room. One of the soldiers dropped his rifle and most of the others put them down, quickly. Thaniel had to pull his watch out of his pocket. He had been aware before that it was getting warm, but it was scalding now. Someone at Aokigahara had turned up the electricity again.

'What … by Christ is all that?' someone said by the last of the unboarded windows.

They all looked. It was so cold outside now that there were ice-crystals in the air, in among the snowflakes. Between them, there was a network of blue light. It was St Elmo's fire again, as usual, but it wasn't trailing any sharp edges now. It was cutting through the air in hair-thin lines. The noise quietened in the camp as everyone there noticed too. The tents looked like they were standing in the middle of a nebula. It glittered inside the office too, in the dust.

Thaniel picked up a packet of icing sugar, one of three sitting on desks still, and emptied it into the air. The blue lines traced themselves through it. They had patterns and crossings, and strange juddering loops. When he thought about turning out the light above him to see it better by, a clear arc traced between him and the lamp. He looked back. Other lines ran from people to the doors.

'It's where we could go,' Six explained, too quiet for anyone else to hear. A light between them flashed just before he lifted her up. 'What you intend – it's all illuminated.'

It was everywhere. Faint arcs traced between the camp and the windows. It might have been bricks they were thinking about throwing. From Vaulker, and from some of the more frightened-looking juniors, there were strong lines toward the back door, even though they must have known they didn't have much of a chance of going anywhere. Among the stronger lines were honeycombs and networks of other, miniature paths. Moving his hand through the icing sugar didn't disturb them. Six put her hand out and made the space around it glow because she meant to open and close her fingers. It flared stronger just before she did.

Thaniel stood still, because turning in circles made a preturn flare all around him. He tried to remember what Grace had called the ghost lines. Fate lines, fate trails. Something. In any case, someone in Aokigahara must have finally realised what they were and cranked up the power.

Other people were doing experiments to see what would make better lights, and so were the men outside, all the fight in everyone forgotten for half a minute.

From the stairs down to Willis's surgery, a narrow clear light line reached up and looped to the front door. There was just time for Thaniel to think it might, despite everything, be Mori, before Takiko came up. There was no sign of Pringle.

'What are you doing?' Thaniel said. 'You can't go outside, you'll be killed. If there's one thing they hate more than the British, it's Japanese who like the British—'

'That's the point,' she interrupted him gently. 'You remember when someone dies. It's a flare. We need it now.'

'You can't. For God's sake – let me do it.'

'Absolutely not. Look, you were right. He's something extraordinary, but I've been charging around like an elephant, like Kuroda, instead of protecting him like ...' She lifted her hand at Thaniel and looked desperately sad. 'Anyone decent. I've been treating him like some monster who just hurts women. Didn't even occur to me that she asked him to do it. I've crushed him. I owe him a chance now.'

'But I'm dying anyway — Takiko!' he called after her, because she had ducked past him and out the door. She didn't bother to shut it and only ran the second she was outside, knowing that over the rambling distance of the lawn he had no chance of catching up with her in the state he was in.

With his pulse echo-chambering round the inside of his skull, he followed her anyway. The cold made his lungs stick. Someone shouted at him to get back inside. In front of him, because she was running, Takiko was trailing St Elmo's fire. It was almost as bright as the line of her intent, stretching like a white-hot wire to the camp.

Sound carried very well over the lawn, which was amphitheatric. He heard her ask to know who was in charge, and from where a big group of people were clustered, working themselves up under banners and torches and chanting, a man came out. He was the same man Thaniel had knocked over on the way into the legation in December, Fukuoka's friend Yuna. They had let journalists into the camp now. Someone took a photograph, and Thaniel could see why. It would be a beautiful photograph, a woman with her hair tugged loose from running, facing down a man a head taller than her, both of them haloed by their intention to punch each other. Despite that, he had to slow down. He felt like an iron cage had closed across his chest. He could hear himself coughing like it was long way away.

'Hurry along before you get yourself hurt,' Yuna was telling Takiko.

'No. You're going to move your men away from this build-ing, and if you hurt me, those thirty journalists there will have it on film.'

He laughed at her. 'The film is melting, you stupid girl. They won't have anything.'

It wasn't true. Thaniel could see it from here. They had brought out old cameras – glass plates, not film.

'Go on then.'

'You think I wouldn't hit a woman?'

She punched him, with real force. It broke his nose; Thaniel heard the crunch. 'Not really, no.'

When Yuna did hit her, he might as well have done it with a hammer as with the sake bottle he really used. It was feral, and full of all the rage that had been building up since before the Constitution. It snapped her head back. She crumpled into the snow. He poured the sake over her and spat his cig-arette out. The flames went up with an unremarkable noise, like someone shaking out a rug.

Thaniel couldn't run. It was like being trapped in one of those foul dreams, the ones where there were monsters, but the air turned to treacle, impossible to push through. It must only have been fifteen seconds or so, but each second felt like hours, and in that time, the fire roared.

He burned his fingertips turning her over. It would have been better somehow if it had been in silence, or if other people had stopped to see, but mostly, people hadn't noticed. With the fire in front of him, he couldn't tell if the journal-ists had caught it. There were eerie blue flickers all across the snow from the future lines, but nothing, not even a glow, from Takiko.

Someone kicked him in the head. He collapsed, nearly grateful. The snow was soft.

'Who's that?' someone else said, with an odd tightness. People were turning away from Thaniel, towards the house. He could only see their boots. Someone must have been coming from that way. 'Yuna – fuck, he's a—'

Blood gushed into the snow, so hot it steamed. Yuna was just in front of him, but he didn't see what had happened. He couldn't see further up than the man's boots. One of the other protesters ran across too and then crumpled right beside Thaniel, his throat slit – not deeply, or even violently, but exactly enough.

Someone leaned down near him. Mori. He touched Takiko's throat, but she wasn't breathing. Thaniel didn't think she had been even before the fire. The man had broken her neck. She wasn't her anymore, just a ruined thing in the snow. It had been so fast: like dropping a glass. Even Arinori hadn't been like that. Thaniel felt like he was watching it all from three feet to one side of his own head. Observant little mechanisms of him were noting what was happening, but there was nothing else, and he couldn't think, or move.

Mori shook Thaniel's shoulder.

'Get up. I can't carry you.'

'I don't think—'

'Get up,' Mori interrupted. He caught Thaniel's hand when he struggled and half lifted him onto his feet. There were protesters watching, hesitating. Mori banged the sword down into the snow to have his hands free. Nobody wanted to see how quickly he could pick it up again. 'Get inside,' he said to Thaniel. 'I'll be back in a few minutes.'

'You're not going anywhere,' someone said, probably with much less certainty than they'd have liked.

Mori shook his head. He didn't seem angry, only pressed for time. 'You can kill me if you want, but there will be men coming for you if you do.'

Camera flashes were still strobing on the left, much closer than before, because the photographers had risked coming in over the lawn to get a better shot. To the right, most of the protesters hadn't even noticed what was going on here; they were still throwing bottles at the legation windows, having fun, because before each throw, the electricity and the snow traced out the bottles' parabolas ahead of them. Dozens of arcs flared every few seconds, flashing and beautiful. They looked like the vaults of an invisible cathedral crypt. Thaniel could only just see them properly. Something strange and blurry had happened to his sight. He could see sounds much more clearly than ordinary things. Concussion, that would be.

The crowd let Mori through. He didn't look back as he disappeared behind the journalists. Thaniel limped towards the legation. The world swam. Someone shouted something into his face with a firework of red and yellow, but he didn't catch what it was. When he reached the door, it was closed. He knocked his fist against it once, then collapsed on the threshold.

FORTY-SIX

Thaniel came to a section at a time. He was still deaf for a long while after he woke. He saw firelight, and the glint of gilt on the books on Willis's desk, but it was all silent. There was a pattern stitched onto the pillowcase, something simple with straight lines. Not a pillowcase; it was one of the pinstripe cushions from the nice couches in the dining room. He was in the surgery. He sat up slowly. Everything was still soundless.

It was freezing. Someone had broken a window and a blizzard was blowing in. The snow was dry and powdery, and, upset with the draught, the fire was smoking.

Willis rushed down. As he did, someone lobbed a bottle at the boarded window. The men outside were playing and teasing each other, in the way you play with the sea; there was a sort of delicious thrill pushing and pushing to see how near you could go before you had to dive in.

'Steepleton, good. Get upstairs. Can you shoot?'

'Where is he?' Thaniel asked.

'I don't know,' Willis said, annoyed. 'Hurry up. Can you?'

'What?'

'Shoot!'

'Yes … yes.'

'Thank Christ, so far it's only Mrs Vaulker and Mrs Henley. Oh. Look at me.'

Thaniel looked.

Willis looked critically into his eyes. 'Bit of a concussion, you'll feel dizzy. But never mind that now, get up there. They've only got hunting rifles. Where did you learn?'

'Home. Dad was a ... gamekeeper, I used to ...' Thaniel shook his head. Talking was difficult. His head ached, but it wasn't as bad as it might have been. There was a bandage around his hand. He puzzled over that until he remembered he had burned it on Takiko.

Her hair had burned. That wasn't the worst thing, but it was what stuck the most. It had gone up fast and bright because it had soaked up the sake, beautiful in the snow, and horrible.

Willis hurried him up the stairs into something like organised chaos in the long dining room. There was no sign of Tanaka and his men – they must have run or gone after Mori – but Mrs Vaulker seemed to have taken charge of a group by the long windows. The windows were boarded up to the height of a person, but she and a couple of others were standing on the tables rammed up against the walls. They were getting ready to shoot over the boards. Six was with them. She was arranging new bullets in a perfectly straight line on the tabletop. At the end of the line she paused and made a smiley face with them instead. Mrs Vaulker snorted and patted the top of her head. Six looked annoyed.

'Where's Takiko?' he said. 'Did someone – find her body?'

'Out there where you left her,' Willis growled. Then, with far more force, 'What the hell were you thinking, letting her go out like that?'

Thaniel stared out that way, through the last pane of glass that Pringle was just covering now. He should have been the one left out in the snow. For a fleet second he wondered if that was what he was for after all, the sacrifice to save a family. Takiko would have been a good mother to Six, and to her son. All lost now.

Mori wasn't so cruel. None of it was meant to be like this. All at once Thaniel could see it.

That instant he had decided to go with Arinori to the Constitution parade had been the important one. He shouldn't have gone.

Vaulker should have been with Arinori. He would have been quicker. Arinori would be alive.

If Arinori hadn't been killed, Thaniel would never have realised that anything was wrong at Mori's end; he wouldn't have realised he was missing, not just absent. He would have had no reason to ignore Mori's message in Aokigahara; he would never have gone back to Yoruji, the one place he shouldn't have been, where Tanaka had seen him in time to produce a body for Kuroda to show the Duke. He'd been trapped inside the legation on murder charges, in that miserable freezing guest room, instead of negotiating with the protesters like he should have been.

There wasn't meant to be any emergency here. No one was meant to be dead on the lawn. It was supposed to be safe.

In one disgusting moment, he realised he didn't feel so panicked and so guilty only because a valiant human being had died. It was because Mori was going to be angry. It was the way he'd felt when he'd got into fights at school and been dragged into the headmaster's office by the collar. Raw shame, and nothing about it pure or good. It was fear of the cane.

Someone threw a brick. One of the windows smashed, spectacularly. Mrs Vaulker bent forward over Six. He'd never thought he would like her. A cheer went up outside and someone kicked at the front door, an incredible bang that made the solid oak groan. A sake bottle with a lit fuse soared in through the broken window. It smashed over the floor and spilled fire across the boards. One of the junior diplomats wrenched down a long curtain to smother it and smoke poured up. It formed ghosts, none clear enough to make out. Someone pushed a gun into his hands and Willis half helped and half lifted him onto the table beside Mrs Vaulker, who nodded.

There was a thump outside that made them both jump, and then a perfect quiet. The protesters stopped hooting. There was no more laughing, only a crackle where a pile of old pine needles was still burning. It was by the last window, where the Christmas tree had sat until last week waiting for the gardener's boy to get round to taking it away. In the torchlight, Thaniel saw that some of the protesters were hurrying away from something before he saw what had made them run.

It was a phalanx of knights. They had stopped just in view, about twenty yards away from the corner of the building. Silhouettes in the lamplight around the tents stopped still.

'Those are soldiers,' Mrs Vaulker said, puzzled.

'That's not army uniform,' someone else said.

Thaniel leaned against the boards. They were carrying a red banner, and though their armour was dark, there was an insignia band on the sleeves. A triangle of dots and a horizontal slash, black on red.

Some of the protesters saw what was about to happen and ran. The soldiers' method of clearing everyone was to set the tents on fire. They went through slowly, like reapers at a moonlit harvest. A few of the younger men tried to fight and got a sword hilt in the teeth for it.

The juniors whooped and cheered. Even Mrs Vaulker relaxed. Four soldiers broke away from the others, flanking a fifth man. They came to the dining-room door and Thaniel eased down to help unblock it, with Vaulker and Pringle. When they opened it, Mori stepped through, and then turned back to bow to the man who must have been the captain. The man looked over Thaniel, Vaulker, and Pringle as though he would rather leave Mori alone on the veldt with only some especially stupid giraffes for help, but he bowed back and turned away.

Thaniel kept his hands behind his back. Mori was studying him, unreadable. He might only have been so tired he had closed in on himself, but Thaniel didn't think so. Thaniel could only hold his eyes for half a second before he had to look down.

'Baron Mori,' Vaulker said, sounding as though he was about to say something awkward and not entirely apologetic.

'Secretary,' Mori said. Like always after any length of time away, his voice was unexpected. It was lower and stronger, and more gold. He raked Vaulker with too intense a scrutiny, and Vaulker looked flustered. Mori hadn't bothered to mask what he thought, which hung quite clear between them even unilluminated by electricity or icing sugar. 'You've let things get out of hand here.'

'These are – your men, are they?' Vaulker faltered.

'They are retainers from my house. I've borrowed them from the Duke of Choshu. Thank you for taking me in, that was very kind.'

'Of course,' Vaulker said again, and begged Thaniel for help with his eyes. 'You're welcome to stay.'

Six had come across nearly straightaway, but she had kept quiet. She pulled Mori's sleeve now and then smiled when he lifted her straight up.

'How are you?' he said gently.

Vaulker looked like he wanted to die.

Six clamped both arms around him and spoke mainly into his shoulder. 'Mrs Vaulker keeps fluffing up my hair. Dad says we're good tea trolls but I think I would be justified in being a man-eating troll in the case of Mrs Vaulker.'

He tipped her back. 'I don't suppose that means you know where the tea is?'

She nodded and made a small noise to be put down on the floor again. 'I'll show you.'

'I'm – afraid the staff fled earlier,' Vaulker said helplessly as Six led the way to the kitchen.

Mori glanced at Thaniel once but ignored him otherwise. And then there was a general easing. The junior diplomats had been watching. It was like a classroom that had almost reached the point of riot, and then gone right back to normal with the return of the schoolmaster. Vaulker seemed suddenly no more authoritative than the fussy prefect from the front row.

Out in the garden, everything was dying down. The Duke's men were combing back through the camp again, looking through piles of canvas to make sure there was no one left hiding. The burnt banners whirled ash into the snow. It was starting to freckle the windows.

Vaulker caught Thaniel's arm. 'Steepleton … if you could … perhaps not tell Mr Mori how badly we all behaved here, I'd be grateful.'

Thaniel looked down at his own arm until Vaulker let go. 'It's Baron, not mister. So when he asks me what happened, I should lie?'

'Well, if you would.'

'No,' Thaniel said, as neutrally as he could. 'I'm going to find something to eat; would you like anything?'

'No,' Vaulker said. 'No, thank you.' He went away along the windows to watch the soldiers.

Mori had found some tea things, and some leftover rice. He set them down on the edge of the table closest to the fire. There were other people, and they were in the process of moving to the seats furthest away by the time Thaniel went across. He moved a chair out. The small scrape it made on the wooden floor made Mori jump. He had been looking at the fire as if he had never seen one before. Six had disappeared again.

'Are you all right?' Thaniel said. He sat down slowly, ready to get up again quickly if Mori told him to go away.

Mori's hands were shaking around the cup, a just-noticeable tremor that might have been cold or shock, or neither.

'Yes. How did you know what to do?'

'I didn't. It was Mrs Pepperharrow.' Thaniel felt like the cane was hovering right above his hand. 'She said we needed to give you a flare.'

Mori nodded slowly. Thaniel saw him breathe in and make an effort to gather the words together. He thought he was going to say something about Takiko, and ask to know how Thaniel had let any of it happen, but it wasn't that at all.

'I can't remember anything. Ahead, I mean I can't remember ahead.'

Thaniel was quiet while he thought about it. 'When did that happen?'

'When I woke up. It was an overdose, they were drugging me.'

'Is it – are you all right, do you need anything?' Thaniel asked, completely insufficiently.

'I'm fine. Just ...' He tipped his head like he could hear something rolling inside his skull. 'Empty.'

There was a long quiet that was full of the fire clicking and the yells from outside. The junior translators and diplomats were watching the Mori knights clear out the last protesters from the one unboarded window, excited now. Sometimes they cheered. They all looked very young.

Eventually Thaniel couldn't keep quiet anymore. 'I'm sorry.' He swallowed, because his voice had splintered. Hardly anyone had noticed what had happened to Takiko; it was what was sticking to him more than her dying. Hardly anyone had even looked. 'I should have stopped her going. But I couldn't catch—' He had to stop himself, because it sounded so spineless. 'I didn't let her go out there for spite. I know it must seem like I did – but – you have to know ... I didn't.'

'It's not your fault,' Mori said. The firelight was making his hair red on that side. His bones were sharper than before and he looked less human than he ever had. He sounded like he was speaking from a long way off.

'It is. Everything's wrong. You were here for her. You were going to have a child with her, for Christ's sake. And now she's ...'

Mori had been shaking his head while Thaniel was talking. 'No – no. I wasn't here for that, that's just the future that
would have come to pass, if you—' He looked away sharply
and then back again. 'If you were to die. You know what grief
looks like, in clairvoyants?'

'No?'

'Recovery. You get over a man dying before he's even half
gone. It's inhuman.' He was quiet. Whatever was coming
next, he had to dredge it up. 'But talking to you, and remembering my children with her – I was going mad with it. I
didn't let them give me an overdose by accident. I did it
because if I hadn't, I'd have torn my own eyes out remembering that while you were still here.'

Mori watched him as if he might have said something else,
but then looked down into his tea. He had his hand around
his own throat, and he was pressing too hard now.

Thaniel touched his knuckles, wanting him to stop.

'Do you know what I was doing in Japan?' Mori asked,
very quietly. 'Because as far as I can tell, all I've accomplished
is a lot of – destruction.' He had to reach for the English.

'I don't think what you were doing is finished yet,' Thaniel
said. He switched into Japanese. A lot of Mori's English
must have been from the future. It must have gone, the
second he lost his future-memory. 'It's all going somewhere.
The electricity and – well, you said something obscure about
microscopes a while ago. I don't know what you really
wanted.'

Mori shuddered and at first Thaniel thought he was
crying, but he was laughing. 'I see.' It died away too quickly.
He looked down and pushed his good hand over his eyes. For
the first time, Thaniel noticed that when they weren't

453

watching the soldiers outside, the people at the windows watched Mori. It was a mix of curiosity and unease, and exactly what would have happened at the theatre if everyone had been smoking back stage, watching the operetta from a side door, only to find that when the fairy king came back to sit with them, he wasn't an actor at all but the actual fairy king.

'I know it must have felt like I was elbowing you aside every second of the way,' he said softly. 'But the reason I didn't tell you anything was that you would have stopped me. For absolutely certain. And ... I don't remember what I was doing, but I do remember knowing I had to do it.'

'I can't stop you doing a damn thing,' Thaniel said. His throat hurt.

'Of course you can. I buckle whenever there's even a chance you'll be angry with me, never mind when you actually do it.'

Thaniel couldn't think of anything to say to that.

The fire cracked every so often. Outside was quieter now. There were still tents burning, but all the protesters had run away. The Duke's men were silhouettes among the flames.

'You've finished talking now,' Six told them, having appeared next to them. 'It's your turn to read again. This is about static induction, it's by Tesla. It's why the lightbulbs work.' She gave Mori a journal. Then, 'Why are you both so upset? There's nothing to be upset about.'

'Six,' Thaniel said, 'when someone's upset, you ...?'

'... consider it an objective problem with a solution.' She looked Mori over. 'Is a cherry bakewell the solution?' she offered, much more humbly.

It made Mori laugh. 'No, you keep it – sorry, where are you getting those in the middle of a siege?'

'Mr Fukuoka is hiding in the larder,' she explained, and gave him half her bakewell anyway.

'I might have to look into that,' Thaniel said. He couldn't think of much in the world he wanted to do less than get up again, but he would regret staying idle if anyone else found Fukuoka first. As he went, Mori told Six he couldn't remember the future anymore and that he might not know some of the difficult words.

'You're thinner too,' she agreed, as if that were the same sort of thing.

———

Thaniel woke up early, struggling out of a dream where he'd still been locked in the room upstairs. Burrs of it held on for a long time, and he couldn't work out at first where he was. He clipped Mori before he remembered he was there. But he was; he had moved the pillow aside so he could lie flat. He slept like someone had dropped him, and silent, but he was breathing when Thaniel touched him. The claustrophobia vanished, really for the first time all week, and the pressure around his lungs lifted so suddenly he felt off-balance. He sank down again and put his head against Mori's shoulder.

From outside, the sound of the river traffic was seeping through the window pane; the barges were going to the sea for the tide. Thaniel lay still for about an hour, listening to the rivermen call and the smoky catch in his own lungs. The sun was soaking warmly through the back of his shirt. For once he hadn't woken feeling like he was arranged around second-hand bones. He got up and lit the fire, and put on extra wood.

On his way back, he paused, because there was a ghost just forming itself on the rug, lying down, asleep. He leaned down gradually and moved his hands through it to clear it. The ghost jerked awake. It made him jump back before he remembered.

That night the soot handprints had appeared on his shoulders. He'd seen his own future ghost.

He edged back into bed. Mori came awake all at once. He frowned and brushed Thaniel's shoulder, where the new sun must have been showing the ugly blast of the bullet scar. It still looked raw and wicked.

'What happened there?'

'Just an accident. I got in someone's way. He wasn't aiming at me.'

Mori didn't ask for specifics. Eventually, he said, 'Does it hurt?'

'No,' Thaniel said. He shifted awkwardly. He had known before that it was horrible to look at, but he'd managed not to pay too much attention. He hadn't looked in a mirror yet. 'It's much better. You?' Thaniel said. Mori was still holding his shoulder. 'How's the memory? Anything ... coming back?'

Mori was quiet at first. 'No. It's a novelty.' He shook his head once against the pillow. 'I was doing it for years. I remember altering things about exactly where those prisons would be built, who would staff them, I remember choosing which carpenter would be hired. It's bizarre not to remember what it was for.'

'It will be something good. Honestly.'

'I'm glad you think so, because a lot of people died while I was arranging them into the right places.' Mori had his other hand around his own throat, the same as yesterday. This time, Thaniel moved it and set his own hand in its place to stop him, much more softly. Mori's pulse was going as fast as a sparrow's, but Thaniel felt him start to ease, and he wondered if it could be possible that Mori had scared himself so badly over the last month that the only way left to feel safe was to know there was someone who could strangle him if need be.

Mori shook his head a tiny fraction. 'I can remember a tax receipt number I got in eighteen seventy-six,' he said, almost laughing.

'There must be a lot of freed up space in there,' Thaniel murmured.

Mori nodded. He was still smiling, just, but it was the way Thaniel would have smiled if he'd woken up and found someone had amputated his arm. There was no use making a fuss, or upsetting anyone, but inside, everything screamed. 'Is that Six's owl?' he asked, towards the window.

Owlbert was perched there, looking pleased with himself.

Thaniel took a breath and realised he owed Six an apology. 'Yeah. He's been waiting for you.'

Outside in the corridor, solid footsteps came their way. Thaniel watched the sound make dull mossy bursts, willing them to go straight past. Mori looked back too, very still. Thaniel didn't say he would get used to not knowing, in case he didn't.

Someone tapped on the main door in the living room. The cotton of the quilt cover creaked as Mori clenched his hands over it. Thaniel touched his chest, very lightly.

'I'll go. Stay there.'

'No – no. I'm all right. Normally when I have no idea what's about to happen, it's because I'm probably about to die. It's just – going to take some getting used to. Better just get on with it.'

He'd always thought that Mori was brave because he always knew what was going to happen, but that turned out to be a serious misjudgement of character. Mori went straight out. He hesitated with his hand on the latch, but only for a second. Thaniel waited a few feet back, leaning against the couch so that at least there were familiar things to turn back to.

It was the guard captain, who had come with some clothes, and with Katsu, who he'd found on the gatepost, sunbathing. Katsu burst out of his hands and coiled round Mori's shoulder straightaway. Thaniel straightened, worried it would make him jump, but Mori only smiled and wound a free tentacle through his hand.

The guard captain looked ruefully pleased.

'This came for you from the Palace,' he said, holding out an envelope stamped with the seal of the Home Ministry. 'They want you for a tribunal later this morning. And that idiot Vaulker.'

Mori nodded. The guard captain bowed, not too stiffly, and left. Mori watched him go, all the way back along the corridor until he turned the corner and disappeared down the stairs. When he let his eyes drop, it was to the envelope.

'I don't know what's inside,' he said. He sounded unnerved. He twisted his head away. 'What a stupid thing to say.'

'No, it's not. Everyone hates ominous envelopes.' Thaniel opened it for him. 'Kuroda is calling an investigative tribunal. "To ascertain how a dangerous prisoner escaped custody" – he is a prick.' He had never liked the bullying wording that permeated English government documents, but Japanese had whole extra levels of language with which to be quietly, snidely, terrifyingly intimidating. He crushed the letter and lobbed it in the fire.

'I don't know what to do,' Mori said quietly.

'They don't know that you've lost your memory. They're not going to leave you alone. If we try to go to the docks, Tanaka will be waiting. You have to go to this tribunal. Talk to Kuroda, you're good at it.'

'Yes,' Mori said. He was watching Katsu wheel off for the fire. Then, 'Can you come?'

'I have to, I'm the only proper translator,' Thaniel pointed out.

'Yes,' Mori said again. 'And then ...'

Thaniel squeezed his shoulder. 'Look, the Duke of Choshu owes you a favour. He should have been looking for you, all this time. I think he must be ...' He had been going to say 'upset', but he couldn't imagine the Duke being upset. 'Very embarrassed.'

'What if he's not?'

'Kuroda convinced him I'd murdered you. Kuroda had a body, and everything; actually it would be worth finding out who that was, you could probably nail him for murder. Kei, Choshu wouldn't have sent his men here if he weren't angry. Kuroda pulled one over on him.' He paused. 'I can't believe this is how it was supposed to turn out. I can't believe you meant for Mrs Pepperharrow to die, or Arinori, but those things are my fault. You arranged everything else perfectly. I think you can trust that the tribunal will be all right.'

'What do you mean, your fault?' Mori said, frowning. 'Arinori is dead? The Education Minister? How?'

'He was shot. Vaulker was meant to go with him to the Constitution parades, but it was me. Arinori's wife thought that you and Mrs Pepperharrow were in trouble, and I went with them because I wanted to know more. And then when the gunman fired, I was too slow.' Thaniel motioned at the bullet scar. 'And then I went looking for you, at Yoruji—'

Mori caught his hands. 'Wait, wait. Did you see the message on the wall, in Aokigahara?'

'Yes, and I – bloody ignored it. I'm sorry. I was scared you were dead, I thought I could find out … I don't know,' Thaniel said, all in an excruciated rush. 'But I went to Yoruji, I was seen, and Kuroda had me arrested. I was sitting locked in a room here like an idiot when I should have been negotiating with the protesters outside. I could have done it, too.' He took his hands back, because they were shaking. 'You should have been safe here, when you came back. There shouldn't have been any protest anymore, never mind a mob. Mrs Pepperharrow would never have had to – she'd still be alive. We would have had time to think of something else, to bring you back to now. I'm so sorry.'

Mori was looking at him as if he'd never seen him before. 'You were worried.'

'I didn't mean for it to get in the way like that, I—'

'About me,' Mori said gradually.

Thaniel choked. 'Are you telling me you didn't factor in me wanting to look for you? That cannot have been a faint chance.'

'Everything was faint, when I was putting this together. I had to guess.'

'So – what, you thought I just tolerated you for the sake of a free room?'

Mori didn't laugh. 'Isn't that what impoverished young artists usually do with old millionaires who fall in love with them?'

Thaniel wanted to splinter into pieces. Part of him sank into a relief like he'd never felt before, but the rest was so shocked that the relief was nearly drowned out. Every conversation they'd ever had rushed across the front of his mind. Suddenly Mori's endless quietness looked much more like grace and deference than indifference.

'Why would you have me in the house if you thought I was like that?' he managed at last.

Mori shifted his shoulder a fraction. 'It was good enough.'

'Good enough—' He wanted to say other things, but they flooded up with a pressure that would have looked like madness if he'd tried to put it into grammar and words. 'I don't *tolerate* you. I can't breathe when you're not here, I can't think, I can't write music properly, I spend my whole bloody life waiting for the post. I never said because I thought you didn't want to hear it. We don't talk about – any of it.'

He looked up when Mori brushed his elbows, and fell still. It was only the touch of a kiss, but it sent burning right down his breastbone and a rush of heat that made the cold room too hot. He leaned up a little and felt Mori's shoulders tip into his hands, then stepped up and eased him nearer. He didn't know he was crying until Mori brushed his eyelashes.

FORTY-SEVEN

The tribunal was held in a grand, bright room at the Palace, full of multicoloured sunbeams from the stained-glass panels in the walls. There were tables and chairs set up in a careful arc, some already filled by quiet men in perfect suits. Willis had tried to ban Thaniel from going, on the not unreasonable grounds that he was in no fit state to think about anything more complicated than lunch, but there was no one else to translate.

The Duke of Choshu arrived with a retinue of soldiers, including the captain who had come to the legation. He introduced himself to Vaulker with a pristine politeness before crossing the room to speak to Mori. Thaniel couldn't hear what Choshu said, but he looked anxious. Mori gave him a cup of tea. Thaniel glanced at Vaulker, feeling more foreign than he did even usually, and caught Vaulker looking at him in just the same way. They drew together.

'Are you up to this?' Vaulker asked uncomfortably. 'I can't catch a single word Kuroda says in Japanese.'

'I'll be all right. It's just how people like him talk. They're like those old soldiers at the Liberal Club who rattle news-papers and cough at you until you understand.'

Vaulker snorted as if he hadn't expected to. 'Well, so long as you're confident. What about Baron Mori? He seems ...'

'He's fine,' Thaniel said, though as he said it he knew he couldn't have sworn it to a jury. Vaulker was right; Mori always moved slowly, but it was gradual now. He had gone to sit with the Duke, and three or four other men who looked familiar and might have fought at the legation yesterday. They all sat angled in the same way, toward Kuroda's contingent. Where the two groups overlapped, in the middle of the horseshoe of tables, there was quiet conversation, over newspapers. The front pages all showed the same photograph. It was Takiko, looking up at Yuna as he swung the bottle. Her intentions were clear in the fate lines – it was obvious he hadn't taken her by surprise. She had been about to hit him back, and in that instant, she looked serene and noble. One of the newspapers had done a sketch based on the same picture, where she was wearing the Japanese flag and the protesters were all apes. Everyone was talking about it. Thaniel recognised a good few of them from the dinner at Mori's house months ago. Yamauchi, Shimazu, Nabeshima. The big, gilded, southern houses, just like the Mori.

'It doesn't really feel like a courtroom, does it?' Vaulker said.

Thaniel shook his head. It was more like a coffee morning than a courtroom, although that might have been because Kuroda hadn't arrived yet. Two of Choshu's men stood behind Mori. They might have been there to stop him running away, but they looked for all the world like they were only there to protect him. Choshu had leaned across to talk to him, one hand on his arm. Mori was listening with an intensity he never normally needed.

The sound of steps came from the long corridor.

'Right, let's get this over with,' Kuroda said. He was on his way to his seat in the centre. 'We're here chiefly on a formality, gentlemen. Keita Mori has illegally left state custody, and—'

'We are here,' interrupted the Duke, in his dry voice, before Kuroda could sit down, 'because a bannerman of my house was abducted, and I was lied to.'

Kuroda looked up slowly.

'My concern,' the Duke went on, unflustered, 'is that if Count Kuroda's disregard for blood has led him to believe that a man temporarily at the helm of the government can steal away a knight and deceive an ancient noble house solely to cover his own tracks, there is no line he would not cross in the correct circumstances even with regard to the royal family.'

He had managed to say 'Count' like it was something pointless you might be handed gratis in a grocery shop.

'Choshu,' said Kuroda, 'a bannerman of yours is no more your property than a fox that happens to wander into your house. In the protection of the state, it—'

'Damn the protection of the state, he's no spy.'

'I didn't say he was a spy. He provided us with intelligence. He's a proven clairvoyant and he owes his service to his country. He refused to lend it.'

Thaniel swallowed. If Choshu agreed, Mori was going to disappear into government vaults. Mori had closed his hands hard over the edge of the table.

'Fairytales,' Choshu said flatly. He hadn't raised his voice once. 'There is no such thing as clairvoyance, as I believe we can all sensibly agree.'

Thaniel looked around. At least four or five people in the room must have known what Mori could do, and that Kuroda was right. But in Choshu's paper voice, the idea sounded idiotic. Eyes were sliding towards Kuroda. 'The Prime Minister is spinning us a fantasy to distract from the fact that he's been using an innocent man to disguise a project that will prove profoundly unpopular should the newspapers find it was of government making.'

'Sit down,' Kuroda snapped.

Choshu didn't sit. He switched into English. 'Dr Carrow, if you'd like to come in and explain the experiments going on in Aokigahara. The ones producing the information Mr Kuroda is so keen to attribute to my bannerman's being *magic*.'

Thaniel hadn't seen Grace come in. She was just by the door with her husband. When she walked out into the middle of the semicircle, there were murmurs about letting a woman into an Imperial council chamber, but Choshu snapped at them to shut up. She spoke clearly and concisely. Someone brought her a small generator. In the silence it was loud and rattling, and there was another protesting murmur, and again Choshu shut them up. When Grace cast chalk into the air, she explained the fate lines around her; one that formed when she intended to walk towards Kuroda, one that lifted above her if she meant to put her arms up. It could have looked like a magic trick, but she was far, far too dry to seem anything like a showman. She was her usual austere self in grey. When Kuroda lost his temper and demanded her arrest for treason, she only pointed out that she was a British subject and he couldn't try her for stealing an apple, never mind treason. It was a cold joke, and it made the noblemen laugh.

'And was it necessary that these tests destroy half the capital?' Choshu asked her. There was an attentive murmur all around him. Even on Kuroda's side of the room.

'No, sir,' Grace said. She was easy, even speaking in front of so many people. She gave lectures; she was used to it, and good at it. 'It could have been done with a great deal more focus, the effects kept isolated to Aokigahara, but our brief was speed over safety. In an ideal world, the generators would have been underground, insulated by the bedrock of Mount Fuji. But they were built hastily.'

She said 'hastily' as if it meant 'criminally'.

Choshu told her then that she could go. Kuroda snapped that he hardly thought the testimony of a foreign woman was worth anything, but then had to shut up when the Duke pointed out in his desiccated way that Kuroda had plainly thought a foreign woman could work on a national defence project. The chamber dissolved into a row where all the colours of everyone's voices clashed and mixed into an indistinguishable brown cloud. Thaniel looked down at his own shorthand. It was a bad idea to take an exact transcript of a fight. It looked crass if it got into dispatches. You were supposed to summarise, softly. He thought about translating it as the fall of Japanese modernism, which was overdramatic, and wrote, 'the gentlemen continue to disagree'.

He looked up when Grace brushed his arm. He smiled.

'You escaped.'

'Oh, the day after you left,' she said. She paused. 'I saw Mori in the papers. I called round to the Duke to see if I could testify here. Akira's spitting nails too; the way he was treated when he tried to look for me. It all adds up.'

'How did you get out?'

She grinned. 'Do you know what? A monk trundled up with his lightbulb cart, and the guards let him in because he was a holy man; then he put me in his cart and trundled straight out again. Man's a genius. What happened to your face?'

'The protesters at the legation.'

'Oh, yes. I saw the front of the *Mail*.' She frowned. 'That woman. Christ. You can even see her intentions in the photograph, have you seen it? She was about to punch him in the head. What a valkyrie.'

Thaniel nodded and didn't try to speak, because he felt like she had jammed her fingers into the bullet scar. She glanced back, because her husband was signalling at her.

'Anyway, Akira thinks there's going to be a fight. I'd better take him home.'

Thaniel watched her go. Because of that, he didn't see exactly what happened next. He was convinced, later, that in his military way Kuroda only meant to call the place to order. He couldn't imagine him hurting anyone actually inside the Palace. But the Duke's retainers were already on edge, and when they saw the gun in Kuroda's hands, he doubted their first thought was a dry shot fired into the ceiling. The gunshot actually went straight over Vaulker's shoulder, because someone had dragged Kuroda's arm down. There was an instant of perfect silence.

'Look, that's enough,' Mori said, as if he were breaking up an ordinary tiff over coffee. And then, quietly but very clearly to Kuroda, 'What would your wife say?'

Kuroda stared at him. If Mori had sunk a knife into his throat, he couldn't have looked more shocked. An interested murmur went round the room, and a kind of fizz.

'Yes,' said the Duke, as dry and immoveable as ever, 'the tribunal will know that Count Kuroda and my bannerman were always close. One can't help but suspect that all this

467

dross thrown at the Mori name is nothing but a thuggish effort to keep him quiet in the matter of the murder of a noblewoman.'

'This is speculation,' Kuroda snapped.

'Speaking of murdered people,' the Duke continued, 'the tribunal is also aware that Count Kuroda gave me a body which he claimed, fraudulently, was my bannerman. We've identified it as the steward of Yoruji, a dedicated and honourable man called Suzuki who, fortunately for us, was recorded in the ghosts at the property dying in defence of his master. Mr Suzuki was a retainer of my house. I will, naturally, be seeking to press charges for his murder. I will also be funding the lawsuits on behalf of the families of the four hundred and seventy-six people who have, thus far, died as a direct result of Count Kuroda's electrical experiment in the greater Tokyo area alone.'

Uproar.

In the middle of it all, Kuroda inclined his head fractionally to Mori. Losing was the first gracious thing Thaniel had ever seen him do.

Choshu's guard captain brought Mori across and said that they should go, and perhaps hurry out of the country when it was convenient.

They spent the brief journey back to the legation trying to calm Vaulker down, but they struggled. He was a terrible off-white, and shivering. There was blood on his cheek – the bullet had skimmed him.

'Thaniel,' Mori said as they pulled onto the legation driveway. He didn't say it with any urgency, but he had just had to catch Vaulker's wrists to keep him from hitting something or somebody in the little space, and Vaulker was much bigger than he was. Vaulker wasn't trying to hurt anyone, but he was saying they had to get out, and what if someone had followed. 'Could you find that tall doctor when we ...'

'I will. Do you want some help?'

Mori shook his head. 'No, he's not strong. What's his name?'

'Tom.'

Mori said it, not loudly enough, Thaniel thought at first, but Vaulker looked at him.

'You're all right,' Mori said. 'No one else is coming. It was only an accident. These are the legation gates, see? You're safe.'

'The men from your clan are still ...?'

'The men from my *house* are still here,' Mori said gently. He smiled. 'Clan. Who arrived here and said, I know, it looks just like Scotland?'

Vaulker nearly laughed. It looked like hypnosis. His hands had eased. 'House like ... the House of Tudor?'

'Exactly. We say House Mori, House Shimazu. It's all the same.'

Vaulker looked down, because he had begun to shake. 'House. That is better, isn't it. Why did people get it wrong?'

Mori squeezed his hands. There wasn't much to see but sky outside the windows from the angle they were at, but then they passed a red banner. 'I think,' he said, very kindly, 'it's the same reason that Tahitian trimaran battleships are called canoes, while the Viking version, half the size and half as skilled, are longships.'

Vaulker smiled and looked embarrassed, and showed no sign of telling Mori it wasn't true.

The carriage slowed. Thaniel got out before it had stopped altogether.

The Duke's men had tidied up since this morning and to distract the ladies, someone explained later, they had invited some of the traders from the floating market to set up on the lawn. Privately Thaniel suspected the ladies were perfectly all right and it was Pringle who'd needed distracting, but nobody wanted to embarrass him.

'Electric torch, sir?' someone said cheerfully, clicking the light on and off to show how it worked. It made Mori jump. There were people everywhere, calling and setting off unexpected noises. Someone had made a whole host of electric flying things that could lift themselves about three feet into the air and then down again, and then up, never stopping. They made a locust buzzing. Someone else had a whole stall of electric watches under a sign that said *never wind your watch again!!*

'Well, that's the first omen of the apocalypse,' Mori muttered.

There were ordinary stalls too, and someone was selling newspapers. Thaniel stopped when he saw the headline. The Russian fleet, or a portion of it, had been sighted just off Yokohama. He looked south. It was only fifteen miles away. Mori had seen too, and turned still.

'It'll be all right,' Thaniel said. 'You wouldn't have set up a war.'

He could see that Mori didn't believe a word.

———

Once Thaniel had fetched Willis to look at Vaulker, he went to the translation office to explain to the juniors what had happened, and found that they were all busy with the telegraphs; the electricity had waned enough for everything to work again, and now there was a rush of messages crackling through the office as everyone scrambled to confirm exactly where the Russians were, and where the British Navy was, and what the hell everyone was meant to do next. It felt bizarre to walk into a room where, quite rightly, no one cared about what had just happened at the tribunal.

'I don't know how to get hold of the Admiralty, sir,' Pringle said when he came in. A few days ago, he would have been panicking, but he said it quite calmly.

'I'll do it,' Thaniel promised, and started the hunt through the huge telegraph directories.

From somewhere very close, one of the other legations, a bell started to ring, loud and urgent. Others joined it, and then a weird, keening siren, electric-sounding, just like the klaxon at the fence in Aokigahara.

Pringle stood up and pointed out the window. Everyone looked. It was just possible to see the sparkle of Tokyo Bay in the distance. Over the water now, there were smoke columns.

Thaniel found the Admiralty codes and yanked a telegraph closer.

Brit. legation in Tokyo here. Reports of Russian fleet firing shots. Can anyone confirm?

There was a long pause. Outside, the sirens howled on. Vaulker ran up from the surgery and everyone explained at once that they were trying to talk to the Navy.

'Quiet, quiet,' Thaniel said urgently, because there was no paper feed in the telegraph, only the dits and dahs of the code.

Then: *Tokyo, this is the HMS Valiance, accompanying the new Japanese fleet out of Liverpool. Russians fired because they saw us. They're trying to stop us getting into Tokyo harbour. Give us twenty minutes.*

They all waited around the telegraph. A couple of diplomats from the Dutch legation leaned in, then from the Chinese, and the American, until the little room was full, and there were murmurs everywhere in four languages. Pringle pushed the window open. Someone had a pair of binoculars and there was a yelp from that direction when a flurry of smoke plumes went up. In the grounds, the people in the pop-up electric market were silent, watching too. That was what stuck with Thaniel later, that no one ran or tried to hide. So much of Tokyo had been in electrical chaos for so long that not many people could have been convinced there was anywhere safe anymore.

'What's better when one's being invaded; to stay put and rely on the fact that this is English soil or to get out?' Vaulker asked softly. He was asking Mori, who had been waiting in silence by Thaniel's chair. 'Can their guns reach this far inland?'

Mori nodded once. 'Easily.'

'How do you know?'

'I was in Canton when the British started shelling.'

'Oh.'

The telegraph rattled. Thaniel translated the code aloud as it came through.

Safely into port. Russians are backing off. No casualties.

Relieved laughter rippled round the room. After a couple of minutes, the sirens stopped. Thaniel twisted back to look up at Mori.

'See? I told you.'

Mori punched him on the arm, very softly. Thaniel caught his fist and dragged him close, just for a second.

It was almost warm, and with one of those strange unspoken group decisions, everyone spilled outside to buy tea and wine from the little stalls on the lawn. The schoolmistress must have given up on doing anything useful, because the children were out too. As Thaniel bought some wine, he saw Six pause, check them both over for any obvious signs of distress, then bob away again once she'd decided they were all right. Mori was waiting at a makeshift table built from old shipping crates, and he smiled when Thaniel gave him the cup. His expressions were coming differently now, more easily, like he didn't have to concentrate to do it. Thaniel had been worried before that Mori would be a different person without that overriding thing that had made him remarkable. But he was exactly the same person, one who had just been allowed to put down a very heavy pack.

The silence unwound, but he still didn't know what to say. Not far away, Six was showing Katsu to the other children. Little electric toys hummed in the stalls. Owlbert, looking bewildered, was hurrying after an electric mouse. Thaniel scanned the grass for the burned place where Takiko had fallen, but it was hidden now under the newspaper stand. Some of the headlines there boasted of a huge naval victory off the northern coast of Hokkaido. The Russians had actually landed troops ashore at a place called Abashiri, only to be repulsed first by thousands of furious labour camp prisoners, some of whom had stolen Russian boats, and then routed by some of the oldest ships in the Japanese fleet, sent there just in time. Abashiri; naturally.

'Is it still February?' Mori said finally.

Thaniel looked up. 'Nearly March.'

'End of the fog season.'

A tingle went over the nape of his neck. 'It is.'

Mori touched their cups together and then sat back a little into a sunbeam, which showed all the red in his hair. It was the deep black red of church music coming up through the floor.

FORTY-EIGHT

London, April 1891

Thaniel let himself out the back door to breathe while he sipped at his tea. There was something silly about a man with hot tea in a china cup outside in hot weather, but the air in the theatre was getting pipe-smokey, even backstage. He propped himself against a poster for the show.

The air smelled of pollen and stone. He put his head back against the warm paper. The sky was just starting to turn mauve with the oncoming sunset. In another few months it would be back to Cornwall to beat the fog, but for now, London was warm and getting warmer, and the spring and the summer seemed like they would stretch out forever. He could have stayed there for a long time, but church bells started to sing out the hour.

After the quiet outside, the bustle in the narrow dressing rooms was much more colourful than it had been a few minutes ago. Because all the windows were open, it was balmy and the girls only had silk wraps on over their dresses. He was supposed to be in an evening jacket but he was down to his shirt and waistcoat, which he was enjoying, because nobody could tell him different. It was his show and he could conduct it how he wanted.

Arthur Sullivan flitted in. He moved fast for such a rounded man. There was sometimes a lasting impression that for whatever proportion he was made of muscle and bone, there was an equal measure of helium. Thaniel was still folding back his cuffs.

'You'll be fine,' Sullivan said. 'It's always a hell of a lot easier conducting your own writing than someone else's. You know how it's meant to go. You know it's good, don't you?'

'It's all right,' said Thaniel.

'I think you'll find it goes down a bit better than all right.'

'Well, don't hex it,' he said, starting to feel embarrassed.

They were in a dressing room tucked off to the side of the Savoy Theatre. The corridor was alive with people tuning instruments and singers warming up. A strain from Mozart's Requiem echoed along from another room. Arthur sat looking through the score with a pencil. He would be playing the piano.

Someone tapped on the door. Mori came in, speculatively. 'Oh, good,' he said. 'I thought you might be the baritones again.'

Thaniel laughed. Mori had no sense of direction at all, although he seemed to enjoy the thrill of that. He kept going to churches to walk the mazes on the floors. He gave Thaniel a glass of wine, saw Arthur and then offered his own.

Arthur smiled and shook his head. 'No, no, no, no need to be so polite, it's quite ...' He trailed off and put the music aside. 'Good grief. My dear fellow. It's him, isn't it?' he said to Thaniel.

Mori looked between them, puzzled. The electric lights backstage brought out his colours and, even in evening clothes, he was brighter than everyone else. He'd taken off his jacket too, and all white suited him. So did his age. He was past that nearly feverish glow of younger health; the time in prison had eroded that and he was more faded, but there was real power across his shoulders now, and that old sense that he might only have been a trick of light in the dust was gone.

'I hadn't actually—' Thaniel began.

Arthur took no notice and shook Mori's free hand. 'I'm Arthur, I'm playing the piano tonight—'

'Yes,' Mori said. 'I've been looking forward to it.'

'Oh, but you usually sit in the front row on the left!' Arthur burst out, as if it were the most significant thing he had discovered all year.

Mori looked down at his hand, which was still trapped in both of Arthur's, but he was too polite to ask for it back.

'God, it's uncanny,' Arthur said, studying him like he was in a glass case. 'My dear fellow, I thought you seemed familiar when you spoke – you have the most remarkable voice, you know.'

'That's very kind,' Mori said, starting to sound like he was enjoying the bizarreness of a whole conversation whose object had managed to remain obscure for so long. The laughter lines had deepened around his eyes. They were always there now, if he stood in bright light.

'Have you heard the whole thing?' Arthur went on.

'No, just bits and pieces.'

Arthur laughed. 'Sorry, this is ridiculous, but I feel I know you quite well. You learned your English from Nathaniel, of course? Hence the, ah, northerly inflection?'

'That's right.' It was less than it had used to be. There was a faint accent under it now, one that could have been from anywhere. It brought a sharpness on a few words, usually the kind of words you read more often than said.

'Arthur, he's got no idea what you're talking about,' Thaniel broke in.

'Oh, but—'

Blissfully a telephone rang in the next room. Arthur hurried out. Mori folded into his chair. He moved more easily now. Thaniel gave him a programme.

'I ... might have put you in the music,' he explained.

Mori didn't say anything and only sat holding the little booklet open on the first page. The theatre had spent some money on it. The title was picked out in gold: the Joy Symphony. Behind his quiet, there was the effort of not saying that he thought describing one person who was not God or the Queen with an orchestra of a hundred and two was no different to trying to do a locket painting with a wallpaper brush.

'He recognised me,' Mori said at last. 'From this. Mr Sullivan.'

'Yes.' Thaniel's insides were churning. 'But – I haven't hung a picture of you in a gallery. There are only about five people in London who could translate your name, so—'

'No, I mean the way you see sound. It's objective. Someone else could see it in the same way.'

'Not the same colours, but the same – gist. I suppose.'

'That's extraordinary.'

'Really?'

Mori kicked him gently. 'Of course it is.'

'Thanks. But it's not a skill, it's just how I see.'

Mori had been looking through the open door through to the next dressing room and the next, where the sopranos were tying each other into their dresses. The tables there were full of flowers and, double framed like that, they might have been something from a painting. His eyes came back and he smiled. He tipped the gold lettering so that it glinted. He kept the pages inclined inward, like he was holding something fragile in them. 'What is that?' he added.

Thaniel looked. 'Easter egg. Want some?'

'It's chocolate?'

'Fry's do them.' He tapped it in half on the edge of the table. 'The altos gave it to me.'

Mori smiled and shared a half with him. It went nicely with the wine. Thaniel watched him and wondered what he would do, if the worst happened and Thaniel's lungs got the better of him. They weren't right; he could tell they never would be. The house in Cornwall belonged to a friend of Mori's who, until Christmas, Thaniel had been pretty sure was imaginary. In his experience only imaginary people disappeared to Peru for ten years, but it turned out that Merrick Tremayne did as well. He'd turned up suddenly, perfectly real, with tattoos, a Bristol accent, and an open invitation to South America. Thaniel liked that idea.

Someone called ten minutes off. Mori glanced that way.

'I'd better find Six. Do your best, yes?' he said in Japanese. It sounded private, and soft.

'I will,' Thaniel said. He wanted to catch his hand, but one of the sopranos was watching, curious. 'On the right,' he added when Mori hesitated at the door.

'I know.' Mori opened the door slightly before Six came through it. Thaniel sat still, feeling like he was hearing bells in the distance. Mori had been waiting for her.

'I thought I'd come and find you in case you'd got lost again,' she reported. Behind her was a woman in a blue velvet gown, which was so unlike her normal style that Thaniel didn't realise at first that it was Grace. 'Oh. This is Dr Carrow. I was talking to her about you,' Six added at Thaniel. 'Well, actually we were talking about electricity, and she told me about a new kind of microscope and something sticky.' She looked back at Grace for help.

'Medicine,' said Grace.

'Sticky,' agreed Six.

Grace snorted, and then nodded a little to Mori, who bowed a fraction back. They didn't exactly hate each other. It was the wariness of two territorial lions. Nobody mentioned to Six that Grace had used to be Mrs Steepleton. 'Six happened to mention that the doctors think you've got tuberculosis,' Grace said.

'I ...' Thaniel shook his head a little, surprised. 'Yes? Why?'

'Well,' she said, 'at the Aokigahara station, we invented a lot of new things with all the electricity everywhere. Just cobbled together. One of them is going into industrial production now. An electron microscope. Its magnification is far superior to an ordinary microscope. I was using it to try and observe ether particles. It's no good for that, but I got talking with a friend in the biology department not long ago, and he's overjoyed, because with the new microscope, he has finally isolated the bacteria which causes tuberculosis.' She opened her hands a little to say, ta-dah. 'He's pretty sure he's got a cure. He's looking for people for the clinical trials. It looks very promising indeed. If you'd like to give it a try.' She came across and handed him a card. 'He's at UCL.'

'Really?' Thaniel asked, feeling like she'd tipped him upside down.

Grace smiled. 'Really. Go and see him.' She glanced back at Six, and then laughed awkwardly, because Thaniel was staring at her. 'Anyway, I'd better leave you to it.' She nodded to Mori again and swept out.

'And us,' Six said to Mori. 'It's supposed to start soon.'

She held the door open for Mori. She didn't rush anymore. She'd shot up in the last year and she was tall enough now to have noticed that Mori was slight, for England. In the street, she walked between him and the road. Thaniel was more proud of that than of any symphony. He'd never noticed before meeting Takiko, but it struck him all the time now that English girls didn't have much chivalry.

He had the newspaper photograph of Takiko on his desk. It was impossible to look at the image without feeling ashamed, but he kept it so that he would keep remembering the debt he owed her.

'Hey,' he said to Mori.

Mori leaned back in.

'Microscopes,' Thaniel said.

Mori smiled. 'Yeah.'

'If there's a cure — you'll have saved hundreds of thousands more people than you hurt arranging it.'

Like always with any kind of praise, Mori didn't look wholly like he knew what to do with it, and only nodded. 'Well. See you soon.'

Then he was gone. Thaniel gazed down at the card. At last, he slipped it into his breast pocket, and then had to sink his head into his hands and laugh. It was nothing, a clinical trial, but even the chance of getting better made him feel so light he could have out-floated a hot-air balloon. He wanted to drop everything and steal Mori away and get drunk at

481

home, and shout at him for being so reckless, and die for him, or live for him, and everything. Over the last few months, he'd felt how his own future had sort of rolled itself up, the way ahead shortening. He could feel his body shutting down, a little more each day. And now, just a thread of it unspooled out and out to the horizon.

Arthur leaned in. 'It's time,' he said. 'Nervous now?'

'Nope,' said Thaniel, who felt like he might be able to fly.

From the stage, the lights made the audience almost invisible. He could only see the galleries. The gilt along them glittered. A stir went through the audience when a couple of the violinists took their lightbulbs from their violin cases to make sure the electricity was working and the filaments lit. He hoped Six had seen. She had helped set it up.

The last thing he saw before the auditorium lights dimmed was Mori, who offered him a one-sided toast. Thaniel turned back to the lectern.

Arthur winked at him from the piano. The choir looked cheerful. Thaniel took a deeper breath, felt the familiar catch in his lungs, clocked the end of the baton against the music stand, and brought in the strings.

HISTORICAL NOTE

This story is mostly fiction. Mori, Thaniel, and Takiko are not real historical figures, and Filigree Street and Yoruji are imaginary. But lots of other things are based on real history.

The electricity towers at Aokigahara are modelled on a real place. In 1901, Nikola Tesla built Wardenclyffe Tower in New York. It was designed to emanate wireless power, based on the experiments he conducted in Colorado Springs – where you really could hold a lightbulb, and watch it light up.

Ether theory was widely considered scientific fact until it was disproved in 1905, by Einstein. This should have been pretty momentous, but he didn't point out that he'd disproved it, because his tutor was so sure that ether did exist.

Kiyotaka Kuroda was notorious for his warlike habits, a huge illegal land deal, and having possibly killed his wife. He was lampooned for the latter in the national press. The rhinoceros cartoon that Takiko Pepperharrow mentions is real.

The Education Minister, Arinori Mori, really was assassinated on the day the new Constitution was announced. It was probably religiously motivated; Arinori was a Christian, and his murderer was a guardsman from the heart of Japanese Shinto, Ise Shrine. A side note here: Arinori is his first name. Correctly I should be calling him Mr Mori, but I wanted to avoid confusion. He's no relation of Keita Mori. In Japanese, the samurai Mori (pronounced Morey) translates roughly to Featherworth; while Arinori's (pronounced Morry) means Woods.

Abashiri prison was one of several huge labour camps active in the 1880s and 90s. Thousands of men, some of them guilty only of political crimes, died in the punishing Hokkaido winters as they built the road system there. Today, the nineteenth-century prison is a museum, and open to the public. It's full of plaques that show prisoners' anecdotes. One is about remembering to rub your nose.

LANGUAGE NOTE

It's easy to translate Japanese badly. Even today, English dictionaries tend to hit too lofty a tone. We end up, when we watch anime and Japanese drama, seeing subtitles that say things like, 'isn't it nostalgic!' whenever anyone says the rather common phrase, 'natsukashi ne!' This is silly. It just means 'I really miss that'.

There's a myth that Japanese doesn't have swearwords, which is prone to give English speakers a strange, romanticised idea of the language. Japanese does have swearwords, but it's also incredibly easy to be rude without swearing at all. The different formality levels of the language are so clear that they actually have names. The highest level of formal language is called *keigo*, which is notoriously hard to speak, because all the verbs change. Teachers love to say we don't have it in English, but we do; it's the equivalent of saying, 'I wonder if you'd like to take a seat?' rather than, 'Park yourself there, mate.' For me, the big difference is that while we're all aware of what constitutes polite language and what doesn't in English, we tend not to demarcate it and name it. We'll tell kids to 'ask nicely', or adults to 'sound professional', but we're only hinting at what we mean. There's such an intense awareness of these distinct registers of speech in Tokyo that sometimes, when what someone has said in Japanese literally just translates as 'no', it *means* something closer to 'sod off' – because saying a flat no, rather than using a proper sentence, is rude.

All this was even more acute in the Meiji period, when events in the book take place.

Particularly in Takiko Pepperharrow's speech, I've tried to show what normal, working-class Tokyo Japanese actually sounds like. I should emphasise *tried*; I only lived in Tokyo for a year and a half, and I'm not a translator. I just eavesdrop in pubs.

ACKNOWLEDGEMENTS

I couldn't have come close to writing this book without the Daiwa Anglo Japanese Foundation. Every year, they send a handful of people out to Tokyo on a nineteen month scholarship. You learn Japanese for a year, live with a Japanese family, and then work at a Japanese company. In 2013, to my continuing bewilderment, they sent me. After my language-learning year, I lived in Hokkaido for a month, at a place called Shari – which is right next to Abashiri. Special thanks to Mitsuru and Katsuya Shishikura, who put up with having me in their attic for that time, and who once drove forty miles to take me out for fish and chips.

Thanks as well to Dr Christine Corton, who wrote a fabulous book about London fog from which I have stolen all my ideas; to everyone at Gladstone's Library, which has copies of every single Victorian newspaper you could possibly want, alongside some wonderful pamphlets about early use of electricity; and also to my brother, Jacob, who is much cleverer than me and sorts out all my plot crises.

A NOTE ON THE AUTHOR

Natasha Pulley studied English Literature at Oxford University. After stints working at Waterstones as a bookseller, then at Cambridge University Press as a publishing assistant in the astronomy and maths departments, she did the Creative Writing MA at UEA. She later studied in Tokyo, where she lived on a scholarship from the Daiwa Anglo-Japanese Foundation, and she is now a visiting lecturer at City University. Her first novel, *The Watchmaker of Filigree Street*, was an international bestseller, a Guardian Summer Read, an Amazon Best Book of the Month, was shortlisted for the Authors' Club Best First Novel Award and won a Betty Trask Award. *The Bedlam Stacks*, her second novel, was published in 2017. She lives in Bath.

@natasha_pulley

A NOTE ON THE TYPE

The text of this book is set in Bell. Originally cut for John Bell in 1788, this typeface was used in Bell's newspaper, *The Oracle*. It was regarded as the first English Modern typeface. This version was designed by Monotype in 1932.